"YOU HAVE NEVER TOLD ME YOU LOVED ME, NOT EVEN ONCE." Sally watched his startled face.

"But that's impossible! Of course I have, I must have! All those things I whisper to you while we make love, the sweet names I call you. Surely you are mistaken!"

"No, I'm not," she said sadly. "I would remember. I have waited so long to hear you say it." To her regret, he did not speak at once. Instead he drew her close again, and his mouth covered hers in a quick but passionate kiss. Sally swallowed hard, as his lips traced her jawline up to her ear. I must not cry! she told herself fiercely. I must not be bitter because he cannot love me!

"Margarite," he breathed in her ear, his deep voice sending shivers racing over her skin, "Margarite, I not only admire and adore you, I do most truly love you."

She drew back a little, to stare up into his eyes. "No," she murmured, as she shook her head and moved away from him. "No! I am not Margarite! I am Sally. . . ."

A HANDFUL OF DREAMS

A
HANDFUL
OF
DREAMS

by

Barbara Hazard

AN ONYX BOOK

ONYX
Published by the Penguin Group
Penguin Books USA Inc., 375 Hudson Street,
New York, New York 10014, U.S.A.
Penguin Books Ltd, 27 Wrights Lane,
London W8 5TZ, England
Penguin Books Australia Ltd, Ringwood,
Victoria, Australia
Penguin Books Canada Ltd, 10 Alcorn Avenue,
Toronto, Ontario, Canada M4V 3B2
Penguin Books (N.Z.) Ltd, 182–190 Wairau Road,
Auckland 10, New Zealand

Penguin Books Ltd, Registered Offices:
Harmondsworth, Middlesex, England

First published by Onyx,
an imprint of New American Library,
a division of Penguin Books USA Inc.

First Printing, August, 1992
10 9 8 7 6 5 4 3 2 1

 REGISTERED TRADEMARK—MARCA REGISTRADA

Chapter One

Ireland—1803

AS SOON AS Sally Desmond was out of sight of the Hall, she stopped running. For a moment she stood still to catch her breath, then the joy she felt at her successful escape welled up inside her, and she flung her arms wide and began to spin. Faster and faster she went, until she was so dizzy she could only fall to the soft turf in a heap of skirts, giggling with delight while she waited for her head to stop whirling and the world to stop dancing before her eyes.

When she lifted her face to the warm sun, she saw plump clouds overhead. They were motionless, and they looked as if they had been painted on the blue of the sky, each one separate from the others and somehow aloof and dignified, like fat old ladies dressed in their best clothes. Sally laughed aloud, amused by her fancy.

She hugged herself, and grinned. She was free! Free to spend this August afternoon any way she chose. She had run away right after dinner, and before her Mam could give her some task—either minding the baby or settling to her needlework, both of which activities she loathed.

Ah, she was the tomboy her da had named her many a time. She knew that well. She also knew how naughty of her this escape was, how she was sure to be punished for it; but right now, at this minute, she did not care. Besides, she told herself, as she buried her bare toes in the thick grass just for the fun of doing it, she had spent all the morning doing chores and studying the history book. Enough was enough.

For as soon as she had awakened this morning she

had known she could not spend all this glorious day inside. She had been impatient right up to dinner time and then, only moments before now, had crept out of the kitchen when Mrs. Ginty's back was turned, hiding her shoes and hose in the shed before running away.

Now no one could see her, nor could she hear them if they called. Ah, she thought, to be sure, it is a great day!

A few moments later Sally jumped up and ran down to the village, as she had intended to do from the beginning. When she reached it, she discovered that the small band of children she played with had a project in mind for this summer afternoon. They planned to dam up the brook that ran through the village, far enough upstream so their work would not be detected for a long time. As soon as the dam was built, they meant to race back and see the fun. They laughed to each other as they fetched stones and branches to make the barrier as strong as possible, trying to imagine what everyone would say and do when the brook dwindled to a trickle, and then finally ceased to flow at all. What fun it would be!

It was Thady O'Brien who had picked the location for their dam. Sally thought there was a better spot just around the next bend, but Thady was the biggest and strongest among them, and a bully to boot. When he made a decision, everyone abided by it. If they did not, Thady had no compunction about beating them until they either gave in to him or ran crying to their mothers.

Sally thought it was most unfair. She knew she was smarter than Thady. Besides, although they were both ten, and the oldest of the children, her birthday came a month earlier than his did. *She* should have chosen the spot. In a better-organized world, one in which there were no bullies, she would have done so.

But there was no arguing with Thady, or pointing this out to him. Sally knew he wouldn't hesitate to pummel and pinch her too, even if she were the squire's daughter.

It had taken a long time to build the dam to Thady's

satisfaction, but once he had given his approval, convinced it would hold, all of them had run back to the village as fast as they could. Once there, however, they saw something so unusual that it drove the dam, and their afternoon's fun, right out of their minds.

For there, standing motionless in the dusty road that ran between the cottages, was a smart carriage. It was painted a shiny black, the wheels picked out in gold. The horse that drew it was a glossy chestnut, and he was tied to a nearby picket.

In the carriage were a lady and gentleman, the likes of whom the village children had never seen. Who were they? they wondered. Why were they here? And why had they stopped?

Thady put his finger to his lips, and dropped to a crouch. Everyone followed his example, and keeping close to the bushes where they could not be seen, they all crept forward so they could eavesdrop on what was being said.

"Well, of all the horrid things! And miles from anywhere, too! I might have known, when you asked me to go for a drive in the country with you this afternoon, that something like this would happen!"

As the lady spoke she tossed her head, and the fashionable bonnet she wore, adorned with several ostrich plumes, was threatened by the height of her indignation.

"Come now, Eloise, where's your sense of adventure? 'Tis no great matter, after all. We have just to sit here and admire the scenery until the groom can have the harness repaired. It is a pleasant afternoon, is it not? This village is most providential. Why, just think! We might have broken the harness far out in the countryside," the British officer who accompanied her said, his eyes twinkling at his lady's pout.

"I hardly consider this collection of hovels a 'village,' and I pray you will not ask me to stroll about it," she said tartly. " 'Admire the scenery,' indeed! Look there, at that pig! Roaming about quite free, and covered with mud as well. How . . . how disgusting!"

"Don't look at it then," the gentleman said, stretching his uniformed arms over his head and yawning. "But this village is no worse than any other in Ireland. And in such a poor country, so torn by war and troubles, what can you expect? I see the church is not finished, although they have made a noble start."

The lady's eyes followed his pointing hand, and she sniffed. "I have yet to see one in this country that is, even in Dublin. The Irish are so feckless! Why do they even begin to build, if there's no money to finish the job?"

"You are severe," her companion said idly, looking about him with interest and ignoring her petulance. It was true, he thought, that the village was unprepossessing. A few poor hovels divided by the dirt road, and at one end the unfinished church and a small commons with a brook winding through it. No doubt the pig had been wallowing in the mud by its banks only minutes ago. He glanced at the broken-down bothy that was nearest the disabled carriage. He wouldn't house his own livestock in such a place, but here he was sure it was home to any number of people, perhaps even that pig as well. He could see a thin plume of smoke above the ragged thatch, noted the broken door and sagging timbers, and he shuddered. That people could actually live like animals, side by side with them, had been a shock to him ever since he had arrived in Ireland.

The racing clouds overhead parted then, and the sun shone down. Oddly, it did not brighten the scene before them. Instead, it seemed to limn the poverty and need and ugliness of the little hamlet in even greater detail.

He heard a hastily stifled giggle, and then several more, coming from behind the bushes across the road, and he smiled to himself.

"Come out now!" he ordered, in his sternest parade-ground voice. "I know you're there. Show yourselves at once!"

A group of ragged children rose one by one, their

eyes wide with apprehension as they huddled close together.

"They stare at us as if we were some strange kind of animal," the lady beside him remarked, raising her handkerchief to her face. "No doubt they have never seen gentlefolk before.

"How very odorous this place is! I am so glad I thought to soak a handkerchief in lavender water before we left on this ill-fated jaunt of yours!"

The officer beside her ignored her. He was inspecting the children much more casually then they were inspecting him, but his eyes brightened when he spotted one of them, a little girl standing somewhat apart from her fellows.

"I say, Eloise!" he said in a voice full of admiration. "Have you ever seen such a lovely child?"

She turned and stared before she shrugged her plump shoulders. "It is impossible to tell," she said coldly. "She is filthy. They are all filthy."

This was not strictly true, for although Sally was as barefoot as the others her gown was less ragged, and she wore a once white apron over it. Indignant at being maligned, she lifted her little chin proudly and returned stare for stare.

The British officer saw that she had long, straight black hair that hung in a tangle over her shoulders, and delicate brows to match. He could not see the color of her large, wide-spaced eyes, but her face was an enchanting oval under the smudges of dirt she sported, and it appeared fair-skinned. Her nose was straight and her mouth small, with a full lower lip.

As if disturbed at being inspected so intently, she hung her head and looked down to where her big toe was tracing a circle in the dirt.

The officer was still staring at her when Sally looked up again, and she transferred her attention to his companion. Her eyes widened. The carriage and the gent were the finest she had ever seen, but the lady! Ah, sure she was more beautiful than a saint! She wore a gown of soft rose, trimmed with a deeper rose velvet, and tight white gloves. Little rose sandals peeped from

beneath the hem of the gown, and she had on pink
stockings. To think of it! Pink stockings! On her blond
curls was set a velvet bonnet, adorned with some sort
of huge, colored feathers, the likes of which Sally had
never seen.

Her gaze went to the lady's companion. She knew
he was an English officer. She recognized the uniform,
the epaulets and braid. There were lots of them about.
When she saw he was still watching her, she felt angered. She'd always been told 'twasn't nice to stare,
but that-there fine gent didn't seem to know that.
With a small hidden smile she dropped him a curtsy,
while around her the other children giggled behind
their hands at the gesture.

"Come here!" he called, waving his tightly gloved
hand to her.

Sally hesitated, for she knew it was not wise to talk
to strangers. But the chance to inspect that shiny carriage and the beautiful lady more closely was much
too tempting. Pushing past the village children, all
whispering now and hanging back, she went closer.

"Outstanding! Here, Eloise, do look at her!" the
young officer enthused, his teeth very white in his
tanned face. "Is she not beautiful?"

The lady called Eloise was a very new bride, and
the only compliments she was used to hearing from
her husband were those directed to herself. She
stiffened.

"Pretty enough, I suppose," she said after another
cursory glance. "Of course she would be vastly improved by shoes and stockings, and a gown that was
not so faded and torn. What she needs most, of
course, is a hot bath. Do people never wash here?"

Sally paled a little at the scornful words, and she
put her grimy hands behind her back. The lady didn't
seem to care for her. She wondered why.

"You are too harsh, dearest. Did you never get
dirty as a small child when you were playing? Even
as perfect as you are now, I cannot believe that!"

His bride smiled a little and turned her shoulder on
the child standing in the dusty road. "Send her away,"

she said, not bothering to lower her voice. "I do not care to converse with Irish peasants!"

"I'm not afther bein' a peasant," Sally said boldly, stung by the lady's assessment of her. As the occupants of the carriage stared at her anew, she went on, "I'm Sally—er, *Margaret*—Desmond, of the Desmonds of Ballyragh. Shure, an' me da's a squire, if ye plaze."

The lady tittered at her broad brogue, at the defiant words delivered in such a gruff little voice.

"Well, Miss Sally-er-Margaret Desmond, how do you do?" the officer asked, raising his hand to his hat in mock salute. "And how old might you be, my child?"

"I'm ten, yer honor," she said, not looking at the lovely, scornful lady anymore.

"When you are ten years more, you'll be a beauty," he told her. "Remember that I said so."

"Hmmph!" his companion sniffed, adjusting her parasol so the sunlight did not fall on her face. "A beauty, will she? I hardly think that likely! In fact, I would be willing to wager any amount that by then she'll have brats hanging about her skirts, and she'll be no beauty at all. Far from it! You've seen the countrywomen here, Thomas! Worn-out and ugly by thirty, every one of them. Why, just look there, at that drab in the hovel door. Perhaps she was just as pretty as this little girl once, but look at her now!"

Sally did not have to turn to know the lady was pointing to Molly O'Brien, come out of her cottage to see the swells. But Molly is old, she told herself, and it isn't her fault she lives in such a wee cottage and has so many babbies. 'Sides, she thought, I don't look nothin' like her.

"A sad fate to contemplate for such loveliness," the British officer mused. "Perhaps, as the squire's daughter, she will find a way to escape it?"

His attention was caught by his groom's hail, and he indicated the man coming up the road toward them. "Here is Marsden now, my dear. We'll soon have the harness replaced, and then we can be on our way. And we shall not be late for the colonel's reception tonight, which I know very well is why you have been fretting!"

Suddenly realizing how late in the day it was, Sally had begun to edge away. Why, the sun was low on Hurley Hill, and she would be missed at home. And she had been told not to play with the village children. Bad enough that she was sure to get a scolding for her dirty clothes, and for going without her shoes and stockings.

"Wait!" the gentleman called, stepping down from the carriage to stride toward her.

For a moment he thought the child might run, she looked so frightened, but as he neared her that defiant little chin came up again and she held her ground.

With his back to the carriage, he reached into his pocket and drew out a gold sovereign. "Here, this is for you," he said in a conspirator's whisper. "Take it and buy yourself some pretty hair ribbons."

Sally knew she was not supposed to take anything from strangers. Not only her mother but Mrs. Ginty had told her that, over and over again. But the gold sovereign was so brilliant in the sunlight, it seemed to beckon her closer.

"I'll not hurt you," the officer said kindly, crouching down so they were face-to-face. "A pretty little girl like you should have pretty things."

He winked at her then and, reassured, Sally smiled. He had nice eyes, she thought. As she took the coin and her grimy fingers closed over it tightly, she bobbed a curtsy in thanks.

He rose and bowed to her in turn, sweeping off his hat and holding it over his heart. Sally could hear the other children's shrill giggles, but she ignored them to curtsy again, deeply this time.

"Thomas! Whatever are you doing?" the lady in the carriage called, her voice testy. "Do leave that child! Come here!"

"Coming, my love," he said over his shoulder. Then he leaned closer to Sally and whispered, "Don't ever get worn and ugly. Will you do that for me? It would be so very unjust if you did!"

"I'll . . . I'll try not to, sor," Sally promised, just before she turned and ran away as fast as she could go. She was afraid the lady would demand the return of the sovereign, it was such a lot of money. Besides, Thady O'Brien had seen the gent give it to her. He'd make her give it up, if he could catch her.

The British officer stared after her flying figure until it was hidden from him by a bend in the road. Only then did he turn back to his carriage and his fretful, impatient wife. To be sure he loved Eloise, and she was a pretty girl, but she couldn't hold a candle to the child he had just been admiring. Three months of marriage, however, had taught him to keep that observation to himself. As he stepped into the carriage and took his seat again, he wondered what would become of the little girl, and he wished her well.

Cutting across a field planted with potatoes, and leaping a small brook, Sally Desmond hurried home, glancing over her shoulder now and then to see if Thady was gaining on her. To her relief, he was nowhere in sight as she raced up the little rise that led to the gates of Ballyragh. Once inside those gates she would be safe, for Thady wouldn't dare come on the squire's land.

The grass grew high on either side of the rutted tracks in the drive she followed, but she did not notice it. Indeed, she could not remember the last time it had been scythed. She scurried up the steps of the Hall and eased the front door open carefully. Just before it creaked, she put her head to the crack and listened carefully. A burst of loud masculine laughter reached her ears, and she shook her head and shut the door as softly as she had opened it.

Going back the way she had come, she made her way around the Hall, bending down and keeping close to the bushes that grew next to its walls. Her da had company, and she didn't want to have to endure some hearty pinches, wet kisses, and slurred questions from his cronies. She had heard Mr. Mannion's coarse laugh above the rest, and she disliked him most of all. He always looked at her so strangely it made her uncomfortable, and she couldn't stand his hands on her.

Just before she entered the yard at the back of the Hall, she tied the sovereign up in a corner of her petticoat. She wished she had more time to look at it, admire it, *gloat* over it, but that would have to wait. It was very late.

She wondered where her mother was. Da wouldn't have cared that her face was dirty, but she knew her mother would scold her for it, and for going without her shoes and stockings as well.

"Mither o' God, will ye be afther lookin' at the child!" Mrs. Ginty exclaimed, as Sally slipped into the big kitchen. Sally could smell some soup cooking, and she sniffed appreciatively.

"An' jest where have ye been, ye imp o' Satan?" Mrs. Ginty demanded. "Yer mither's been lookin' fer ye this hour past. An' dirty as a wallowin' sow ye be, and ye auld enough ter know better, too!"

Sally was pouring a mug of water from the pitcher, and she did not answer until she had downed the contents of it. Wiping the back of her hand over her face, and smearing the dirt there, she said, "Jest down in the village, playin'."

"I thought yer mither told ye not ter hang around there no more," the cook said, as she turned away to stir a pot that threatened to boil over. "Yer in fer it, Sally, fer it's that late."

Sally poured more water into a basin and proceeded to wash her face and hands. Behind her she could hear the cook going on and on, scolding her, but she did not listen. She was wondering how much you could buy with a sovereign, and looking forward to the next fair, or when the tinker should come round again. And she wondered as well how she was to explain such wealth to her mother, and where she could possibly hide it so it would be safe. Eight-year-old Mary was forever poking through her things, and Joseph and Michael, although still little boys, could not be kept from anything.

"Where's yer shoes, then?" Mrs. Ginty asked sharply. "Shoes cost money. That angry the squire'll be, if ye lost them. Aye, ye'll be in throuble then, lass!"

"I left them in one o' the sheds. I'll fetch them in a moment. Is there anything ter eat? I'm that hungry!"

"Since ye run off today, yer mither sez yer not ter have none," came the stiff reply.

Sally ran to the old woman and put her arms around her spare waist. "Ah now, jest a wee bit?" she begged. "I'll not be afther tellin' on ye!"

Mrs. Ginty shook her off, but she nodded to a basket of rusks on the center table. Sally grabbed two, before the cook had time to change her mind. She was just swallowing the last crumbs when her mother came into the kitchen, Andrew wailing on her shoulder.

"Oh there you are, naughty child!" Mrs. Desmond said, looking distracted. A woman only in her late twenties, she seemed years older. Five children and several miscarriages since she had married at sixteen had aged her considerably, as had her husband's growing poverty and almost constant drunkenness. Once she had been a lovely girl, as lovely as Sally appeared she would be, but those days were long behind her. Times were hard now, and she saw no chance that they would ever improve.

She patted the baby's back absentmindedly, before she raised her hand to brush the hair back from her brow. "Here, Sally, take Andy for me. I must sit down for a moment, and every time I do he wails even louder!

"Mrs. Ginty, the master wants a light supper for him and his friends. Nothing special, of course," she added, looking a little nervous as she noticed the cook's suddenly truculent mien.

"That it couldn't be, mum," Mrs. Ginty told her. "Holy saints in hiven! There's nothin' much ter be had, never mind it be special!"

Mrs. Desmond sank down at the big deal table and put her head in her hands. Both her daughter and the cook watched her, Sally wondering if she was going to cry, as she so often did. This time, however, she straightened up after a moment. "Just make do with what you have. They won't care, the state they're in."

Mrs. Ginty sniffed. "Well, an' why are ye afther tellin' me that, mum? I know it as well as ye do."

Her mistress looked as if she meant to scold her for her pertness, but instead, Mrs. Desmond's attention was caught by her daughter's bare legs and dirty feet, as Sally walked the baby up and down the kitchen.

"Sally! You'll be the death of me, so you will! I've told you and told you, yet still you insist on going about like the lowliest peasant. You're a Desmond, Sally, a *Desmond*! And the name still means something in County Wexford, even now. Wherever are your shoes and hose?"

"They're out in the shed, Mam," Sally said. "I'll fetch 'em afther Andy quiets down."

"*After*, not 'afther'!" her mother wailed, putting her head down on her arms and beginning to sob. Sally and Mrs. Ginty exchanged a glance before Sally went and patted her mother's shoulder softly.

" 'Deed, I'm that sorry, Mam," she said. "But it was such a nice day, an' well . . ."

Mrs. Desmond did not even raise her head. "What's the use?" she asked, despair in her voice. "Why do I even bother? You look like a peasant, you talk like a peasant—why, you even run off to play with those dirty little villagers every chance you get! Whatever was the use of me teaching you to read and write, insisting you practice your curtsy and manners, so that someday—"

She sobbed again before she raised her head and spun around to face her unsatisfactory daughter. "Someday," she said again, slowly and quietly this time, "someday, Sally, you will be wed. I'd have you wed well, to a man of wealth and standing and breeding. Indeed, with your face, I still expect a fortune for you, no matter what the family has come to. But if you continue on the road you seem so intent on traveling, I fear all my efforts, all my dreams for you, will be for naught."

"I'll do better, Mam, I promise ye—er, you," Sally said, bewildered by all this talk of "someday," and a little frightened by the intensity in her mother's eyes, by her pale, tear-streaked face.

Mrs. Desmond only stared at her and shook her head. "Here, give me the baby," she said, holding out her arms. "Quickly, now! Fetch your shoes and hose. And wash your feet before you put them on! I'll need you to watch your brothers, for Katty must help Mrs. Ginty with the supper. And it's the least you can do, after running off to play all afternoon."

Sally curtsied, and grabbed a huckaback towel from the drying rack before she ran from the kitchen. She did not want to linger, for Mam had been so strange! And whatever had she meant, going on so about "someday"? That time when she supposed she would have to marry seemed a lifetime away.

When she had her shoes on Sally made a face, for they were tight and pinched her feet. She'd hardly liked to mention the fact to her mother, for her shoes were not a year old yet and she knew there was no money for another pair. Not this year. But as she trudged back to the hall she realized her feet had been growing as fast as the rest of her. Her face lit up as she reached the kitchen again. Sometimes Mam let her wear her old slippers in the house, even though the big toe was out of both of them and the backs were worn-down and flattened.

As she ran up the stairs, she wondered if a sovereign was enough money for new shoes. But then she shook her head. No. No matter how uncomfortable her feet were, she would not waste anything so shiny, so marvelous, on something as commonplace as new shoes.

The sovereign was meant for pretty things: hair ribbons, or lace, or . . . or maybe even a new book! A book of her very own, with crisp, clean pages and no dog-eared covers like her mam's few.

Sally had seen such a book but once in her life, the

day her mother had taken her to town in the dogcart to buy her new shoes. It was a picture book, displayed in the window of a small shop, and she had eyed it longingly. But when her mother had shaken her head, a tight, closed-up expression on her still pretty face, Sally had turned her back on it. She knew there was no money for books. There was barely enough for necessities, and sometimes not even for food. For somehow the rent from the tenants grew less and less, and da's man, Mr. McGillicuddy, shook his head over it. And, Sally suspected, over her da's nonchalance as well. The last time Mr. McGillicuddy had been here at Ballyragh, she'd heard da say to him that there was no need to fuss over it, for no mortal man yet had been able to get blood from a stone. Times were bad for everyone.

She had seen his face as he'd mounted his horse, and it was so black she hadn't run to wave good-bye to him, even though she was a favorite of his.

Sally sighed as she went to the nursery. Mam had told her only this week that Mr. McGillicuddy had left da's employ. She remembered how Mam had shaken her head and sighed when she'd said that although it would be a savings, Mr. Desmond himself now must see to the rents. And it was not at all a fitting thing for him to be doing. Not a *Desmond*, and he the squire!

Sally doubted her da would have any more luck with the tenants. Mr. McGillicuddy was known as a hard man, and if he couldn't pry the rent out of the tenants how could her good-natured da do it? Especially since he'd be more likely to step inside a hovel, accept a wee drop of comfort, and rise an hour later unsteady on his feet and with pockets as empty as when he'd stepped in the door. Emptier, perhaps. He had such a soft heart, he'd be more apt to give away what few coins he had at the first tale of woe.

When Sally came into the nursery, the little boys jumped up from the floor where they had been playing. Katty, the dour-faced maid, was repairing some of their clothes, but she was quick to put the sewing away.

"Mam wants ye down in the kitchen, Katty. Me da has asked fer a supper fer his friends, and Mrs. Ginty needs yer help," Sally told her over the clamor her brothers were making.

"Bejasus, an' does she now?" Katty muttered, pushing Michael away from her skirts so that she might pull his thumb from his mouth. "Narsty, Mikey! Narsty boy!" she scolded.

Sally shrugged as Joey pulled her into the room. She did not hear the snap of the door as it closed behind the maid, or the clump of her feet as she plodded away down the uncarpeted passage, muttering to herself about this extra work.

"What ye been doin', Sally?" Joey demanded. "Wuz ye afther down ter the village all this time?"

Sally ruffled his hair and smiled at him. Joseph was a handsome little boy, with hair and eyes as dark as her own and with her regular features. Five now, and the oldest son, he held himself above his brothers, little Michael and baby Andrew.

"Aye, I was there," she told him. "An' if yer very good, I'll tell yer all my adventures. But what about a walk first? We'll go an' visit da's horse, an' the baby pigs, all right?"

Joey nodded eagerly, for he had been cooped up in the nursery all afternoon. Katty was not one for taking walks, not when she had a chance to sit down.

Sally saw that Michael's eyes were wide. At two, he was terrified of the huge animal his da rode, and he always cried when he was taken anywhere near him. Now his face was beginning to pucker, and Sally said hastily, "Never mind, Mikey! We'll find Mary first, an' you can stay with her. An' when we come back, I'll tell ye a story."

"About the dragon?" Joey asked, his dark blue eyes lighting up.

"No, not the dragon. That one frightens Mikey," she added, bending down to whisper that information in Joey's ear alone.

"Baby, baby!" Joey taunted, as Michael's thumb

crept back into his mouth and his big round eyes filled with tears.

"That's enough out o' ye, Master Joseph Desmond, Junior!" Sally said tartly. "Whist now! Leave Mikey alone! Ye were jest sich a one yerself not long ago. Come along then."

She hoisted Michael to her hip and he put his head on her shoulder. As she went down the stairs, Joey plodding after, Sally thought how heavy Mikey was getting. She wouldn't be able to lift him in a little while, even though he was not a fat child. None of them was fat.

Mary was practicing her penmanship, but when Sally bribed her with the story she would tell later she put the pencil down and accepted Michael's care without demurral. Sally had discovered only a couple of years ago that she had a gift for making up tales, and the more she invented, the more popped into her head. Dragons and princesses, castles and fairies—at first stolen from one of mam's books, but lately all of her own invention. Her sister and brothers would sit spellbound for as long as she chose to go on, and it kept them quiet when da was sleeping mornings, or carousing with his friends.

Just before she entered the kitchen, she heard another gust of laughter from the back salon which was her da's private room. Someone broke into song, and she realized da's cronies were getting to the stage where her mam would make sure all the children were out of earshot. The warm stories would begin soon, and the oaths and arguments. Sometimes there was fighting, too. It is the drink, Sally thought sadly. It made some men quarrel and eager to pick a fight, but it only made her da more sentimental and prone to weeping.

Much later, as she snuggled down under the blankets on her side of the bed, Sally could hear the men taking their noisy leave. Only a few minutes later she also heard her father struggling up the stairs, humming a little under his breath. She steeled herself. She knew he would come into the room to kiss her and Mary good night, and she prayed that tonight he would be quick about it and move on to the nursery and the babies. Sometimes he sat down on the bed and woke her up to hug her and weep over her, and that made her feel hot and nervous, and somehow ashamed.

Tonight, however, his kiss was almost absentminded, and he was quickly gone. Sally sighed, wrinkling her nose at the sweet, stale smell of the whiskey that clung to him. She could tell from her sister's little snores that she was fast asleep, and now, for the first time, she could think about her sovereign.

She had hidden it under a loose board in the unfinished solarium. That room was to have been her mother's wedding gift, but somehow, after the roof was on and the underflooring done, all work had stopped. Now it was no more than an open porch, and deteriorating all the time from the wind and the rain that blew through it. Sally often wondered if her mam minded. She had never said, but then Rose Desmond had never criticized her husband. And as da had pointed out, it was the thought that counted. He had certainly intended to give his darlin' Rose a solarium fit for a queen, he said.

Sally thought it was the perfect hiding place, for no one went there. But what was she to do with her sovereign?

If she spent it, even for something as wonderful as a new book, it would be gone and she would never see it again. But if she kept it she could take it out anytime she wanted, and she could hold it in her hand and dream as she admired it. And perhaps it would bring her good luck! Why, perhaps that British officer had been a wizard in disguise! Perhaps he had stopped in the village on purpose, just to give her the magic sovereign that would change her whole life! Perhaps she was to become a princess, or—

Sally giggled softly, recognizing her own vivid imagination at work. But even if she was making up stories again, the sovereign might still bring her luck. Lots of people had lucky pieces. Even Mrs. Ginty was never without her rosary, one that she said had been blessed by the Pope himself. And Katty swore by her rabbit's foot.

Sally yawned and snuggled into her pillow. Yes, that's what she'd do. She would not spend her sovereign on foolish things. Instead she'd keep it, because maybe, just *maybe*, it might be magical after all.

Chapter Two

1808

IT WAS FIVE more years before Sally had her next talisman, years that had not been kind to the fortunes of the Desmond family.

She was on her hands and knees in the garden next to Ballyragh Hall, digging potatoes for dinner, that summer day when she was to learn what the future held for her.

Such a shame, she thought, as she unearthed a mound. The potatoes needed at least another month to reach normal size. If they kept on digging them up now, what would they all eat this winter? And the pig had sickened and died only last week, so there would be no pork to salt down. Thank heavens the cow continued to give milk!

She heard someone approaching, and she glanced over her shoulder as she shook away the earth that clung to the potatoes. It was her sister Mary, and Sally saw that she was sulking again. Idly, she wondered what had set Her Highness off this time.

"Mam wants to see you," Mary said in a voice full of rage. "I'm to finish the digging."

Sally smiled to herself as she rose to her feet and wiped her hands on her apron. Mary hated outdoor work. At thirteen, she was well on the way to becoming the perfect little lady her mother had always wanted. Except, Sally thought, the way things were now, no one needed a perfect little lady.

"What's it about, Mare?" she asked, as she handed over the gardening apron.

Her sister shrugged as she tied it on. "Don't know.

Mam was closeted with Da for ever so long this morning, and when she left him she was crying."

"Mam is always crying these days," Sally said matter-of-factly. "Well, best I go see what she wants. Mind you take only the biggest ones, Mare! An' only enough fer dinner!"

"Dinner!" Mary said, viciously attacking the soil with the trowel. "Praties and buttermilk are not dinner!"

"It's more than some have," Sally reminded her over her shoulder as she ran lightly away. As usual now she was barefoot, but the soles of her feet were so callused that she did not feel the stones beneath them, or the occasional sharp-leafed weed she trod on.

She found her mother in the nursery, putting baby Agnes down for a nap. Sally studied her curiously, hoping for a clue as to the summons. Rose Desmond was thinner; the two latest babies had taken their toll on her looks. Forsythe, the next to youngest, sat on the floor nearby, his vacant expression never changing as he moved a block from side to side. Sally knew he would do it for hours if he was not interrupted.

She was afraid that poor Forsythe was not normal, and she was beginning to worry about baby Agnes, too. Agnes cried all the time, and she was so sickly.

"You wanted to see me, Mam?" she whispered.

Her mother put a warning finger to her lips, and nodded toward the door. After Mrs. Desmond had scooped Forsythe from the floor, Sally followed her obediently. To her surprise her mother led her to her own bedchamber, and she began to wonder what it was all about. She could not recall having done anything to displease her mother lately, and her days of running off to the village to play were long past. Now it was Joe who escaped there every chance he got, with Mikey tagging after him as fast as his seven-year-old legs would carry him. It was from them that Sally had learned the village had a new bully these days. Always hungry, and disgusted with his family's poverty, Thady O'Brien had run away to Dublin that spring.

"Sit down, Sally," her mother said, pointing to a faded armchair. As she took the seat, and her mother continued to stand before her, cuddling Forsythe in her arms, Sally wondered at her expression. It was not that she looked sad and defeated, or had those two vertical worry lines between her brows that were a permanent feature of her face now. She always looked that way these days. No. Today there was something else, something like apprehension reflected in her face, and Sally felt a shiver at the base of her spine.

"I've something to tell you, my dear," Rose Desmond said, as she turned her back and walked to the window to look out.

"Yes, Mam?" Sally asked, wondering why she was hesitating so.

"Your father thought it best for me to prepare you, and so I shall."

She paused, then she squared her shoulders and took a deep breath. "Mr. Mannion has asked your father for your hand," she said quickly over her shoulder.

"What?" Sally asked, horrified, and sure she could not have heard correctly.

"You heard me," her mother replied, turning to face her at last. "Leo Mannion wants to marry you as soon as the banns can be called, and your father has agreed to it."

"He did what?" Sally cried. "Oh no, no! I won't be doin' it! I hate Mr. Mannion, ye know I do! He's a therrible, awful man! How could Da even think o' sich a thing?"

Before her mother could reply she hurried on: "Besides, I'm only just turned fifteen! Mr. Mannion's almost Da's age—old enough to be me father. He's *old*, Mam!"

As she put Forsythe down on the bed and handed him a spool from her work basket to play with, Rose Desmond's pale cheeks reddened. Leo Mannion, at thirty-four, was just her age. "Many men marry younger girls," she said evasively, coming to sit down across from her daughter.

"But . . . but I don't want ter marry—not fer ages! I'm . . . I'm not ready fer it, Mam!"

"At first I thought so myself, but as your father pointed out, I was only sixteen myself when I married. You've had your menses for two years now, Sally, and you've a woman's figure. You're ready."

"But not ready fer Mannion!" Sally protested. In a flash she was out of her chair to crouch by her mother's knee. "Don't make me do it, Mam! Ah please, don't! I tell ye I hate him, so drunk an' crude! An' he's always touchin' me, tryin' ter feel my breasts an' my bottom when he catches me alone. It . . . it makes me feel sick. Oh, please, Mam, *please*! Not Mr. Mannion!"

The tears were streaming down her cheeks now, and Rose Desmond put a work-roughened hand gently on her daughter's hair. It had come loose from its ribbon and hung in a dusky curtain around the perfect oval of her face, framing her horrified, wide blue eyes and trembling, tender mouth.

Ah, but she is lovely, Rose Desmond thought, her own eyes filling with tears. Once I dreamed of her marrying well, to a man of wealth and breeding—a good man. And indeed, a girl as beautiful as Sally deserved such a match. But it was not to be. Remembering some of the things her husband had told her this morning, her lips tightened, and she took her commiserating hand away.

"It must be, Sally," she said, trying to keep her voice steady; stern. "You may have heard Mr. Mannion inherited a large sum of money recently. He'll give you a good home, with plenty to eat and pretty clothes."

"I don't want them!" Sally interrupted. "Not from him!"

"And he's offered your father a goodly settlement for you, one thousand pounds," her mother went on, as if she had not spoken.

Rose Desmond removed her daughter's clinging hands from her knee, and rose to pace the room. "We need that money, my dear. We need it desperately," she said, her voice stronger now. "Indeed, without it, I do not see how we are to survive the winter. There are no rents coming in, and—"

"There aren't any rents comin' in because Da's afther bein' drunk all the time now, an' he doesn't bother ter collect them!" Sally said quickly. "You know how he is, Mam! An' if we're so poor, how does he always seem ter have the money ter buy his whishkey, answer me that?"

Rose Desmond ran to her and slapped her face hard. "You're never to speak of your father in that disrespectful way again, do you hear me, miss?" she demanded. "Never!"

"But . . . but, 'tis true!" Sally wailed, both hands flying to her stinging cheek. "You know 'tis true, Mam! An' if he would but stay sober, an' call on the tenants as he should; if he wouldn't be so soft with them; if he'd *demand* the rents an' threaten ter throw them off his land if they won't pay what's due, I wouldn't have ter marry Mr. Mannion!"

"There's more to it than that, Sally," her mother said, fighting for control. She saw how distraught her daughter was, and she forced herself to make allowances this one time. More quietly, she went on, "There are the boys to educate, and all of us to feed. Besides, I fear Forsythe is going to need special care all his life, and Agnes is so sickly. There's no money now for a doctor, or medicine, and without both I know she'll die."

She paused, but when her daughter had nothing to say she continued, "That's the way of it, Sally. There is nothing else we can do. I can't write to my sister again, and beg her aid. She's given me all she can. You're the only one who can help us now. You should be thanking God a wealthy man wants you; thanking Him that you can help your family in their hour of need. 'Tis your duty."

"No!" Sally cried again, clenching her fists by her

side. "No, I can't! I love ye all, an' I'm sorry, indeed
I am, Mam, but I cannot marry that dreadful man! I
will die if I do!"

"Nay, you'll not die, Sally," her mother said, shaking her head sadly. "You'll grow accustomed. Wives
do. It's . . . it's not so bad, truly. And you'll live
comfortably with him, and when you have babies—"

"I don't want his babbies! I don't want anybody's
babbies!" Sally interrupted. As her mother's brows
rose she hurried on: "Ah, an' don't ye think I can see
with me own eyes what marriage is like? A babby a
year, or a miss, an' nothin' but gettin' older and more
careworn and exhausted an'—"

Mrs. Desmond looked shocked. "Children are God's
gift! You should be ashamed of yourself!"

She flushed then, the high color at odds with her
pale, lined face. "Besides, there may not be that
many. Mr. Mannion is often in his cups and . . . and
well . . . he won't be able to bother you then."

Sally ignored this comforting remark. Leaning forward in her earnestness, she asked, "Ye would do this
ter me? Ye would sell me into the same kind of marriage with a sot that ye have had to endure?"

"You are impertinent, girl!" Mrs. Desmond said
coldly. "I love your father. I always have. He can't
help what he's become, no more than he can help the
hard time we're having these days. If he takes a drop
or two, it's only to console himself for his failure to
do better for us all."

"A drop or two!" Sally repeated, incredulous.
"Why, Mam, an' do ye call it a drop or two when he's
well on the way ter bein' sodden by early afthernoon?
An' he has ter be put ter bed night afther night? Holy
mither!"

"I have no intention of discussing this further. You
will hold your tongue!" Mrs. Desmond said, her color
still high and her lips tight. So upset was she, she even
forgot to scold Sally for cursing. "You will do as we
bid you. Your father has already accepted Mr. Mannion's generous offer. The banns will be called for the
first time this coming Sunday."

Horrified, Sally stared at her mother. Seeing the implacable look on her face, she whirled to leave the room. Mrs. Desmond called after her.

"Stop! You are not to speak to your father of this, 'tis not fitting!" she said to Sally's rigid back. "No, instead you'll put on your Sunday dress and your shoes, and come with me to town. Mr. Mannion has been generous with you as well. There's money for your bride clothes, and best we see to them at once."

She held out her hand to her unseeing daughter and added, "You'll feel better, Sally, when you see what pretty things I intend to buy you. Indeed you will."

Sally waited to hear no more. She ran from the room and pounded down the stairs, almost upsetting Mrs. Ginty as she tore through the kitchen. The old cook opened her mouth to protest, but just as quickly closed it. She knew what was afoot, and was truly sorry for young Sally. But she knew that what must be, must be. And perhaps, with a bit of money, they'd be able to hire another maid. Katty had left long ago, tired of working without wages. Mrs. Ginty sighed as she stirred the thin soup. She'd have gone with her, but she had no other place to go. Bejasus, but things had come to a pretty pass at Ballyragh! she thought, shaking her head sadly.

Sally ran straight from the Hall through the stable yard, past the field where her sister had just finished digging. She ignored Mary's called question, looking neither to the left nor right as she flew. Once or twice she stumbled, for her eyes were so filled with tears she could hardly see the way she took. Marry that drunken brute? Sleep beside him, and give him the right to put his hands on her night after night? She could not! She could not!

Rose Desmond was much relieved when Sally finally came home at dusk. All afternoon she had tried to tell herself that there was nothing to worry about, that Sally was a good girl. She would not do anything foolish. No, surely she would see her duty plain, as

soon as she had wept and bewailed her fate alone for
a while.

Mrs. Desmond would have spoken to her husband
about it, but to avoid any trouble Joseph had gone
out. By the time he reached home late in the afternoon he was so gone with the drink he could not speak
coherently, could only weep and shut himself into his
room. Poor man! she thought tenderly as she went
away. He feels it terribly too, I know he does. He
adored Sally, called her "my morning star." He had
told his wife once that although he knew it was wrong,
he could not help loving this daughter best, for she
reminded him so of her mother when he had first
courted her.

Rose Desmond herself had not liked this marriage,
and she had objected to it as strenuously as possible
when Joseph had first proposed it to her. Leo Mannion, besides being much too old for a fifteen-year-
old girl, was every bit as coarse as Sally had claimed.
Long a drinking companion of her husband's, he had
never married. He raised horses on a run-down estate
nine miles to the east, with a few stable hands to help
and a couple of maids to cook and to clean. The
money Joseph told her about he had inherited from
an uncle of his in England, and the talk was that with
that inheritance he had become a wealthy man.

But to marry her lovely daughter to him! She tried
to tell herself that Sally would become accustomed,
but she was not at all sure of that. Sally had made no
secret of her distaste for this particular friend of her
father's, and once she had even complained to her
mother when Mannion had caught her outside the
Hall when she was only twelve, and insisted on kissing
and fondling her. Knowing her husband could not be
counted on to handle the matter with any authority,
Rose Desmond had then steeled herself to have a few
severe words with Leo Mannion herself. He had blustered and denied everything, but he did keep his
hands to himself from then on.

However, one thousand pounds was one thousand
pounds, and the Desmonds were all but destitute. The

only difference now between them and the villagers and tenant farmers was that they lived in Ballyragh Hall. Perhaps, with Leo Mannion's settlement, there might be enough money to set in train some necessary repairs to the Hall. The roof was leaking badly on the northwest corner, and there was dry rot in some of the floors.

And with the settlement she could summon a doctor for Agnes; see to sending Joseph junior and Michael to Dublin for their education, before they forgot they were the squire's sons completely; put enough food in everyone's mouth, and clothes on their backs.

She had finally agreed to the marriage. Much as she loved her firstborn, Sally was only one, and against her claim were those of the six other children, all of them in dire need.

It was a great shame, but there was no other way. Rose Desmond could not begin to count the hours she had spent on her knees, praying that her husband would reform—stop drinking, and learn to be harder and more assertive. Then, when she had seen there was no chance of that, she prayed for a miracle. Leo Mannion was not a very prepossessing miracle, but there was no denying he was one. Without his money, they all would starve.

She thought Sally looked very pale and sad as she sat and ate her supper of soup and rusks that night, but she was glad to see that the girl's earlier defiance had disappeared. She would take her to town early tomorrow for her bride clothes. Mary could watch over Agnes and Forsythe. In fact, when she learned of the reason for their outing, and of the family's change of fortune, she probably would be happy to do so.

Sally was indeed resigned. When she had run away, she had gone as far from the Hall as she could. Finally, a stitch in her side had forced her to sink down beside a small brook to rest. Lowering her head in her hands, she had wept until there were no more tears to weep. It was unfair, she told herself, cruel! She would not do it! They could not *make* her do it!

But eventually, as the afternoon wore on and every wild idea she had for escape was considered and rejected, she came to accept her fate as something she was powerless to change. Her da had taken the money; indeed, knowing him, he probably had already spent some of it on his whiskey. And it was true the Desmonds were in a bad way. Still, if there had been one place she could have run to for safety, Sally knew she would have done it in a minute. Since her only relative was her mother's sister, who lived many days' travel away, that was not possible. Outside of her lucky sovereign she had no money, and with the number of beggars and thieves and spalpeens roaming about the countryside, her chances of reaching her aunt's house unscathed were so infinitesimal as to be next to none. Besides, she knew her Aunt Dorothy would send her back the very next day. She had met the lady only once in her life, but she knew that such a rigid, proper person would never give shelter to a runaway. It would be unthinkable.

Of course there were the nuns, but since the Desmonds were Church of England, Sally did not think the sisters would be inclined to shelter her. Why should they?

As she had come slowly home in the gloaming, Sally thought long and hard about her future as Mrs. Leo Xaviar Mannion. She supposed she would get used to it. She supposed you could get used to anything. And perhaps, after a bit, Mr. Mannion would get tired of her and leave her alone. Her own da spent little time with his wife, after all, and Mannion was just such a man as he. In the afternoons and evenings he liked to go "rambling about," as the saying had it, from house to house and from pub to pub, being sociable. And when he did come home at last, the worse for drink, she would be fast asleep. She would just have to endure him until those happy days arrived.

The three weeks of the bann-calling passed faster than any Sally had ever known. She had only had to see Mr. Mannion alone a few times during those three weeks, and she had swallowed the bile she felt rising at his loose, familiar kisses and his wandering, fondling hands. She did not realize it, but she had her mother to thank for that. Mrs. Desmond had assured the eager squire that once her daughter was married she would not be so shy, but, calling attention to her tender years, she had begged for his understanding as she kept Sally very much at her side. Although disappointed, Mannion had agreed. It would not be long now. He could wait.

Besides, he was feeling very much the cock of the walk these days, accepting all his friends' vulgar congratulations on the prize he had captured, laughing at their lewd jokes, and winking in response to the sly smiles he was favored with. Ah yes, he knew he was envied, all right!

And when he saw Sally in church the day of their wedding, dressed in the fine clothes his money had bought for her, he had been stunned anew by his good fortune. The girl was an uncommon beauty, worth every penny he had spent to get her! Conscious of the admiring whispers he could hear, he preened himself, well pleased.

By the time the party Joseph Desmond had given in celebration after the ceremony was over, Mannion was feeling less cheerful. All through the party Sally had stayed as far away from him as she could get, and it was only by clamping an arm tight around her waist that he had been able to keep her by his side. White lines bracketed his mouth when he felt her cringe at his touch, before she remembered herself. Further, she had behaved as if she were at a funeral. She had not wept, of course, but neither had she smiled—not once. And her face was so white and still, her eyes so resigned yet despairing, that it was obvious even to those who had been dipping heavily into the whiskey punch that she had not come to him willingly. Forcing himself to smile and be pleasant, he still saw the women's scornful looks, heard the men's whispers and hastily stifled laughter, and he seethed, even as he pretended to be well pleased and called for yet another glass, and then another.

Her father was nowhere to be seen when Sally kissed her family good-bye. She could only be glad of it, for her feelings for him had undergone such a great change. *Weeping, no doubt he is, with a large glass of his whishkey to keep him company,* she thought bitterly. *Whishkey I bought him. I hope he remembers that!*

She did shed a few tears herself when the wedding guests called their good wishes, and when she saw that Mikey's thumb had gone to his mouth for comfort now that he was losing his favorite sister. The unfamiliar gold band on her left hand reminded her, however, that she must wipe her eyes and cry no more. A moment or two later Mannion's chaise was taking the turn out of the gates of Ballyragh, and it was done: Ballyragh was no longer her home. She must make the best of it.

She stole a glance at her new bridegroom, almost for the first time that day. Mr. Mannion obviously had dressed with great care for his wedding. His linen was so white, it had to be new, his plum-colored coat well brushed, and his boots highly polished. She had never seen him looking so neat. She knew he was not unhandsome. He was tall and loose-limbed, with regular features that were only slightly blurred and reddened with the drinking he had indulged in over the years, and when he bothered to reveal it he had an attractive smile.

As she looked at his face, she was startled to see his black expression and tightly compressed lips. All the jovial smiles and the jests he had treated the guests to were gone, as if they had never been.

But why did he look so angry? Sally wondered, much confused. Now that he had what he had wanted for so long, she had expected him to crow over her.

"Is—is there something displeasing ye, sor?" she ventured to ask.

Mannion spared her one furious sideways glance before he whipped the horse to a faster pace.

"Whist!" he said roughly. "Ye'll find out when we get home, an' not before. Keep yer mouth shut!"

Sally grasped her hands together even more tightly in her lap, and stared straight ahead as the chaise thundered along the winding country road. She hoped Mr. Mannion would not overturn them, for surely at this pace they would both be killed. And even dreading this marriage as she was, she did not want to die. Remembering all the punch he had consumed she said a small prayer for her safety, even as she continued to wonder why he was upset. Perhaps someone had said something he had not liked at the party? Perhaps the drink had made him surly?

She did not see the green fields spinning past them, nor the hills in the distance, and as they careened through a few small hamlets she did not respond to the waves and cheers of the villagers, all of them come out of their cottages to see the bride.

She had never been to Mr. Mannion's estate, and she looked at the large brick house he pulled up before with vague interest. This was to be her home, now and forever. It was seedy-looking, its small gardens neglected and full of weeds. Beyond it were the stables and paddocks, and the usual plot planted to vegetables.

A stableboy came running to take charge of the lathered horse, and Mannion jumped down and came around without speaking to him.

Sally found herself lifted from the perch and swung to the ground without ceremony. A large, firm hand at her back propelled her up the steps and through the door that had swung open to welcome them. The maid who stood there gaped at them before she bobbed a curtsy and scurried away.

Mannion paid her no more heed than he had the stableboy. Grasping Sally's hand, he pulled her up the stairs so fast she almost tripped over her new skirts.

Not until he had shoved her into a large front bedroom and slammed the door behind them was she able to look at him.

But before she could speak, ask him again what was wrong, he slapped her so hard her head rang. She staggered away from him to fall heavily against a large bureau.

"Slut!" he roared. "Make a mockery o' me, would ye? Well, ye'll pay fer it!"

He came toward her again, fists raised, and, bewildered and frightened, Sally asked, "What do ye mean, sor? I—I never did that!"

"Didn't ye just, and ye my bride? All my friends there at the weddin' party was laughin' at me, while ye drooped around with sich a look on yer face, 'twas like a murtherer being led to the gallows! An' not one smile outta ye all day! *Ye*, what cost me over a thousand pounds! Where's yer gratitude?"

He hit her hard again then, with his fist this time, and Sally found herself screaming at the sudden pain in her jaw.

"Oh, don't, I beg ye, don't hit me no more!" she pleaded, trying to back away from him and protect her face at the same time.

He grasped her arms so tightly that she gasped. As he shook her hard he snarled, "I meant ter treat ye kindly, take the throuble not ter frighten ye, but ye don't deserve that. Not now, ye don't!"

He let her go, but only so he could shove her toward the big four-poster bed against the wall. "Take yer clothes off!" he ordered, shrugging out of his coat as he did so. "I'd rip 'em off ye, 'cept I know well what they cost me, and I've no mind ter ruin 'em fer the likes of ye, ye ungrateful little bitch!"

Sally stared at him aghast. The room was full of the afternoon sunlight that was streaming through the front windows. She had never expected anything to happen till much later, when it was dark and the household asleep. But she was sure the maids could hear every word he bellowed; why, probably even the stable hands could hear him, too. She had never been so ashamed.

"I said take yer clothes off, and quickly, too! It'll go worse fer ye if ye don't. I'll beat ye till yer bloody, I will," he told her, sitting down to remove his boots and throw them one after the other across the room.

Sally's teeth were chattering, and her hands were trembling as she obeyed. Her new chip bonnet and the pretty white muslin dress trimmed with pink ribbons were removed and placed over a chair. Her lace-trimmed petticoat followed. She dared not look at Mr. Mannion, although she could tell from the sudden quiet in the room that he had stopped what he was doing to watch her. She felt the heat come up her body and suffuse her aching face, and she wished she might die. Her head still rang from his blows, and her arms smarted where he had gripped them so cruelly.

She lowered her head to remove her sandals and the pink stockings that were just like the ones the English lady had worn that day long ago when she had had her sovereign. She remembered, even in all her pain and humiliation, that they had been the only article of clothing her mother had bought her that she had felt any interest in at all.

Clad only in her thin chemise at last, she sank down on the bed. Her legs were shaking so, she was afraid they would not hold her up.

"Take that off, too," he said, his voice quieter now but still full of rage.

Sally could not force herself to move. Instead, she wrapped her arms around her breasts and sat shivering with terror. And still she could not look at him.

Wearing only his breeches, he came to her all in a rush and pulled her to her feet. One hand held both of hers above her head, while the other yanked the chemise up and away from her.

"Ye'll learn ter obey me, missus, or ye'll be the sorrier fer it!" he said, as he pushed her down on the bed. Sally barely had time to draw breath before he was on top of her, his hands cruelly squeezing her breasts and his legs prying her own wide apart. His kiss, when it came, was brutal. She gagged and choked, and he drew back to slap her again, hard.

Half-delirious with pain, Sally almost fainted, but the shock of the invasion of her body brought her to her senses. She could not help screaming with the pain of it as he pummeled her over and over, faster and

faster, until she was sure she was about to be broken
in two. It seemed an endless time to her in her agony,
but in reality it was only minutes before he gave a
guttural cry and collapsed on top of her, all his heavy
weight crushing her down in the bed. She could not
breathe, she knew she was bleeding, and she was sure
she was dying.

He raised his head after a moment. "Open yer eyes,
Missus Leo Xaviar Mannion!" he panted in a rough,
uneven voice. "Look at me!"

Sobbing, and gasping for breath, Sally made herself
do as he ordered. She saw the triumphant look on his
face, smelled the whiskey he had drunk, and his
sweat, and she tried not to vomit.

"Aye," he said, nodding to her. "I've taken yer
purse, an' yer my wife now. Ye'll learn ter like it. Or
else.

"An' if ye don't learn ter please me, smile fer me,
I'll beat ye till ye do."

Sally saw his eyes narrow as he stared down at her
naked, violated body. The slight change of his expression made her breath flutter in her throat with fear.
Not again! she prayed. Dear God, not again!

Her prayer was not answered. Sometime later,
Mannion rolled off her and rose to button his breeches
and collect the rest of his clothes.

When he was dressed, he came back to the bed.
Sally lay huddled where he had left her, a fist in her
mouth to still her sobs. He pulled that fist away so he
could study her white, tear-streaked face, see the
bruises already darkening the fair skin where he had
hit her.

"Worked up an appetite fer supper an' a glass or
two, I have," he said in his normal tone of voice. "I
see ye don't care ter join me. No matter. I prefer ye
here. Don't bother ter dress."

Sally held her breath until the door had slammed
behind him. Still she dared not move, until she heard
his booted feet clattering down the stairs. Only then
did she roll into as small a ball as she could and give
in to her tears. Her jaw ached, and when she touched

it gingerly she could feel the lump there. One of her eyes ached too, so badly she dared not investigate. Finally, she gained enough courage to put her hands between her legs. She was sticky with blood and semen, but at least she was in one piece, although she could not have told you whether that was an advantage or not.

An hour later she heard a timid knock on the door. She sat up, heart pounding, grabbing the quilt that had been placed on the bed and pulling it tightly around her.

She could not speak, and when she did not answer another knock the door opened slowly. The little maid she had seen when she'd first entered the house put her head around the door. Her mouth dropped open and her eyes widened when she saw Sally's face. Shaking her head, she slipped into the room carrying a can of hot water and a towel. Quickly, as if she feared being discovered there, she placed them on the washstand and hurried back to the door. She hesitated as if she meant to speak, but a roar from below made her start and hurry away.

Sally forced herself to get up and go and wash. There was a mirror over the washstand, but she did not look into it. She did not feel she could ever look into her own eyes again, not after what had happened to her. She felt fouled, dehumanized—her spirit broken.

And, she told herself sadly, this was only the beginning. It wouldn't do any good to tell herself that things might get better, that she might find a way to temper Mannion's anger, keep him from beating her again. She knew he would do so, and she also knew that she was not strong enough, or brave enough, to stop him.

No, she was neither strong nor brave—and how it hurt to have to acknowledge that. She, Sally Desmond, who had always thought of herself as intrepid, unafraid of anything, had been humbled in a matter of minutes by a beating and a rape. She realized now that women were vulnerable in ways she had never imagined, and that they were utterly at the mercy of men and their whims. It was a hard lesson.

Well, she told herself, she would recover from this beating, and the next one, and the next. She was strong. She would not die. But she also knew that some important part of her had died today. It was something more than mere innocence, and no matter how long she lived she would never be able to bring it back to life again. She could not help but mourn its loss.

Chapter Three

THE MARRIAGE LASTED for three months.

Mannion had not bothered Sally again on their wedding night, for by the time he had staggered upstairs, muttering and cursing, he was too drunk to be interested in anything but sleep.

The next morning he had seemed sheepish, and had avoided her eye, even though he was still in the devil's own temper. He had gone to the paddocks, and outside of his solitary dinner he had not come back to the house all day. Sally had rested, nursing her bruises, before she dressed and went to make the acquaintance of the maids.

At supper, Mannion still would not look at her. Sally did not even have to wonder why. Her face was a mass of livid color, her jaw was misshapen, and her right eye was completely closed.

Her appearance, and his shame at being the cause of it, had not been enough to keep him away from her that night, however. Sally gritted her teeth as he fumbled her night robe up to her waist. To her surprise, it did not hurt anywhere near as much as it had the first time. But later, as she lay there clutching the edge of the feather bed, to avoid any more contact with him where he lay sprawled in the hollow at the center, she was still revolted. She thought she had never heard any more wonderful sound than his first loud snore, when it came at last.

She discovered early in her marriage that Mannion would not allow her to leave the house, not even for a walk on his own land. Sally was sure it was because of the way she looked, and she didn't care. Given the condition she was in, she certainly didn't want anyone to see her any more than he did.

She was sorry when the bruises faded. He asked her once, after he had had a few glasses of whiskey, why she wouldn't smile or at least look pleasant, and she had told him coldly that her jaw hurt so badly she could not smile. In fact, she had added, it was hard for her to chew her food. He had colored up at her answer, and had not pressed her again. Yet she knew that when she looked again much as she had the day she'd married, she'd no longer have any excuse. And she had nothing to smile about.

He came to her regularly—at night, and sometimes first thing in the morning. Only when she had her menses was she free of him. She found she could not restrain that small involuntary shiver of revulsion when he touched her, and that seemed to anger him anew. He began to beat her again, although he was careful now to leave her face unmarked. It was not much of an improvement, Sally thought, as she took a shallow breath one morning after he had kicked her and cracked a rib.

The maids, Sue and Aggie, were no help to her, but Sally could not fault them for that. They were as frightened of Mannion as she was, especially when he was drunk. When she had first arrived at the farm, Sally had seen the marks of old bruises on their faces and arms. Her advent as mistress here must have been a relief to them, for it had meant Mannion had someone new to vent his quick anger on.

After ten days of seclusion on his farm, Mannion took up his old life again. He slept late, then worked around the horses with his three stable hands for most of the afternoon. Twice a week, however, at three, he would storm into the house, yell for hot water, wash, and change his dirty clothes. His horse would be waiting when he came belowstairs again, and without a word to Sally he would be gone, rambling about to visit his friends. Sally came to dread those days, for when he returned late at night he would invariably be furious.

She wondered what people could be saying to him to get him in such a temper, and why, when they did so, he took it out on her. Pretending to be asleep when he came to bed did her no good at all. He just pulled her out of bed and proceeded to kick and to punch her until she screamed with pain.

She had heard about the Horse Fair that was to be held near Waterford in late October, and knowing that Mannion planned to go, taking several of his horses to sell or to race, she looked forward to it even more eagerly than he did. He would be gone for three days, maybe more if the sales pleased him. Looking ahead to those three blessed days alone was her lifeline to sanity.

Sally tried to be a good wife. She oversaw the complete cleaning of the house, made sure her husband's meals were hot and tasty and served on time, and that his linen was freshly ironed when he called for it. But Mannion did not seem impressed by her efforts, and once, when she had placed a small bouquet of late garden flowers on the dinner table, he had thrown the whole into the fireplace. It was true he had been in his cups then, but even so, Sally never repeated that small domestic gesture.

The night before he was to leave for Waterford, Mannion did not go out. Sally was forced to sit in the main room with him, busying herself with some mending. Every so often she would steal a timid glance at him. He was drinking heavily, and looking blacker than ever. She knew he'd feel all that whiskey when he was pounding over the country roads tomorrow, and she was glad. She only hoped he would not drink so much that he'd be forced to delay his departure.

When he rose unsteadily at last, and came toward her, all her inward defiance faded, and she felt the now familiar terror well up in her breast. Her breathing grew shallow, her mouth dry, and she could feel perspiration coming out all over her body. Mannion had a crop in his hands, one he had bought only that day in New Ross, and she eyed it with misgiving. He had never used anything but his fists and his feet to beat her before. Surely he did not intend to horsewhip her!

"Bitch!" he said roughly as he pulled her to her feet, scattering her sewing around her feet. "Bitch! I'll show ye!"

"No, don't, please don't!" she cried, trying to twist away from his hard grip. "Oh, whatever is wrong? What have I done now? Please, please, just tell me, and I'll try ter do better!" she pleaded.

"Better, ye say? Aye, an' the divil will find himself in hivin before ye do that!" he snarled. He pulled her close, so close she could see the tiny brown flecks in his red-rimmed hazel eyes, the bristles of his beard— smell his hot, fetid breath.

"Ye want ter know what's wrong, missus?" he asked. "Why, it be that every time I go ter town, or even about ter see my friends, everyone asks fer the bride. Mere manners, ye say? Aye, but *ye* don't have ter see the smirks on their faces, *ye* don't have ter hear them whisperin' behind me back, as I do, so I know they're laughin' at me! Laughin' 'cause they know, yeah, somehow they know, ye don't want me an' ye never did!"

He shook her then, and Sally bit her lower lip. There was no sense in pointing out to him that that was not her fault, for he had always known it yet he had married her anyway. She had found in these past ninety-four days of marriage, each one carefully counted, that if she spoke back to him it only went worse for her.

He pulled her over to the hearth, and taking a length of cord from his pocket he proceeded to tie her hands to the low-hanging beam over her head.

"What . . . what are ye doin'?" she whispered. "Oh please, fer God's sake, don't hurt me again!"

His answer was to rip the gown open down her back. Her chemise followed. Sally struggled with her bonds but she could not get away, and as she waited for what she knew was coming she seemed able to hear every little breath he took, every little crackle of the peat fire before her. The sound of the lash as it whistled through the air was louder than thunder in her ears.

The pain of this beating was unlike anything he had ever inflicted on her before. Screaming and begging for mercy, Sally was unaware of the blood that was soaking into the gown bunched about her waist. Again and again he hit her, until her back was flaming so with pain, it burned much more brightly than the sullen turf fire did.

Finally, mercifully, she fainted.

Mannion stopped his stroke in midair when he saw her body sagging loosely beneath her bonds. He left her hanging there while he went back to the table and poured himself another glass of whiskey. Through the red film that seemed to cover his eyes, he saw how badly he had hurt her. The welts crisscrossed each other, and most of them were bleeding.

Ah, but he had a fearsome temper, he knew. A shame it was, a cryin' shame. But it were all her fault, the slut, he told himself. He'd married her in good faith, an' spent a lot o' money ter get her, an' wot was his reward? A surly wife who never talked to him, who acted, in fact, as if he were someone off a dung heap, one who never wanted a romp in bed. Aye, an' one who even dared to cringe away in horror when he touched her. Well, he'd shown her, hadn't he? Served her right, the bitch! he thought, as he poured himself a last glass "fer the road-like."

When Sally did not recover consciousness after several minutes, Mannion had the grace to feel a little uneasy. He got up and staggered over to her, carrying the knife he had used at supper. He soon had her cut down, and when she collapsed in a heap on the floor, he picked her up and laid her on the settle, facedown. He even arranged a pillow under her head before he knelt beside her, concerned now. By bending his head closer he could just catch her thready breathing, and immediately he felt better. She'd do. She were a strong lass, fer all her little waist an' dainty figure. He noticed a wool throw on the back of the settle and he put it over her. He even made up the fire so she wouldn't feel the chill.

She'd do better down here, he told himself, as he took his candle and went to the stairs. Besides, he couldn't have 'er bleeding all over the bed, or possibly wakin' him with 'er infernal cryin', now could he? He had a journey to make on the morrow, and he wanted an early start. He'd need a good night's sleep for that.

When Sally came to, she was blessedly alone. Her back was on fire still, and when she tried to move the wool of the throw irritated the open wounds so, it was all she could do to stifle a scream. She saw she was lying on the hard settle before the fire. There wasn't a sound in the room. Either Mannion had gone to bed, or he had passed out on the floor behind her. She did not dare move, in case he had. She might wake him.

She could not sleep. All that night she lay there alone in her agony, and when the first graying of dawn began to lighten the room she had made her plans. She would go home. She would not stay here any longer. If she did, it would be only a matter of time before he maimed her, or killed her. And even if he didn't, she knew that if she stayed she would most surely kill him. Somehow, some way, she would have to kill him, and she wanted to die on the gallows no more than she wanted to die at his hands.

Mannion left only a short time later. Sally heard him above her, moving around and dressing, then clumping down the stairs and roaring for his tea. Only then did he come over to the settle and bend down.

"Ye awake?" he asked, his voice still ragged with sleep.

Sally nodded a little. She did not open her eyes. It seemed an endless time before he straightened and moved away.

When Aggie came in with his tea and scones and porridge, she gasped. Sally heard the harsh slap Mannion gave her before he said, "None o' that, now! She got what she deserved.

"When I'm gone, you see ter her. She'll need some salve fer her back. I'll expect her ter be better when I get home, so best ye take care o' her, girl, or it'll be the worse fer ye."

Sally made herself lie motionless, counting the minutes as she did so. She heard him eating, and drinking his tea, and the chink of the crockery when he touched it. She heard him when he pushed his chair back and got up to urinate out the front door, bellowing for the lads to bring the horses as he did so. Still she did not move. Get out! she ordered him silently. Just go!

Wary, she did not move when he slammed the door behind him. He might have forgotten something. He might still come back.

Aggie came in minutes later, making clucking noises as she set down another tray. Sally opened her eyes, and screamed when she felt the maid trying to pull the throw off her back.

"Aye, I know it hurts, missus, but there's no help fer it," Aggie muttered. "It's all dried on with the blood, an' I got ter get it off."

"Get warm water then, soak it off," Sally managed to say. "An' get Sue ter help ye."

The two maids worked as carefully as they could, but Sally fainted again before they were through. Perhaps it was just as well, for she did not feel any pain when they washed her cuts and put the salve on them. She came to herself just as they were lifting her in order to put a soft old chemise over her head.

"No!" she cried, frightened that she might have to have the undergarment soaked off, too. "Leave it open ter the air! It . . . it will heal faster!"

Sue nodded. "I'll get ye some tay, missus, an' I'll lace it with whiskey, so I will. Ye could use it," she said gruffly, as she put the throw over Sally's legs. It was damp, and stiff with dried blood, but Sally knew she couldn't lie there naked. Out of the corner of her eye she saw Aggie bundling up the ruined gown, and the basin of red-stained water and dirty cloths. She shuddered.

After she had sat up and drunk several cups of the

doctored tea, Sally felt better. She had planned to leave today, but she knew that was not possible now. There was no way she could stand to have clothes on her back, no way she would be able to walk all the way to Ballyragh. And she knew she had to walk. The stableboy who had been left to care for the rest of the stock would not help her, nor would the maids, for fear of Mannion's anger. Sally knew they were sure to be beaten anyway when he returned and found her gone, and she was sorry for it, but perhaps he would go easier on them if they could say they had had no knowledge of what she had planned to do.

She would have to wait until tomorrow. She hoped that would give her enough time to reach home, and she prayed, even harder than she had for Mannion to leave the house, that the Horse Fair would be a resounding success for him. If it was, if he sold his horses for a good price and picked up some promising new stock at a bargain, if he met a convivial friend to drink with, he might linger there. He might even meet a pretty, willing wench, and forget his wife. Sternly, she told herself that making up happy endings for stories would do her no good now. She must plan for the worst that could happen.

Staggering to the table and sitting well away from the back of the chair, she ate some breakfast before she let Aggie help her up the stairs. She collapsed facedown on the feather bed. It smelled of Mannion, but she was too tired and sore to care.

She was awake well before dawn the next day. She had dozed off and on all the previous day, trying to build up her strength, and she had made herself eat hearty meals. During the times when she was awake she planned what she would wear, and what food she would take from the larder. An old gown would be best, she thought, and over it that dark blue shawl her mother had knit for her. She would call less attention to herself dressed that way. She would need another shawl to wrap the food in, and she must wear her shoes. The soles of her feet had grown soft these past three months of being housebound. But she would take none of her wedding clothes—no, not even the pink stockings. Nothing *he* had given her, nothing at all, except, of course, his wedding ring—and her bloody back.

She dressed as quickly as she could. She had to stifle a cry when she put an old chemise on, for it rubbed against the still raw welts on her back. It can't be helped, she told herself as she buttoned her gown over it. Bending and stretching to put on her hose and shoes hurt her too, but she set her mouth in a hard line and persisted. Checking the bureau one last time, she saw her gold sovereign in one of the drawers and she picked it up. It was hers. It had nothing to do with Mannion. And she might need it, and not as a lucky piece either, she told herself, as she put it in her pocket. A fine lucky piece *it* had turned out to be! No, it was not magical. It was only money after all.

Coming down the steep stairs hurt so much that for a moment she could only cling, panting, to the newel post at the bottom. Dear God, suppose she could not do it? Suppose she couldn't even get as far as the road? She put up her chin. She'd *crawl* to Ballyragh if she had to, but she'd get there.

Sally had counted on the maids sleeping late now that their master was away, and as she had suspected there was no one in the kitchen. She put as much bread and cheese in her shawl as she dared, hoping Sue would not notice it was missing. She hoped as well that both maids would not be suspicious when she didn't ring for them. Perhaps, if she were very lucky, they would not even investigate for some time, maybe thinking that a good sleep would help her back heal faster.

She did not look behind her as she started down the drive. She was leaving, and no matter what she had to do, she was never coming back. She was so stiff that every step she took was painful, but she concentrated on putting one foot in front of the other, over and over again. She was young and strong. She could do it.

She did not stop to rest until she was well away from the farm. She had cut across a field to a small lane that led west. She did not know this part of the county, but she knew that was the direction she had to travel. And she did not dare stay on the main road that Mannion had used to drive her here on the wedding day. Someone might see her, someone who would remember her. The fewer people she saw, the better.

Of course, Sally knew it was impossible to escape notice entirely. Too many people were tramping the roads, looking for work. She almost always heard them coming, though, and she was quick to conceal herself behind a hedge or a tree until they were safely past. When a few did surprise her she pulled the shawl well forward to hide both her hair and her face, and she pretended she was a cross old woman who could not be bothered to stop and pass the time of day. Because she could only walk stooped over anyway, her disguise stood her in good stead. No one bothered her.

By dusk she was exhausted. She had no idea how far she had come, or even if she was traveling the right road, but she knew she had to stop for the night, to rest. There were no farms near, but it would be safer to sleep out anyway. She found a small copse, and after eating a little and drinking from a nearby brook, she curled up in her shawls on her side and tried to sleep. She knew she had been missed by now, and that knowledge preyed on her mind. Maybe the maids had even sent the stableboy off to tell Mannion of her disappearance. If only they would wait for his return—oh, please, let them wait!—she still might be safely home in time.

Sally had to spend another night in the open. Her back had hurt more and more during the next day's trek, forcing her to rest often. She could tell from the trickle of blood she felt that some of the welts had opened again. She cried that night from more than pain and exhaustion, however. She cried because she could go no faster, and it was taking her too much time. Why, Mannion might be close behind her even now. She was frightened.

She was on her way at dawn, and after an hour's plodding—one foot set doggedly after the other—she smiled for the first time.

She had reached a crossroads she recognized, one she had passed often on the way to town. She would have to travel cross-country from now on, for she was far south of Ballyragh. She knew it would be harder on her that way, but she was driven by the need for haste. Besides, the sky looked threatening; it was going to rain soon.

Although she was wet through, and near the end of her strength, when Sally saw the gates of Ballyragh before her late that afternoon she almost fell to her knees in relief. No! she told herself as she struggled forward, fiercely dashing a hand across her eyes to wipe away her weak tears. I must not stop yet!

The front door was closest, but she was afraid her da might have company, so she made her way around to the back.

"Jasus, Mary, and Joseph!" Mrs. Ginty exclaimed, hands to her heart as Sally staggered into the kitchen and collapsed on the floor. "Missus Desmond, mum! Come quick!"

"Be quiet!" Sally ordered, as she struggled to crawl over to the bench by the table. "No one must know I'm here! Fetch my mam."

Mrs. Ginty crossed herself and scurried away, and Sally pulled herself up to the bench. She dropped her head on her arms on the table, and she was almost asleep when she felt her mother's gentle hand on her shoulder. She screamed at the touch.

"Sally! What is wrong with you?" Rose Desmond asked. "And what are you doing here?"

"I've come home, Mam. I'm never goin' back," her daughter told her.

Mrs. Desmond began to wring her hands. "Now, Sally, you know that isn't possible. Why, you're a married woman now, and your place is with your husband. It's . . . it's not that I'm not that glad to see you, but you cannot stay. Just think of the settlement! We can't give it back, and . . ."

Sally struggled to her feet, grasping the edge of the table for support. Her head spinning, she said, "No, Mam, I'm not goin' back. Besides, I've earned that settlement, every penny of it.

"Mannion beat me. He's beaten me so bad I've been feared I'd die sometimes. I've walked all the way here in pain fer three long days ter get away from him, an' nothin'—nobody—can make me go back."

Rose Desmond leaned closer. She saw something in her daughter's face that had not been there three months ago, and she had to put her hand over her mouth to keep from crying out. No one of only fifteen years should ever have such old eyes, she thought.

"But—but you can't stay here, Sally!" she whispered. "Mannion will just come and fetch you home, and we can't stop him."

"If he touches me again, I'll kill him," Sally said, her voice flat and menacing. Behind her, she heard Mrs. Ginty calling on her saints to forgive the lass for even thinking such a thing. Sally didn't care about forgiveness. She meant it.

"I don't want anyone ter know I'm here yet. Is Da home?" she asked, in the stunned silence that had fallen.

"Why, yes, but I fear this is not a good time for you to talk to your father, for—"

"I know, Mam. I'll see him termorrow.

"I don't think I can manage the stairs. It's me back. He beat me with a crop, and it's all bloody cuts."

As Rose Desmond exclaimed Mrs. Ginty said, "Put 'er in my room, mum. 'Twill make it easier ter tend her. Jest ye go an' lie down, lass. I'll bring some salve fer yer back, an' some hot soup."

"Yes, that would be best, I suppose," Mrs. Desmond said. "I'll help you, dear."

But when she had helped Sally to undress, and had seen her back, Rose Desmond burst into tears. As she could only sob helplessly, it was a thin-lipped Mrs. Ginty who had to wash the cuts and apply the salve;

Mrs. Ginty who spooned the soup for her. "Lie still now, lass," she said as she took the empty bowl away. "Ye didn't do yerself no good at all, at all, walkin' all that way, the shape yer in. I fear there'll be scars from it."

"Oh, that beast!" Mrs. Desmond wept. "My beautiful Sally! But *why*? *Why* would he do such a thing?"

The cook took her firmly by the arm. "Come away, do, mum," she said, as she herded her to the door of her little room off the kitchen. "She's almost asleep now. Time enough ter ask termorrow."

Sally slept straight through to the following afternoon. When she woke she was still in pain, but now she was able to smile, for she was home, safe home at Ballyragh. Her first question was of Mannion, and her relief that he had not appeared as yet was obvious.

As she ate some food, still in bed, Sally told her mother everything. "Ye see, Mam," she concluded, "Leo Mannion's not like Da, all weepy and sentimental when he's drunk. No, he turns mean then. An' he thinks everybody's laughin' at him fer marryin' me. It's then he beats me. Why, he beat me the minute he got me back ter his farm after the weddin', an' then he made me take off my clothes fer him, an' he—he . . ."

Her mother's choke gave her pause, and she took a deep breath and said more quietly, "I won't go back to him, Mam. Not ever."

Horrified at the story, Rose Desmond agreed, but still she was perturbed. Sally's place was with her husband. She did not see how they could stop him from taking her back. But to her great surprise, Mannion did not come hotfoot to Ballyragh to fetch the runaway home. Instead he sent a letter to his wife, asking her to return to him, and he promised he would forgive her if she did.

Sally was not fooled. She had spoken to her father, early enough in the day so he would be sober and remember it, and showed him her back. By his furious reaction she knew that even as weak a man as Joseph Desmond would stand by her in this.

Accordingly she sent Mannion a curt reply, telling him she had no intention of ever coming back, and threatening to go to the courts about it if he bothered her again. For a safeguard, she told him a doctor had seen and treated her back, and he would swear to her story of abuse. To everyone's relief, Mannion was heard from no more.

If Sally could have erased the three months of her marriage from her memory, being home at Ballyragh would have seemed the same as if she had never been away at all. After her back had healed she slipped into her old routines: working with the little boys on their lessons, minding the babies for her mother, and helping Mrs. Ginty in the kitchen. She refused to discuss the marriage with her sister Mary, and eventually Mary stopped asking about it. But Sally could not forget those three months. She might have escaped Leo Mannion, but Leo Mannion and his treatment of her would be with her to the end of her life.

The winter months went by and spring came, but still Sally stayed very close to home. She would not even go to the village or to town with her mother, lest her husband see her and try to take her back by force. He must be furious with her! Since everyone in the county knew she had left him, those whispers behind his back must have turned into loud guffaws, the little smirks into wide grins. How he must hate it, and—especially—her. She would take no chances, for she knew only too well how he would punish her for having made him a laughingstock, if he ever got his hands on her.

A company of British soldiers had been stationed in a large new barracks nearby that spring, and Sally often saw one or two of them in the distance as they rode the countryside, looking for the illegal stills that abounded in the county. Like the smugglers on the English coast, Irishmen saw no reason for paying a tax on liquor they could make themselves.

The red-coated soldiers had been very much a presence in Ireland since the United Irishmen had been suppressed in 1794. They were here to keep the peace, put down the frequent demonstrations, and subdue any desire for Irish independence. Inspired by the American and French revolutions, the Irish were restless.

The senior officer in charge of the barracks was an older man, who'd even called at Ballyragh one afternoon. Sally had just come downstairs as he was leaving, and she met him in the hall outside her father's room. No doubt he had been inquiring where Da obtained his whiskey, Sally thought, as she dropped him a curtsy and prepared to pass.

The officer seemed startled by the sight of her, but he smiled at her kindly as he bowed and asked her name. When he learned she was a Mrs. Mannion his surprise was evident, but Sally was not tempted to smile, nor did she as they exchanged a few pleasantries about the clement weather.

Colonel Peter Jenkins was much struck by the squire's daughter. Surely she was the most beautiful girl he had ever seen in all his fifty-three years. Why, his own pretty daughter couldn't hold a candle to her! But still, he wondered, as he took a courteous leave of her, what she, a married woman, was doing living in her parents' home. For that matter, she didn't even look old enough to be wed! These Irish had some strange customs, to be sure.

He decided he would like to learn more of her and resolved to call on Squire Desmond of Ballyragh again. The man was a sot, but an amiable one, and the only man close to the colonel's age among the gentry in the immediate neighborhood. Indeed, the squire had already invited him to come again, any time he liked; had assured him he would always be given a welcome there.

As he rode away, the colonel wondered what there was about the squire's daughter that set her apart from other girls her age. It was not her brogue or her deep little voice, no, not even her breathtaking loveliness and graceful figure. Ireland abounded with handsome women, as gracious and charming as they were attractive. Of course this Mrs. Mannion was very young, that was true, but it was not that either.

He decided it was partly an intriguing air of mystery which clung to her that set her apart; that, and her quiet demeanor. There was nothing of the coquette about her, and she had extraordinary poise for one of her age and upbringing. Would that his daughter Anne had such self-possession!

But above all, he thought, it was a certain look in her dark blue eyes. It was a wary, considering look she had, as if she were weighing a man for good or for ill, no matter what his age, ready to forget him in a minute if he fell short of her standards. And, her look told you, she would not be at all surprised if he did.

What had happened to her in her brief lifetime, to give her that wariness, that knowledge of all men's frailties?

The colonel was amazed at how very much he regretted that she'd had to learn such a hard lesson, so lovely as she was.

Chapter Four

1809

COLONEL PETER JENKINS became a regular visitor to Ballyragh after that. He was disappointed at first when he saw so little of young Mrs. Mannion, but it was not long before he had most of her story from her father. By careful questioning one afternoon, when Joseph Desmond was well on the way to insensibility, he heard all about her marriage to a man over twice her age, the generous settlement her parents had received for her, which was the reason the marriage had been agreed to at all, and—although not in any great detail of course, for the squire was weeping gustily by that time—a few vague reasons for why she had come home again. The colonel was disgusted by the tale—disgusted and appalled. To think that that lovely child had been as good as sold, and at fifteen, no less! he thought hotly, all his paternal instincts coming to the fore. No wonder she was so cool and quiet. No wonder she looked untrusting. It was too bad.

In the following days he continued to seek young Sally out. He knew he was missing Anne, who at nineteen was not much older than Mrs. Mannion. Sometimes he would find her taking a walk around the grounds, and he would join her. As they walked he told her of his daughter, and answered all her eager questions about England and Anne's life. She was soon "Sally" to him, and he was pleased when she finally began to smile for him; pleased he could bring a little happiness into her bleak life, become a man she could trust.

One morning, stopping at the hall to leave a special

gift of old brandy for her father, Jenkins found her trying to teach her oldest brothers their lessons.

Neither Joey nor Mikey thought much of lessons, and their attention was quickly distracted by the colonel's entrance, with his beaming, good-natured face adorned by the unusual mustache that, once seen, could never be forgotten. Mikey had often had to leave the room in a fit of laughter when the older British officer appeared, for the colonel, although what hair he had left was iron-gray, sported a luxuriant, bright-red brush above his mouth. For some reason, Mikey found this hilarious. This particular morning he could not control himself either, and seeing how confused the colonel was, Sally dismissed both boys.

As they ran laughing from the room, and she collected the battered schoolbooks and exercise papers, she shook her head in regret at their manners. The colonel, who had seen her brother Forsythe once, said quickly, "You must not feel it so, Sally! Many families have more than one simple member. Nothing at all to be concerned about, my dear child! Why, I have a cousin who had to be put away because he, er, he . . ."

Here he coughed and changed the subject. Sally stared at him in amazement. When it occurred to her that he thought Mikey an idiot, she had to laugh herself. "No, no, there's nothing wrong with Michael, sor," she finally got out. " 'Tis just that . . . that . . . oh, dear, I don't know how ter say it!"

"Say what?" the colonel asked, coming to take the pile of books from her hands.

"May I be truthful, sor?" she asked, her eyes steady on his.

"But of course you may," Colonel Jenkins assured her, putting the books on a table nearby.

"It's yer mustache, sor," Sally confessed, her lower lip quivering.

Encouraged by the sight of her mirth, Jenkins prompted, "My mustache? He finds my mustache amusing? But—but why? Surely he has seen one before, has he not?"

"Well, yes, but not like yers. Ye must admit it is unusual, and it is rather a . . . a contrast."

The colonel smiled at her and chuckled. "Yes, I daresay it does look a bit strange. Couldn't believe it myself, when I began to grow it years ago. I had dark brown hair then. But m'mother assured me it was just the same for my grandfather. Must run in the family, you know."

Sally was relieved he had not been offended. Sometimes older men were stiff with their dignity, and she didn't know the colonel that well. Smiling back at him, she said, "I must ask ye ter excuse me now, sor. I'm after bein' late ter wait on me mither."

The colonel followed her to the shabby hall. At the door, she held out her hand. "I'm that sure my da will be upset he was not belowstairs ter receive ye, sor, but in his place I do thank ye fer yer gift."

"I hope I shall see you soon again, Sally," Jenkins said as he bowed. "Perhaps I might take you for a drive one afternoon? Ireland is a beautiful country, never more so than in the spring. It is so green. I have never seen the like, and I wish Anne were here to see it as well. How she would enjoy meeting you!"

"Thank ye, I . . . I wish I could," Sally told him. "But it wouldn't be possible. I never leave Ballyragh."

Before he could inquire as to the reason for this strange behavior she had curtsied and opened the door for him, and he was forced to go away.

He thought of her statement often in the days that followed, and wondered about it. What a narrow, restricted life she led for a young girl—no parties or balls, no excursions or amusements! When he compared it to the myriad entertainments his daughter considered her due, he found himself pitying Sally Mannion sincerely; more so, perhaps, because she did not appear to think herself an object of pity.

It was in early July that the Desmond family was once again thrown into turmoil. Joseph Desmond, made aware by his wife's gentle reminders that the marriage settlement was fast disappearing, and that

there would be no more money to come after it was
gone, made a last valiant effort to collect the rents.

It was a fruitless endeavor. His tenants, long left to
their own devices, had almost forgotten they owed
him rents at all, and they looked so amazed and indignant when he demanded them that he was discouraged
and went home to get thoroughly drunk. For once,
however, he persisted, riding out each morning as
soon as his aching head would permit him to sit a
horse.

The local farmers were undergoing a difficult time
that summer. The potato crop was going to be a poor
one, due to an unusual drought in the spring and a
severe late frost, which had struck just as the first
tender shoots of the plants were poking up through
the soil. A large percentage of the crop had died, and
the poorer farmers especially had no money to spare
to buy more seed potatoes. They were going to be the
worst off, since most of them cultivated only this one
crop. It was all the sustenance their families had
through the long winter months.

Already foreseeing the famine to come, they were
in no good humor when their squire came around,
blustering and pretending to be stern as he demanded
that they pay several years of accumulated debt. The
squire's action was ill conceived, of course, for such
payment all at once was impossible, even in good
years. But he was not a practical man, and he had
wanted this all to be over with quickly.

The farmers began to mutter, there were some
threats, and once someone even took a shot at him as
he rode his land. Indignant, Joseph Desmond called
in the troops. Colonel Jenkins questioned everyone
diligently but he could discover no culprit, nor could
he persuade anyone to inform on his neighbor. As the
tenant farmers saw it, it was *us*—the poor, downtrod-
den laborers—against *them*—the landed gentry and
the British troops. On the advice of the colonel, Desmond took to carrying a loaded pistol whenever he
went out, and he wondered, in a rather bewildered
way, why things had changed so. He had always been

on good terms with his farmers. Why, many a misty afternoon had he spent with one or the other of them, before a snug peat fire in their cottages, enjoying a glass or two or three in complete harmony.

Sally had been amazed to see how her father applied himself, and she wondered if it was anything she had said or done. Perhaps her impatience at his drunkenness and ineptitude had shown more clearly than she had known. Or perhaps it was because he was at last feeling some shame for what had happened to her, and was trying to atone for it. She had been curt with him when, on one of her first nights home, he'd come to her room to kiss her and weep over her. She'd told him that such behavior was inappropriate now, for she was grown, and a married woman. She had asked him not to come to her room again as well, and weeping even harder he had agreed, even though he shook his head and bemoaned the loss of his darling daughter. Perhaps her banishment of him had bothered him more than she knew.

But no, it wasn't that, she told herself cynically. I'm sure I had nothing to do with it. It must have been merely that he was alarmed that his constant supply of whiskey was in danger of being cut off.

Whatever his reason Sally prayed he would persevere, for she, as well as her mother, knew what a bad case they would all be in if he did not succeed. Sometimes, however, she wished Mr. McGillicuddy were still here, or if not he, some other equally hard, decisive man, who would demand the tenants' respect, force them to pay what they owed. Sally's childhood adoration of her big, handsome father had died long ago.

On the particular day the trouble came Joseph Desmond had been drinking even before he rode out, to give himself courage. He was not going to stand for any more malingering, he told himself as he stamped to the stables. No, indeed! Today he would inform his tenants that they must at least pay something, or he would have them thrown off his land.

He found three of them in front of John Reilly's

bothy, talking among themselves over large jars of comfort. Still mounted, and eying those jars with longing, the squire delivered his ultimatum. One of the hotheaded Reilly sons, who had listened to many a long, heated discussion about the squire's sudden unreasonableness and greed, jumped from his seat and grabbed a nearby pitchfork. As he advanced, brandishing it and cursing, the squire lost his head.

What happened was not entirely his fault. He was befuddled with drink, and frightened—stunned as well, for none of his tenants had ever cursed him to his face before. Afraid for his life, he pulled his pistol from his jacket pocket, raised it, and fired. He had had no intention of killing the boy, as he explained later, and his bullet would never have found young Reilly's heart if his horse had not shied in alarm just then, and if the lad had not jumped sideways, trying to avoid the shot.

A great uproar ensued. Mrs. Reilly knelt by her son's lifeless body, keening and wringing her hands, the other children began wailing, and the men advanced on him with whatever weapons they had to hand. Joseph Desmond beat a hasty retreat under a hail of stones.

By suppertime he was under arrest for murder, and detained at the Ballyragh barracks until he could be transported to the prison at Waterford.

There was nothing anyone could do about it, Colonel Jenkins told a distraught Rose Desmond and a white-faced Sally that evening. The squire had fired on the boy, and he had killed him. He would have to stand trial, and he was afraid the outcome did not look promising.

In fact, he added, he had detailed troops to guard Ballyragh Hall. Tempers in the neighborhood were high. There was no telling what the peasantry might do to the family for revenge.

"But what are *we* ter do?" Sally whispered. Although her eyes were intent on his face, Jenkins knew she was not seeing him at all.

"Have you no relatives you could go to in your

affliction? Just until things calm down, that is?" he asked. "Perhaps the squire has a brother, cousins?"

"There is no one, no one!" Rose Desmond moaned. "We shall all perish! Ah, my poor innocent babes!"

She stopped then, and looking up into her daughter's face she said timidly, "Of course, there is your husband, Sally, and he is family now. You could ask him if we could—"

"No, never!" Sally replied, so loudly that Jenkins was startled. "I'll never ask him fer anything! How could ye even suggest sich a thing, Mam, ye who know what he did ter me?"

"But the children, Sally! They might all be burned in their beds!"

"There now, ma'am, no need to take such a dark view of things," Jenkins interrupted in a bracing voice. "I hardly think that likely, not with the troops to see to your safety. But I must admit I cannot keep them here forever. If only there were some place you could go until all this has blown over."

Sally had been thinking hard while he spoke, and now she said, "I think you had better notify Aunt Dorothy, Mam. She has helped before."

Her mother's tear-streaked face brightened slightly. "But of course! My dear sister! I shall write to her at once, if you would be so kind as to post the letter for me, Colonel."

The colonel said he would be delighted to do so, and after a short time spent trying to reassure young Sally while her mother wrote the letter, he took his leave. Idly, as he rode back to the barracks, leaving the first group of soldiers to guard Ballyragh behind him, he wondered what would become of the Desmond family now. He hoped, for Sally Mannion's sake, that after this Aunt Dorothy had been consulted she would find a way to give them all succor, so the girl would not have to suffer any more than she already had.

Ten days later, Mrs. Dorothy Duffy arrived at Ballyragh Hall in a large traveling coach. She was accompanied by not only her coachman and groom but two outriders as well.

When she had not had an immediate reply to her letter Rose Desmond had begun to fret, and it was with great relief that she now welcomed her sister, falling into her arms and weeping uncontrollably. There had been no news from the prison at Waterford either, but that nice Colonel Jenkins—such a dear, kind man!—had assured her it might be some time before her husband came up for trial. She worried about him no less than she worried about the fate of her children, but now that her sister had arrived she was able to place the whole burden on her capable shoulders.

Dorothy Duffy was shorter than her younger sister but she was built on much more solid, imposing lines, and she dressed so fine that the Desmond children were in awe of her. Sally knew her to be prim and proper, and very proud of her consequence, and as her mother introduced the children to her Sally wondered what Aunt Dorothy—and her uncle as well—really thought about taking on the care of so many relatives. It was very good of them!

Mrs. Duffy kissed baby Agnes, shook her head sadly at Forsythe's vacant expression, accepted Joe, Andy, and Mikey's shaky bows, and gave Mary a warm smile. Sally she treated as just another adult, and her greeting to her was cool and contained.

She said nothing of her plans for the family until she and her sister were alone much later.

"I have discussed this problem with Archibald, Rose," she began, as she settled herself in the best chair in the shabby parlor. She saw her sister leaning forward eagerly, and inwardly she sighed. Shiftless, the whole lot of them! she thought, wondering why, with all her troubles, Rose had felt it incumbent upon her to produce such a brood.

It was strange how things had turned out. At one time, when the handsome young Joseph Desmond had come a-courting, she had envied her sister, wished that he might love her rather than the beautiful Rose.

She had had cause for many years to be glad he had not. Looking at that sister critically now, she could only pity her. Rose was careworn and old before her time, with all her good looks gone, and all because her husband could not stay away from the drink. Archibald Duffy might not have had Joseph Desmond's virile good looks, or his abundant charm and winning smile, but he was worth a dozen of him, she thought smugly. He was an astute businessman, a worthy personage who was much respected in Limerick, and his fortune, made in shipping and real estate, had grown rather than diminished through the years. She herself had been careful to see that there had been only three children of their marriage. A daughter first, then a son and heir. She had had no intention of having any more children, but there had been one surprise, a little boy they named Theodore who was now the darling of her heart. Would that her sister had been so restrained!

"And what did dear Archibald say?" that sister was asking now. Mrs. Duffy put her musings aside and replied, "He is agreeable to seeing to your family's welfare."

She saw Rose Desmond's eyes close in relief as she sagged in her chair, and before she could begin to weep and proclaim her gratitude, Dorothy went on quickly, "One of his farms outside Limerick is empty at the present time. It is small, and not what you have been used to, no doubt, but I am sure it will be suitable. Eventually, things will return to normal at Ballyragh. Joseph junior is almost eleven now? No doubt after his schooling, he will wish to come back and claim his inheritance. Mr. Duffy has agreed that until that time he will put a bailiff in charge, to care for the hall and to see to collecting the rents for you. Your tenants will either pay or they will have to go, so they can be replaced by honest, hard-working men. I was never more shocked than to hear how they had attacked your husband! Things have come to a pretty pass here, indeed!"

"Indeed they have," Rose Desmond said sadly as

she wiped her eyes. "My poor Joseph, wasting away in prison, and all for an accident!"

Privately, Mrs. Duffy thought it the best place in the world for him—incarcerated, he would have to accept the help of his competent brother-in-law in setting the estate to rights—but she did not say so.

Instead she went on, "We will be on our way as soon as you can be packed. We will be crowded in the coach, but we will manage. You will not be able to bring the servants, however. You must give them notice tomorrow."

Rose Desmond appeared startled. "There is only the one, a Mrs. Ginty, our cook. She has been with us for years, and I cannot like to turn her out now. She is old, Dorothy, and she will not be able to find other work. And I . . . Well, I have no money to pension her off."

Her sister's mouth tightened and then she shrugged. "I see no reason why she cannot stay here, then. The bailiff and his wife may well want to keep her on, and until they come she can keep an eye on the place for us. I understand there have been threats?"

Mrs. Desmond nodded. "Yes, that is true, and I suppose it would be best. Probably Mrs. Ginty would not care to move away from the place she has lived all her life. And it will not take me long to pack. Sally and Mary will help. They are good girls, and Sally especially is such support for me!"

Her sister looked down at the hands she had clasped in her lap, and the sight of them, much be-ringed and well cared for, stiffened her resolve. "You remind me, Rose, that we have not discussed Sally. Of course my invitation does not extend to her. She is a married woman with a perfectly able husband to see to her care. Truly, I found it incomprehensible that you permitted her to leave him last year and return to make her home with you. However, she shall not continue to do so. That, I would never be a party to. You will inform her that she is to go back to her husband, preferably tomorrow."

"Oh, I cannot do that!" Rose Desmond cried, looking distraught. "Leo Mannion is a dreadful man. He abused her, beat her terribly! If she returns to him, he will do so again. I fear for Sally's life!"

"Nonsense!" Mrs. Duffy said briskly. "You exaggerate, Rose. You always did. No doubt the girl has been dramatizing her state. We will not regard her. Her place is with her husband."

In vain, her sister pleaded that Sally be allowed to live near Limerick with the rest of the family. Mrs. Duffy remained adamant. Rose and the other children would be provided for. Mrs. Sally Mannion would not.

Dorothy Duffy had had no such intention during her journey here, but only one look at the girl's lovely face and handsome figure had convinced her that helping this particular niece was something that must be avoided at all costs. Archibald Duffy was the best husband in the world, kindly, steady, hard-working, and considerate, but his wife was well aware of his secret flaw. She had discovered it early in their marriage when she had caught him with the prettiest maid. Since that time she had employed only older women, whose best qualification for the position had been their lack of good looks.

And there was no denying, Mrs. Duffy knew, that as her husband had grown older he had grown even more susceptible, and to younger and younger women as well. It was deplorable in a man of his years and dignity! Why, he had one now who was not even twenty, tucked away in a discreet little house on a quiet Limerick street. Mr. Duffy would have been amazed at how much his wife knew of his supposedly secret liaisons.

That wife also knew that her beloved Archibald would only have to see Sally for all to be lost, and she was not a woman who took chances. What her husband did on his evenings out, or on his business trips, was one thing, and she had come to accept this weakness of his long ago. (At least he did not drink!) But in his own home, among his own family, there must be no scandal. There were Rosemary and John, and dearest Theo to consider, and her own reputation as one of Limerick's leading hostesses as well. No, Sally Mannion would remain on Ireland's east coast, far from Limerick and her both silly and vulnerable uncle.

When apprised of her aunt's ultimatum by a tearful Rose Desmond, Sally turned pale. Because she could not believe anyone would be so cruel, she made haste to seek her aunt out for a private interview. Surely it was only that her mother had not explained the situation to her clearly. Surely when Aunt Dorothy learned the true state of affairs, she would relent.

But Mrs. Duffy did not relent. Coldly, she told Sally that she was making a great to-do about nothing. All men were difficult. It was only a matter of discovering how to manage them skillfully. She was sure Sally would learn to do so, and be much happier when she had accepted her obligations at last.

And if it was her niece's disgust at what happened in bed, she herself could testify that one became accustomed in time. Naturally it was distasteful. Every good woman knew that. But it was a necessary evil, and one that must be borne stoically, for neither she nor her husband were prepared to bear the cost of supporting another man's wife. Indeed, she was surprised her niece expected them to do so.

She even went so far as to remind Sally of her wedding vows, how she had promised before God to forsake all others and keep herself only unto him as long as they both should live. It was more than time, Dorothy Duffy said as she rose to terminate the interview, that her niece began to honor those vows. She suggested Sally start packing at once. She would be happy to lend her the coach for her return journey in the morning.

She left Sally in despair, for there was no one she could turn to, no one who would help her. And when she went to plead for her mother's assistance, Rose Desmond said she had no choice but to concur with her sister's decision. How could she not? she asked, her eyes pleading for her daughter's understanding. The babies had to be considered, and the welfare of the older children as well. She was very sorry for Sally, but perhaps Mr. Mannion might be different now? Perhaps he had learned his lesson?

Sally left her surrounded by her packing, and weeping her easy tears. As she ran down the stairs, desperate to escape the Hall, she realized anew how weak a woman her mother was, even as she acknowledged that in this instance she had had little choice. But to be abandoned by her, by all her family, so coldly! It was dreadful.

She spent the afternoon wandering around the grounds of Ballyragh, trying to think of what she might do, where she might go. No matter what her aunt said about vows and the sanctity of marriage, she would never go back to Leo Mannion. That was to walk meekly to her doom, and she had no intention of doing that. Anything in the world was better, including starvation. But what was she to do?

Colonel Jenkins discovered her sitting on the top step of a stile sometime later. Smiling and waving to her, he dismounted and tied his horse to the hedge nearby before he came to sit down beside her. It was then that he saw her distraught air, her pale, set face, even what he suspected was a trace of tears on her cheeks, and he took her hands in his and held them tightly.

"My dear Sally! What is the matter, child? How can I help?" he asked.

Sally stared at him, considering. He looked kind and concerned, and by asking he had given her more sympathy than her own family had done. For a brief, stabbing moment, she even wished he had been her father, and she was hard put to choke back a sob. She did not attempt to evade his question. Perhaps he could help. God knew, there was no one else.

Without preamble she told him of her aunt's arrival, and what had been decided for the family. And then she told him that she was not to be included, that she had been ordered to return to her husband. She gave all the reasons she would never do so.

"I do not know what I am ter do," she finished,

pulling her hands from his and putting them over her face. "Shure, an' I can't change me aunt's mind. She is firm about this. So there is nowhere fer me ter go, no one ter help me. I . . . I am alone, and I am penniless."

Colonel Jenkins's eyes narrowed, and he made a conscious effort to control his features, although he was sure that the horror he had felt in hearing her story was written plain for her to see. "Sally, my dear child," he said. "Let *me* help you."

Sally lowered her eyes to stare at him, and her face became very still, almost wary. "Ye? Ye would help me? But—but why?"

"Because I have affection for you, and I sincerely pity you."

He paused then to clear his throat, and he did not look at her as he went on. "I have killed while in the army, not once but many times. My life has been all destruction, aye, and my only son's as well. He was an army man too, but he died young in a training accident. Perhaps this opportunity is God's way of allowing me to atone, of giving me the chance to save someone. Please, Sally, let me see to your care."

He paused again, but when she had no comment he went on, "I have been planning on selling out for some time. I want to return to my home in England, see to my estate, be a real father to my daughter. I would take you there with me. My wife is dead, but my sister lives with me and Anne. They would both welcome you."

Sally listened to his earnest words in confusion. She wanted to trust the colonel so much, so much! But she was afraid, and she doubted whether even a man as good as this British officer seemed to be could be telling her the truth. Take her away from Ireland? Bring her to his own home, treat her like one of the family? Care for her, feed her, and clothe her? Why? Why was he being so magnanimous? Surely not because he wished to make amends for a misspent life! Could he have a secret, underlying motive she knew nothing about, one he would not reveal until she was deep in his debt?

"Sally? Do you agree? I understand this will be a painful step for you, to travel far from your home, your family. But there is no other way. You must never return to your brutish husband. And you have my promise that you are more than welcome. What say you, child?"

Sally stared at him, considering. There was nothing in his hazel eyes but concern, nothing on his lined face that spoke of duplicity. But still she hesitated, feeling somehow as if she were about to step into an abyss so dark and fathomless she would never be able to find her way out. *Could* she trust him? Could she?

She had to draw a deep breath before she whispered. "Very well then, yes. But—there is one thing. . . ."

His gray brows rose a little. "Yes? What is it?"

"I . . . I must have some money first," she managed to get out past dry lips. "I am so afraid, ye see, that in spite of yer promises and kind intentions, that ye will turn out ter be just sich a man as me—me husband. And if ye do, I will have ter leave ye. Fer that I will need money."

Colonel Jenkins first felt indignation that she might think him capable of such entrapment, then horror, and finally understanding, when he remembered the tale she had told him of her marriage. Of course she did not feel she could trust men—any man—no matter how old or how sincere. Whenever he thought of her being abused by that drunken brute, strung up and horsewhipped, he felt ill. Sally Desmond Mannion had every reason in the world to be suspicious. But what he would not give to have Mannion before him right now, stripped to the waist and strung up! How he would relish flogging the man until he screamed for mercy, after what he had done to this lovely child!

"How much money would you require?" he asked.

Sally put her head to one side to consider. "I . . . I would have ter have ten pounds," she told him finally, turning her head away to hide her blush.

To her surprise, Colonel Jenkins chuckled before he took her hands and squeezed them reassuringly. "You innocent, Sally!" he said. "And how far do you think you would get on ten pounds?

"No, no, do not bother to tell me!" he went on, unbuttoning his tunic and drawing out his purse to give her ten one-pound notes then and there. "Believe me, I shall see that you have the same amount of pin money I give to Anne, and take care of all your needs, but here! Take this now, if it will make you feel better. I do understand, you see."

Before she could even whisper her thanks, he went on, "I shall set my plans for selling out of the army in motion at once. Until I have done so, you are to stay at Ballyragh Hall with your Mrs. Ginty. When that is done, I shall come and take you away—to Dublin first, and then to England."

He went on then, telling her again how much she would enjoy his country, and how happy she would be at last. Sally listened, still in a daze. For better or worse, she had taken the final step. She could only pray she had chosen well.

The colonel left her late in the afternoon, after squeezing her hands and smiling at her fondly. Sally smiled at him a little in return and he nodded, as if he knew she needed time to get used to their new relationship. He would not press her, he told himself as he strode to his horse and mounted. But someday soon, he would have the great pleasure of seeing that wary look of hers disappear forever, watch her blossom into a trusting, lovely woman. He could hardly wait.

As he rode away Sally kept her smile in place, was even able to wave good-bye to him. But when he had gone she sank down on the grass and began to cry, hating herself as she did so. This arrangement she had made was all wrong, and she knew it. The colonel was a stranger. She had no call on him, none at all. And yet she had accepted his suggestion because it was all she could do. And by doing so, she had at least ensured her immediate future.

She admitted to herself that she was not at all averse to leaving Ireland and making a fresh start somewhere else, far from the hateful Leo Mannion. And she was looking forward to meeting the colonel's daughter Anne. She hoped they would be friends. She had never had a friend.

His description of his home, called Beechlands, had also intrigued her, and made her eager to see it. The British colonel obviously was a man of some substance. Perhaps it would all work out for the best. Perhaps she would come to love his family, and they, her. She hoped so with all her heart, for if that were to happen she knew she could then stop feeling so worthless and unloved. So abandoned.

Chapter Five

SALLY AND MRS. GINTY stood on the steps of Bally-ragh Hall to say good-bye and wave the travelers on their way, when the Desmond family left two morn-ings later. Sally was almost glad to see them go. She had had to endure a painful interview with her mother and her aunt when she had announced that she was not going back to Leo Mannion, but was accepting the help of Colonel Peter Jenkins instead. That inter-view had left Rose Desmond close to hysteria, her aunt tight-lipped and haughty, and Sally drained.

"Oh, no, no, no, Sally!" Rose Desmond had cried, reaching out to her daughter in her distress, and turn-ing pale with shock. "No, you must never do so! You are a married woman, and—"

Dorothy Duffy waved an imperious hand, and her sister fell silent in mid-sentence.

"And has this—this *British colonel*—told you what role he has in mind for you to play, niece?" she asked, her voice awful.

Sally was well aware of her aunt's insinuations, but she made herself look straight at the lady and keep her voice steady as she replied, "I am to be a compan-ion to his daughter, treated as one of the family," she said.

Her Aunt Dorothy snorted. "How very naive of you to accept such farradiddle!" she said. "I can assure you that the only companionship you would be called on to give would be to this selfsame colonel, flat on your back, my girl, and late at night. The old goat!"

Ignoring her mother's shocked gasp, Sally opened her mouth to refute her aunt's statement, but that lady was in full spate now and would suffer no interruptions. Leaning forward in her chair, and pointing a stern finger at her niece, she swept on, "You are comely, and I do assure you, Sally, men are all the same, no matter what their age. And as for him feeling *fatherly*, I can tell you it is no such thing! Men never change. They are all animals until the day they die. *Fatherly*, indeed! Hmmmph!"

"It is not so! I know the colonel is not like that! He is kind, and he cares fer me as he does his own daughter!" Sally protested.

Her mother waited to see if Dorothy had anything more to say. Observing her flushed face, those tightly compressed lips and stern eyes, she ventured to say, "But even if what you tell us is true, you know what people will say, Sally! People always put the worst interpretation on everything. And so they will say you are his mistress, and you a married woman! Why, you would be accused of committing adultery! And what of your good name? Ours? You are a Desmond! I cannot permit you to take such a heedless step. To think you would let a stranger pay your keep! Why, you would be no better than his pensioner!"

Sally ignored her aunt's sniff by turning her back on her. She evaded her mother's clutching hands, but as she looked into her horrified eyes she was overcome by anger.

"But how can it be that ye are so upset?" she asked coldly. "Afther all, it was ye an' my father who sold me in the first place, an' ter a man ye both knew I loathed. An' lest ye forget it, Mam, ye and Da received a great deal o' money fer doing so, did ye not?"

She waited, but when her mother had no reply she rushed on, "An' ye alone were willing fer me ter go back ter him, ye alone who would have condemned me ter a life o' beatings an' abuse, till one day he managed ter kill me, or I, him. An' ye did this only because me aunt here said ye must. Ye were wrong, Mam, *wrong*! Ye should have stood by me, but ye did not.

"Well, I have no wish ter die, and so ye have no

more say in me life. I will make the decisions about what I do an' how I behave from now on, an' I will do so only ter benefit meself. The Desmond family cast me out; well, the Desmonds will get no more sacrifices from me!"

Rose Desmond buried her face in her hands, sobbing and rocking to and fro in her distress. In a quieter tone Sally said, "Colonel Jenkins is a kind man. He is takin' me ter his home in England, an' he promises I will never want."

Hearing once more her aunt's scornful sniff, and her mother's muffled words about the loss of her reputation, she flung out her hand. "Argh! Do not prate ter me about 'reputations' again, either o' ye! Dear God, I do not intend ter suffer more, die even, fer sich a worthless thing as that!"

With her silent, disapproving sister watching, Rose Desmond continued to plead and cajole, until finally Sally left the room in self-defense. An hour later, everyone in the Hall knew of her decision. Mary had stared at her, eyes wide with horror, and the little boys had avoided her. Only Mrs. Ginty had pressed her hand when they were alone together getting supper, and said, "Ye do wot ye has ter, lass, an' niver mind. A foine future ye would have had with that brute o' a husband of yers. Jasus save us!"

As for Sally's Aunt Dorothy, she never acknowledged her niece in any way from that moment on. It was as if Sally had ceased to exist for her.

Even this morning, when she had swept past Sally to take her seat in the carriage, she had ignored her. Rose Desmond had wept again, clutching Sally in her arms until her sister spoke to her sharply, telling her to make haste. As the carriage pulled away Sally could hear all the children bawling, baby Agnes leading the chorus. Waving good-bye, she thought about the unpleasant journey her aunt was about to undertake, crowded into a carriage with a brood of noisy, restless children, and she was able to smile a little to herself, over the ache in her heart. Serves her right, the proper old prune! she thought.

Colonel Jenkins came to see her that afternoon, to tell her he was off to Dublin first thing in the morning. "I have apprised Lieutenant Smythe, my next-in-command, that you are here alone in the Hall," he said. "He will make sure no harm comes to you, for the troops are to remain, by my order, until I have you safely away. But may I suggest you stay indoors? If your husband has heard of your mother's departure, he might well try to take you back by force."

Sally assured him she would take the greatest care, but still the colonel did not go away. Instead he remained standing before her, twisting his gloves and looking somewhat grim.

"There is something else, sor?" Sally asked finally.

He coughed, and he did not quite meet her eye as he said, "Young Percy Smythe is a very good fellow, you know. Trust him with my life. But . . ."

He coughed again, and Sally stared at him, perplexed.

"Percy's a devil with the women, though," he said, all in a rush. Suddenly he came to stand close to her, so he could take her shoulders in his hands and gaze down into her eyes. "Sally, child, I beg you will have a care, and not be taken in by him! He is persuasive, and he might well try to, er, to . . ."

Sally made herself smile. "Of course I will not!" she said firmly. "But I thank ye fer the warning, sor. Forewarned is forearmed, is it not?"

He looked a little easier then, but still he promised to return as quickly as he could. As he hesitated, Sally held her breath. Was he going to kiss her? *That* way? Was Aunt Dorothy right after all? She steeled herself for disappointment, and she felt a flood of relief when he only picked up her hand and kissed it quickly.

"Adieu, my child," he said. "Be prudent, now!"

Sally nodded and curtsied, and he was gone.

He did not return for almost two weeks. Sally spent the time helping Mrs. Ginty clean the Hall so it would be ready for that bailiff her uncle was sending. Since Mrs. Ginty was not given to idle conversation, Sally had a great deal of time to think as she did so. Lieutenant Smythe had called every day, and Sally had

seen immediately why the colonel had been worried.
Smythe was a handsome young officer, with the fair
curls of an angel, but there was hot lust in his eyes
whenever he looked at her, and he had a seductive
smile. He treated her with a familiarity she could only
deplore silently, while her behavior to him was so cool
it bordered on incivility.

Sally reminded herself that the lieutenant must
think he knew very well what the colonel had in mind
for her, and she had no way to dispel his misconcep-
tions. She supposed she must accept his assessment of
the situation, treat it as part of the price she had to
pay if she was to have any future at all.

Colonel Jenkins came back to Ballyragh one evening to tell Sally that all was in train, and they could
be off the next morning early. He gave her a large
parcel and a bandbox, saying he hoped she would approve his choice of traveling ensemble, for it was just
what he would have chosen for his daughter. A little
stunned, Sally accepted his gifts, feeling truly commit-
ted as she did so.

Early the following morning she was dressed in the
royal blue cambric gown and matching bonnet. The
dress was not a perfect fit, but it was much more
elegant than any other she owned. Her old clothes
were packed neatly in a small trunk.

As she stood on the steps of the Hall with Mrs.
Ginty while the colonel strapped her trunk to the back
of the carriage, Sally felt great sadness. She was leaving Ballyragh, and in spite of all the unhappy things
that had happened to her and to her family here, she
regretted her departure. Ballyragh was virtually all she
had ever known. It was her home, but she knew that
in all probability she would never see it again. No,
nor her family either. Today was to be the final good-
bye, and after sixteen years, it was hard. As hard as
to step blindly into an unknown future, one that might
bring her more evil than good. She had no way of
knowing.

As she brushed the tears from her eyes, Mrs. Ginty
advised her to stop acting so wet. Her own eyes were

suspiciously bright as she went on, "Off ye go now, Sally, an' good riddance ter the past, is wot I sez. Shure an' I'm sairtain ye'll be all right. The colonel's a good man. I can sense it."

Sally hugged and kissed her before she tucked five of her ten pounds in the cook's pinny. She knew the old woman would need it if the bailiff turned her out.

Mrs. Ginty wiped her eyes on the back of her sleeve. "Ochone, it's jist I'll be afther missin' ye, lass," she admitted. "Yer a good girl. But there now, no more gaggin' fer ye with an auld woman. The colonel's waitin'. God's blessin' on ye, aye, an' all the saints, too. I'll pray fer ye."

As the colonel's carriage turned out of the gates Sally looked only at the road ahead, trying not to think of the last time she had left, with her new husband. She would not remember that or look back—no, for it was done and she had made her choice. Taking a deep breath and praying she had made the right one, she turned to Colonel Jenkins and forced a smile. He was watching her somewhat anxiously, and when his hazel eyes lit up in return she was glad she had made the effort.

They reached Dublin three days later, for the colonel had maintained a spanking pace whenever the roads were clear. True to his word, Sally had her own bedchamber, and a maid to wait on her at the inns where they stopped for the night. The colonel did no more than press her hand when he bade her good night.

During their journey he talked to her and treated her very much like a daughter, even scolding her when he did not think she had eaten enough of the inn fare, or bidding her to wear a warmer shawl on a cool morning. Sally felt herself beginning to relax.

During the days while they waited to sail, the colonel took her sightseeing. Sally was fascinated by the city of Dublin, built on a hill as it was, with the Hill of Howth to the north. Dublin's streets were airy and spacious, and the houses that lined them, mostly of red brick, were tall, stately. She especially admired Fitzwilliam Square, with its gardens filled with flowers and foliage, and she was awed by the grand hotels and shops, the theaters and churches. Dublin was crowded with all manner of people—beggars and merchants, travelers and thieves. Idly, she wondered if Thady O'Brien was somewhere in the vast throng.

The colonel told her that when she saw London she would find that city much more impressive, but Sally did not see how that could be. She had never imagined Dublin could be like this—it was so different from Ballyragh village, or even New Ross.

The colonel also took her shopping, buying her all manner of gowns and fripperies. When she protested his extravagance, he told her she had to be well dressed for the family's sake. Sometimes Sally was uncomfortable in the fancy shops, for she caught the knowing glances of the lady clerks, saw their thin-lipped smirks. But invariably, by the time they were ready to leave, everyone was all smiles. From the gowns this colonel selected, and his manner, it was obvious to all that he was very much a relative of this stunning young woman.

The voyage down the Irish Sea and St. George's Channel was a pleasant one, and another new adventure for Sally. There was just enough wind to speed them on their way, and Sally found sea travel exhilarating. And the day-long journey by private carriage from Bristol to Beechlands, situated as it was near Tiverton in Devon, was of constant interest to her.

How tidy England was! she exclaimed, her nose all but pressed to the side window of the carriage. Why, just see the hedges that enclosed the fields, the prosperous cottages in the neat villages they passed through! Surely everyone here must be very rich, were they not? Why, even the peasants lived better than they did in Ireland! And hark! Wasn't that a church bell she could hear?

As Sally pointed to things, exclaimed and asked questions, the colonel leaned back on his side of the carriage and smiled at her in happy contentment. She was such a contradiction, he thought. So untried and childlike in her naiveté, yet this same child had a seductive body and a beautiful face that he was sure he would have to defend from every buck in the neighborhood of Beechlands. Still, he was pleased with the quick decision he had made on the top of a stile in a dreary Irish field. He would keep her safe.

Of course Sally was shy with him still, and wary, but he could sense her defenses crumbling, little by little. And all his kindnesses, his gentle acts of concern, were met by a radiant smile of gratitude. He was glad he had offered to help her; glad he had been so magnanimous.

If anyone had asked Sally what she thought of her new situation, she would have told them it was much better than she had imagined it could be, or had had any reason to expect. Yet, deep inside, she knew she was still waiting to be disillusioned. It was as if everything were too good to be true, and eventually she would have to pay for present happiness.

They reached their journey's end in the late dusk, and Sally was not able to see much of Beechlands as the carriage rumbled up the drive that led to the house. The flambeaux on either side of the door were lit, however, so the colonel knew that his letter telling of their arrival had been received.

He wondered what his sister, Honour Jenkins, thought of all this, his bringing a strange girl to stay with them for an indefinite period, and his requesting that this young Mrs. Mannion be given one of the best bedchambers. But now, remembering his sister, he was not too concerned. Honour Jenkins was a woman who accepted the things life dealt her without question, who saw only what she wanted to and not a glimmer more. He had marveled before at the blinders she used to avoid having to deal with anything unpleasant.

And yet, to look at her, you would have thought her the sternest martinet in the world. She was tall and of a heavy build, the type of woman who exuded dignity and propriety. In reality, however, she was neither dignified nor imposing. Not to put too fine a point on it, she was dithery. All her concern was for the management of the house, and with an excellent housekeeper to see to the details, she did very well at that. But rather than she chaperoning his daughter, Jenkins had always thought it was Anne who took care of her, from finding her handkerchiefs and misplaced lists to calming her agitation at every small disaster, and assuring her that of course her dear brother would not care that there was no potted hare for his tea, even if it was his favorite.

Lord, how coming home reminded him! the colonel thought as he smiled. No, Sally would have no trouble with Honour. As for Anne, well, she had always been somewhat of an enigma to him. He hoped she would like Sally, but he would just have to wait and see.

He jumped from the carriage before the groom had even let down the steps, to look around with satisfaction. The old place appeared to be just as it had been the day he had left some months ago, and he was well pleased. Tomorrow he would ride his land and greet his farmers, perhaps even stop in at Craigbourne Manor to see his old friend, Sir George. And then there was his agent to see, and he must not forget to call on the elderly Nathaniel Bates and his wife. . . .

As Sally stepped down on the groom's arm she saw how abstracted the colonel was, and she took the time to look around. Her eyes widened. What a very large house this was! she thought, feeling a tremor of nerves. It was so long and rambling! And was that a wing over there? She could hardly make it out in the gloom. But before her were steps leading to imposing double doors. Such well-scrubbed marble steps they were, too. Such shiny, painted doors. She felt very provincial suddenly, very *Irish*.

The colonel came to take her arm, issuing orders over his shoulder about the disposal of the baggage as he led her up those steps to give the knocker a mighty crash.

He smiled down at her then, and he would have spoken, but suddenly the door was flung open and a slight girl threw herself into his arms.

"Father!" she cried, as she kissed him all over his

face. Laughing, he tried to fend her off. Behind them, Sally could see an older, gray-haired man beaming fondly at them both.

"How glad I am to see you at last! It has been so long!" the lady exclaimed in her lilting soprano.

"Now stop that, Annie," Colonel Jenkins growled. "At least let me bring Sally into the house before you set up such a ruckus. Ah, there you are, Bailey! Have the footmen see to the baggage, will you, there's a good fellow?"

As he spoke he ushered Sally into a large, candle-lit hall. It seemed very grand to her, with its large mirrors, polished furniture, and soft rugs. She had never seen any place so clean.

The lady he had called "Annie," and who she knew was his daughter, turned to greet her, and Sally saw her eyes widen. "Oh my, how beautiful you are!" she said, in a voice filled with awe. Sally blushed.

"Yes she is, truly, but where are your manners, hoyden?" her fond father asked. "Let me make you known to my impossible daughter, ma'am. And this, of course, Anne, is the Mrs. Sally Mannion I wrote to you about who has come to stay with us. I am hoping you will be friends."

Anne smiled at her so warmly that Sally smiled back at once. When she would have curtsied, Anne Jenkins took her hand in hers instead and pressed it. "I do beg your pardon, Mrs. Mannion," she said, her twinkling hazel eyes giving the lie to her formal words. "I have been looking forward to your arrival, and I am delighted you are here."

"Where's your aunt?" her father asked, as the grooms came in with the first of the trunks.

"She is speaking to the cook about dinner. For some reason she feels we must have Dublin herrings tonight, in honor of our guest, although where she thinks cook can procure them at this hour, I have no idea. But you know Aunt!"

"Indeed I do," her father said, as he offered an arm to each young lady. "Shall we go to the drawing room? A glass of wine would be welcome after our journey. Bailey?"

"At once, sir," the gray-haired butler assured him, raising his hand to summon one of the footmen who had somehow materialized at the back of the hall.

Sally struggled to look at ease. Why, she had never even suspected that men could be employed as indoor servants, for surely it was not so at home. At home people kept maids, and the only male servants worked outdoors in the stable or on the farms.

But these servants were vastly superior to them. They were all of them dressed in sober black suits, and their white linen would not have shamed the King himself. How very unusual! The colonel must be even more wealthy than she had thought, to be able to afford such singular servants.

"Do sit down near the fire, Sally," that gentleman was saying now. "The evenings grow chill. And allow me to take your stole and your gloves."

"Thank ye," Sally whispered, as she handed these articles to him. His eyes reassured her, and she was able to relax a little.

"Was it a pleasant journey?" Miss Jenkins asked, as she took the seat opposite. "I quite envy you the experience, for I have never sailed; never been abroad, you see."

Sally nodded. "Yes, ter my surprise it were," she said. "I was that afraid that I'd be afther bein' sick, but it were no sich thing, praise hivin!"

She saw Miss Jenkins's eyes begin to twinkle again, and her hand creep to her mouth to hide her smile, and Sally wondered what she had said that was so funny.

"Yes, Sally does have an Irish brogue, Anne," her father told her, as he turned to the tray of glasses and decanters a footman was placing on a table nearby. Nodding his dismissal, and pouring them all a glass of sherry, he added, "No doubt she will soon lose it, now she is in England."

"I shall be glad to help you," Anne Jenkins told

Sally. "It . . . it is not quite the thing here, although I am sure it was much admired in Ireland."

"Well, ter be shure, I don't know about that," Sally said. "It's jist the way I've always spoken, although me mither did try that hard ter break me o' it when I was younger. I . . . I would be glad ter have yer help, Miss. I . . . I thank ye."

"Oh, you must call me Anne!" the girl exclaimed. "We are to be friends, are we not? My father has said so."

Sally nodded and sipped her sherry. She did not like the taste of it, but she supposed she must drink it, to be polite.

"Peter! Dear brother!" a large woman exclaimed, as she entered the room and hurried toward them. "That I was not in the hall to welcome you! I am so distraught! Do say you will forgive me?"

The colonel took the lady into his arms and hugged her while he assured her he had taken no offense. When she would have continued to bemoan her lapse, he cut her short and introduced her to Sally.

Oh dear, Sally thought as she rose and curtsied, studying the lady as she did so. The colonel's sister was even sterner-looking than her own Aunt Dorothy. With a sinking heart, Sally wondered if the lady would countenance her remaining here, becoming one of the family. Perhaps she would insist that Sally go away. That would be bad, to be sure, but at least she had enough money now so she would not be penniless when she was turned out, Sally told herself.

To her surprise, the lady said in a flustered voice, "So happy. I do apologize though, Mrs. Mannion. There will be no herrings. Dear, dear!"

"Do sit down and stop fretting, sister," the colonel told her. "No one cares about herrings, not when I am sure you have arranged for the usual excellent dinner to be served. No, no," he added, holding up his hand as she opened her mouth to reply. "Do not tell me. I want to be surprised."

Turning to their guest then, he said, "I am sure you must want to rest before dinner, do you not, my child?

It has been a long day. Anne? Would you show Sally
to her room?"

His daughter jumped up at once, and came to take
Sally's arm. "Of course, Father," she said, as she led
their guest away. "I'll see to it she has everything she
needs, Aunt Honour. You stay here and talk to Father. I am sure you are longing to hear all his
adventures."

"And you are not?" the colonel asked, sounding a
little offended.

"But of course I am," Anne told him. "Those few
that are suitable for my girlish ears, that is! I know
the stories you tell, and how you change them when
I am listening!"

She left the room laughing, and she squeezed Sally's
arm as they went to the stairs. "How ridiculous men
are, including my father," she confided, as they began
to climb the flight. "You see how hurt he was to think
I did not care to hang on his every word?"

Sally was so taken aback by the candid Miss Jenkins, she could think of nothing to say. It did not
matter, for the irrepressible girl went on, "But there,
no doubt I should not laugh at him, nor ask the *real*
reason you have come to live here, no matter how
anxious I am to discover it."

"Do . . . do ye object, like?" Sally asked.

Miss Jenkins laughed again. "Of course not! I think
it will be fun, don't you? And now I have seen you,
I understand why my father was so quick to befriend
you. You are very beautiful."

As she had been speaking they had traveled down
a long corridor to the front of the house, and now she
opened a door and ushered Sally inside. The room was
already candle-lit, and there was a small fire blazing to
take off the chill. Sally had only a dazed impression
of thick rugs, graceful furniture, and rich velvet
hangings.

"This is to be your room," Miss Jenkins explained,
going to light more candles on the dressing table. "I
am right across the hall. I see that your trunks have

been brought up. I'll just ring for a maid to unpack for you."

"No, please, don't ye be doin' that, Miss Jenkins," Sally said quickly. "I can unpack fer meself, an' . . . an' I would prefer it."

Anne Jenkins shrugged. "Very well, but even if you do, you will need hot water."

As she rang the bell she said, "You do realize what everyone in the neighborhood is going to think of your being here, don't you? That you are a very young mistress of my father's? And are you, by any chance? You can tell me!"

As Sally stared at her, appalled, Miss Jenkins came back to her side, looking anxious now.

"Forgive me, I should not have asked that," she said, sounding contrite. "But I do so want us to be friends, and able to be honest with each other, truly I do. I don't have many friends, you see. I'm . . . I'm different from the other girls around here, and none of them likes me very much.

"But in my eagerness to get close to you, I am afraid I have offended you with my questions, my free conversation. Do not be shy with me, I beg you. You must learn to tell me at once if I say or do anything you do not like. Will you promise to do that?"

Sally took a deep breath. "Yes, I promise ye," she said, even as she wondered about the strange Miss Jenkins. She had not been at all surprised to hear she was not well liked. Such bluntness as she had would not sit well with many people. Indeed, Sally admitted she found it rather unsettling herself.

By the end of only one week at Beechlands, however, Sally was not only easy with Anne Jenkins, she had come to like her a great deal. They were much in each other's company, for the colonel was busy with the estate and his friends, his hunting and fishing and falconry. And since Miss Honour Jenkins was completely absorbed by the housekeeping, Sally would have been very lonely indeed, as the weeks stretched into months, had it not been for Anne Jenkins.

The two spent every minute of the day together, walking and talking, and having what Anne called "lessons." At nineteen, and three years the elder, she was very much the teacher, and she seemed to revel in the role. She worked hard to rid Sally of her brogue, and introduced her to literature, art, and music as well. Sally, who could not play an instrument or sing, was much in awe of Anne's prowess on the pianoforte and harp; her clear, true soprano. And when they went sketching, and Sally tried to follow Anne's instructions, she could only laugh at her childish efforts. Compared with Ann Jenkins's graceful watercolors and charcoal sketches, hers were a joke. Only on rainy days spent in the library did she feel at all her new friend's equal. She had always loved to read, although her selection at Ballyragh had been limited in the extreme. But here, in the long library with its globes and maps, its walls of books and comfortable chairs, she was in heaven. And when she finished a book there was the added pleasure of being able to discuss it with Anne, weighing its merits and learning of its author, for Anne was a fount of information.

It was only fair, Anne told her one morning, when Sally was bemoaning her inability to find Turkey on the globe. For Sally was so beautiful, more beautiful than any girl Anne had ever seen.

"Saints preserve us!" Anne had said, pulling down her mouth and looking severe. "An' are ye afther bein' that selfish ter be wantin' ither accomplishments as well? Bejasus!"

Sally could only laugh at Anne's accurate imitation of her brogue, and shake her head helplessly. She had never rated her beauty high. She did not do so now. What she really would have liked would to have been more like Anne, talented and clever and educated.

Reticent as Sally was, it was a long time before Anne had the whole story of her early life, but when she did hear it, she was horrified by the tale. She held her new friend's hands tightly when Sally told her of her forced marriage at fifteen, the beatings and abuse, and how she had left her husband with her back in ribbons. Sally told her what had occurred later as well—her father's imprisonment, how her family had abandoned her, and how Colonel Jenkins had come to her rescue, for which, she said fervently, she would always be grateful.

Anne's face was white as she leaned forward to put her arms around Sally and hold her fast. "Oh, my dear, but what a terrible, terrible thing to happen to you! *Men!*" she added, her voice full of disgust.

"It does not seem at all fair that *men* have so much power over us, don't you agree?" Anne went on, all in a rush. "Why, they, in their infinite wisdom, decide everything, treating women as chattel, or mindless little idiots who have to be told what to do for their own good. And have you noticed they never talk to us of serious things? Oh no, for those subjects are reserved for their august fellow males. Has any man ever consulted you when he had a problem? Of course not! In fact, I notice men barely speak to us except of inanities! And we are both of us intelligent, well-read. More so, I daresay, than most of *them*! And just see what men did to you! Ruined your life, and all for what?"

She paused to take a deep breath before she hurried on, "You know, my dear, none of this would be so in a better world, no indeed! In a better world women would have control of their own money, and they would be able to decide for themselves how they would live, and where, and with whom. And they would be able to speak of any subject under the sun; not have to hide their superiority. Perhaps they might even be able to do so without having men around to chafe at them, and bother them. I have often thought this, and now I know I was right!"

Sally shook her head at Anne, so vehement in her indignation, so sure of the truth of what she said. Fierce Anne, with her quicksilver wit, her intolerance of stupidity, was a girl unlike any she had ever known. But such things as she expounded could never be, and Sally knew it. Accepted it, even, as Anne would never do. But Anne might fret and fume over the status quo till Judgment Day, and she would not be able to change a thing. Wiser, Sally realized there was nothing to do but bow gracefully to the inevitable. Women were dependent on men, for men held all the power. It had always been so. Probably, it always would be so. She wondered that Anne, who was normally so astute, could not see that for the fact of life it was and submit to it—stop fighting for something that could never be. If she did not, sooner or later she would be hurt. And Sally, who now held Anne dearer than she had ever held her own sisters, did not want her to be hurt.

The winter months at Beechlands were pleasant ones. Colonel Jenkins had gone up to London on business right after the new year, and he planned to be gone for some time. He had not suggested Anne and Sally accompany him on this trip; indeed, he had tried to pretend it was only a tedious chore and a great bother to him.

But Sally was not fooled. The colonel had been unable to hide his pleasure that he would soon be gone, gone to his friends in town, and away from all the constraints of the country. As old as he was, he had still been like a little boy pretending he did not want the treat as he had frowned and grumbled about the necessity of the journey. Sally thought him very transparent and uncomplicated, so easily satisfied as he was with simple pleasures. He ate, drank, hunted, and rode, all with the same gusto.

Although Sally was at ease with him now, and with his sister too, she knew that in his world she was just a pleasant reminder of his benevolence. Her living at Beechlands was no hardship to him, wealthy as he was, and since she never bothered him, he was able to bask in his good works and feel a true Christian.

She had met the neighboring gentry by this time, and if she was accepted with enthusiasm by all the gentlemen for miles around, the ladies were much less welcoming. Just as Anne had predicted, Sally could tell they doubted she was married at all, and suspected she must be the colonel's mistress. Either that, or a love child of his whom he was forced to care for. Neither role made her fit for polite society, but since the entire Jenkins family championed her they could do nothing but accept this Mrs. Mannion as well, no matter how it galled them. Nothing, however, could make their reception of this suspect sister of theirs anything but tepid, and a few of the older ladies refused to acknowledge her at all.

Anne explained that it was because they were jealous of her beauty, and her friend was not to heed them, but still it hurt Sally to be whispered about, and ignored. She knew it was not because of her Irish brogue or her manners, either. Anne had succeeded in ridding her of the brogue long ago, and she had taught her impeccable manners; fit, as Anne had said with a smile, for the Court itself. Sally had learned to keep her head high in company, on occasion even resorting to a convenient deafness.

It was not only the gentry who gave her trouble. The servants at Beechlands were quick to question her visit, and all the maids sneered at her for her Irish background and her poverty. The footmen—even the bootboy!—were much warmer, but Sally was not fooled. She saw the calculated interest in their eyes as they studied her face and her figure, made clumsy attempts at familiarity. She was quick to check their presumption with a slightly raised brow, something she had learned from watching Anne. But the barely hidden contempt, the assumption that she was no better than they were and perhaps less so, was always there.

In time, a sort of armed truce went into effect between the servants' hall and the master's "charity case," as she had heard herself called behind her back. She was offended, but there was nothing she could do about it, no way to change it, so she was forced to rely on dignity and pride. It was very hard, but when she was tempted to the blue devils she reminded herself that anything was better than starvation, or the

life she would have led if she had returned to Leo
Mannion.

Beechlands itself required a great deal of study on
Sally's part. The mealtimes with all those courses, the
plethora of china and crystal and plate! The formality
that was observed between the inhabitants of the
house, the whole posture of the wealthy as they went
about their business, so self-assured and easy in their
station. The etiquette required for tea parties, calling
days, the occasional ball, the christenings and funer-
als, the visits to the sick bearing fruit or flowers, and
church attendance. Especially church. The colonel insisted that everyone in his household go to church
on Sundays, and he conducted morning and evening
prayers every day. Anne shook her head at his sudden
devotion to religious observance, saying she could not
understand it at all, for he had never behaved so
before.

All of this was an education for Sally, and one she
thanked Anne for providing, for she had only to watch
her friend to see how to behave. But oh, it was all
such a long, long way from that barefoot girl in an
Irish field, digging praties for dinner, whom she had
once been!

She knew she had learned well, but still she suspected that in spite of her new clothes, her new accent, and her new manners, she was that girl still, and
always would be.

And then she would tilt her chin at Fate and tell
herself she was being silly. That girl was gone forever,
and, as Mrs. Ginty had said, good riddance to her!

But in spite of her bravura, she knew there was
nothing she could do about her reception here by all
classes. As a poor pensioner dependent on charity she
did not deserve the servants' respect, nor did she belong with the proper married ladies and their virginal
daughters. Aware of her situation as she was, she
would have refused each and every invitation if Anne
had not insisted that she accept them.

"For I shall have no fun at all if you are not there,
my dear Sally," she had said. "But just having you

with me, hearing the absurd things I am hearing, knowing that later we can laugh at them together, is all that makes these dreary parties worthwhile."

She had run to Sally and kissed her then. "Oh, Sally, I am so lucky you came here! I do love you so much," she had whispered.

Warmed by her fervent affection, Sally had smiled and agreed. Dear Anne! How could she refuse such a simple request from her only friend? Anne had made Beechlands more than a haven. She had made it a home. Her only home, now.

Sally had written to her sister Mary soon after her arrival in England, but it was several months before she had a reply. Mary wrote briefly and stiffly of the family. At the end of her note she had said she could not write again, for it had been decided that Sally was now as dead to them as their father. Thus it was that Sally learned that Squire Joseph Desmond had indeed been hung for murder at Waterford Gaol.

She tried to weep for him, but after everything that had happened to her Sally could not mourn her da, no, nor even the loss of her family overmuch. She knew Anne was all she had now, but Anne was the finest friend and ally in the world. *She* was the lucky one, to have been brought here safely and to have found her, and for that she would be grateful to Colonel Jenkins all her life.

Chapter Six

1813

As COLONEL PETER JENKINS stood at the drawing room window of Beechlands, he smiled at the sight of the two girls who were strolling toward the house, arms about each other's waists. As he watched they paused, and his daughter Anne began to talk fervently, completely forgetting that it was teatime and they were being patiently awaited.

"What a charming picture they do present, to be sure," he remarked to his sister, as she fussed with some knickknacks displayed on a table nearby.

"Hmm?" she asked absentmindedly, intent on deciding whether the amorous porcelain shepherd looked better beside or in front of the Sevres vase.

"Anne and Sally," he told her over his shoulder. "Do come and tell me if I am not right."

Obediently, Honour Jenkins came to his side to peer out into the gardens. The two girls were laughing merrily now, and as the older couple watched, Anne leaned closer to kiss her friend's cheek and put her head on her shoulder.

"There now, could anything be more attractive?" the colonel demanded.

"As you say," his sister replied. "Er, how long has it been since Sally came to live with us, brother?"

The colonel seemed disconcerted by the sudden change of subject. "Why, now that you mention it, almost three years," he said, looking amazed. "How strange that it has been so long! I swear, it is as if it were only a month ago that Sally came here."

"No doubt," his sister agreed, sighing a little.

"You must admit she is easy to house, just like one

of the family," her brother said defensively. He had heard that sigh.

"Very easy. In fact, she is a delight. Always so calm and pleasant and well-bred, so willing to help with whatever needs to be done. Why, only yesterday, she found a pair of embroidery scissors of mine that I lost weeks ago, and never thought to see again. Indeed, I am very fond of Sally Mannion. She is a good girl."

Her brother was smiling and nodding, and after a moment she went on, "It is more than past time for you to begin arranging Anne's marriage, brother."

Startled once again by another change of subject, he turned to stare at her. "Anne? Marriage? Why on earth do you mention that now?"

"No particular reason, except that it has been on my mind of late. Anne is twenty-two now, and she should leave your house and set up in her own, with a man to care for her and give her children. If she is going to do so, that is."

"Twenty-two! I had not thought her so old!" the colonel exclaimed. "Has she shown any partiality for anyone in the neighborhood? Tim Mason? Reggie Wardwell, perhaps?"

Honour Jenkins sighed again. "No, she has not. She is more apt to make fun of all their gallantry than encourage it. And that is wrong. Besides, she is too close to Sally—much too close. It . . . it is not fitting."

"Surely you make too much of it!" her brother scoffed. "Of course they are the best of friends! I have been delighted that it is so. We all live so closely here, it would have been uncomfortable else. And Sally has been as good for Anne as Anne has been for her. My daughter, no doubt from observing Sally's calm good sense, has ceased to astonish with her wild remarks and strange behavior, and the young, gauche Irish girl Sally once was has matured into a self-assured young lady who can hold her own in any company. I am very pleased that my charity has had such happy results. I will admit, however, that I do not understand the girls' sudden passion for learning French and German.

Whatever good will those languages do them, down here in Devon?"

Honour Jenkins did not reply. She was peering through the window again. Still clasping each other's waists, Sally and Anne had paused again to admire the roses. "No doubt you are right," she said at last, as she rapped sharply on the pane to attract their attention. They turned as one and waved. The colonel saw Sally say something to his daughter, then release her to pick up her skirts. Smiling, Anne followed suit, both of them running lightly over the grass in a childish race to the house.

Minutes later, breathless and windblown, Anne Jenkins came into the room. "I do beg your pardons, Aunt, Father. We quite forgot the time. Have you been waiting long for your tea?"

"Not so very," the colonel told her, as his sister rang for the tray. "Where is Sally?"

Anne settled down on a sofa, arranging her skirts around her. "She went up to tidy herself. I told her it was not at all necessary, since we are only family today, but she would not listen. She is such a stickler for proper appearance!"

"You would do well to emulate her," her fond father said pointedly, eyeing her riotous brown curls and wrinkled gown.

"Pooh!" Anne said, making a face at him. Sally came in to join them minutes later, followed by a footman bearing a heavy tray.

It was toward the end of teatime that the colonel suddenly remembered something. "We must expect a guest soon," he announced. "On my last stay in London, I ran into an old friend of William's from his years at Eton. You do recall Harry Tredman, Viscount Reath, don't you, Honour? I know he came to stay here with my son years ago."

Miss Jenkins considered, her dignified face composed. "Yes, I do remember him. Surely he was that nervous little fellow who could never sit still, and was forever getting into the most dreadful scrapes?"

"He does so no longer," her brother assured her,

patting her hand. "He tells me he is married for the second time now, and he has several children."

He coughed then, as if to stop himself from saying something unsuitable, and his daughter's hazel eyes danced. She looked across the tea tray to Sally, and both girls smiled. So much in each other's company as they had been, they were able to exchange thoughts, and Sally could see at a glance that Anne had several interesting possibilities about what her father might have revealed, had he not remembered his company.

"My, yes, little Harry," Honour Jenkins remarked, in the slight pause that ensued. "I recall he fell off the stable roof and broke his arm, took great delight in jumping out from behind curtains to startle the maids, and managed to offend the vicar so, I could not show my face in church for a month. I was delighted when his visit came to an end."

Her brother chuckled. "Yes, I agree Harry was a handful. But what fun he and Will had as boys! They were as close as brothers, which is why I extended the invitation when I learned he would be in the neighborhood. How good it will be to reminisce with him! We must lay on a party or two, make sure he has good sport while he is here, lest he grow bored with an old man's company. He is to come in two weeks' time."

"Still, I admit I am surprised he accepted," Anne said with a little frown. "He did not care enough to come for the funeral, now did he?"

"Anne! You are too pert!" her father scolded. "I am sure he had a very good reason for missing it."

Anne shrugged and changed the subject. "Do you care to join Sally and me for a ride tomorrow, father? We intend to take a lunch and go toward the Blackdown Hills."

"I must beg to be excused. I have business with my agent then. But the weather appears to be holding. I am sure you girls will have a pleasant canter. Mind you take a groom with you, now, Anne."

As Anne chaffed her father for insisting on a male escort, Sally sat quietly and wondered why Miss Jenkins was so quiet today. She hoped the older lady was feeling well. Twice this past hour Sally had surprised her staring at her, and looking severe. But that is probably my imagination, she told herself, as she rose and excused herself. Miss Jenkins always looks severe. No doubt she is only wondering where she left her favorite shawl, or her smelling salts.

Harold Tredman, Viscount Reath, came to Beechlands on the appointed day two weeks later. He was driving a handsome black phaeton, with his valet and his luggage following in a coach that also trailed his riding horse. From the library windows both Sally and Anne saw the entourage sweep up the drive, and Anne laughed scornfully at the sight. "My, what pomp!" she said. "I begin to dislike this boyhood friend of my late brother's excessively, although in all honesty I cannot remember him at all. Of course I was very young when he visited before."

"No doubt your aunt kept you confined to the nursery for safety while he was here," Sally remarked. "He sounded rather a daunting little boy, did he not?"

"Yes he did, but I can see he has outgrown such childish traits with a vengeance. We shall not have him falling off the stable roof this visit! Why, anyone can see he is a man of *great* importance! No doubt we shall have a formal time of it, Sally, all curtsies and courtesies." She sighed. "It is too bad, his coming here to cut up our peace."

Sally did not reply at once, for she was watching the viscount as he stepped down from his phaeton to look around. He was a man of above medium height and wiry build, and he was beautifully dressed under his caped driving coat. As he turned she caught a glimpse of his profile: the hawk nose, firm jaw, and high cheekbones. He looked the complete aristocrat.

"Hmmm?" she asked. "Did you say he would cut up our peace? How on earth can he do that? Surely he will spend the majority of his time with your father, and we shall be left to our own devices, just as we always have been."

"No we won't," Anne said gloomily. She was

frowning now, and Sally raised a delicate brow. "I just know he'll fall in love with you, and he'll monopolize your time, and I'll never get to see you," Anne told her, her lower lip pushed out in a massive pout.

Sally laughed. "How silly you are, my friend," she scolded. "You sound like a jealous suitor, and how very ridiculous that is."

"Is it?" Anne asked idly, hanging her head and staring down at her clasped hands.

"Yes, indeed it is, and you know it.

"I beg you to remember the viscount is a married man—twice over. And I am married, too. Your father will soon set him straight on my situation."

"We shall see," Anne said. "I pray you will not quite forget me, Sally."

"Goose!" Sally said lightly, as she moved away from the window. "Have you finished that novel that the colonel had sent to us from London? Tell me what you thought of it."

Successfully diverted, Anne settled down to discuss *Sense and Sensibility*. Since she had been royally entertained by this new author's satirical wit, nothing more was said of the just arrived Lord Reath.

But all her fears were realized that evening, when the viscount had the pleasure of being introduced to Mrs. Sally Mannion. For although he was too sophisticated to make it apparent, it was plain to a watchful Anne that he had been properly bowled over by Sally's beauty. By the time they all rose from the dinner table his admiration for Sally's intelligence, wit, and manners was obvious as well.

Anne tried not to frown as she went to the pianoforte to play.

As Sally stood beside her, to turn the pages of the music for her, Anne noted that the viscount never took his eyes from her dearest friend all through the performance. He is certainly mercurial for a married man, she thought, as she rose to his applause later. But then I suppose I should only pity him, for he is just a man, with all a man's failings. And Sally is so very outstanding.

Suddenly Anne was glad that Sally was married. She knew she did not want to share her with anyone other than an absent, almost forgotten husband. But no man could begin to appreciate her, she told herself, not as I do. Men were so shallow. They wanted a woman only for their own physical satisfaction, callously ignoring her other, more wonderful traits. Sally especially deserved so much more: devotion, love, intellectual communion, a deep concern for everything that affected her. All those things she herself gave Sally so unstintingly, and with such joy in the giving.

To Anne's disgust, the viscount remained at Beechlands for well over two weeks. During his stay, the colonel found himself rather more in his daughter's and Sally's company than he would have liked. To be sure they were adorable young creatures, and he loved them both, but they had no place in men's business. And yet Anne and Sally always seemed to be included in every outing—why, once they had even come fishing with him and his guest. He had never heard of such a thing!

Of course he realized it was all Harry Tredman's doing, for as easily as had his daughter, he had seen how the younger man was attracted to Sally. As careful as the colonel always had been of Sally's reputation, he certainly never felt a qualm about leaving the viscount alone with the girl. Anne was not so sanguine, however, and she managed to remain at Sally's side throughout the visit.

One afternoon, however, when Anne had been forced to respond to a desperate appeal from her aunt, leaving Sally unattended in the garden for a few minutes, their guest happened upon her there.

"Ah, can it be you are alone at last, Mrs. Mannion?" he asked in his amused drawl, as he bowed to her and smiled. Sally rose from the rustic seat where she had been reading with Anne, and curtsied.

"I cannot believe that Miss Jenkins has finally deserted you, ma'am," he went on, before she had a chance to speak. "The two of you have been all but inseparable! But come, will you stroll with me a while? I should like to see the gardens in your company."

"If you would care for it, m'lord," Sally said, obediently putting her book down on the seat she had just vacated.

Idly, the viscount picked up the book, and his brows rose. "Alexander Pope's *An Essay on Man*, hmm? You continue to astound, ma'am. I had not thought women interested in such subjects. I am pleasantly surprised."

"Are we not allowed to educate ourselves, sir?" Sally asked, reluctantly laying her hand on his outstretched arm. She ignored the tensing of the muscles that she could feel there, right through his coat.

"But so few women avail themselves of the opportunity," he replied. "And surely, for one so beautiful as you, it is unnecessary. But of course, you know you are beautiful. Allow me to tell you you would fulfill your purpose on earth to perfection, just standing about so you might be admired."

"As if I wanted to be applauded for my looks," Sally said scornfully. "That is ridiculous! I would rather be noted for my intellect, knowledge, good sense, compassion—oh, for a thousand more worthy things than my appearance!"

"I stand corrected," he said, almost meekly.

Sally stole a suspicious look at his face. He was staring down at her, his eyes so intent they made her nervous. He did not smile. The viscount was much taller than she was, and yet suddenly she felt closer to him than she would have liked.

"Your husband is still in Ireland?" he asked next. In spite of the new topic, Sally was glad he had changed the subject.

"Yes, I imagine he is," she said, looking ahead of her now. "We do not communicate with each other.

"Do notice the roses, m'lord. That deep red color is superb, don't you agree? I have never seen them finer."

"Outstanding," he concurred, although Sally was

aware that he continued to watch her, with never so much as a glance at the rose beds.

"Whereabouts are you from in Ireland? Who were your parents, and how did you come to marry this Mr. Mannion, a gentleman you so quickly became separated from? How did that happen?" he asked in his abrupt way.

"I do not care to discuss my marriage with anyone, sir. It is a painful subject for me, and . . . and a private one."

He nodded, as if he'd suspected as much, and went on, "Do you intend to remain at Beechlands much longer? It seems such a waste, to have one such as you languishing unseen in the country."

"My . . . my plans are uncertain. Certainly I would like to stay. I have grown very fond of the family and this is my home now."

"Sally, my love, wherever are you?" They both heard Anne's voice calling, and Sally turned gratefully toward the sound.

"You must excuse me, sir. There is Anne, concerned for me."

Harry Tredman sighed, a look of annoyance crossing his features so swiftly that Sally wondered if she had only imagined it.

"Certainly," he said politely. "I know well that Miss Jenkins has the prior claim. Allow me to escort you to her, ma'am."

As they strolled back the way they had come he said, "Let me tell you something, Mrs. Mannion, and before we reach the ever-vigilant, ever-present Miss Jenkins."

He paused, and grasping Sally's arms he turned her toward him, his thin, strong hands firm.

"No matter how you may deride yourself, you remain the most beautiful woman I have ever seen," he said. He sounded so cold and matter-of-fact that Sally stiffened.

"You are perfect in every way. So perfect, in fact, that I find myself searching for just one tiny flaw. But alas there is none, to show that you are only a mere mortal like the rest of us. Your features, taken separately or as a whole, shame the most exalted dream of womanhood—your skin is like alabaster, your hair, dark silk. Even your eyes, so handsome yet so considering as they look out on the world, are outstanding. And your form, your grace of movement . . . You were wrong, you know. You should sit enthroned, so that you may only be admired, worshiped even. And I do not think that too strong a word."

"M'lord!" Sally said, deeply embarrassed. Anne called to her again, and she looked down at his hands. He let her go, albeit reluctantly.

As she curtsied, she noticed he never took his eyes from her face. She was glad to leave him and run away to Anne.

She was nervous the next time they met, but he never said anything so strange to her again, nor did he try to seek her out alone. After a few days she told herself that he had only been testing her, like other men she had encountered here. When he had discovered there was no chance for him, he bowed to the inevitable and discontinued his pursuit. She was glad. At least he had not been blatant about it! There had been one gentleman who had asked her bluntly what he would be required to pay for the privilege of gaining her bed. That episode, occurring as it had at a crowded reception, had required all the countenance she had been able to muster to avoid an ugly scene.

The viscount was a strange man, and while there were some things she liked about him there were others she could not admire. In his favor it could be said that he was quick and intelligent, and vastly amusing with his stories of London and society—the lettered men, musicians, and artists of the age, many of whom he knew personally. She could listen to him for hours then, for he was a master storyteller. And he had beautiful manners, and an almost reverent regard for her comfort. But there was no denying that he was eccentric, even volatile. Sometimes his mood could change in a minute, from a laughing good humor to black, brooding introspection. It made Sally uneasy.

She knew the viscount to be a man in his thirties, but she also had observed that he seemed able to act whatever age fit the situation he found himself in. He could be as gay and boyish as a youngster, as middle-aged and soldierly as the colonel, or as solemn and opinionated as the testiest octogenarian. It was not precisely as if he were aping the manners of others, he simply seemed to become one of them, much as a chameleon changes color to fit its environment, and just as easily. Somehow, such a trait was disquieting. If you could strip away the facade, what manner of man would he be?

Sally did not know how he did it, but after watching him charm some starchy matron, their heads close together as they exchanged on dits, or bend to catch an elderly gentleman's quavering words with all his attention given, she had to admit the viscount could do it with ease.

The unknowing would never suspect how easily he could become bored, how eager for yet another adventure, another scene, another occupation, but Sally knew. She had wondered before why he remained at Beechlands for so long. It was obvious he was not a country person. Without ever having seen London, Sally knew the city was his proper milieu; a place that pulsed with vibrant life and change, with both good and the evil that was greed and pride and status.

Harry Tredman was an enigma to her; she doubted she would ever understand him, even if he stayed for months. However, when he took his leave of them at last, she could only be relieved. Perfect guest that he had been, it had not been comfortable for her at Beechlands while he was in residence.

Anne was delighted to see the back of her father's guest as well, and she gave him her warmest smile when she said good-bye. His brows rose in pretended astonishment, but his eyes were knowing. Anne found herself blushing, something she scolded herself for later. Why, she had not blushed for years! What on earth was the matter with her?

* * *

Nothing more was heard of Viscount Reath for several months, and both Anne and Sally almost forgot he existed. They had mastered French now, and they could rattle away at great length to each other, as easy in that language as in their mother tongue. It made it possible for them to discuss their company openly, without that company ever knowing they were being mocked. Sally felt uneasy doing it, but Anne enjoyed it so, she did not object.

Anne had persuaded her to try her hand at writing as well, as a way to pass the long, dreary winter months, and Sally had begun a novel. She smiled to herself sometimes when she read over her work. It seemed so childlike, so simplistic, when compared with the fiction she was used to reading now. But Anne admired it, and said it was better than a great many published books. *She is too prejudiced, I know, but I shall consider it an exercise,* Sally told herself as she settled down to another morning's struggle with her pen.

In April, the colonel had a bulky letter from the viscount. He smiled when he opened it, but he was not smiling when he put the closely written sheets down on his desk some minutes later. He did not mention the letter to anyone, but from that time he was often preoccupied, and apt to frown when he thought no one was watching him.

Sally noticed his abstraction, but she could tell he did not care to speak of it. Knowing him well now, she realized he would have made it more obvious if he did. Careful questioning of Anne brought her no closer to discovering what was wrong, for Anne had never even noticed the change in her father.

Honour Jenkins was more perceptive, however, and so she was not surprised when she was summoned to the library one afternoon.

"You see, it's this letter I had a few days ago from Harry Tredman, Honour," her brother began, carefully patting the top of his head, as if to ensure that each of the few strands of hair left there was in its proper place. "I don't know what I should do about it, and I rather thought you might advise me in the matter."

Not waiting for his sister's nod, he plunged on, "It seems Viscount Reath's wife has died. Only two months ago, in fact. I did not know, else I would have written to console him. But it appears he does not mourn her overmuch, for he has proposed to take Sally away from us, and he is prepared to pay me the magnificent sum of ten thousand pounds for the privilege of doing so."

"Ten thousand pounds?" his sister asked, her mouth falling open in astonishment.

"Yes, quite a princely sum for her, wouldn't you say? I . . . I do not know what to do. I am very fond of Sally, you know that. Indeed, I think of her as a daughter who is only a little less dear to me than Anne. But it is not as if I could not bear to lose her. And I cannot deny that the money would be very welcome."

He sighed and threw up his hands. "To be sure, I am on the horns of a dilemma. Young Harry is as rich as Croesus, and he is titled. Sally would have a better future with him, an assured income, and it is not as if she could ever marry again, not while her husband lives. Besides, she is only a poor Irish squireen's daughter, and not one of us. It is ludicrous to consider her reputation.

"But still . . . somehow it seems like pandering to me, and that is repulsive! He . . . he does not tell me what he has in mind for her, but I think we can assume he means to make her his mistress. As a right-thinking man of principle, I am tempted to deny him for that reason alone."

As her brother compressed his lips and looked stern, Honour Jenkins stared down at the hands she had clasped tightly in her lap. "Yes, it is an unsavory situation, for Sally is not a slave to be sold at whim, even by you, her benefactor. However, I admit myself would be very glad if you would agree to the viscount's scheme, or to any more honorable one that sent her away from here forever. Very glad, indeed."

Her brother stared at her, his hazel eyes intent on her sad, stern face. His own face was drawn and tired, and the brilliant mustache he still affected seemed an odd adornment to it. "But I always thought you liked the girl, Honour! Indeed, you have often told me you do. Why would you wish her gone?"

His sister rose and came to take his hands in hers. She looked around before she spoke, as if to make sure the library doors were closed and they were quite alone. "It is not my feelings for Sally that motivate me in this case," she told him. "It is because of Anne. She has become ever more infatuated with Sally Mannion, even to the point of madness. And understand, I am not speaking only of a romantic friendship between two girls here. You must know this yourself, for how many times has Anne told you, over and over again when you bring a new suitor to her attention, that she will never marry and leave Beechlands? The reason she will not do so is because she is deeply in love with Sally."

She saw he had flushed and was about to speak, to deny the truth of what she had told him, but she shook her head. "No, let me finish, Peter. I know you do not think I see the dark side of life, and perhaps that has been true in the past. It is a weakness of mine, a way of avoiding unpleasantness, and I admit it. But in this situation I cannot help but see, and I know that what I see is wrong. And no amount of denial or procrastination will make it go away. It has gone too far.

"Do you remember when you went to Bristol a few weeks ago?"

Once again, startled by his sister's habit of changing the subject, the colonel could only nod.

"It was at that time that Anne began to try to sleep in Sally's bed. She claimed she was afraid of a storm one night. Anne? Afraid? She has never been so before, not even as a small child. And the next night she had a headache, and the next she came across the

hall claiming she could not sleep . . . Oh, she had any
number of reasons to gain her end.

"To her credit, Sally finally told her she must not
come to her late at night again. I don't know why,
but I did hear her say so. She told Anne she could
not sleep if she had to share a bed with anyone. I saw
Anne was disappointed, but she had to bow to Sally's
wishes, and so I did not have to bring it to your attention. Not then.

"No, wait. There is more. Only a few days ago, I
chanced upon a poem Anne had written to Sally and
left lying about. I read that poem, and if you had done
so as well, Peter, you would have thought it had been
written by a lovesick man, not a woman friend, no
matter how "romantic" she was. You see, it spoke of
desire for the loved one's body, of a physical longing
for completion that no woman should ever seek of
another. That such a thing is impossible did not even
occur to her.

"You and I know this is wrong, and if Sally remains
here it can only get worse. To be fair to her, I do not
think Sally even suspects the direction Anne's affection for her has taken, although Anne herself is
well aware of her passion—revels in it, even. Why else
would she have left that poem lying about for anyone
to see? She no longer wants Sally to be her friend.
She wants her to be her lover.

"And rather than try to conquer this sin, this, I
could even say, sick aberration, Anne persists in her
ardor.

"Even if you do not accept the viscount's offer,
brother, I beg you to send Sally Mannion away, far
away from Anne, lest finally your daughter does
something so singular it brings down censure on the
whole family, and ruins us all. I know her, and believe
me, she is capable of it."

There was silence then, and the colonel pulled his
hands from his sister's to go and pace up and down
the library, deep in thought. Honour Jenkins waited
patiently. She felt emotionally drained by the tale she
had had to tell, and very, very old.

"You are so sure of this, Honour?" he asked finally, his good-natured face shocked. "But to think my own daughter would . . . It is so bizarre! Why, even now I find it hard to believe!"

"No one can choose where they will love, Peter, nor whom, nor which sex," Honour Jenkins told him wearily, as she settled her heavy body in a chair. "It is truly unfortunate. But perhaps, if Sally were not here, so close, so tempting, Anne might come to see her transgression for what it is, a dark sin that she is perpetuating. And out of sight, out of mind. Let us pray that old maxim will prove true in Anne's case."

"Yes, I must agree with you there. Very well, after what you have told me, I see I have no choice in the matter. Sally will have to go, and as soon as possible. The viscount intends to come here for my answer in two days' time. He will stay but overnight, and he begs me to agree and make all as easy as possible. But if Anne feels as you say she does, I do not think it will be a pleasant visit."

"No, it cannot be that. Thank heaven, however, that it will be brief." She paused before she said, a little diffidently, "How think you Sally will take the news?"

Her brother looked stern. "It does not matter how she takes it! She must go! To think that my bringing her here, all my kindness and my wish to do the Christian thing, has turned on me like this! That Anne, my own dear daughter, should be led into sin by one like her! It shall not be! Sally Mannion must go!"

He spoke almost as if he were alone, but his sister understood. His words, his whole attitude, revealed his distress. She had known he would be distraught at what she had to tell him of his daughter—she had expected it. And compared to that awful revelation, taking the viscount's money was a minor problem. After all he could still refuse to do so. For it did not matter whether Peter loved Sally Mannion as a daughter. He would have to send her away. Anne was family—flesh of his flesh—and family came first.

"When the girls return from their ride, will you

please send Sally to me, here?" he asked. "Please make sure that Anne does not accompany her."

"Certainly, Peter," she said as she rose. She hesitated, wishing she might go to him and kiss him, hold him close for a moment, but wisely, she did no such thing. Instead, she let herself out of the library quietly. Her brother needed to think, and for that he had to be alone. As she closed the door behind her, and went to tell Bailey that his master had asked not to be disturbed, she prayed that Peter would handle the thing well. What Sally would think of it she had no idea, but then, she told herself, Sally was in no position to make demands. She must have known that her days at Beechlands might be numbered; must have been prepared to go away someday.

It was too bad, yes, but Sally Mannion was not their responsibility. They had taken care of her for three years, seen to her every need; indeed, coddled her in luxury. Surely she could not quarrel if their support was withdrawn, especially in this instance.

As Honour Jenkins went into the front salon to keep an eye out for the girls as they rode up the drive, so as to be able to intercept them, she wondered if Peter would reveal to Sally the real reason she was being sent away. She almost wished he would not do so, but she could see no way this information could be kept a secret from her. Or from Anne . . .

She shuddered.

Chapter Seven

"YOU WISHED TO SEE ME, SIR?" Sally asked, as she entered the library an hour later. She smiled as she came toward him, swinging her riding hat in one gloved hand.

She looked so lovely—so *innocent*—the colonel thought bleakly. The exercise had brought a delicate flush to her cheeks, and her handsome eyes sparkled. The dark blue habit she wore fit her to perfection, clinging to her lithe waist, her high bosom. How could it be possible she was the devil's tool?

But stay! Perhaps her beauty was meant as a snare for the unwary. Why, he himself, a widower in his late fifties, and a pious, respectable man, had occasionally had to stifle lascivious longings for her. Of course! He could see it clearly now. Naturally the devil would be clever enough to employ someone lovely and alluring to do his evil bidding.

And not content with seducing every male past puberty who ever set eyes on her, what must she do but trap poor, naive Anne in her coils as well?

Aware she was staring at him, he said, "Sit down. I must speak to you of something important. Hear me out."

"Of course, sir," she said, looking slightly bewildered as she took the seat he indicated, facing the desk. She wondered why the colonel looked so forbidding. Even so . . . so indignant.

"I have received a letter from Viscount Reath," he began stiffly, as he moved some letters on his desk and avoided her eye. "He has asked me to let him have the care of you from now on."

111

He glanced up in time to see her hand creep to her throat, and he prayed she would not make a scene. Quickly, to forestall it, he went on, "I have given his proposition a great deal of thought, and I have decided, finally, to agree to it. You have been here a long time, over three years in fact, but surely you knew your visit was never meant to be a permanent solution to your problems. This should come as no great shock to you."

He waited, but she only stared at him, her blue eyes wide with disbelief. So unmoving was she, she looked like a beautiful statue, and it made him uneasy.

"Young Harry will be here the day after tomorrow," he said, wishing she would speak, or cry, or— or something. "That should give you ample time to pack and prepare."

Still she had no comment, and he felt himself flushing. It angered him, and he said in a harder voice, "And if you think to quarrel with my decision, let me tell you it is all your fault! You have been an unwholesome influence in my house, bringing with you a stench of evil—unspeakable sin!"

Warming to his subject, he went on, "Before you came here this was a Christian home, one known for its godliness and piety. You have tried to turn it into a den of iniquity! I tell you I have no intention of letting the devil walk freely here! You will go, and the sooner the better!"

"Go?" she whispered, completely ignoring his ranting. She did not understand what he was saying; indeed, she had barely heard him in her distress. "Go?" she repeated. "You would send me away, just like that?"

"How dare you question me, ma'am?" he blustered. "Have you forgotten all I have done for you? Why, I saved you!"

"So you did, and I loved you for it," she said sadly. "And yet now, it appears, you would turn me out."

The viscount's aristocratic face came to mind then, and she remembered his words to her in the garden.

She had known he wanted her, but she had thought he had gone away and forgotten her. But go with him?

"What will you do if I refuse?" she asked swiftly, feeling a little spurt of anger at being so summarily dismissed, and in such a way, too. "Oh, of course I must leave if you order me to, but I do not have to agree to go with Viscount Reath, merely because you two have contrived my future. I am not a possession of yours because you saved me once, to be disposed of at will, and you cannot hand me over to him and expect me to be all smiling complaisance. The very idea!

"And *why* does he undertake my care? Have you considered that? As a Christian act of charity, as you have told me you did? I think not! And you yourself could not possibly believe it. We both know his reason very well. No, sir, I shall not go anywhere with that noble gentleman, and you may tell him I said so!"

"Do you have enough money saved so that you can live alone without protection?" the colonel asked. Very well, he thought. If she wanted to be blunt, he could certainly accommodate her. And who was she to question men's arrangements, and try to make him feel guilty? Obviously, the devil was at work again! He could hardly wait for her to be gone.

Sally bit her lip and lowered her eyes. She had some one hundred pounds put aside from her allowance. But while that amount of money would have seemed a munificent sum to her once, she was older and wiser now, well aware of how quickly it would be gone. And then what would she do?

She was alone. She had no family to return to, no friend save Anne. But Anne would help her, she knew she would, she thought, feeling a quiver of hope. Perhaps Anne could even loan her some money—no, that was thinking stupidly! Anne had no money of her own. All that she had came from her father's largesse.

Sally's mind was running in circles, and she felt so ill she had to grasp the back of the chair for support as she rose. "I am not sure what I will do. I must ask for some time to consider this before I give you an answer, sir," she said, concentrating on keeping her back straight, her head high, and her voice steady.

"You were wrong to agree to this without consulting me, sir. I had expected a little more consideration from you. For I may have been a charity case to you, but you have never owned me. Kindly remember that women are not 'things,' to be disposed of at will."

He rose and leaned on the desk facing her, his generally good-natured face almost purple with fury. "Enough!" he thundered. "You may tell me your decision in the morning. You are not to join the family for meals from now on. I shall have trays sent to your room until you leave. And you are not to see Anne again, not even for a moment. I forbid it!"

"But I must," she said swiftly. "I have to tell her what has been decided, say good-bye. Anne is my dearest friend!"

He shuddered and held up both his hands, as if to ward off something evil. "Do not speak to me of *friendship*, you . . . you . . ." He paused as if to gather himself, then pointed a stern finger at her. "Leave me at once!"

Sally stared at him for a moment, uncomprehending, but his expression did not change. She did not understand, no, not at all, but seeing how adamant he was, she picked up the train of her habit and walked swiftly to the door.

As that door closed behind her, Colonel Jenkins sank down behind his desk again and buried his face in his hands. Dear God, how difficult that had been! To have to talk to one such as she, with all her smooth-faced innocence, knowing she was, in truth, the devil's handmaiden. But he had vanquished her. God had been on his side!

He reached for the brandy decanter beside him and poured himself a large drink.

And to think she had dared to berate him for making arrangements with the viscount for her future. After spending three years in sin, corrupting his only daughter, what could it matter who she went to now? At least Harry Tredman was male!

Reminded of Anne, he shook his head, a look of utter disgust contorting his features. How far had it gone? Surely not too far for him to redeem her. He was reminded he would have to speak to his daughter, explain Sally's departure. He prayed he would not have to tell her the real reason. Somehow he must keep her away from Sally, make up some story for her that she would accept. Old soldier that he was, he knew he would rather have faced a cavalry charge alone than lay the truth bare to Anne.

But when Sally Mannion was gone—with or without Harry Tredman—he would set about matching Anne with some hot and handsome fellow—and quickly, too. All his daughter needed to take her mind from this unspeakable connection she had been enticed to was a virile man, one who would show her what love really was, over and over, night after night. He would insist she marry, so she might learn that a woman's true happiness came only from a man, and from having a home and children of her own.

As for Sally Mannion, when she realized that she had no other choice but the viscount, as he expected she would in time, he would be the richer by ten thousand pounds. He felt no revulsion at taking that money now. Indeed he felt the family had earned it, deserved it, even, after what she had done to them.

Upstairs, alone in her room, Sally paced up and down, telling herself she must think—*think!* She had been ordered to leave Beechlands, and so she must go. Not with the viscount—no, never that! But what could she do, else?

She wished she had saved more of her pin money, but it had been impossible to do so. Beechlands itself, the local society, and the parties she attended had meant she had to be well-dressed. And there had been other expenses, and gifts for Christmas and birthdays, as well as the trinkets and books she had had to buy lest Anne should buy them for her. Anne was always giving her presents. She had had to reciprocate. No, she had wanted to, for Anne, but dear God, she had never thought that someday . . .

She could go back to Ireland. It was much less expensive to live there. And perhaps she could get a position as a governess. She had heard the Irish were wild for English governesses, and Anne had certainly taught her accomplishments. Not sketching or music, to be sure, but French and German, the use of the globes, literature, and most importantly, an impeccable English accent. Perhaps she would end up trying to rid a number of Irish children of their brogues, even as Anne had done for her. How ironic that would be.

But now, knowing how susceptible men were, she rather doubted that any sensible woman would care to introduce her into a household that contained a husband, perhaps grown sons. No, she could never be a governess.

Perhaps she could finish her novel, get it published, and start another.

Sally shook her head. How could she live alone? She would have to hire a companion, and maids, and she could not afford to do that. And somehow she suspected it was harder to get a book published than she had imagined. She herself had not thought her writing unusual or strong.

Her head was beginning to ache, and she rubbed her forehead.

It appeared she had little choice in the matter after all. All her brave words to the colonel about making her own decisions about her future had been only that—words. Once again, she could not put herself in danger of starvation, just out of stubbornness. Unless she could think of another way, she would have to go with the viscount after all. Despairing, she slumped in her chair. So, she told herself, all of it *was* all too good to be true, wasn't it? But what else did you expect, you silly creature?

If only she understood why she was being sent away, why the colonel, who had always appeared to care for her, had talked so wildly and looked so grim.

What had changed? Why would he do so? She could not remember doing anything that might have upset him. She had always been careful to remain in the background, as unobtrusive as possible.

She wished she had listened to his words more carefully, but she had been so shocked and stunned by his ultimatum that the angry flood of words had washed over her without comprehension. What was it he said? she asked herself, her brow creased in a frown. *Think*, now!

A quick, impatient rap on the door caused her to turn. Anne came running in, slamming the door behind her. She was smiling, her hazel eyes glowing in a way Sally knew well. Anne had just had a marvelous idea, and she could not wait a single minute more before she discussed it with her friend.

"Sally? What are you doing up here all alone? Oh, never mind! I must tell you something. Aunt sent me off on the silliest errand after our ride, and as I was coming home from the Ames's cottage I started to think about God.

"Why do you stare at me so?" she asked, teasing. "I do occasionally think of Him, you know. I am not a heathen! How could I be, since Father has become so very pious?

"To be truthful, though, it was really because Granny Ames went on and on about Him. You know how she is. Well, she did so today, till I thought I would scream!

"But that is neither here nor there. And never mind that my father is waiting for me in the library. He can wait, for this is more important."

She sat down in the chair facing Sally's and reached out to grasp her hands. Earnestly, she went on, "Granny kept prating on about 'our Heavenly Father,' but tell me, Sally, why shouldn't God be a woman? Who decided He was a man? Tell me that, if you can!"

She sat back, triumphant, and Sally could not help smiling a little, even in all her distress. Dear Anne, imagine questioning such a thing! But that was just

like her friend, with her intelligent, inquiring mind.
She had never been able to just accept things.

Sally studied her. As usual, Anne's nut-brown curls
were disarranged, and her riding habit rumpled. Anne
cared nothing for feminine fashions; in fact, she
scorned all of woman's vanities. Her thirst was all for
knowledge. And although sometimes she could hurt
with her careless words, and on occasion was outspo-
ken to the point of rudeness, her loyalty, once given,
was true and unswerving. Now, as she waited for an
answer, her lips were parted, and her pretty face
intent.

"I don't know," Sally said. "I . . . I have never
thought of it."

"Well, stupid, *men* decided. Isn't that obvious?

"Men would never worship a Heavenly *Mother*!
How incongruous that would seem, when they consider the universe revolves around *them*! And yet
women have many more godlike qualities. After all,
they are the care-givers—they bring forth life, they
preserve it. But men . . . ah, men are destroyers,
eager for war.

"I thought of this all the way home, and I was sure
you would agree with me. Certainly the God of the
Old Testament, the Jehovah, is masculine. Think of
the sins and the laws and that 'eye for an eye' business. But I am sure the God of the New Testament
that Jesus tells us of is feminine. That God is kind,
forgiving, and loving. What think you? Do you
agree?"

"I haven't the faintest idea," Sally said. "It seems
somewhat irreligious to me."

"Yes, but only because we have always been taught
to pray to Our *Father* Who art in heaven," Anne said
impatiently.

She stopped suddenly and tilted her head to one
side, and the animation on her face faded. "What is
it? What is amiss?" she asked.

She saw Sally hesitate, and she grasped her hands
so tightly that Sally almost cried out. "I know there

is something wrong, very wrong! I can see it in your eyes. Tell me at once!"

"Your father is sending me away," Sally admitted, her lips dry. She could no more have refused to tell Anne than she could have stopped breathing, and it didn't matter what Colonel Jenkins wanted.

"*What?* Sending you away? Where? And why would he do that?"

Sally pulled her hands free and rose to pace the room again. Somehow she knew it would be easier to speak of it if she was not looking into Anne's clear eyes, her concerned face.

"Viscount Reath wants me, and your father has agreed to it," she said baldly. "The viscount is coming the day after tomorrow. I have to go with him."

"Oh no, you do not!" Anne said, her voice firm. "The very idea! It is obscene! I shall go and speak to my father this minute, and when I am through with him he will see how unspeakable such a thing would be. Don't worry, my dear. I'll make all right!"

She turned to run to the door, and Sally called after her, "Wait! It will do no good to speak to the colonel, none at all. He is angry with me for some reason, and . . . and his mind is made up."

Anne stopped and turned toward her again. "Sally, you disappoint me," she said, shaking her finger playfully. "You appear to have given up without even trying. Father would never do such a thing, not when he learns how unhappy it would make me, and you as well."

She stopped then, and frowned a little. "It is not that you *want* to go with Tredman, is it? Want to leave me?"

"Of course not, my dear friend," Sally assured her. "I shall be miserable. But truly, I have no choice. Your father brought me here out of kindness and charity, and if he wants to withdraw that charity I cannot refuse to leave. And he is adamant that I must go."

"No," Anne whispered, her eyes huge in her pale face. "No. It must not be. I cannot bear to lose you,

Sally. You shall not leave me, you shall *never* leave me! No, no, *no!*"

Her voice had risen with each word till she was screaming, and Sally looked uneasily to the door. She was sure everyone in the house could hear Anne and she longed to quiet her, although she had no idea how she was to do that.

Anne came to her then and clung to her, babbling of her love and devotion, and Sally was confused. This Anne was someone she did not know. Her words were wild, unconnected, her face so clenched and distorted that the tendons in her neck showed clearly. Tears filled her eyes and ran unchecked down her cheeks.

"Shh, my dear," Sally said, trying to speak calmly and evenly. "It does no good to carry on so, and it will make you ill. I have little choice in the matter. I must agree. I have no family anymore, and only a small amount of money saved. It has little to do with the viscount. If your father wants me to leave, you do see I could not stay, even if there were no wealthy lord waiting in the wings."

"No, I will not listen to you!" Anne cried, shaking her head in denial. "You shall not go! I could not bear it! I shall *die* if you leave me!"

She clung to Sally even more fiercely, putting her head on her shoulder. As the taller of the two, Sally looked down at her. Anne was on the edge of hysteria. She must do something. But what?

"Listen to me, listen!" Anne said all in a rush, as she clutched Sally closer. "I love you, Sally! I love you better than any man ever could! I want to live with you, make you happy! I can do it, I know I can! And we will be together always, lovers whom only death can part!"

She reached up then and pulled Sally's head down, to kiss her full on the mouth. To Sally's dismay, it was not the kind of kiss one woman normally gives to another. No, this was a lover's kiss, and a long one.

Wrenching free, Sally stumbled away. "No, stop it, Anne," she gasped. "You don't know, you *can't* know, what you're doing!"

As Anne just stood there, holding out her arms and looking pathetic, Sally suddenly remembered things she had conveniently forgotten. All those many other kisses of Anne's—hadn't she herself always been the one to draw back first? And the way Anne liked to run her fingers slowly up and down her arm, tickle the back of her neck, brush her hair with slow, caressing strokes—even the way she had sought her bed a short while ago. Sally had put a stop to that. It had made her uncomfortable to have Anne putting her arms around her and cuddling close, with only thin night robes between them. And once, she had felt Anne's hand on her breast. It had been then that she had told her friend she must not come to her room late at night ever again. She had done so because she had been uneasy, although she hadn't known why.

Now, however, it was all too clear to her, and she was horrified. Yes, Anne loved her, but not as Sally loved in return, as a friend. No, Anne loved her—or she wanted to—as a man would. Sally wondered if the colonel knew, and then, in her shame, she was sure he did. His words came back to her in fragments: *Satan . . . unwholesome influences . . . evil.* But she was not like that, she was not! she protested still. Oh, no! Dear God, no!

As Sally stared at Anne, all the horror and revulsion she felt at the thought of such an alliance was mirrored in her eyes.

"Don't look at me that way, darling," Anne cried. "You must not! It is killing me! Oh, I am sorry I startled you, but you'll see. When we are truly together, I'm sure you will come to love me, too. And I'll make Father give me some money, and we'll go away from here, far away where no one knows us. I promise I'll make you happy."

Sally could only shake her head over and over as she retreated backward, step by careful step. "No," she said. "Never."

She held her hands before her, as if to ward off this once dear friend who had become a stranger to her.

Anne watched in disbelief, her fist going to her

mouth before she abandoned the effort of stifling her emotion and screamed. It was a desperate scream, primitive and wild, and, pressed against the wall now, Sally felt the hair rise on the back of her neck.

Before Sally could even consider going to her, or ringing for help, Anne had whirled and run from the room. Sally could hear her wailing cry all the way down the stairs, how she shrieked her father's name before she slammed the library door shut behind her. Sally was sure that Anne was mad, and she shivered again.

Staggering forward, she grasped the bedpost for support as a pair of wide-eyed maids peeked around the door. She had to force herself to go to that door and close it. The maids looked avid for whatever dark story might be gleaned there, but she had no intention of telling them a thing.

Alone now, she felt so ill she knew she was going to vomit.

No one came near her for hours. Sally lay on her bed exhausted, her empty stomach still queasy. She heard the commotion in the downstairs hall, then Anne's keening again as she was carried to her room. Later, she heard footsteps passing to and fro before her door, the tinkle of glass against glass, the murmured words of the servants, even Miss Jenkins's unsteady voice and the colonel's terse replies. Sally huddled under her covers, quivering.

Eventually, a maid knocked and came in with a tray of supper. After slapping it down on the table, she made up the fire and lit some candles in the dark room. She did not speak to Sally, nor did Sally so much as open her eyes. She did not have to see the scorn in the maid's eyes to know it was there. Her hatred was obvious from her disapproving sniffs, the clatter she made. It even seemed to emanate from the crackling of her starched apron when she moved, from the way she slammed the door behind her as she left. And she had not removed the basin, or the chamber pot.

Sally could not eat anything, but she did drink several cups of strong tea, heavily sweetened. That calmed her stomach, gave her new heart, but she still felt chilled deep inside. It was then she began to cry, softly and helplessly. Poor Anne! she thought, rocking a little and hugging herself in her misery. My dear friend! I hope she will be all right. But I did not know—how could I? It was not my fault, as the colonel claimed. Was it?

She did not leave her room all the following day. Trays were brought to her, and water to wash with; the fire was attended and candles provided. Even the basin and chamber pot were dealt with finally. Sally spent the time packing her trunks, trying to forget the turmoil she felt and all those questions she had that now never would be answered.

It was dusk when Honour Jenkins knocked and asked for a moment of her time.

Sally bade her come in, and as she curtsied her eyes were anxious. "Please tell me, ma'am," she begged. "How is Anne? I have been so worried!"

"She is under heavy sedation. The doctor feels it would be best if she remains so until you are gone," the older woman said, putting some parcels on a nearby table. She seemed old and weary as she looked around and indicated a chair. "May I?" she asked.

Unable to speak, Sally nodded, and Miss Jenkins sighed and settled heavily into her seat. "In spite of what my brother believes, you did not suspect, did you?" she asked.

Sally shook her head. "No. No, I had no idea."

"I thought as much. But you do see, don't you, that even without that ten thousand pounds the viscount has promised my brother for you, you would have to leave anyway?"

"Ten . . . thousand . . . pounds?" Sally asked slowly. "He is going to *buy* me?"

Honour Jenkins looked stricken. "Oh, dearie me," she murmured. "You did not know that, and now I've let the cat out of the bag. My wretched tongue!"

Sally's anger was running strong and true now, and

it steadied her voice as she said, "I am glad to learn of it, ma'am. But how I have come up in the world!"

When she saw that her visitor only looked confused, she rushed on, "Oh yes, for when my parents sold me to my husband, he only gave them a thousand. Now I am worth ten times that. My *value* has increased exceedingly, wouldn't you say?"

Miss Jenkins made no move to answer her, and when Sally saw the fright and dismay in the older woman's eyes her anger died at once. None of this was Miss Jenkins's fault. She must not take out her fury on her. It was the colonel she wanted to rake down, and, of course, the arrogant viscount.

She took a deep breath and said more calmly, "Does the doctor feel Anne will recover, ma'am?"

"He—he does not know. All we can do is pray that she does, pray that this madness has not gone too far and she can be saved. Know I do not blame you, Sally. I always liked you, in spite of . . . of . . ."

As her voice died away in confusion, Sally paled. "I thank you for your concern, ma'am. I see I must go with Viscount Reath, so Anne will never see me again. It is all I can do for her now, and for her sake I will not hesitate."

The older lady waved a tired hand to the table, where she had left the parcels she had brought with her. "You remind me. Those came from the viscount, with a message to my brother today. He will be here very early in the morning, and although he had intended to stay overnight he has agreed, in the circumstances, to leave immediately. He has asked you to wear the clothes he sent. You can be ready?"

"Yes, certainly," Sally said, her throat tight. She wished she could have asked to see Anne one more time, but she didn't know how she could voice such a request, or whether such a visit might upset Anne. She decided to write her a letter instead, and ask Miss Jenkins to give it to her when she was calmer. For no matter what had happened, or how Anne regarded her, she was still her best friend, and dearer to her than any other person on earth. She would never forget her.

Honour Jenkins rose. "I shall have a maid wake you at six. And now I will bid you good-bye, Sally. I cannot say I am sorry to see you go. No, I cannot say that, for it would be a lie. But I am sorry for *you*. More sorry than I have ever been for anyone in my life. You poor, poor child! There is a forfeit to be paid for beauty, as you have seen. I never realized it before."

Sally's chin came up. "There is no need for your pity, ma'am. I am doing what I have to do, as I have been doing all my life. The colonel's rescuing me three years ago, and giving me sanctuary here, was but a brief respite for me. I . . . I have every reason to be grateful for it. I need no pity. No, I beg you give all your pity and all your prayers to Anne. She is the one who needs them.

"I intend to write a letter to her tonight. After you read it, I pray you will see fit to give it to her when you feel she is able to see it. I would not like Anne to think I had just gone away, so callously."

Miss Jenkins nodded and left the room. Sally stared after her for a long time before she went back to choosing those few favorite books that were all she could fit in her trunks, and to thinking of what she might say to Anne in her letter.

Much later, when the packing was done and the letter finally written to her satisfaction, she found herself thinking of the one thing she had been firmly suppressing all these hours—those ten thousand pounds. Cynically, she wondered if the colonel would have tried to find some other method of banishing her to gain them, if Anne's mad love for her had never become known. Even as good and pious as he was, she would not put it past him. After all, it was a princely sum, and one more needy men would have killed to obtain.

And so I have been sold again, she thought drearily as she stared into the fire. But what I told Miss Jenkins is true. I have come up in the world. The viscount is wealthy, true, but I do not think he will beat me. No, for he would not care to damage something he had to pay so dearly to get. And he was always kind and considerate to me when he was here before.

She rose from her chair so suddenly that she almost overturned it. No! she told herself fiercely. She would not count on that, or on any man's word, ever again. Men were not to be trusted, neither as loving fathers or new husbands; not even as kindly old Christian gentlemen.

And most certainly not as the sort of volatile dilettante the viscount appeared to be. It was up to her, and only to her, to safeguard her future, and from this time on she would do it in whatever way she had to.

And in doing so, she told herself coldly, she would trust no one. Neither man—nor woman.

Chapter Eight

IN THE MORNING, she discovered that the parcels the viscount had sent her contained black mourning clothes. Her mouth twisted as she stared down at them. Was this some macabre joke? she wondered. She did not know Harry Tredman well enough to know if he would consider taking her away from Beechlands swathed all in black, amusing, but if that was what he had thought, she considered his sense of humor appalling.

Still, obediently, she donned the garments. First the fine white lawn chemise, then the black silk petticoats lavish with lace, the encompassing black silk gown with its drifting panels and jet embroidery. There was even some modest jet jewelry. The bandbox contained a smart black satin bonnet, complete with plumes and heavily draped in veiling. She was glad of that veiling. It meant she could avoid everyone's eye on her way down the stairs, through the hall, and out the door for the last time.

She was ready and standing at the window when the viscount's carriage drove up, and she watched his tall, wiry figure as he jumped down to stride up the steps. It seemed an endless time before she heard a footman coming up the stairs, and she waited breathlessly for his knock on her door.

Once admitted, she indicated her trunks silently as she swept by him to the door. She saw it was James. He had always been the kindest of the footmen, but from his compressed lips, his narrowed eyes, she could see he was regretting that kindness now. As he muttered "wicked Jezebel!" under his breath she knew he was blaming her for his Miss Anne's deviance, and her collapse.

Honour Jenkins was not in the hall, nor was the colonel. Sally was glad of that. Only Bailey and the footmen were there, and none of them was looking at her.

And of course, there was Harold Tredman, Viscount Reath. Sally stole a glance at his face as she rose from her curtsy. He was not smiling. Indeed, he was very pale, and his set face was stern.

"Mrs. Mannion," he said, bowing. "Permit me to offer you my sincere condolences on the death of your grandmother. I am delighted to be able to be of service to you, escorting you to your ship at Bristol. I know how anxious you must be to rejoin your family."

Sally had no idea what he was talking about, or even why he was saying what he was. He must be aware that the servants knew very well why she was being sent away, and what they all thought of her now. What then was this farce he was playing? Still, she made herself nod as she put her hand on his arm. He led her to the door.

"Hurry those men along with Mrs. Mannion's trunks, Bailey," he said over his shoulder, as they went down the steps to his waiting carriage.

He handed her into it himself, then stood back to supervise the loading of the baggage. Only when all was secure did he join her inside. As the carriage started down the drive Sally stared straight ahead, as she had done when she left Ballyragh three years before. Just as she had that day, she knew this would be a final leavetaking. She would never see Beechlands again. Indeed, with her stomach still churning, she did not want to see it again. Ever.

But she could not dwell on what had brought her to this pass, sad though it was. She had other things to do now, things she had thought long and hard about through an almost sleepless night.

She drew a deep breath and turned to face the viscount. Even though he was staring at her she knew he could not see her clearly, and she had no intention of raising her veil. No, for the things she must say now would be far more easily said masked.

"I believe we have a great deal to discuss, m'lord," she began, proud that her voice did not quiver.

"As you say," he agreed. "Fortunately, we have a long way to travel alone together, in which to do so. Should you like to begin?" he asked, courteous as always.

"Yes, I would. I would ask what arrangements you have in mind for me. I understand you offered Colonel Jenkins ten thousand pounds? I am sure he accepted the sum, and although that is all very well for him, what of me?"

"What of you? You expect to be paid?" he asked in a lazy drawl.

Sally peered at him through her veil. He had sounded almost amused, and surely the corner of his mouth was twitching as if he were trying not to laugh. Well, he would discover this was no laughing matter. She clutched her reticule closer. In it were her hundred pounds, her small amount of jewelry, and the sovereign she had been given as a little girl. All that she had of value in the world. No, she told herself, setting her mouth. I have something more valuable than all of that. I have beauty. Beauty men want. Since I have no other way to survive but by using that beauty, I shall do so more wisely from now on.

"I believe it is customary to be paid," she told him. "However, I must say I resent the colonel being given such a munificent sum for *my* favors. What has he to say about where I bestow them? I was not his slave, nor had he the right to sell me to anyone!"

"I thought perhaps he would not have let you go without some, er, incentive. I am sorry if this has seemed like a business transaction, more sorry than I can say. I only chose to do the most, er, *expedient* thing."

She shrugged. "I wonder you did not think to ask me directly, then. It might have saved you a great deal of money."

"I would have been delighted to speak to you, my

dear Mrs. Mannion," he said cordially. "However, I knew there was no chance you would have agreed to my proposition. Now honestly, would you have?"

He did not wait for her answer, but went on, "No, for you were far too comfortable at Beechlands, and then there was Miss Jenkins and her, ah, friendship."

"You know of Anne's fondness for me?" Sally whispered.

"I saw it clear when I visited last," he told her. "Her father told me the whole this morning. He was, as you know, horrified; in fact, he considers you an evil influence, sent by Satan to corrupt his daughter."

"I know that. He told me so."

"Well, he has great hopes he can cure Miss Jenkins of her unwholesome attraction for you, if you are least in sight, not luring her on. I myself do not think he has much chance of that. The girl is truly besotted. Incidentally, you are not to write to her or attempt to communicate with her in any way from now on. The colonel has forbidden it.

"Miss Honour Jenkins tells me you claimed to have no idea of your friend's love; that you thought of her only as a dear companion. Is that true?"

Sally nodded, for she could not speak of it. Not to him. Not to anyone.

"Unfortunate, but something that cannot be helped," he said, sounding easier. His voice had lost its cold severity as he went on. "You are too lovely, ma'am, for members of either sex to ignore you. But you know that very well."

"Yes, now I do," Sally said, lifting her chin again. "And it is because I do know it that I will not accept your protection as naively as I accepted Colonel Jenkins's kind offer of sanctuary. At that time I was younger and I was desperate. I am neither young nor desperate now."

She saw he was smiling down at her. "How old are you?" he asked.

Startled, Sally replied, "Why, I just had my nineteenth birthday."

"So, you are nineteen! Such a great age," he said, sounding amused.

"Nineteen is quite old enough to understand the ways of the world, if you have seen rather more of them than you bargained for," she said. "What I have seen, and your bribe to the colonel, tells me I am worth a great deal of money to you."

She drew another steadying breath. "Be so good as to tell me exactly what you have in mind for me, sir. And what renumeration I can expect. I can then tell you if it would be satisfactory, or no."

"How sordid all this is," he complained, sounding bored. "And far from the mark as well. I hate haggling. I never engage in it.

"As for my intentions, why, I intend to marry you, of course. As Lady Reath, you will have a goodly settlement, as well as an annual allowance of three thousand pounds for your dresses."

"Marry me?" Sally echoed, stunned. "I must tell you, I do not care for the jest, m'lord!"

"It is no jest. I have wanted to marry you ever since I first saw you."

"Very fine talking, sir, when you know there is no chance of it. Lest you have forgotten, I am, and most irretrievably too, married already."

"At the moment you are," he agreed. "But as soon as you tell me of your husband, and where he can be found, I shall send an envoy to him, begging him to divorce you. I believe I can, ah, ease the way for him not only to agree, but to be happy to do so."

"More money thrown away?" she asked swiftly. She was more than a little angry now, sure he was playing with her for his own amusement. "I do not believe you, or any of this. Why me? I am only an Irish squire's daughter, and I have seen how the English look down on the Irish. Furthermore, my father was hung for murder; the family is impoverished. You are a noble lord, with a fine title, wealth, estates. Why would you marry me?"

"Because I must. How else can I be sure of having

you beside me always?" he asked, as if it were the most logical reason on earth.

"You would have me believe that you are that much in love with me?" Sally asked, her voice openly scornful.

Now it was the viscount's turn to shrug. "I have no idea. I do not think I have ever been in love. I wanted my first wife with a boy's hot, heedless passion, and later, I married my mistress because that woman had given me three children and another was on the way. I thought it the least I could do for such devotion, to make the last one of them legitimate. Now, of course, she is dead too, and I want you. But love you? Who can say?"

"I do not love *you*," Sally told him with a great deal of satisfaction.

He laughed with genuine amusement. "Of course you do not. You hardly know me. But I do not require love in any case.

"By the way, have *you* ever been in love? Ever felt desire for any man?"

Sally bit her lip, more glad than ever of her heavy veil. "No, never," she admitted softly.

The viscount nodded, as if he had already known what her answer would be. "Of course not. You, my dear, are a goddess, and above such earthly, mundane things."

"If you do not require love, what do you require?" Sally asked, to change the subject. She wondered as she did so if the viscount was quite sane.

"If I love anything in this world, it is beauty," he told her seriously, if obliquely. "Beauty in art, music, literature, and especially in the human form and face. But there is so little perfection to be found in mankind. You are the first woman I have ever seen who is perfect. Naturally, connoisseur that I am, I must have you. As to what I require of you, it is simple. Only that you remain as beautiful and desirable as you are now, so I might admire you, and know that there is no man on earth who does not envy me."

"How can I promise that?" Sally asked, sure now

the viscount was mad. "Most assuredly I shall grow old someday, and this beauty you admire will fade. It happens to everyone, man or woman."

He nodded. "But by the time you do, my child, I do not think my eyesight will be so keen. You are just turned nineteen. I am almost thirty-five."

Sally was forced to smile a little at his logic, although she did not believe a word he said. Harold Tredman was a nobleman with a proud name. Why would he marry her? It was ludicrous, even if he had indeed married his former mistress after his first wife's death. Perhaps that lady had been as highborn as he was himself, not the nameless little Irish girl she was.

Sally stiffened. She reminded herself she could not trust him. She could never trust anyone again. The viscount could say he was sending someone to Leo Mannion, pretend he was trying to obtain her divorce, and she would have no way of knowing if it was true. Perhaps he only wanted her to believe he was seeking to marry her, as a way to make her more eager for him, and accommodating.

Besides, in spite of his intelligent words, his easy, educated drawl, she really did suspect he was insane. Speeding through the morning behind his well-bred horses, however, gave her no opportunity to escape him. She would have to humor him until she found a chance to make good that escape. Till then, she would have to bide her time; pray he would not become violent.

"And what do I do, where do I stay, while you are persuading my husband to release me?" she asked coldly. "With you?"

"Certainly not!" he said, in a voice just as cold. "You are to be my wife. As such, all the proprieties must be observed. It is why I brought you mourning to wear. When we stop at inns along the way on our journey to London, you will be a widow I am escorting to her family. Do not ever lift your veil in company, not even before a servant. No one must see your face, or know your right name. And that reminds me. Were you christened Sally?"

"No, Margaret. I do not know why I was called Sally, but Sally I have always been."

"Margaret . . . Margaret . . ." he mused. "Much more suitable, but still not perfect for one such as you. Let me see . . ."

He turned to stare out the carriage window at the lush farmlands they were traveling through. Once again Sally could see his profile, so sharply drawn, so elegant and sure, and she stared at it, mesmerized.

"I have it," he said, turning back to her and smiling. "Margarite! Margarite Desmond. We shall dispense with your married name. It is a little premature, but why not? And 'Mannion' is impossible. It is as common as Sally, and you, dear lady, are most *un*common.

"As to where you will stay, my dear Margarite, I have rented a house for you in Manchester Square. It is fully furnished and staffed, right down to your lady companion. Mrs. Fairfax is a distant second cousin of mine. I pray she will not bore you to death while she lends you consequence. I myself will call on you only as any gentleman might call on his chosen lady, and you will never see me except in Mrs. Fairfax's company. Does that quite satisfy you?"

"I begin to believe you are serious!" Sally exclaimed, startled but trying to sound amused.

His brows rose. "Naturally. I never lie. What is the sense of it? Lies only make trouble in the end. I shall expect you to be as honest as I am myself, not only with me but with everyone you soon will meet in society. Believe me, it will smooth your path."

He picked up her left hand then and calmly removed the black glove she wore. Sally stifled a protest as he took off her wedding band.

"And now, shall we dispose of this tawdry little token, ma'am? I do assure you my wedding ring will be much more suitable for your lovely hand. Sapphires, I think, and diamonds."

He turned Mannion's ring around and around in fastidious fingers. "How deplorable," he murmured. "Not even precious metal. Why, it is already losing its thin wash of gold."

In only a moment he had opened the window beside him and tossed the ring to the wind. Sally thought to complain of his high-handedness, but remembering that she must humor him she held her tongue. Besides, she told herself, as he wiped his fingers on a handkerchief, she didn't need that particular talisman to remember her marriage and the brute she had endured it with. Those memories would be with her always.

"Now tell me, if you please, of this parsimonious husband of yours," he said calmly. "Everything about him, including the most important piece of information of all: where he can be found."

It took almost a week to reach London. The viscount did not insist on a fast pace, and their frequent stops for meals and refreshments were often prolonged if he saw something he wished to investigate— a church or a guild hall, even a pretty little village. In spite of herself and her nervousness at being in his company, Sally began to enjoy the journey. The viscount was a fascinating companion, as erudite and amusing as she had remembered. True to his word, he left her every evening to the solitude of a comfortable bedchamber, and the services of a maid, at whichever inn he had graced with his patronage.

Sally was surprised to see that his valet preceded them in another carriage, which carried such comforts as the viscount deemed necessary on a long overland journey. She was tempted to scorn such nicety at first, but after only one night spent on the smooth linen sheets the valet provided for their beds she had to admit such luxury was a treat, as were the special wines, delicious sweetmeats, fine perfumed soap, and soft, immaculate towels.

London itself stunned her. It made its presence known many miles before it came into view, first from the acrid smell of sea coal that permeated the air, then by the dark cloud that hung over it on the eastern horizon. The viscount explained that the cloud re-

sulted from the smoke issuing from thousands of
chimneys.

Traffic increased apace as they traveled nearer. Besides the abundance of carriages and coaches, there
were the carts and drays of the country folk bringing
produce to market. Often all traffic was slowed by
large numbers of cattle being herded to Smithfield for
slaughter, or by gaggles of geese, their webbed feet
tarred to enable them to make the long walk from
some rural pond to a wealthy man's dinner table.

When the viscount's carriage finally reached London itself, it became entangled in a great press of
traffic in Baker Street. Sally was alarmed. So many
vehicles of all kinds, almost touching—so many, many
people in this one street! And where has the sky gone?
she wondered. She felt stifled by the tall buildings,
built so close together they seemed like imprisoning
walls.

And it was so noisy! Newspaper sellers' bells, street
vendors, shrill little girls selling flowers, and bellmen
calling the news of the day over the din. A fist knock-
ing on the window beside her startled her, and she
stared with horror at the grimy-faced man, missing
most of his teeth, who waved a placard at her. Harry
Tredman told her to ignore him; he was only giving
out playbills.

As the carriage inched forward, she heard their
coachman bellow. He was answered sharply by another roaring voice, and for a moment the wheels col-
lided and the carriage rocked. As they pulled clear
Sally smelled a composite aroma of roasting chestnuts,
manure, cockles, and hot pork pies. Surely London
was madness personified!

She kept her hands clasped tightly in her lap so the
viscount could not see how they were trembling, and
she concentrated on not cringing toward him in her
distress. Her companion was calm; indeed, he appeared so bored by it all that obviously there was
nothing to worry about. But still it was a relief to
Sally when the carriage finally turned into Manchester
Square, and the noise and confusion abated.

The house they stopped before was as dignified and solemn-looking as its neighbors, grouped as they were around a tiny park. Sally thought it couldn't hold a candle to Dublin's Fitzwilliam Square, and for a brief, stabbing moment she was homesick.

Still, she looked around with pretended interest as the viscount ordered the grooms to unload her trunks. As he escorted her up the steps the front door of the house opened, and they were greeted by an elderly butler, who bowed them inside.

"Jackson, is it not?" the viscount asked abruptly. "Ah, yes. This is your mistress, Mrs. Margarite Desmond. After you have seen to the disposal of her baggage, fetch Mrs. Fairfax to us."

The butler bowed and Sally nodded, but she was given no opportunity to speak to him, for the viscount was leading her to a salon off the entrance hall, ushering her inside, and shutting the door behind them.

The salon was tastefully, if austerely furnished. To Sally it had the look of the rented house it was, for none of its previous tenants had left so much as a hint of their presence. Flowers would help, she thought, and books and prints; even a slight disorder would be a welcome relief.

"Now, Margarite, before we are interrupted by my cousin, let me tell you what I plan," the viscount began, and she forced herself to concentrate. He had gone to take a place by the fireside, and now, as he leaned against the mantel, he watched her closely.

"Tomorrow morning you are to go to Madame Clotilde's in Bond Street. She is London's finest modiste, and she is expecting you. I have already selected the patterns and materials for your new gowns, but she will need to take your measurements."

"You did that?" Sally asked, indignant at his high-handedness. "But perhaps I would prefer to choose my own gowns!"

He nodded, his narrowed eyes never leaving her face. She was still veiled, and he made an impatient gesture. Obediently, she raised the veil. It had more

than served his purpose—and hers. There was no
more need to employ it.

"You may choose as many others as you like, but
you will not refuse these gowns I have selected. You
are but new-come to town, and can have no idea what
is suitable. And since I don't know if this Cousin
Emily of mine has any taste at all, I prefer not to trust
her judgment."

"You—you do not know her well?" Sally asked,
amazed.

His brows rose. "Certainly not. I do not think I
have set eyes on the woman more than once or twice
in my life. I do not associate with bores or poor rela-
tions. Why should I?"

Sally had no answer to his arrogance, and after a
moment he went on. "I have opened an account for
you at my bank, Wellings and Bourne, in the city.
You have five thousand pounds for whatever expenses
you may incur, and for the housekeeping. Apply to
Mr. Bourne personally for your needs."

A timid knock sounded on the door then, and he
turned impatiently. A tall, thin, older lady hesitated
there, and Sally thought she had never seen anyone
with such a straight back. Why, she did not look as if
she could bend, never mind sit down.

"Come in, cousin, come in!" the viscount said, as
the lady lingered on the threshold. "Let me make you
known to Margarite Desmond, the lady I wrote to you
about. And this, of course, my dear, is your chaper-
one, Mrs. Emily Fairfax. You are not to go anywhere
outside this house without her. Do you understand
me? Nowhere, not even for a stroll around the
square."

As Sally nodded and curtsied, she studied the
woman before her. Her thin face was wrinkled and
plain, and although she smiled slightly her pale blue
eyes looked timid, almost frightened. Why? Sally
wondered.

"I am delighted to meet you, Mrs. Desmond," she
was saying in a soft, apathetic tone. "I am sure we
shall deal extremely well together."

"Whether you do or not, you are to be inseparable," the viscount interrupted. His elderly cousin turned toward him at once.

"Certainly, m'lord—er, Harry. It shall be as you say. Can we persuade you to stay and dine with us?"

He shook his head. "No, I'm for St. James's Square."

He came toward Sally then, and took her hand to kiss it. "I shall, however, do myself the honor of taking tea with you tomorrow, Margarite. And, er, with Cousin Emily as well. As soon as your gowns and ensembles are ready we shall drive in the park, attend the theater and concerts, be seen here, there, and everywhere so you may meet society.

"Perhaps you had better replenish your wardrobe as well, cuz. Send the bills to me," he added, his generous words at odds with his grimace as he studied her simple, outdated gown.

Mrs. Fairfax cringed. Ignoring her, Harry Tredman looked around and frowned even more. "This may be perfectly respectable, and all very well as rented houses go, but it is not the showcase for your beauty that I demand, Margarite. Trust me to send my envoy to Ireland first thing in the morning. The sooner I have you away from here, the better."

He turned and walked rapidly to the door. "My farewells, ladies. A pleasant evening."

Both women stood very still until they had heard the outer door of the house close behind him. Only then did they face each other, in equal trepidation.

Mrs. Fairfax waved a thin hand toward a sofa. "Do you care to take refreshment, Mrs. Desmond?" she asked. "Or perhaps you would rather go to your room and rest? Traveling is so fatiguing!"

Sally was feeling not only nervous but suffocated, and she was quick to agree to the latter course. No doubt she would get to know the viscount's elderly cousin very well if she was to go nowhere without her, but she did not feel able to face that just yet.

"It was a long journey," she said with a little smile.

"If I might have a cup of tea brought to my room? And I should like to rest till dinnertime."

"Certainly, madam, a wise decision," Mrs. Fairfax said, her pale eyes looking anywhere but at her charge. "Dinner is served at nine."

Sally nodded, although she was startled by the lateness of the hour appointed. Nine in the evening? Good heavens, in the country they had—

She pushed that thought out of her mind. Beechlands, and all it represented, must be forgotten. Curtsying to her frightened new bodyguard, she left the room.

A footman took her upstairs to a large front bedchamber. A middle-aged maid was already there, unpacking her clothes. She introduced herself as Windle, saying the viscount had chosen her to be Mrs. Desmond's dresser, and then she proceeded to inspect her new mistress with a keen eye.

Sally was a little disconcerted at being studied so carefully by this servant, but at last the maid's thin lips curved in a pleased smile and she nodded.

"Indeed, it is just as the viscount assured me, when he stole me away from Lady Billings," she said, nodding in satisfaction. "You will be the most famous beauty of the decade, ma'am, when we have dressed you. I shall, of course, attend you and Mrs. Fairfax on your shopping expedition tomorrow. You may rely on my taste and experience to choose those accessories that are the most becoming. And I shall personally summon the best hairdresser to see to your coiffure. Most satisfactory! I am content!"

For one mad moment Sally was tempted to express her gratitude for this condescension in a low court curtsy, but she stifled such levity, excusing the maid from her chores by telling her she would like to be alone for a while. As soon as Windle had left and the tea tray had been delivered, Sally had her solitude.

She made herself eat something, drank the hot tea. She was not hungry. She had not been hungry for several days.

As she sat there, blessedly alone at last, she began to think, as she had promised herself she must. She had not tried to leave the viscount on the journey here. For one thing he had watched her too carefully, and for another she knew such an attempt was doomed to failure. He would have been able to locate her easily in the country. But here in London it would be another matter, and simple for her to disappear if she chose to do so. But she must make that decision before tomorrow. She could not take anything from him, neither gowns nor money, if she intended to leave him. It would not be ethical. She had to decide what to do—now.

She shrugged as she poured another cup of tea. She felt like a leaf drifting idly down a slow-moving stream, purposeless, riding the currents, letting herself be taken wherever the stream was going. It bothered her, this lassitude, but she suspected she was still in a state of shock, after what had occurred at Beechlands. Even now, thinking of Anne and wondering how she was faring, she had trouble believing that it had all happened, even that Anne had really felt that way about her.

She remembered the letter she had left for her, and how difficult it had been to write. She had thrown several sheets of paper on the fire before she had been satisfied. In her final effort, she had told Anne that she would always remember her as her dearest friend, and she hoped that eventually Anne would forget what had happened between them that fateful after-noon and find the happiness she deserved. Happiness, Sally had written firmly, that could never be attained with her. What Anne had wanted was not right, but she was sure, after a period of reflection, that Anne would come to see that for herself. She closed the letter with her love and her gratitude for their friendship.

Sally had not been happy even with that attempt; she was not happy now. In retrospect she saw it as a poor, stilted effort. Pray Anne could read between the lines, see what had been in her heart that had been so very hard to say!

She sighed and went to the window, to hold back

the draperies so she could stare down into the square.
It was quiet, with few people or carriages abroad, but
London itself was not. Even the brief glimpse of it
she had had today had shown her it teemed with un-
fortunates—beggars and thieves, starving children and
young prostitutes with no future ahead of them but
a death before their time, miserable and alone. She
reminded herself that at least she did not have to end
up that way. No. She had been offered a way out.
But could she trust Harry Tredman, Viscount Reath?

She recalled that the viscount had kept his word to
her. He had not touched her, beyond a courteous
hand to help her from the carriage or up a flight of
stairs. But even if what he had told her was true, even
if he did intend to marry her, would she agree to it?

All during the past week, as they had journeyed to
London, she had tried to get to know him better, to
take his measure as a man. But she had to admit she
was no closer to knowing Harry Tredman than she had
been before. He never spoke of himself, his family, his
background, and she had hardly liked to ask. He had
been amusing, attentive, even quiet when he sensed
she did not wish to converse. There had been very
few brooding moods to mar the trip, but she reminded
herself that she was too new an adventure for that.
He might become bored with her, as she sensed he
became bored with everything sooner or later, but that
would not come for some time. And he seemed sincere in his wish to marry her. Why else would he have
gone to so much trouble? Spent so much money?

But what was she to do?

She was sure he would not fail in his quest to find
Leo Mannion, sure he would be able to buy her freedom. He was not a man who failed at simple things
like that. And if she did marry him, she would be
safe. Being a wife was vastly superior to being a mistress, for she could not easily be discarded.

And she would be Viscountess Reath. Safe,
wealthy, an assured place in society. A lady. She
knew she would be a fool to turn this opportunity
down, to run away, try to escape. And, she told

herself coldly, she was not a fool. Not anymore. But still . . . still . . .

What if the viscount really was not sane? What if he had a fierce temper, and beat her as Leo Mannion had? His aristocratic, haughty face came to her mind, and she shivered a little. If she agreed to be his wife, she would be taking a fearful chance.

She told herself that that was why she hesitated. She had spoken truly on the journey. She did not love Harry Tredman. Indeed, she was sure she would never love him. He was as foreign to her as someone from another world.

But what difference does that make? she argued. He was her best chance for security, and he had told her he did not require her love. And it was not as if she would ever love another man. She had put all her girlhood dreams away a long time ago. Her eyes grew sad and her mouth twisted when she recalled those dreams. They had been hardly grandiose, or impressive. No, they had been only a tiny handful of dreams, and now they were gone. She must make the best of the life she had left to live.

As she stared down into the square, she saw a little boy come around the corner. He could not have been more than five years old, no older than her brother Forsythe was now. The child was moving slowly, holding onto the palings as he came, and feeling cautiously before him with each foot before he took a step. She realized he was blind. At last he stopped, and pulled his cap from his head to hold it out before him in silent, piteous appeal. There was no one near him, but still Sally watched him as he stood there, patiently waiting. Poor little boy! she thought, stirred to sympathy. What a pathetic picture he makes!

She hoped someone would come along and drop a penny in his cap. He was so thin, so ragged and dirty. How long would he last in this huge metropolis? And what chance did he have of escaping whatever Fate had in store for him?

She sighed and dropped the draperies to move closer to the cozy fire. Rubbing her arms and hugging herself, she realized that she was in no better straits than that little blind boy. The future—her future—was hidden from her, too. It was a frightening thought.

Yet even though the prospect frightened her, she knew then that she would accept the viscount's proposal. For whatever fate had planned for her, she would be better prepared to face it as the wife of a wealthy English lord than as a little Irish nobody named Sally Mannion, who had a mere one hundred pounds and a gold sovereign between herself and starvation.

God helps those who help themselves, she reminded herself, her lips tightening again. And so, in this instance, shall I.

Chapter Nine

THE VISCOUNT CAME as promised the following afternoon, bringing with him that air of lordly assurance, bordering on arrogance, that had become familiar to her. As always he was dressed carefully, today in the tight pantaloons, snowy linen, and beautifully tailored coat and vest that proclaimed the wealthy man about town.

Sally and Mrs. Fairfax received him together in the drawing room. Sally had decorated it with floral arrangements, had even had the furniture moved to less formal, more comfortable groupings.

As the viscount bowed to her, and studied her face with that intent look she was beginning to recognize, he smiled.

"A vast improvement, Margarite," he complimented her. "Remind me to send you some trinkets to display as well. They will help."

Emily Fairfax had gone to ring the bell for tea, and as she came back timidly he waved her to a seat. "You must tell me how you have spent your day, ladies."

"But of course we went to Madame Clotilde's, as you ordered, sir," Sally said, before her chaperone had a chance to speak up. She had learned a little of Emily Fairfax at their dinner together last evening, and she had divined much more than the lady had meant to reveal. Mrs. Fairfax was a widow of long standing and little fortune. She had wed beneath her, a naval captain who had died at sea shortly after their marriage. Now she had become the viscount's pensioner. It was easy to see that Harry Tredman frightened her to death, so Sally knew she must be desperate for the money he was paying her to play companion, or she would never have been here. She herself had resolved to do all she could to help the lady, for although she had no liking for her, and could not foresee ever having any affection either, she did pity her her dependence—and her helplessness.

"Such charming garments as you have chosen for Mrs. Desmond, sir," Mrs. Fairfax put in. "So stunning, so rich. I was quite lost in admiration!"

"And do you approve my choice of maid, Margarite?" he asked.

"She is very competent," Sally admitted, although a little frown creased her brow as she said it.

His own brows rose. "But . . . ?" he drawled.

Sally looked straight at him. "She is also very domineering. In fact, I felt just like one of the dressmaker dolls Madame was showing me. I was not allowed to have any opinion, or say, in anything, from sandals to bonnets to stoles. I do not believe my taste is that despicable!"

"Certainly not, but I must beg you to, er, put up with this haughty paragon. She is much sought after, you know. Wait and see how she will present you for a ball, or a court engagement. And when you know your way about more, you can easily put her in her place."

Tea was brought in then by the two footmen, supervised by the elderly butler. Sally smiled at them all as they bowed themselves out.

"Mrs. Fairfax, would you do the honors?" she asked, thinking to keep the lady busy and out of the viscount's line of fire.

She need not have bothered. For the most part, he ignored his relative for the rest of his visit.

"And did Madame have a gown that was suitable for this evening?" he asked Sally, as he took the cup his cousin handed him.

"Yes. It required but few alterations," Sally said. "The aqua silk, m'lord. She told me it was one of your first choices."

He nodded. "In that case I shall dine with you, and

take you to the theater. There is a revival of a play I am sure you will enjoy, and the divine Sarah Siddons is to give one of her last performances. Rumor has it that she is about to retire."

He put his cup down and reached into his pocket to remove a blue velvet box. "Wear these with the gown, Margarite," he ordered as he handed it to her.

Reluctantly, Sally undid the clasp and opened the box. It contained a set of pearls, all perfectly matched: a long double necklace, matching bracelets, and ear bobs. Stunned, she looked up at him in confusion.

"How very lovely," Mrs. Fairfax said in her wispy voice. "But m'lord, do you think it entirely correct to be giving Mrs. Desmond jewelry? One would not want others to put the wrong interpretation on your generous gift, and I—"

"My cousin reminds me that I forgot to tell you my envoy sailed today on the afternoon tide. He was fortunate to find a vessel going directly to Dublin. I expect we shall have word in a month or so."

"But m'lord! Mrs. Desmond is still a married lady!" his cousin made so bold as to say. Her voice trembled a little at her temerity, and when he turned to stare at her she subsided at once.

"I believe Mrs. Fairfax is correct, sir," Sally said. "The pearls are beautiful indeed, but I should not accept them now."

He made an impatient gesture. "Oh come now, Margarite. I refuse to be hedged about with social niceties. Who is to know I gave them to you? Is 'Lord Reath' graven on every pearl?"

He paused before he added more slowly. "They will complement your beauty, and pearls are such a *chaste* jewel, are they not? I consider them a perfect gift for my intended bride."

Mrs. Fairfax opened her mouth to speak, and just as quickly closed it. Sally stared at the viscount for a long, long moment. Something she saw deep in his eyes made her nod at last.

"Good," he said, smiling a little now. "I detest arguments. They are something, like haggling, I never engage in. Would you pass me the cake plate, my dear?"

Teatime passed slowly for Sally, but it seemed no time at all before Windle was dressing her and arranging her hair. The famous hairdresser was to come the following morning, and until they had the benefit of his expertise the maid's own talents were taxed. Still, when Sally looked at herself in the pier glass at last, she could hardly believe her eyes. The aqua gown clung to her figure so perfectly it was embarrassing. But she had to admit she looked very well in it, and as the viscount had said, the pearls were the perfect accessory.

Dinner was a quiet meal. Mrs. Fairfax said little, and the viscount seemed abstracted. Sally, herself, in her new finery, was feeling shy.

She was unprepared for her reception at the Theatre Royal, Drury Lane. After admiring the domed Corinthian rotunda, and the beautiful double staircase, she had scarcely taken her seat in the viscount's box before she felt as if every eye in the house was fastened on her, and the whispers she heard quickly turned into a babble of conjecture. Harry Tredman ignored it all as he smiled and waved to his friends before he took his seat beside her. Mrs. Fairfax, however, turned pale.

Several gentlemen came to the box during the intermissions to be presented, an act which the viscount performed with aplomb. But as he did so, he left no doubt in anyone's mind that Mrs. Desmond was to be the next Lady Reath.

Sally was surprised to see that she knew one gentleman. Mr. Harcourt had visited Devon the year before, and she had met him at several parties. He had been one of her most fervent admirers.

Now he was quick to remind her of that fact, before he turned to the viscount and said, "Harry old son, if I had known you would be so quick with this beauty, I would never have told you of her as soon as I returned to town. Did you go there immediately, to capture her?"

Harcourt's admiring smile made Sally uneasy, for there was little respect in it. Suddenly she realized that he thought she was the viscount's mistress. But of course, she reminded herself, he had known her as Sally Mannion, not Margarite Desmond.

How would the viscount handle this? she wondered.

"But of course I did," Harry Tredman said easily. "Mrs. Mannion has taken her maiden name of Desmond again. And I have had inquiries set about in Ireland. There is good reason to believe her husband has gone to his glorious reward."

His face darkened, and Sally felt a chill on her arms as he added, "Or wherever men of his stamp go when they die. As soon as we have proof he is dead, we shall be married."

Mrs. Fairfax made a small, distressed sound which no one heeded. Indeed, Sally did not even hear it. What did the viscount mean? Leo was dead? How could he know?

"Alas, that I did not think of that," Mr. Harcourt mourned. "But you are to be congratulated, Harry. I am sure Mrs. Mannion—er, Desmond—is the most beautiful woman London has ever seen."

"I am aware," the viscount agreed. "And since I was the one who brought her here to glorify the scene, I can bask in my role as philanthropist. Good of me, don't you think?"

Mr. Harcourt chuckled, and the other gentlemen in the box smiled knowingly. Harry was a wit, there was no denying that, they told themselves, as they bowed and excused themselves when the lights dimmed.

Sally would have questioned the viscount, but he put his finger to his lips. "Later," he murmured.

After he had taken the ladies home Sally asked for a minute of his time, and he followed them into the house. Dismissing the servants, she took him once again to the drawing room, accompanied by the watchful Mrs. Fairfax.

"What did you mean at the theater, sir?" she asked,

as soon as they had been seated. "About Leo Mannion's death?"

"I have no idea if the man is alive or not," he answered coolly. "But after what you have revealed of him by your tight-lipped silence, I can only hope he is."

Sally looked startled. She had said little to the viscount of her married life, and nothing of the beating or the abuse. She had only said that her husband was a drunkard. Harry Tredman was very astute.

"Did you indeed come into Devon expressly to meet me, as Mr. Harcourt implied, sir?" she asked next.

"Of course. He was so enthusiastic, I had to see you for myself. I contrived that invitation from Colonel Jenkins in order to do so."

"Why, we all thought you had come to reminisce with him about your friend—his son!"

"Talk about William for more than a minute? Never! After our years at Eton I made sure that we never saw each other again. He was a bore. No, it was to meet you, and you only, that I made that long journey into Devon. Are you flattered, my dear?"

Sally was not required to answer, for suddenly Mrs. Fairfax spoke up. She looked worried, and there was a suspicious hint of color on her wrinkled cheeks.

"Dear cousin, I fear you have not considered," she said. "Even if poor Mr. Mannion is deceased, it must have been a very recent occurrence, or surely his wife would have known of it. And your own lady wife has been dead but a short two months now. Of course there can be no thought of marriage between you two for at least a year. Whatever would people say?"

The viscount stared at her, and his voice was cold as he said, "I would remind you, cuz, that you are here to guard Margarite's reputation, not to take me to task for social lapses. I do beg you will remember that. I do as I please. I always have. Margarite and I will be married as soon as it is possible to do so without committing bigamy. Is that clear?"

Mrs. Fairfax hesitated, wringing her hands together,

and he added smoothly, "Of course, if you feel such a thing personally abhorrent, or an impossible dese-cration of your high standards, I shall be happy to replace you."

Sally stole a glance at her companion. Mrs. Fairfax had lowered her eyes to her lap, and her shrinking posture showed that she was completely cowed.

"No . . . no. Not at all. I . . . I beg your pardon," she whispered.

Sally was relieved when Harry Tredman turned to her again. "I am glad you asked me to come in, my dear, for I must tell you something. There has been a change in my plans, and I am forced to go away for a while; indeed, perhaps for as long as a month. A business matter, you understand."

Sally did not understand in the slightest, but she nodded, even feeling a little relieved that she would be alone again, free of his disturbing presence. Then she remembered that she was in London, and London frightened her. What was she to do all that time? The thought of being cooped up with Mrs. Fairfax was a dreary prospect. She forced herself to forget all those happy hours she and Anne had spent together.

"While I am gone, I think it would be best for your butler to deny you to any, ah, callers you might have. The bucks will discover my absence ere long, and I don't trust a one of 'em. See to that, cuz. Be firm."

As Mrs. Fairfax nodded, looking happier now, he went on, "I do not intend for you to curtail all your amusements, however, Margarite. There will be your fittings at the dressmaker, and you will want to ex-plore the shops and libraries—see all the sights. To make that easier, may I suggest you don your mourn-ing again? No one bothers sorrowing widows they can-not even see."

Sally's lips curved in a little smile at his cleverness. Yes, her weeds would be a perfect disguise.

She looked up as the viscount got to his feet, and she rose immediately. As he took her hand in both of his and pressed it gently, he stared down into her eyes for a moment that seemed endless to Sally. "Have a care for yourself, my dear. I shall try to be as quick as I can," he said. "And if you want for anything, notify Mr. Bourne at my bank. He will be acting as agent during my absence."

He raised her hand to his lips and kissed it before he bowed to her. As he strolled to the door he said over his shoulder, "Know I quite rely on you, cuz, to keep Mrs. Desmond safe for me. Do not disappoint me."

The door closed behind him before Mrs. Fairfax could even begin her disjointed promises.

Almost five weeks passed before Sally saw Viscount Reath again. To her surprise, the time went by quickly. There was so much to see and do in London. She even grew accustomed to the shadow that was Emily Fairfax, and learned to ignore her when her conversation grew tedious. And then there were the magnificent libraries, and the thrill of being able to buy the latest books as soon as they were printed. She devoured all the journals as well.

She was more comfortable in town now that she knew her way about, although she was still disquieted by the number of beggars and child prostitutes she saw, some of them not even in their teens. And whenever she noticed the little blind boy holding out his cap in Manchester Square, she sent a footman to give him money. She knew it was more a sop to her conscience than anything else, but it did make her feel better to be able to help him, even a little.

Sally discovered early that the viscount had been right. A few days after he had gone away, several of the gentlemen she had met at the theater left their cards on the shining table in her front hall. Jackson was firm about refusing her to each and every one, and at last they tired of their fruitless pursuit and ceased to come again.

She was at home early one afternoon, engrossed in a new book of essays, when Harry Tredman reappeared without warning. She had heard the knocker on the front door, but had ignored it as usual. Suddenly the drawing room door opened, and he stepped inside.

"Margarite," he said as he came toward her, holding out his hands. "Forgive me for coming to you like this, in all my travel dirt, but I could not wait to see your lovely face again, and reassure myself that you were all right."

Startled, Sally rose, her book falling unheeded to the floor.

"You're back!" she exclaimed.

"Obviously," he said, taking her hands and bending closer to look deep into her eyes. Whatever he saw there must have pleased him, for he smiled.

"Do sit down, my dear, and let me feast my eyes on you," he said, as he took the chair opposite. "But where is my cousin? Shirking her duty?"

"She always rests at this time of day," Sally told him. "And since no one has ever gotten past Mr. Jackson, on guard at the door, there is no reason for you to feel uneasy. I beg you will not tax her about it. You know how you frighten her."

"Silly woman," he murmured. "What can she possibly expect me to do to her?"

"Give her a tongue-lashing, at which activity you excel," Sally told him. As his brows rose she realized she had spoken without thinking, and she made haste to add, "Er, I hope your business went well, sir?"

He did not answer for a moment, and since he had not taken his eyes from her since entering the room, Sally began to feel uneasy. As she watched him his face became very still, stern even, and she wondered at it.

"You remind me. I have glorious news," he drawled. "From Ireland, where I have been all this time."

"In Ireland?" she echoed, one hand going to her throat. She could feel her heart begin to race.

"Ter be shure, mavourneen," he said in mock brogue. "I went to find Leo Mannion."

"But . . . you told me you had sent an envoy to do that. Why would you bother to go yourself as well?"

"I would not have done so, had your dresser not

had a few words with me when I came to tea the afternoon after we arrived here."

Sally was perplexed. Whatever could Windle have said to him to make him look so dangerous?

"She told me that while she had been helping you undress that first night, she saw some scars on your back. Whip scars. You did not tell me of those, Margarite."

"I never thought of doing so," she said, amazed and angry. "Surely Windle takes too much on herself, to be reporting such things to you!"

"Not at all," came his swift rejoinder. "She was only following my orders. I wanted to know everything about you, my dear. *Everything.*"

Suddenly, Sally remembered how he had told her he wanted to marry her because he admired beauty so, and because she was perfect. Was he angry because her back was scarred? Angry enough to break the engagement and send her away, even though the scars were few and barely noticeable now? She pushed all thoughts of what she would do in that case to the back of her mind, as he leaned toward her and said, "Tell me. Did Leo Mannion whip you?"

Sally could only nod, her dark blue eyes troubled.

He leaned back and crossed his arms over his chest. "I thought as much. And that was why you left him, wasn't it? Because he abused you?"

He barely waited for her to nod again before he went on. "I did indeed go to Ireland, but not to induce Mannion to divorce you, my dear Margarite. No, I went to kill him for what he had done to you."

Sally gasped. His voice had been flat, menacing. She was stunned to see his grim smile.

"Fortunately, I was not put to the trouble. I discovered easily enough that your husband died four months ago, falling from an upper window while in a drunken stupor."

She looked at him questioningly, and he continued, "But not from one of his own windows. No, he fell from the top floor of Waterford Gaol. It seems he had been carousing with several of his cronies just before the, ah, accident occurred. No one bothered to investigate, since he was going to be hung the next morning for murder anyway. He had been tried and found guilty of beating one of his maids to death."

Sally closed her eyes, her face paling. Dear God! Sue? Aggie? And if she had not escaped him when she did, it might well have been she herself who died in that horrible way. She felt so dizzy she was afraid she was going to faint, and she prayed she would not.

"Here, drink this," she heard the viscount say, and she opened her eyes to see him with a glass of wine he had poured for her.

He put it to her lips, then waited until she had swallowed some and the color had come back to her face before he gave the glass to her and moved away.

"Since I cannot imagine anything more unlikely to cause you distress than learning of your husband's demise, I take it you are upset at the servant's fate?" he asked as he took his seat again. "But she must have known what manner of man he was. She could have left his employ at any time.

"I beg you to forget the incident! I dislike the sadness I see in your eyes. Besides, we have something else to discuss. Our marriage. It could go forward apace now, except, that is, for one major obstacle."

He paused, and Sally held her breath. Was the volatile viscount about to dismiss her? Having gone to Ireland, perhaps even having seen Ballyragh, had he decided she was not suitable after all? He knew about her scars now; knew she was not perfect.

"That obstacle, and very important it is, too, is that the alterations I have been having made to my townhouse in St. James's Square are not completed. Especially those in your own rooms, my dear. I would not bring you there until they are as lovely as you are, for any lesser setting would not be worthy of you. If you only knew how I have dreamed of seeing you there, the ultimate, the most glorious of all my beautiful possessions!"

Once again, Sally wondered if the viscount was truly sane. What was he thinking? He could not *own* her!

No one could ever *own* another! And he was an educated, astute man except for this one obsession he had with beauty. Reminding herself again that marrying him was her only option, she tried to steady her breathing.

"I shall leave you now, so that I may see how the decorating progresses. Hopefully, it will not take much longer. Until then, we shall resume our meetings. I will be back at five to take you to the park, and since I plan to drive an open sporting carriage, we can dispense with Mrs. Fairfax's company. Please tell the good lady she may be serene. There isn't a man on earth who can be less than a gentleman when tooling a high-bred pair through London's busy streets. Both hands, you see, must of necessity remain on the reins."

As he rose, he shook his head and chuckled at some joke only he was able to understand. "Finish your wine, Margarite," he ordered, tilting her chin up with one hand. "And please wear the gold driving ensemble I chose for you. You will be superb."

Only after he had been gone for some time did Sally carefully put the still full glass down on the table beside her. She was confused and uneasy. She would not think of the maid's painful death anymore, but she could not ignore Leo Mannion's. It had set her free at last. Of course, this freedom meant that the moment when she would become the viscount's bride was fast approaching. And she did not imagine, now that he was back on the scene, that his redecorating would take any time at all. He would see to that.

What would marriage to him be like? she wondered. Ever since she had known him, he had done no more than kiss her hand. What would he be like, naked and in a passion? Strangely, she wished he had kissed her, caressed her, before now. If he had, she would have had some idea of what to expect. This . . . this *limbo* she was in was unsettling. And remembering some of his wilder statements, how he had looked and sounded when he said he had gone to Ireland to kill Leo Mannion, made her shiver still. Once again, the black un-known lay before her.

Sally took a deep breath and bent to retrieve her book. Carefully smoothing the crumpled pages, and shaking her head at her carelessness, she tried to for-get Harold Tredman, Viscount Reath. At least for the short time that was left to her.

Later, when she had been informed of the viscount's return, and Leo Mannion's death, Emily Fairfax turned even paler than usual. She did not, however, attempt to stop Sally when she left the room to dress for her drive in the park.

As she ran up the stairs, Sally considered the fear-ful, proper Mrs. Fairfax. Even in these past five weeks of her exclusive company, she had not come to know the woman any better. She sensed that Mrs. Fairfax did not approve either of her or her decision to marry the viscount. And although she was a model chaper-one, and spoke pleasantly when spoken to, she had not made any attempt to reach a closer relationship. When she was finally relieved of her duty, Sally was sure she would leave Manchester Square and travel back to her cottage in Kent with a sense of great relief.

But perhaps it was her own fault they had not been closer, she thought. She knew she was still mourning the loss of Anne and her friendship. Perhaps if she had made more of an effort, it could have been easier for them both. But she knew she never could have done it, not as heartsore as she still was.

Anne, oh, Anne! she thought with longing. How are you now, my dearest friend? Well again, I hope? Has your aunt given you my letter yet? What are you thinking, feeling? Do you miss me as I miss you?

Sally shook her head as she rang for her maid. She knew that what Anne had told her about her love was true. Of course she is missing me! she scolded herself.

But still she said a little prayer that Anne might recover, to forget her and take up her life again. It would be different for Sally. She could never forget, nor did she want to. Anne would always be a part of her for the rest of her life. Her friend.

When Windle came in, Sally remembered how quick she had been to speak to the viscount, to tell him about those scars. And she admitted that if she was indifferent to Mrs. Fairfax her dislike for Miss Windle was profound, and had been even before she had learned of her carrying tales. Abruptly, she ordered her to lay out the gold driving dress, and the plumed hat that completed the outfit.

As Windle bustled about, all importance and full of chat about sandals and gloves and a parasol, Sally told herself that one of her first acts as Viscountess Reath would be to dismiss this maid. Competence was not nearly enough, not in your closest personal servant. For that, she would demand loyalty. She supposed she would be able to pay for it, after all.

For a week, the viscount came to see her every day. Some evenings the three of them went to the theater, or to concerts. Sally truly enjoyed the concerts. She had never heard professional musicians perform, and she was captivated by the beauty of their music.

The viscount also took tea with them, or occasionally dinner, and during the daytime there were drives or strolls in London's parks. He was quick to introduce Sally to everyone in the ton as his future bride, a quiet smile of satisfaction on his finely drawn face as he did so. The gentlemen were openly envious, and fervent in their congratulations, but Sally saw that many of the ladies the viscount favored with the confidence looked startled. It was the same reception she had received in Devon, but somehow it had ceased to matter to her. They did not approve of her? Who cared? She would be a viscountess, and as such, must be acknowledged, she told herself. Besides, she didn't want friends anyway. Not anymore.

Harry Tredman arrived in Manchester Square one June morning while the ladies were still at breakfast. Mrs. Fairfax seemed flustered by his unexpected appearance, but Sally merely indicated a seat and asked him if he would care for coffee. His eyes were admiring as he took the seat and nodded.

"Well, cuz, I have great news for you," he began, still looking at Sally. A sunbeam limned her profile as she turned away to reach the cream pitcher for him, and he seemed entranced by the sight.

Reminded by Mrs. Fairfax's sharp little gasp of the other person at the table, he turned to her and said, "You must begin packing, cuz. Margarite and I are going to be married tomorrow morning at St. George's, Hanover. Of course you will be Margarite's attendant, but right after the ceremony you will be free to leave. I know you must be anxious to return to that village in Kent—er, what is its name? Never mind! Just think, you can be on your way there tomorrow."

"But—but I cannot be ready as soon as that," Emily Fairfax said, looking flustered. As was her custom, she sat stiffly on the very edge of her chair. Sally realized she had never seen her lean back against any cushion, no matter how weary she was or how late the hour. She wondered if she would travel all the way to her village in the same posture.

"There is so much to do. . . . Why, I must return my library books, and I must see about a place on the stage, and there is all the packing to do. . . ."

Her voice died away, and she wiped her mouth nervously on her napkin. In front of her the steam from her coffee was dying away, but Sally knew she did not dare pick it up and drink it lest she spill it, she was so distraught.

Amused, and more than a little sorry for her, she said, "But surely there is no need for such haste, sir. Couldn't Mrs. Fairfax stay here until such time as she is ready to depart?"

The viscount frowned. "Why, I suppose so, if she cares for it. The lease for the house is paid to the end of the month, the servants engaged for like time. I only thought it would be what she wanted."

As Mrs. Fairfax murmured "Too good!", Sally asked, "And what time is the ceremony?"

She was struggling to keep her composure, for she felt nervous and uneasy.

"At eleven. I have arranged for it to take place in one of the smaller chapels. So much more intimate, you know, for a private ceremony."

"And where do you plan to go on your wedding journey?" his cousin ventured to ask.

"We are not taking one," the viscount said absently. "I cannot wait to see Margarite in my house. It has been ready for three days now, my dear, but I wanted to be sure the odor of paint had completely dissipated before you entered it, my queen."

Sally tried to smile. In only a little over twenty-four hours, she would be Harry Tredman's wife. She put her toast down untasted. She had most assuredly lost her appetite.

When the viscount had been announced Mrs. Fairfax had been reading the newspaper. Now her eyes strayed to its pages again. They were open to the obituaries, which she always read first as a sort of duty before she allowed herself to look at the Court News.

Suddenly, she started and cried out. Both Sally and the viscount stared at her. "Oh, dear me!" she said in a voice of horror. "Oh, how dreadful! But m'lord—Harry—you cannot have known, poor boy!"

"Known what?" he asked, putting down his coffee cup.

"This announcement! It is of your beloved father's death at Darlington Hall! Why . . . why, your marriage is impossible now! How sad that you should learn the news in such a way—and at such a time!"

"Do calm yourself, cuz," he said, as he patted her hand. "I have known of his death since yesterday."

As a horrified Mrs. Fairfax opened her mouth, he continued, "Do spare me any condolences, ma'am. You must have known, or at least have heard of, my father. Since that is the case, you cannot possibly imagine I would feel anything but a great relief at his demise."

"But—but he is *dead*," she whispered, as she fumbled for her handkerchief.

"Yes, he is," Harry Tredman agreed, his voice rich with satisfaction. "And in mentioning it, you have spoiled my greatest surprise for my bride. Shame on you."

He turned to Sally then, and she was stunned to see the light that danced in his eyes. "Madam, you will not be a viscountess after all," he told her, bowing a little. "No, indeed. Tomorrow at eleven in the morning, you will become the Countess of Darlington. Isn't that splendid? And so much more worthy of you! I only mourn that he was not a duke."

"Sir!" Sally said, almost as shocked as Mrs. Fairfax. "You would not marry two days after your father's death! How could you do such a thing?"

"Easily, as you shall see. I hated my father. I haven't seen him in years. I have felt only relief since hearing the news," he replied. Still watching her face, he said over his shoulder, "We shall excuse you now, Cousin Emily. Please leave the paper. I haven't seen it yet."

Trembling with outrage and chagrin, Mrs. Fairfax did as she was bade. Her sideways glance at the viscount, as she scurried to the door of the breakfast room, was as horrified as if she were regarding a wild beast.

As the door closed behind her, Harry Tredman chuckled. "That was very bad of me, wasn't it? I know I should try to curb this unholy itch I have to shock the good lady, but I cannot, I positively cannot, resist!"

"You still intend to marry me anyway? Tomorrow?" Sally persisted, ignoring his wide grin, the rueful shake of his head.

"As you say." All the levity was gone from his face in an instant. Now it was intent, serious—severe. "I must have you safe—mine," he said slowly. "The longer I wait, the more impatient I become. It will be tomorrow."

He picked up her hand and kissed it. Sally sat speechless.

"If you have quite finished breakfast, may I suggest

you go up and don something more appropriate? My
carriage waits. We are going to Rundell and Bridge,
to collect your wedding gift from me. I am so glad I
ordered the entire parure. I cannot wait to see you
wearing them, although, of course, not all at once.
Diamonds, my dear, and sapphires to match your
eyes. The most impressive tiara, a necklace, bracelets,
a brooch, and last but not least, your wedding band.
Hurry now," he urged, as he rose to hold her chair.
"I shall wait for you here. Jackson! More coffee!"

To her surprise, Sally found Mrs. Fairfax pacing
nervously in her room. She dismissed an avid Windle,
even waited until she had heard the maid's reluctant
footsteps going away, before she asked the older
woman how she might help her.

Emily Fairfax shook her head. "Mrs. Desmond!
Please, you must not marry tomorrow! The scandal,
the gossip! Somehow you must find a way to stop
Harry from this mad start. He will be ostracized from
society for years, and you as well. Please, for the sake
of the family, I beg you!"

As she clutched Sally's hand in her own thin dry
one, Sally tried to smile. "I quite agree that it is not
at all seemly, ma'am," she said. "But what do you
imagine I can do to get him to change his mind? You
know him, even better than I do."

Mrs. Fairfax looked around wildly, in order to avoid
Sally's eyes. "I—I don't know," she admitted. "Perhaps if you said you could not possibly consider it for
at least six months? He loves you. Surely he would
do as you wished!"

"I doubt it. I have already tried," Sally said wryly.
"Besides, he doesn't love me at all. He only wants
me."

She had spoken without thinking, and now Mrs.
Fairfax's wrinkled cheeks burned with color. "In that
case, I shall leave you," she said, as she hurried to
the door. "But I cannot, I *cannot* stand your witness;
no matter what Harry does to me, I cannot!"

"It is quite all right. I understand," Sally told her.
Deep inside, she was relieved. The thought of having

this desiccated, disapproving older woman beside her at her wedding ceremony had not been a pleasant one. Anyone, even a complete stranger, would be a more suitable choice.

Just before the door closed behind her visitor, Sally said, "I shall see that the viscount does not punish you for it. Don't worry!"

Poor Mrs. Fairfax, to be caught in such a muddle, she thought, and then she smiled a little ruefully. No, she found she did not pity her after all. Rather, she admired the lady for her firmness in upholding her standards, even in the face of her terror. For of course she was right. This marriage should not be performed, not yet. A death in the family seemed such a bad omen for it.

And surely a marriage so singular, so strange, needed all the good luck it could possibly garner.

Chapter Ten

AT ELEVEN THE next morning, dressed in a gown of palest blue with a huge matching silk bonnet, and wearing at least some of the magnificent jewels the new earl had lavished on her, Sally Desmond Mannion became Margarite Tredman, Countess of Darlington. She acquired several lesser titles as well, which she had not even known about. The groom had as witness one of his friends, a gentleman she had not met before, Sir Thomas Avery.

She herself was attended by a Miss Lydia Fullsham, a large middle-aged lady from Northumberland who happened to be in the church at the time, admiring the brasses, on this, her first visit to the metropolis. Miss Fullsham declared herself thrilled to assist at the bridal. So thrilled, Sally noted with a little amusement, that she even sobbed at all the appropriate times.

As for the bride herself, she felt vaguely detached from the entire proceeding. It was as if she were watching the ceremony from a back pew, and not standing beside Harold Tredman at all. She said her vows in a low voice, allowed the earl to place the wedding band on her finger, and took his arm to walk to the vestry to sign the register as if she were not really there. She most certainly did not feel married, perhaps even less so than after her wedding to Leo Mannion.

It was only with a great deal of difficulty that Miss Fullsham was persuaded that a gala wedding breakfast was not in the offing, which event, Sally saw, she would have attended gladly—and no doubt dined out

164

on the description of for months after her return to
Northumberland.

Sir Thomas managed the lady with aplomb, offering
to take her in his own carriage to her next destination.
Sally liked the way this gentleman's lazy eyes crinkled
shut in amusement as he made the suggestion, which
Miss Fullsham was so quick to accept, before he shook
the earl's hand and gave his best wishes to the bride.
She also endured a hearty kiss and a hug from a blushing Miss Fullsham, who could be heard telling Sir
Thomas as he led her away that never, no, positively
never, had she ever seen such a beautiful bride! Sally
was unable to hear his reply, for by then the earl was
joining her in his town carriage and the grooms were
putting up the steps and shutting the door.

"There, that's all right and tight, then," he said with
satisfaction, as he patted the pocket where the wedding certificate reposed.

Dressed as he was in impeccable morning clothes,
he intimidated Sally, and as the carriage took them
on to St. James's Square she could think of nothing
whatsoever to say.

"Margarite, Margarite! Don't look like such a wist-
ful waif, I beg you," he told her, taking her cold hands
between his to chafe them. "There is nothing to worry
about, my dear—but you'll see."

Sally tried to smile at him, but she was reliving another wedding day and its aftermath, and there was a
coldness around her heart.

"And now you are mine, truly mine," Harry was
saying, and she forced herself to concentrate. "Let me
tell you what to expect so you will not be surprised,"
he added, picking up her hands to kiss them slowly,
one after the other.

"The entire staff will be assembled in the hall when
we arrive. Of course they cannot wait to see you,
although ostensibly they will be there to offer their
fealty and congratulations. Wayland—my butler—will
speak for them all, and I will thank them in your
stead. You have nothing to do but smile and nod and
look as beautiful as you always do. Then we two shall

enjoy a festive luncheon. Just think how festive, freed of Emily Fairfax's presence! Afterwards, I want to show you over the house. You must tell me if there is anything you want changed—anything you do not like. But I will be surprised if you have any complaints, beauty."

He chuckled a little before he went on. "By then no doubt you would like to rest for a while. Windle is still in Manchester Square, overseeing the removal of your clothes, but there will be another maid to wait on you."

Sally nodded, wishing she could think of something—anything!—to say. But she could not help wondering what the earl would be doing while she "rested."

As if he had read her mind, he said, "I myself have some business with my bank. The succession, you understand. And I am afraid we will have to travel into Hertfordshire tomorrow. I have to attend the funeral and hear the will, much as it pains me to do so. And I suppose I must take full possession of the Hall, see to it that my mother retires to the dower house immediately. Don't be concerned. We stay there but overnight."

"Surely you cannot be thinking of banishing your mother on the day her husband is to be buried!" Sally exclaimed. "Why, she must be overcome with grief!"

He laughed, long and hard. "I doubt that, my dear," he said when he could speak again. "She hated him even more than I did. As for forcing her to relinquish the Hall, believe me when I say I shall take great pleasure in the act."

He saw her shocked face, and as he patted her hand he added, "She's a nasty bitch. Indeed, it's a toss-up as to which parent I detested the most.

"But come! We won't discuss her, not today. In any case, you will soon see her for yourself.

"Ah, here we are now. My dear Margarite—welcome to this one little part of your kingdom."

Dazed and stunned, Sally let him assist her from the carriage. She was speechless.

In the quick glance that was all she had time for, Sally saw that the houses here were much more impressive than those in Manchester Square, and that the park the houses surrounded was graced by a large equestrian sculpture of some long-gone dignitary or royal. Idly, she wondered who he had been.

Lord Darlington helped her up the marble steps to the house, his hand cupping her elbow in his usual solicitous way. As if by magic, the front door opened slowly, and they stepped into a vast hall. There was a graceful stairway on each side that met in a gallery above, and in the center the most magnificent yet delicate crystal chandelier that Sally had ever seen. The hall was full of servants, and every eye was fixed on the new bride in awful concentration. Sally forced herself to look around slowly, and even managed a smile.

She was welcomed by the butler in a sonorous, plummy voice. He seemed almost overwhelmed by the seriousness of the occasion, and when at last he was done he introduced her, one by one, to the entire staff in order of precedence.

Sally did not dare look at the earl as he began to respond, lest she lose her composure. How grand it all was! And how incongruous, when you considered what a quicksilver, irreverent man Harold Tredman was.

To her surprise, his short speech of thanks was measured and serious.

She was taken by one of the upstairs maids to a small anteroom, to remove her bonnet and freshen up before luncheon. Her groom waited for her in what he told her was the morning room. The table had been set for two, wine was chilling, and there were flowers everywhere. Sally saw that they were to be attended not only by the butler, but two footmen as well. It was not her idea of a cozy meal à deux, but the earl did not appear aware of the company as he seated her next to him.

In fact, Sally noted with amusement, he talked to her throughout the meal as if they were completely alone. This was not at all embarrassing, however, for

he was no more amorous than he had ever been. Sally
was able to enjoy her delicious luncheon.

When they had finished, he escorted Sally through
each and every room. She could not help but be impressed, for surely it was the most beautiful house
she could ever have imagined, and it was filled with
beautiful things—paintings and sculptures, porcelains,
silver and gold pieces, all executed by the outstanding
artists and craftsmen of the time. A veritable treasure
trove, all set in rooms decorated with the finest furniture, carpets, and rich hangings of brocade and dam-
ask and silk. *And to think I once thought Beechlands
imposing,* Sally remembered. *How very naive I was!*

The earl saved her own spacious rooms for last.
They were at the back of the house, overlooking a
garden, made private by high brick walls. There was
a graceful elm tree there, flower beds and gravel
paths, even a small fountain crowned by a winsome
marble statue of a young girl pouring water from an
urn into the basin beneath.

But it was the rooms themselves that drew her most
appreciative gasp. Decorated in silver, dark blue, and
palest apricot, they were sumptuous with flowers,
silks, and satins. The bedchamber ceiling sported a
mural of nymphs and cupids at play. There were several large gilt mirrors adorning the walls, and in the
sitting room an elegant Chippendale writing desk and
an inlaid table of some exotic woods Sally did not
recognize.

"You are pleased?" the earl asked, his voice eager.

He was just like a little boy waiting to be praised,
Sally thought, as she turned and smiled at him. "They
are beyond lovely—the loveliest rooms I have ever
seen," she said softly.

Harry Tredman smiled at her as he took her hand.
"Then they are worthy of you, and I am content."

He raised her hand and kissed it before he said, "I
shall leave you now to settle in and rest, my dear. If
you need anything, ring for a maid. I shall be here to
join you for dinner."

Sally nodded, wondering again about her strange

wedding day and her equally strange bridegroom. Surely it was not customary for a new husband to leave his equally new wife to her own devices for several hours! But then, she reminded herself, she was more than happy to have it so. From the moment they had entered these rooms, and most especially the bedchamber with its huge, graceful bed draped in satins and brocades, she had been uneasy.

She wandered back to the windows that overlooked the gardens. How very different all this was from that day four years before, when Leo Mannion had brought her to his neglected farmhouse, dragged her up the stairs, and—

No! She would think of that no more! That was over, long gone, and best forgotten. Whatever his faults, the earl was no Leo Mannion. And thank the Lord for that!

They dined early in the large formal dining room. The earl intended to take her to the theater that evening, to a play they had yet to see. As they ate he told her about the playwright and some of the actors, and he said that as soon as she grew more accustomed he would look forward to the salons she would give for the artists and playwrights and musicians of the day.

"And the authors as well?" Sally asked eagerly, her veal piccante forgotten. "I should so like to talk to Miss Austen, and Wordsworth and Scott—oh, a score of them!"

"I cannot promise you Jane Austen, beauty, but I am sure I can persuade some of the others to attend. You shall be famous, you know."

As she looked skeptical, he added, "Oh yes, you will. I'll see to it."

Sally laughed at him, feeling lighthearted for the first time the entire day.

Her unease came back after they had returned from the theater. The earl escorted her to her rooms, kissed her hand, and turned her over to the superior Windle, now duly installed and quite prepared to reign supreme in the servant's hall as the new countess's dresser. Sally wished she might have another maid, but she knew that was impossible, at least for a while.

Her rooms were even lovelier in candlelight and fireglow. Windle helped her to undress and bathe, but when she held out a filmy night robe and negligee, Sally questioned her about them.

"Oh, ma'am, so romantic, is it not?" Windle gushed, although her hard little eyes were shrewd. "The earl had these made for you, especially for tonight."

Sally eyed the pale blue chiffon and satin garments with misgiving. Even wearing both of them, they would still be transparent. Or as good as. Still, she supposed she must put them on. Her husband had chosen them for her. What else could she do? She shivered, however, as the soft fabric slid over her nakedness.

She was quick to dismiss the dresser, saying she preferred to brush her own hair that evening. Windle nodded and curtsied, but still she lingered. Sally raised imperious brows. Surely Windle was not going to instruct her on how to behave on her wedding night, was she? she thought, although she would not have put it past her. But Windle finally left the room without another word.

After Sally had brushed her hair smooth, she sat at the dressing table for quite some time. The house was quiet now. She wondered how long it would be before the earl—Harry—came to her, and she told herself that she must try—try very hard—not to let him know how distasteful this part of marriage was to her.

When the door between their rooms opened much later she was standing beside the fire, staring down into it. At once she looked to where his tall, wiry figure lounged against the door he had just entered. She was surprised to see that he was still fully dressed. He had not even removed his cravat, or his evening coat.

"Ah, yes," he said slowly. "You are as beautiful as I knew you would be, Margarite."

Still he made no move to come to her. He only stood there, devouring her with his eyes. Trembling a little, Sally wondered if he was waiting for her to go to him, but she could not make herself move in that direction, nor did she feel she could say one word.

"Turn around for me," he said, his voice low, husky.

Mystified, she forced herself to do as he asked.

"Slowly. Much more slowly," he ordered.

Sally was beginning to feel alarmed. What strange ritual was this? she wondered, even as she obeyed him. Even near the fire she felt a chill, she was so frightened. Why was he asking this? What was he going to do?

"I am humbled by your beauty, my dear," he said when she was facing him again. "Go to bed now. We must take coach very early. Windle will wake you at six. A pleasant night's sleep, countess."

He made her a low bow and left her, the door closing softly behind him. Transfixed, Sally stared at that door for a long, long moment.

What was the matter? Why didn't he stay with her, and consummate this marriage that had cost him so much time and effort and money? Surely that was why he had been in such a hurry to wed at all? Wasn't it? But he had only looked at her and gone away. She did not understand him. She wondered if she ever would.

She knew he was not incapable of the act. He had had children by both of his previous marriages. What was there about this one, about *her*, that was so different?

As she removed her negligee, climbed into the huge bed heaped with soft pillows, and slid down between the silky-feeling sheets, she told herself that someday soon she would find out what the earl really wanted of her.

They were on the road to Hertfordshire the next morning at eight. Sally had intended to wear her mourning again, and she was stunned when she saw

Windle lay out one of her most colorful gowns: a bright cherry muslin, trimmed with matching bows. But when she questioned the suitability of this garment for a funeral, Windle said the earl had ordered it himself.

"Aye, m'lady, and the cherry straw. I'm to take your royal blue satin for this evening, and the sapphire and diamond set as well, all of it," Windle said, shaking her head as she scurried about. Sally frowned a little as she sat up in bed to drink her chocolate. It was deplorable that the earl should mock his father this way, no matter how he had felt about him and his mother, too, but she supposed she must bow to his wishes.

She ate her breakfast in her room as she dressed, and when she came downstairs, followed by Windle clutching the jewel case and a footman bearing her overnight satchel, the earl was waiting for her. He was attended by his valet. Sally had thought before, on their journey to town, how unusual a servant he was for the fastidious earl. Even taller than his master, the valet was so thin and bony that Sally had the irreverent thought that if he turned sideways, he would disappear completely. And he had a homely, rough-hewn face, and very large red hands. As she had before, Sally looked from him to his impeccably turned-out master, wondering how he managed it, ham-handed as he was. When she saw her interest was embarrassing him and causing him to flush, she was quick to look away. Poor man, she thought again. He cannot help how he looks.

Virtually the entire drive was spent in silence. The two servants sat facing back, staring out the windows of the carriage, and although they never took their eyes from the road fast disappearing behind them Sally was always aware of their presence. As for the earl he had little to say, and after a few commonplaces about the weather he lapsed into deep, brooding silence. Eventually, Sally put her head back on the squabs and closed her eyes.

Just before noon the carriage slowed and turned

between a pair of large, ornate gates. As it traveled up the drive, the earl shook off his air of abstraction and said, "So, we are here," in such a colorless voice that Sally felt uneasy.

The carriage rounded the last bend and drew up in a large courtyard, before a massive building of gray stone. As the grooms hurried to let down the steps the earl remarked, "Horrid, isn't it? I have always thought so myself. But don't worry, my dear. We will never come back again."

As a groom opened the door he added, "Of course, I suppose I must be buried here someday. What a ghastly thought! Remind me, Margarite, to be sure to live a very long time."

He held out his arm, and Sally stepped down. She had to agree with him. Darlington Hall was a depressing sight. And even though it was June there were no flowers to be seen, no gardens of any kind. There were only masses of dark ivy beds, and some cypress trees stark against the sky. What a setting this would make for a novel! she thought. Some gothic tale complete with ghosts and ghouls, a taciturn masked villain, a lovely but helpless heroine! Then she took herself firmly in hand, lest she begin to weave one of her tales. This was serious. And, she admitted to herself, she was not looking forward to it at all.

"Lord Darlington. Sir," the elderly butler said in mournful tones as he bowed them in.

"Well, Detts, I see you haven't changed a bit. Still the gay, mad jester I recall from my youth, are you not?" the earl asked, as he handed the man his hat and his gloves. "Where is she?"

"The countess awaits you in the drawing room, m'lord," the butler said in his colorless way. Sally wondered if he was mourning his late master, or if, as Harry had implied, this was his normal manner of speaking.

"We'll go along there, then. No need to announce us. Instead, see that our attendants are taken to our rooms, then order the servants here to start packing my mother's things. She is to be moved to the dower house by dusk, and by my order she is never to set foot in the Hall, ever again."

He paid no attention to the butler's assent, nor that man's puzzled glance at Sally. It was plain to her, however, that her arrival had not been anticipated.

The drawing room, although shabby, was massive. Sally had expected it to be as gloomy as the entrance hall, but to her surprise bright sunlight streamed in through every window. Over beside the empty fireplace a man and a woman were seated, deep in conversation. They looked up as the earl entered with Sally on his arm, and the gentleman rose ponderously to his feet. He was tall, red-faced, and very fat. As they walked toward him Sally could see that the woman, who remained seated in a high-backed chair, was just as massive. If she was indeed the earl's mother, she looked nothing at all like her aristocratic son.

"You're too late!" the woman crowed in a shrill, high voice. She sounded pleased. "We planted him at dawn, the little worm! The vicar was most upset at the irregularity of it, but he's gone now, along with all those others who came later to gape. *Detts! Detts, I say!*"

Sally jumped as her screamed command echoed through the room. Not waiting for the butler to make an appearance, the countess bawled, "If any more idiots come to console me, send 'em away! I'll see no one!"

She turned then to her son, and said with a smile of satisfaction, "You missed it! But since you didn't take the trouble to come yesterday, I don't know any reason why I should have had to wait about for you."

"I must thank you for sparing me the ordeal. I had not remembered you so thoughtful," the earl said coolly. "Your promptness has relieved me of a tiresome chore. And I had more important things to do yesterday. It was my wedding day.

"Madam, may I present the *new* Countess of Darlington? And this, my dear Margarite, is the now *dow-ager* countess."

As his mother peered at her, all smiles gone, Sally curtsied. She regretted her bright cherry gown, the frivolous hat, even though the dowager herself was dressed in a wrinkled, outdated gown of purple velvet, heavy with tarnished gold lace and food stains.

"I see you expected me to be surprised!" the lady said, trying for a recover. "But I assumed she must be your new wife, for I was sure that not even you would dare bring your latest whore to the funeral. Who are you, girl?" she asked, turning to Sally.

"She was a Margarite Desmond," the earl replied before Sally could speak. "From Ballyragh, County Wexford, Ireland."

"Well, I'll be damned! An Irish nobody! Oh, how delicious!" the dowager crowed, falling back on her cushions and chortling.

"Now, now, Desdemona, you can't know she's a nobody," the gentleman beside her scolded.

"Course she is! All the Irish are nobodies," she retorted.

"Well, I don't see that it matters," he went on, smiling at Sally as he did so. "She's a lovely thing, a lovely thing! And I've no doubt you shall wear her like a jewel upon your breast, nephy. Or should that be a jewel upon your heart? I've no turn for these bookish allusions, but you get m'drift. Do present me, so I may kiss the bride."

"I'll present you, but you stay right where you are, for you'll not touch her, you old lecher," Harry Tredman said calmly. "My dear, to my infinite sorrow, this is my uncle, Bartholomew Worth."

Sally curtsied again, her eyes lowered. Whatever is the earl about, to be insulting them so? she wondered. And what a singular family for him to have!

"Since you appear to have lost what few manners you might once have possessed, madam, I shall pour Margarite and myself a glass of wine. It was a tiresome, dusty journey."

As he moved away to do so, he added over his

shoulder, "But I am surprised to see you sitting about here, when you have so much to do. Know you will sleep in the dower house tonight, both of you, and never come here again. I have already given Detts my orders."

"Leave the Hall? I?" the lady asked, her raddled jowls jiggling in indignation.

She rose to her feet then. She was so fat that it was a slow process, and by the time she was standing her face was almost purple. Sally concentrated on not cringing away. The dowager had to be at least six feet tall. She loomed, a massive, threatening figure, even over her taller, slim son.

"You cannot cow me as you used to do, madam, and I advise you not to offer me any violence. I might forget I am a gentleman," the earl said, sounding only amused. As he handed Sally a glass of Madeira he went on, "I remind you that I am Earl Darlington now, and whether I like it or not, this is my seat. And since it is, I want you out of it. I will be obeyed, you know, even if I have to have you carried out, screaming invective. Dear me, I wonder if I have enough able-bodied servants here to do the job? I never thought of that."

The dowager raised a large fist and shook it at him. "I'll not go till I'm damned well ready, you bastard!"

"Unfortunately for you, that is one thing you cannot call me, madam," the earl said. He sipped his wine before he seated Sally beside the fireplace. His mother might not even have been in the room for all he acknowledged her, but Sally was all too aware of her heightened breathing, the little stream of spittle that ran down her chin, and the dark malevolence that seemed to seep from every pore of her ugly, obese body. She tried hard not to shiver.

"I take it the lawyers are here?" the earl asked, turning to his uncle.

"Yes, waiting for you in the library," Bartholomew Worth said, frowning a little. "Come now, Desdemona, calm yourself before you become ill. The boy has the right of it, y'know, deplorable as it may be.

But I don't know what people will say when they learn you were turned out in such a way, sister. Unfortunate!"

Harry Tredman's laugh was bitter, mirthless. "Those few who know my mother will be delighted for me, and consider it no more than her due. And since my wedding day followed so swiftly upon my succession, the high sticklers will snub me as always. Not to worry. They've been doing it for years, so nothing will change. And it's never bothered me a whit.

"Shall we adjourn to the library, and get this over with? I've other things to do with my time than stand about here, exchanging pleasantries with you both."

Sally had to speak up then. She did not think she could bear to stay with the earl and his unpleasant relatives any longer. "If you would permit it, sir, might I be excused?" she asked her new husband. "I would feel very much in the way, and the reading of your father's will has little to do with me, after all. Perhaps I might go apart and rest?"

"Exhausting wedding night, eh?" the dowager asked slyly. "Never let you alone for a minute, did he? After that, and the drive here, I imagine you're sore as hell."

Sally paled and tightened her lips. And then she remembered that the earl had once said he expected her to be as honest as he was himself. She took a deep breath and put her wine down on a table before she rose and walked toward the dowager, her chin tilted in defiance. "You, madam, are a revolting woman," she said evenly. "I asked to be excused because I did not care to remain in your company a second longer than I had to. Harry? If you would be so good?"

His eyes, dark and stormy only moments ago, gleamed now with amusement and delight as she came and took his arm. Behind them as they walked down the long room they could hear the dowager's shrill sputtering and her brother's soothing mumbles, but they ignored both of them.

Once they were again in the hall, the earl bowed and kissed her hand. "Well done, my dear, well done!

You were superb! Here, Detts, take the countess to her rooms. See she has everything she needs, including a light repast. I shall be with you as soon as my tiresome business is concluded, Margarite."

Windle was already installed in the rooms the butler escorted Sally to upstairs. The maid looked disgusted by the dust, threadbare carpets, faded draperies, and the musty odor that hung in the air. Sally had to agree none of it was very pleasant.

"I do beg your pardon, m'lady," Detts said. "We, er, we did not expect you, having no notion of the wedding, so to speak, and we had no time to prepare. Perhaps you would rather wait in the smaller morning room—have luncheon? Please ring when you are ready."

Sally nodded and he bowed, but still he did not go away. She looked at him curiously. He seemed nervous, and she noted his hands were trembling.

"There is something more, Detts?" she asked, trying to help him.

"Yes, m'lady, there is," he said, more strongly now. "I—we all here—are delighted that young Harry—er, I mean m'lord—has succeeded to the title, and that his mother is removing to the dower house. The Hall needs so much done to it, for not a thing has been changed since she came here as a bride forty-five years ago. Do you think . . . that is, have you any idea . . . er . . ."

He took a deep breath and rushed on, "Will you and the earl be in residence soon, ma'am?"

Sally felt sorry for Detts. He was an old man, and probably he had served this unusual, difficult family all his life. She hated to be the one to tell him, but she felt she had no choice. "I am so sorry," she said. "I do not believe the earl intends to make Darlington Hall his primary home."

The butler sighed, his gloomy face even sadder. "Well, I suppose it was only to be expected," he muttered. "Never happy he was here, never, not even as a nipper he weren't."

He seemed to recall his dignity then, for he bowed

again and left the room. Just before the door closed behind him, a piercing scream sounded from below. Both Sally and Windle started, but the butler did not even flinch. No doubt such alarums were a common occurrence in the Hall.

The luncheon she was served in the inferior morning room was adequate, if not inspired. Obviously, the dowager had not spent any time planning a meal for the mourners at the funeral. Again Detts attended to Sally's needs himself. During the meal more screams and curses, louder now, could be heard coming from the direction of the library. It seemed that whatever the late earl's wishes concerning the disposal of his estate had been, they were not at all pleasing to his widow. Sally was delighted she was not any closer to her.

After her meal, Sally went outside to explore the grounds. She felt stifled in the Hall, a most unwilling prisoner. And as gloomy and neglected as the grounds were, at least there was fresh air to breathe, and she could escape the dowager. She had never imagined that any woman could even known such language, never mind use it!

She found the remains of what must have been a pretty lake at one time, and not trusting the rotting gazebo that faced it, she sat down on the soft grass nearby and rested her arms on her knees, so that she might study the vista before her. As she did so, she made idle plans for the Hall if the earl should change his mind. First, a complete top-to-bottom scrubbing was in order, with all the carpets and draperies carted away to be burned. Then, fresh paint in all the rooms. The furniture would have to be re-upholstered, and polished to a fare-thee-well, she thought, and as for the grounds—extensive gardens, a new, airy summerhouse here, and the lake cleared of weeds. And no more cypress trees!

"How pensive you look," she heard her new husband say, and she straightened and turned toward him. As he joined her on the grass he said, "That pose would make an interesting painting. But I think

I prefer to have you done in a ball gown, wearing your
jewels. I want no memories of this damned place!"

Sally saw that his face was pale, and there were
lines around his mouth and on his brow.

"It is over?" she asked.

He nodded, brooding as she had done at the quiet
sheet of water before them. "As you say. My father
had the last laugh, though. He left my mother only
his esteem for a worthy adversary, and forbade her to
remove so much as a single candlestick from the Hall.
No doubt you heard her reaction. I'm sure they must
have heard her in the village."

"Will she have enough to live on?" Sally asked.
Much as she disliked the woman, she didn't want her
to be in need.

"Oh, she has money of her own. Both of 'em do.
It was all just spite." He paused before he added,
"The lawyers have left. I did not even ask them to
remain for a luncheon, since it was obvious they could
hardly wait to be gone. I'd leave here right now myself, but until *she* is safely off the premises I must
remain."

"What will happen then?" she asked, curious. As
he stared at her, she explained. "I mean what of the
servants, the Hall itself? Will you lock it up? Leave it
deserted?"

"I wish I could. How it would gall her to see the
mansion closed and empty, while she is forced to
make do in the dower house! But I suppose I must
keep it habitable. There is my heir to consider. Reginald is fourteen now, and he might well want to live
here someday, since he has none of my unhappy memories to disturb him. I'll keep a few of the younger
servants on for that, and pension the others off. My
agent will tend to it. Most certainly, *I* shall not."

As her son had ordered, the dowager was gone by
dusk. Sally was relieved that the woman did not have
to be carried cursing and screaming from the Hall,
after all. It was something she had been dreading.

Perhaps her brother had spoken to her, convinced

her it was no use, she mused, as she watched from a window while that man and a footman heaved the lady into a carriage for the short drive to her new residence.

A cart had taken all their clothes and personal effects away during the afternoon, and a few servants had been assigned to them until the dowager could engage her own staff. The earl had given her two weeks in which to do so.

Their solitary dinner that evening was served in the large, formal dining room. Sally felt ridiculous in her elaborate evening gown, all aglitter with the tiara and other jewels as she was, but she had nothing else with her to wear. The earl had smiled for the first time that day when she came down the stairs to join him, and he had told her she was surely the most beautiful thing that had ever graced these depressing walls.

"And even though I know it was foolish of me," he told her as they walked to the dining room, "I wanted to see you formally attired and bejeweled here, just this once. Do you imagine I did so because I wanted the Hall itself to regret the countess it could never have? That seems rather a singular reason, even for one with my convoluted mental meanderings. But to be truthful, I don't know why it is so important to me," he admitted, shaking his head as he held her chair for her.

Later, when the servants had been dismissed after a quiet meal, the earl asked Sally to remain with him while he drank his port. She was more than happy to agree.

Before he could lapse into silence and begin brooding again, she asked, "Would you tell me of your family, m'lord? Explain them? If it is not too painful a subject for you, that is."

He glared at her for only a moment before he shrugged. "Yes, I suppose you do deserve an explanation, after what you have been put through today. Let me see. Where should I begin?"

He thought for a few minutes, idly moving his wine glass in circles on the mahogany table before he said,

"It was an arranged marriage of course, between my mother and father. From what I have learned of it both of them resisted it strenuously, but her father wanted the title in the family and my Grandfather Tredman coveted her fortune. That fortune was a considerable one, you see, made from wool, coal mines, shipping.

"Unfortunately, the coerced couple loathed each other on sight. My father was a short man, and as you have seen, my mother, a Long Meg. 'Little worm' was the least of her pet names for him. As for him, he called her 'the ugly, rich Maypole,' and often told anyone who'd listen that he'd rather go to bed with a giraffe. They must have been a charming couple, don't you think?"

When a shocked Sally had no reply, he sipped his wine before he continued. "I wasn't born to their union for almost ten years. I was told they were both drunk the night I was conceived, my mother especially. Maybe that's why she always hated me, because she felt she'd been tricked. She'd made very sure, you see, that she didn't have children, lest she give her husband the satisfaction of an heir. There were certainly none after me.

"To say my childhood was miserable would be to understate the matter to an extreme. Oh, I was not physically abused. I was either ignored and neglected, or fought over. I soon grew to prefer being ignored.

"But my father saw to it I had a governess, tutors. Not from any concern for me, of course. He did it to spite her, and for the title."

"Why didn't they separate? Live apart?" Sally asked. "After you were born, there was no need for them to stay together any longer, was there?"

"No, no need at all. But in some strange way they seemed to need each other. It was as if they fed on their hatred, that that hatred gave them both a purpose in life; made them strong. Eventually, they poisoned everything and everyone around them. All those malicious tricks they played on each other! All those sly insults, those screaming, vindictive arguments!

"My father refused to take my mother to London as she wished—forced her to remain here. She retaliated. The Hall grew dingier, dirtier—meals were a disgrace. When my father ignored such tactics she began to gain weight, stopped bathing. But nothing she did was any use.

"Their few friends finally ceased to visit, when they realized they were only being used as pawns, an audience for humiliation. And my Uncle Bartholomew sided with the countess, while my Grandmother Tredman championed the earl. Those two kept the fires stoked whenever there was any hint they might be dying of their own malignancy."

Sally was not only stunned, she was horrified. The Desmonds might have been poor, but she had always known love as a child. In all of this hatred, hadn't there been *any* love at all for the helpless little boy who had been Harry Tredman? Not even from his grandmother?

When she asked the earl about that lady, he shook his head. "No, because she disliked me, too. First because I was half-Worth, and the Worths, for all their wealth, were only merchants, in trade. Then because I grew so tall, like my mother. Not that that endeared me to *her*. I had my father's eyes, his features, you see, and so my face was a constant reminder to her of her one moment of weakness. As for my dear, dear uncle, yes indeed, he wanted to love me. He tried to seduce me when I was eight."

The earl finished his port and poured himself another glass. Sally shuddered. Such evil, she thought. I never even knew such evil existed in the world!

"My uncle was, er, indiscriminate in his tastes," the earl went on. "My father claimed he would sleep with any one, man or beast. In fact, he accused him and my mother of being lovers. I don't know about incest, of course. Knowing my father's vicious tongue, it may well not have been true."

Sally took a sip of water, for her mouth was dry. As she did so, she stole a glance at her new husband. He was pale, but his face was composed. In fact he looked detached, almost as if he were talking nothing but commonplaces. She wondered how he did it.

"Well, it is over now, and best forgotten, put away," he said. "Children *are* survivors, you know. That's why I made friends with William Jenkins at Eton, boring as he was. And I cultivated other boys too, to get invitations to their homes during the vacations. Anything—even demeaning myself—was better than coming back here. I was determined to get away and live my own life, as soon as I gained my majority and came into my title. And that, of course, is what I did. Today is the first time I have been back here in almost fourteen years."

In the silence that followed his confession, Sally wondered if the reason Harry Tredman surrounded himself with beautiful things was that he had seen so much ugliness in his lifetime. Or did he do so because he preferred to love inanimate objects, considering them worthier of his regard than the people he had known? She felt so sorry for him that she turned impulsively and stretched out her hand to him.

He did not take it. Instead, his face impassive, he looked deep into her eyes. When he saw the pity there, he stiffened. "Come, come, beauty! All this happened a long time ago, and I never think of it anymore. Nor would I have tonight, if you had not asked me about it. Do not place too much significance on my sad childhood. I would remind you, countless have had worse."

As he rose and came to hold her chair, Sally asked shyly, "But was that why you were in such a hurry to marry me, sir? Because you knew your father was dying, and you wanted to be sure your mother would never reign here alone, even for one day? Did you indeed marry me only to make her the dowager countess?"

His hands tightened on her chair back as he stared down at her. "As I promised I will give you an honest answer, even though that answer will show you I am not a good man. Yes, I did marry you to spite her;

at least, partly for that reason. I had another, more important one, but we will not speak of it now."

As he drew back her chair and Sally rose, he added, "Perhaps I may even be able to tell you that reason some day. Stranger things have happened.

"And now, my beautiful bride, I suggest we both get to our beds and try to get what sleep is possible in this awful place. As I am sure you can understand now, I want to be away from here as early as we can manage it in the morning."

Chapter Eleven

THEY WERE BACK in town before noon the following day. Sally had been delighted when the gates of Darlington Hall disappeared behind them, perhaps even more so than the earl. But his mood lightened all the way back to London, and he beguiled the drive by discussing the party he planned to give to introduce his new countess to the ton. As he talked Sally was even able to forget that Windle and his valet were sharing these confidences with them, although she was feeling more than a little trepidation about her reception by society. The earl seemed to have no such reservations, and he waxed enthusiastic about the decorations, the food, and the gown she must wear for the event.

That evening they attended a concert by Karl Czerny, who was making a rare appearance in England. Afterwards, the earl took her backstage to meet the great musician. Sally was thrilled when Czerny kissed her hand, and vowed he must compose a sonata in honor of her beauty.

What did it matter if society didn't like her? she asked herself on the return drive to St. James's Square. To think an accomplished musician like Czerny would smile at her, even offer to write a piece of music for her!

She went to bed, still elated. The earl did not come to her room that night, not even to look at her, but she did not notice. She hadn't even heard Windle's directives about the gowns she should wear on the morrow.

In the days that followed, however, Sally began to

wonder anew about this strange marriage she was sharing. The earl was everything that was kind, considerate, and gracious. He never failed to compliment her looks and her gowns, rarely forgot to give her his complete attention, and he took her almost everywhere with him. But he never kissed more than her hand, nor did he touch her except to help her in the way even a strange gentleman would.

Sally was confused and a little worried. She even began to question whether he really found her attractive or not. He didn't want her, that was obvious, but if that was the case why, *why* had he married her? And some evenings he went out alone, claiming prior commitments, and leaving her to a book for entertainment. He never told her where he was going, or whom he was seeing, and Sally hesitated to question him.

It was after one such evening that she resolved to have it out with him. She waited until she knew he had come home and was in his rooms before she knocked on the door that separated them. Her heart was racing and her breath came short, but she told herself she must not be a coward. Not now.

He opened the door for her himself, looking slightly surprised at the intrusion. Tonight Sally was wearing one of her own night robes, covered by a satin wrapper that was primly closed to the throat.

"If I might have a few minutes of your time, sir?" she asked.

"Certainly," he said courteously, holding the door wide in welcome, and smiling at her a little. "I must say I don't care for that color on you, Margarite. But then, I have never been fond of pink."

She looked down at her wrapper in confusion before she put up her chin and marched into his room. It was completely masculine in feeling, as different from hers as night is from day, with its heavy dark furniture and crimson hangings, fine Oriental carpet, and huge armoir on one wall. She could see a book he had been reading lying open on a table near the fire next to a large wing chair, a glass of wine beside it. His evening coat was laid on the bed, which was turned down invitingly. She averted her eyes from that piece of furniture.

"A glass of wine?" he asked, gesturing to the decanter. Sally shook her head.

"Then at least be seated, my dear, while you tell me what this visit is all about," he said, waving toward the chair across the hearth from his own.

As Sally sat down, she wondered if she had given this whole matter enough thought. She had not even considered how she was to go about it, she had only been courageous enough to know that she had to try. As he waited, she thought frantically.

"I wish I could read your mind, Margarite, but alas! as a mortal man I am not capable of it. Come now, speak up! Nothing can be that bad, or that painful, now can it? And I would remind you, you can tell me anything. I am your husband."

Thankful for the opening, Sally hurried to say, "Yes, you are, but then again, you are not. I—I do not understand it, and I must."

The earl sipped his wine, regarding her over the rim of the glass as he did so. The glow of the fire cast flickering lights and shadows over his strong, high-cheekboned face, giving him an almost diabolical look.

"But what is there to understand?" he asked easily. "I do not come to you, but what of that? I have my heir—three of 'em, in fact."

"But I thought . . . You know it is not normal, nor . . . nor is it right. You are a man," Sally went on bravely. "Why don't you come to me, love me? I . . . I certainly expected you to do so."

He put his glass down and leaned forward to take her hands in his, chafing them when he discovered how cold they were. One of his fingers touched her pulse briefly, and when he felt its racing beat he smiled to himself.

"Don't be afraid," he said softly. "But tell me, do you really want me to come, or are you just concerned because it is unusual? I'll have an honest answer, if you please."

"I don't know," she whispered. "I . . . I have never thought about it." She paused and swallowed before she said, "But no, I suppose I don't want you, or . . . or anyone."

"Of course you do not, for in spite of your early, disastrous marriage you are as unawakened as any virgin."

He let her hands go, to rise and move away from her a little. Speaking from the shadow he said, "And that is how it should be. You are a goddess, not a woman. As such, and as beautiful as you are, you were meant only to be admired. Most certainly you should never be pawed about, or used by men, myself included. I am here to protect you from that. And it is for that reason I do not make love to you, my dear. Because it would demean you.

"It is kind of you to be perturbed about me, and I thank you, but please do not be. I have a very adequate mistress for my needs. She should not concern you. No one in town knows about her, for she is not your common demimonde. She neither attends their revels, nor flaunts herself about town. In truth she is a respectable widow, who has been more than accommodating this past year." He paused for a moment, and then he said, his voice colder, "However, even though I do not choose to bed you, I must insist you allow no one else the privilege either."

"But of course I won't! The very idea!" Sally exclaimed, much shocked.

"I am delighted you are so nice," he said calmly. "Not that you won't have offers aplenty, my dear, for all men are not as careful of goddesses as I am. You must refuse each and every one. As usual, I will not tolerate deception, especially in this instance."

He came back to her then and drew her to her feet. For a moment he held on to her hands, looking down into her still troubled face. "Go to bed, goddess," he said softly. "Dream of the gods, your only true mates. And be easy in your mind. The marriage we are sharing is exactly the marriage I desired."

He raised her hands and kissed them before he took her to the connecting door.

Once alone, Sally climbed obediently into bed, but she did not go to sleep for a long time. How strange the earl was! she thought. She had never in her life heard anything so ridiculous as the nonsense he had just spouted to her. A goddess, was she? He was beyond belief! She was flesh and blood and completely human, with every human failing and, she hoped, a few human strengths. But if he wanted to pretend she was not, that was certainly his prerogative.

And to be truthful, she was both relieved and yet also in some strange way, disappointed. Relieved, because she didn't really want him or any man. Yes, that had been an honest answer she had given him. She had been more intent on "doing her duty" than anything else.

Yet she was disappointed, too. Was it because it pricked her vanity a little, to think he could ignore her charms so easily?

Sally sighed and rolled over to her side. So he had a mistress, did he? A discreet widow, tucked away in a cozy backwater, unknown to anyone else? How . . . how charming for him! she thought, as she punched her pillows and tried to compose herself for sleep. How very, very convenient! He certainly had thought of everything!

Alone again in the adjoining bedchamber, Earl Darlington settled down in the chair by the fireplace, his book and wine forgotten as he stared into the flames.

Carefully, he reviewed Margarite's unprecedented visit, what she had said and how she had looked—the fast beat of her pulse. And as he remembered, a tiny smile curved his lips. At last, he told himself, a beginning at last.

The earl had provided Sally with a pretty mare, all glossy black, which he had purchased for her at Tattersall's. As soon as the habits he had ordered for her had been delivered, they began to start their days with a canter in Hyde Park before breakfast every pleasant morning. Sally quickly learned to control the playful little mare in the busy streets, but she was always glad when they reached Rotten Row and there was nothing to worry about but other riders. One late June morning, as they cantered toward the gate at Hyde Park Corners, heading home, they found themselves hailed by a rider just entering the park.

The earl smiled, and motioned to Sally to pull up as the other gentleman came abreast of them. Sally recognized Sir Thomas Avery, he of the pleasant, lazy eyes who had been such a help on her wedding day, and her smile for him was warm.

"Thomas! Well met," Harry Tredman said. "Margarite, you remember Sir Thomas Avery, do you not?"

"But of course I do," Sally said. "Tell me, Sir Thomas, did you have much trouble . . . er, disposing of Miss Fullsham?"

"Fullsham? Fullsham?" the earl asked, perplexed. "Who is Miss Fullsham?"

"Your countess's bridesmaid. So to speak, that is," his friend told him. "I am ashamed of you, sir. To think you could forget such an accommodating, important person.

"But to answer your question, m'lady, I have to admit I did have a devil of a time with her. She invited me to join her for luncheon at her hotel, since we had been 'choused out of a wedding breakfast.' Her exact words, 'pon my honor! When I invented a previous engagement, she tried to set a date for the following day. I was forced to lie about a fictitious journey. And then, of course, I had to leave town lest the lady spy me out, still in London."

He sighed wearily. "The things I do for you, m'lord. To be languishing in the country during the Season! I have only just returned, and every time I step outdoors I pray Miss Fullsham has returned to her home in the north."

"Strange," the earl mused. "I never knew you to be a timid soul. I would have thought you able to handle any female with aplomb."

The two shared a quiet chuckle before he went on. "But know you have all my thanks for your part in our wedding."

"I understand congratulations are in order, Lord Darlington," Sir Thomas said next. "So, you are the earl at last."

"Yes, my father died two weeks ago. But we should not be keeping the horses standing about. Come and dine with us, and I'll tell you all about it."

A date and time were decided on, and the three parted company. Sir Thomas's eyes were warm as he bade the new countess good-bye, but when he was riding alone again he grew thoughtful. Margarite, Countess Darlington, was a beautiful woman, but there was something else about her that went beyond beauty. Something that spelled a mystery. And in some strange way, she looked familiar to him.

He shook his head. Surely if he had seen her before, he would remember her. What man would not? He resolved to find out where Harry had met her, how he had courted her, and where she was from. She was a stranger to the ton, and that was unusual in itself. Where had she spent her childhood? Why had she not been presented at Court? Her wide-spaced blue eyes haunted him for the rest of the day.

Sir Thomas Avery became a frequent visitor in St. James's Square from that time on. Occasionally he accompanied the newlyweds to the theater, or a concert, and when he learned of the gala evening the earl was planning for his bride he was the first to say he would be there.

Invitations had been sent to most of society, and Sally was relieved to see that very few people refused to attend. She was having a new gown made for the occasion, of white satin with silver trimmings. Harry had insisted on visiting the modiste with her, to inspect the patterns and make his choice. Sally wished he trusted her to order something suitable by herself, but she was glad of his company even so, for it meant that she could dispense with the domineering Miss

Windle, whom she was loathing more and more each day.

Sally was not permitted to assist in the preparations for the gala, although she could not help but be aware of the amount of work necessary to ensure a successful evening. The cleaning and polishing and rearranging that went on, the long discussions of the food and wine to be served that the earl held with his house-keeper and butler, the extra crystal and plate that was rented and delivered, the elaborate floral arrange-ments for every room, each carefully coordinated to complement the decor—it was astounding. The earl had hired two groups of musicians to play, not only in the ballroom but in the entry hall as well. After the guests' carriages had finally inched their way to the front door, and they had descended to the red carpet laid over the steps, sheltered by an awning above, they would be greeted by the sounds of music as they entered the Hall.

Sally knew there were to be extra grooms to direct traffic, and to hurry the carriages on their way once they had discharged their noble cargoes, and inside extra maids and footmen would be on duty to take care of stoles and top hats and canes. One of the salons on the lower floor had been set aside for the ladies. It had been furnished with its own set of maids, discreet screens to hide the closestools, and long pier glasses for the primping and preening necessary before the ladies felt confident enough to climb the stairs and be introduced to the new countess all London was discussing.

On the evening of the party, Sally stood beside the earl on the gallery at the top of the double staircase. She had a perfect view of the proceedings below as Wayland announced each guest in his plummy, sono-rous voice.

"The Duke and Duchess of Barrington . . . Vis-count and Viscountess Fleming . . . Lady Rogers, Miss Rogers, Caroline and Agnes Rogers . . . the Earl of Dent . . . Mr. and Mrs. . . . ." The names rolled

out, one after the other, a seemingly endless litany of
them.

Sally returned the superficial smiles, and heard
the drawled phrases—"So happy to meet you,
m'lady"; "My very best wishes on your marriage,
countess"; "Harry, you sly dog, where did you find
this beauty?"; "You are to be envied, sir!"; "I
would not have missed this evening for the world!";
"Naughty Harry! But I suppose you will be forgiven
in time"; "So kind of you to include us . . ."

And on and on they came, the women all richly
dressed in silks and satins and dainty muslins, their
persons adorned with flashing jewels, their elaborate
coiffures secured with gold pins or large plumes or
lace, and their faces painted. And the gentlemen were
no less grand in their form-fitting evening clothes, the
white of their linen dazzling the eye. Over them all
hung a miasma of scent, some of it masking the body
odor of those who considered excessive bathing an
unnecessary chore.

As on her wedding day, Sally felt somehow divorced
from the entire proceeding. She smiled and chatted,
listened and nodded, but she did not feel a true part
of the festivities the earl had planned so carefully to
display her charms. It was as if she were watching a
play she had read, knowing beforehand what lines
would be recited and by whom. She even felt able to
read everyone's mind. That ugly dowager, all smiles
and honeyed words, had loathed her on sight, as so
often the ugly do dislike others lovelier than they.
And this thin, stiff gentleman, with his pursed mouth
and steely eyes, held not only her but Harry as well
in contempt for their all too hasty marriage. That
young lady over there was carefully pricing everything
Sally wore, while her father, seemingly all aged goodness, was mentally undressing her.

Although she could not hear the conversation of the
guests as they moved about the ballroom, she knew
what it consisted of. Conjectures about her origins,
her suitability (or lack of it) for this exalted position,
how she had managed to snag the wily earl, how much

she would realize financially from the match, the cost of her jewelry, the dimensions of her waist, hips, and bosom—even the size of her feet! It went on and on.

She held her head high—a necessity, graced as it was with the magnificent sapphire-and-diamond tiara. Harry had insisted she wear the entire parure again, and although she had resisted the show she had to admit she looked very fine. Windle had earned her salary this night. And because she had, Sally looked as wealthy and correct as anyone there, which only made the ladies dislike her more.

She saw she would have no trouble with gentlemen of any age. The younger were all too obvious in their attraction to her, so obvious she expected her husband to give them a set-down. He did not do so, however. Instead, he only smiled a mocking little smile of ownership as he watched them inspecting her. The older gentlemen were more subtle, but Sally knew their thoughts were just as lustful as those of their younger counterparts. She disliked the entire proceeding, for she felt like some exotic bird of paradise, put on show as entertainment for the ton. Something bizarre—a curiosity, not a woman.

As the evening wore on, she began to think she would never be able to stop smiling. Surely the muscles of her face had hardened in place. Still, once released from the receiving line she made herself move among the guests, and she chatted and listened before moving on. Never once did she sit down, or linger, nor was she invited to do so.

Sir Thomas Avery was there, of course, his lazy eyelids hiding his thoughts. Sally had only a minute or two to converse with him, but when she left him she felt better. He, at least, seemed to understand what she was going through, and when he pressed her hand it was in silent commiseration for her ordeal.

She could see that Harry was well pleased, very well pleased indeed, and his most urbane, sophisticated self. No guest was neglected, no matter how boring or tiresome or unpleasant they might be. He swept all before him, willing them to enjoy themselves and applaud not only his efforts but his choice of bride. And such was the force of his personality that he succeeded, albeit superficially.

Refreshments were served by an army of footmen—sparkling glasses of wine and spirits dispensed with lavish hands. Over the din of noisy conversation and gay laughter, the musicians strove mightily to entertain with strings and reeds and harpsichord.

The ballroom grew warmer and stuffier, the enveloping scent of flowers and perfumes and bodies more stifling, but still Sally smiled and allowed herself to be admired, ogled, leered at, and studied minutely. That was her role in this play, and she must perform it.

It was doubtful, however, whether anyone in the vast crowd had a more unpleasant time of it than she did, and no one was more relieved than she when the last carriages had been called for in the small hours of the following morning.

As soon as the last guest had been ushered from the house, she sagged against a wall and closed her eyes in exhaustion. The earl was quick to put his arm around her in support.

"Can it be you have had nothing to eat, my dear?" he asked. "Nothing to drink? Come, we will go into one of the smaller salons and I'll have the servants bring you something before you seek your bed. Wayland!"

He gave terse orders before he led her away. After the butler had brought a tray and left, closing the door behind him, the earl settled her in a comfortable chair and took a seat across from her.

"You were magnificent, beauty," he told her, his voice warm. "A queen, a goddess, so beautiful you did not seem real! All I ever wanted you to be, my countess. I was much envied. Thank you.

"I only worry that it was too much for you. Here, do try the lobster patties. Have a cake!

"I should have remembered that—what an ordeal it would be for you to be meeting so many of the ton all at once, making endless conversation with strangers.

Forgive me that I put you through it, although it was necessary. It will be easier next time."

Sally sipped her wine before she waved a weary hand. "It was nothing, sir," she tried to say lightly. She refused to even consider a "next time." "A momentary fatigue, that is all. After a good night's sleep I shall more than recover, although I pray you will not insist on an early-morning canter."

He smiled at her as he lifted her hand and kissed it, his lips lingering in adoration. It was quieter here, the only reminder of the evening being the distant clatter of the servants as they began to put the house back in order again. Sally could feel herself relaxing.

"You shall sleep all day, m'lady, if that is what you wish. And now, I think it more than time that you were in bed," he said, as he rose to his feet.

Obediently, Sally got up too, only to find herself being picked up and carried. She supposed she should have demurred, for she was perfectly capable of walking, but she did not. Somehow, she felt comforted and safe in the earl's strong arms. As he mounted the stairs, she rested her head on his breast. She could hear the beat of his heart under her head, smell the scent he wore, and she closed her eyes.

Once in his wife's room, the earl rang for Windle to assist her and bowed himself away.

When Sally woke, early in the afternoon, she found her bedchamber filled with vases of deep red roses. On the breakfast tray she had ordered, there was a small parcel and a note. The parcel contained a jade carving of a Chinese empress. It looked very old, very valuable. Sally was sure she had never seen anything so precious, and she set it on the table beside her bed with reverent hands. The note thanked her again for a memorable evening, made more so, the earl claimed, by her presence.

He wrote too that he hoped she had slept well. He himself was out calling on the noted artists of London, so that he might arrange to have her portrait painted, as a permanent memento of the evening. Not, he assured her, that any mortal artist, no matter how talented, could possibly do justice to her beauty.

Their days continued in much the same pattern as before—the early rides, the strolls and drives through the park, fittings and shopping, visits to the libraries, museums, and sights. Now of course they were often out to parties in the evening, or invited to tea or a musical reception. London was growing thinner of company as the Season wore down, many in the ton having left for their country estates, but still the Earl and Countess of Darlington continued in residence at St. James's Square. Sally was also involved in the sittings necessary for her portrait. As a kindness, the earl said, he had chosen Sir Thomas Lawrence, for having anyone as beautiful as Margarite, Countess of Darlington, as his model would more than make up for his usual sitters, whom he was forced so often to flatter.

Sally tried to tell herself she was content and busy, but deep inside she knew she was not. There seemed to be a lack of purpose to her days, a dearth of anything meaningful or worthwhile. Sometimes she felt so edgy and unnerved she was hard put to hold her tongue, a situation exacerbated by the talented but opinionated Windle.

She had never spoken sharply to the maid, but one evening, when she had ordered Windle to lay out a particular gown and she discovered she had chosen another, Sally could swallow her resentment no longer.

"This gown is much more suitable for evening, m'lady," Windle said in her positive way, as she held it up. "For even though you and the earl dine alone, you must remember your position. I think the pearls with it, and the dark red satin slippers."

"You overstep yourself, Windle," Sally told her coldly. "I prefer the violet muslin I chose earlier. Get it out for me at once!"

The maid had looked affronted, although she did as she was bade. But when she returned from the dressing room empty-handed moments later, she said she had discovered a rip in the hem of the muslin that would make it impossible for the countess to wear after all.

Seething and tight-lipped, Sally had allowed herself to be dressed in Windle's choice before she marched downstairs to her husband, her lovely face set in mutinous lines. She was easy with him now; indeed, they sometimes shared a camaraderie that amazed her, it was so comfortable. Almost as comfortable as she had felt with Anne. Not that Harry was anything like her dear friend—oh no! He was too much the man for that—a fact she could never seem to forget.

Pushing Harry's disturbing masculinity to the back of her mind, Sally lost no time telling him what was bothering her, her voice shaking with rage as she paced up and down the drawing room. "I tell you she must go, sir! She is impossible! And I won't be dictated to by a servant! The very idea!"

From his seat by the fire, the earl studied his angry wife. "Very well, you may give her notice tomorrow," he said. "I shall engage another maid for you. Now do sit down, Margarite. You make me weary with your fierce striding about. And if you are not careful, you'll split that gown to the knee."

Fully enraged still, Sally whirled on him. "What do you mean, *you* will engage another maid? She is to be my servant, is she not? I shall do it! And furthermore, sir, from now on I must insist on being allowed to order the meals, oversee the housekeeper and the other servants—do all those things any wife is responsible for. You have treated me like a little know-nothing long enough! And how am I to learn how to go on, if you will not even let me begin? I can assure you I am capable. I watched how it was done at Beechlands for three years!"

He waited for a moment, his expression courteous, before he said, "Have you quite finished, my dear? I would hate to interrupt you in full spate, as it were."

When Sally just stood there, still seething, he said, "Good. Now let me assure you, first, that this is not Beechlands. That was only a pleasant little country estate. This is the home of the Earl of Darlington, and there is a vast difference between the two.

"Besides, I cannot allow you to get involved in such mundane matters, goddess. To think of you fretting about the cost of coal, the number of wax tapers we use, the price of silver sand! To say nothing of dealing with a maid's toothache, or an underfootman's sick mother. The very thought is repulsive to me!"

All Sally's anger dissipated in an instant, and she sank down in a chair across from his and burst out laughing. He watched her, a faint frown across his brow, until at last her amusement had faded away to a few weak chuckles. As she wiped her eyes on a handkerchief she said, "Forgive me, I couldn't help it! But how ridiculous, when you consider I used to go barefoot, dig potatoes, milk the cow, mind the babies for my mother, and help Mrs. Ginty with the cooking! I fear that although you have made me a countess, m'lord, part of me will still be that poor little Irish girl who didn't always have enough to eat, and very often had only one decent dress to her name."

The earl rose and came to put his hands on both arms of her chair, leaning down to look deep into her eyes. His expression as he did so gave Sally pause.

"If you would please me, Margarite, you will forget all about that little Irish girl," he said slowly. "She lived in another time, another place. I wish her long gone. You will never want again, never be required to lift your hand to anything. You are the Countess Darlington now. Promise me—right now!—that you will never, *ever* mention your Irish upbringing to me again."

A little frightened by his intensity, Sally nodded, "Why—why of course, Harry, if it bothers you so. I—I did not know," she said.

He smiled at her and straightened. "Shall we go in now? I believe I heard the bell some moments ago."

As they ate dinner and discussed their day, Sally could not put the earl's directive from her mind. She was almost glad he was going out alone this evening, even if it was to his mistress, for she wanted to think over what he had said. Why was he so adamant about this one thing? Why did it upset him to such a degree? She did not understand.

She had little time to consider it later, however, for shortly after the earl had left the house the butler announced the arrival of Sir Thomas Avery.

"I told him as how the earl was not at home, m'lady," Wayland said. He sounded slightly outraged as he went on. "The gentleman persisted, and asked for you. Shall I . . . shall I deny him?"

"Certainly not," Sally said, pleased that Sir Thomas was here. He was a nice man; she liked him very much, and she could use the company. First Windle and then the earl had upset her, and she knew she would have trouble sleeping tonight. Perhaps a few minutes with Harry's friend would change her mood.

Wayland bowed, although it was plain he did not approve this visitor. Moments later, Sir Thomas came into the library.

"How kind of you to receive me, ma'am," he said as he bowed.

After Sally had asked him to be seated, and ordered a glass of wine for him, she said, "Not kind at all, sir! I needed someone to take my mind from things tonight. I was feeling blue-deviled."

"Lord Darlington being unavailable," he commented, as he sat down near her.

"Yes, Harry had another engagement," she admitted, unaware of her little frown. "But I know it is silly of me to be so upset at a domineering maid!"

When he questioned her she told him of Windle, and she began to feel better when he was chuckling in amusement at her description of this very superior lady's maid and her forceful ways.

"But I am to give her notice tomorrow," Sally finished. "How delightful that will be! It is bad of me, but I must admit I look forward to it a great deal more than I should."

"Was it only this Windle person who upset you?" he asked softly. "Forgive me, but I could not help but notice the depth of your chagrin, and I do not think one servant could be enough to cause it, no matter how aggravating she was."

Sally felt her cheeks grow warm. "I . . . I cannot speak of it further, sir," she said, in a stiff little voice. "But come! Did you wish to leave a message for the earl? I should be glad to deliver it for you."

"It is not important. I only wondered if he was going to ride tomorrow morning. I've a new hack, and I'd like his opinion."

Sally promised to convey the message, and then for a half hour or so the two sat and chatted of plays they had seen, and the current London scene.

Thomas Avery had yet to discover Lady Darlington's background, and it teased him still. He knew by now that Harry had met her in Devon, where she had been living with friends. He even knew she had been married before, and that she was Irish. But he could not question his friend further, and he hesitated to ask the lady herself. She was a very private sort, not given to confidences, he thought as he rose to take his leave.

But as he strolled toward St. James's Street he told himself he would find out, one of these days. There was something about this marriage that did not ring true to him, and Harry and his countess were unlike any newly married couple he had ever known. It was obvious that Harry revered his bride and placed her on a high pedestal, and equally obvious that Lady Darlington looked up to him in return. But still they were different—unusually so. For all of Harry's smiles for her, and the warmth in his eyes when he looked her way, there was never that current between them, those private little glances that he had observed in other newlyweds. Nor did the earl's hand linger when he had occasion to touch her. She might have been his sister, or an elderly aunt, for all the caresses he gave her.

Surely it was a most singular marriage they shared, Sir Thomas thought, as he went up the steps of White's Club. And tonight he had discovered the countess was upset, and with more than just her maid. With Harry? he wondered.

Just then he was greeted by Raggett, the proprietor of White's, and he put the puzzling earl and countess from his mind as he went in search of a game and some serious gambling.

But it would be true to say he had no intention of forgetting it. For anything that affected Margarite, Countess of Darlington, affected him, and he knew it, just as surely as he knew how much he had come to love her himself in the few short weeks that he had known her.

Chapter Twelve

MOST UNFASHIONABLY, the Tredmans remained in London till mid-July, but even though so many others had gone it was unusual if the post failed to bring Sally impassioned notes, or poems to her eyes, her grace, or her beauty. Sally was disturbed by these tributes, but when she sought her husband's advice about how to stop them he only shrugged.

"Why bother, my dear?" he asked. "It amuses the gentlemen—makes them happy. Surely you would not deny them the privilege of adoring you from afar, now would you? It is such a harmless pastime for them."

The two were in Sally's rooms at the time. The earl had formed the habit of coming in in the mornings while she was being dressed and having her hair arranged. At first this had disturbed Sally no less than her new abigail, a Miss Preston, but they soon grew accustomed to it, and to the earl's suggestions as well.

Now, as the maid applied the tongs to the curls of her mistress's coiffure, Sally stared into the mirror. She could see Harry's reflection as he lounged in a chair behind her, his chin propped up in his hand as he studied her.

"But somehow it seems unfair to them!" she persisted. "Shouldn't I write to them—a cold, formal note—asking them to stop? What if they take my silence as a tacit acceptance?"

"They won't do that. Er, Preston, that curl you just finished needs pinning up."

"Yes, m'lord," the dresser murmured, her capable hands already busy at the task. She was a middle-aged woman of great sense, with steady, calm gray eyes.

Sally had liked her on sight, although the earl had not given his approval until he saw how well Preston turned his countess out.

"It is the fashion to conceive a passion for an unattainable woman, Margarite," he continued. "All the young men do it, and I am sorry to say, a few of the sillier, older men as well. Such a passion makes them feel safe."

"Safe? I don't understand," Sally said, turning her head this way and that as she inspected her hairdo, Preston having stood back and folded her hands.

"But of course. For if they are in love with you they are in no danger of being required to love another, thus saving themselves from the dreaded finality of matrimony," he drawled.

Sally whirled on the stool and chuckled. "But how lowering to think I serve only as protection for them! It makes me feel rather like an umbrella!"

She rose and took off her wrapper, as Preston held out a sprigged muslin gown. As the maid dropped it over her chemise and petticoat, careful not to disarrange her hair, the earl said, "A most admirable purpose in life for you, goddess. I do assure you, you have saved many a young man from being marched up many a church aisle this season."

He studied his wife, as she sat down for Preston to put on her hose and her sandals. Margarite was lovelier than ever, he thought. That pure profile, those beautiful eyes. It was no wonder half the men in London were mad for her, and he was content to have it so. He knew there was no danger she would lose her heart to any of them. Not this particular countess. Not yet, at any rate, and pray God, not ever.

He wondered then whether the careful plan he was pursuing would be enough to make her lose her heart to him. It had been all he could think of to do, to make her forget the past and that disastrous first marriage. It was why he had ordered her never to speak of Ireland again, for if she did not, she might forget her brutish husband more easily—and sooner.

Oh, he had called her a goddess, pretended he did

not want her except as a lovely object to be admired, but he had lied. Lord, how he had lied! he thought, knowing how much he cared for her, how much he longed for her to be his wife.

"You have a fitting this morning, my dear?" he asked, his voice only a little unsteady.

"Yes, Madame expects me at ten. Preston goes with me."

As she rose and the maid knelt to adjust her skirts, he said, "You might inspect some patterns suitable for country gowns. It is almost time for my annual visit to my estates. We go to Norfolk first, then into Warwickshire, and finally to East Sussex. That is where Reath Court is, and it is my favorite. It has the added charm of being close to Sir Thomas Avery's estate. He has asked us to be sure to be there in September. He plans a house party.

"Come to think of it, I'll cancel my morning appointments in the city, and take you to the modiste's myself. That way I can see for myself what Madame has in stock that would be suitable. Preston, you will be excused."

The maid nodded and curtsied before she took herself away, her arms heaped with Sally's nightclothes and a charming but discarded bonnet. The earl had preferred a white chipped straw this morning.

Sally's lips tightened a little as she remembered that. How she wished she could be honest, and tell Harry that she wanted to choose her own clothes, even argue with him when he vetoed her selections in favor of his own. I have a mind, good taste—I am not a doll! she told herself for perhaps the hundreth time. But she did not say so aloud. Dressing her as he wished seemed to please Harry. And, she reminded herself, there was so little she could do to please him.

Suddenly she wondered why wanting him to be happy had become so important to her, and when? Because she admitted it was important, even if she couldn't understand her reasoning.

Afraid he might see the confusion in her eyes, she turned back to her dressing table. As she picked up her reticule and gloves she asked, "When do we leave for the country, sir?"

"In a week or so. Whenever we can be ready. I have sent messages ahead, so they will be expecting us."

"You do not go to Darlington Hall?" she asked, as she came to stand beside him. She saw his eyes grow wintry, saw his sudden frown.

"No," he said. "Most definitely, no."

"What of your children, m'lord?" she asked next, putting her hand on his arm. "Where shall we see them?"

"See 'em? Why should we?" he asked absently, admiring her soft skin, her full, rosy lower lip.

"But surely you intend to visit them!" Sally exclaimed. "You told me they were in the country. And since we will be going there too, I assumed . . ."

"Never assume, my dear," he interrupted. "I hardly think my first wife's dear parents would be prepared to welcome you—or, come to think of it, me either. As for my second wife's brats, only one of 'em is legitimate. I see to all their care and I receive regular reports on their progress. What more could be required?"

"But they are your children, and their mothers are dead! Of course you should see them! They must miss you dreadfully. Please, if you will not go to them, might we not have them come to visit us? I should so like to make all their acquaintance."

He looked stunned. "Margarite, you must be jesting. Even the thought of you surrounded by a pack of grubby brats is appalling."

She tilted her chin at him. "I am not jesting at all, m'lord. Putting aside the fact that it is your duty, I should think you would take the greatest care that your children do not grow up hating you, as you hated your father."

For a moment she was sure she had gone too far, for his face grew stern and his eyes icy. Then, as she looked at him, worry coming into her eyes, he relented. "We shall see," she said shortly, holding out

his arm. "Shall we? Madame awaits. *Griffen!* My hat
and gloves!"

His tall, bony valet hurried from the earl's rooms
bearing these articles. As usual, when he looked at
Sally, he flushed.

Wisely, Sally said nothing more of the earl's children and a possible visit, nor did she protest when he,
and he alone, chose her new country gowns. He had
such exquisite taste, it would have been mere petulance if she had. Madame promised to set her entire
staff to stitching that very afternoon, and she was all
smiles as her best customer took her best advertise-
ment away over an hour later. Her custom had increased tremendously once it had become known that
she was the one who had the dressing of Countess
Darlington.

Ten days passed before the Tredmans were on their
way to the earl's Norfolk estate, some six miles west
of Ipswich. It was cooler in the country, and since
London had become unseasonably warm as the summer continued, Sally was delighted to leave it far behind. As usual, the earl traveled with every comfort.
Their personal servants, Griffen and Preston, rode in
a separate carriage along with the various trunks and
boxes, and linens, wines, and such delicacies as could
be obtained only in town. The Tredman's hacks were
being brought along too, and the earl's sporting carriage, tooled by a groom. It all made an impressive
show, Sally thought, stifling the pang she felt remembering how she and Anne had watched just such a
cavalcade sweep up the drive to Beechlands only
months ago. How distant that day seemed now.

She forced those memories to the back of her mind
when Harry began to talk to her. As usual at the start
of a new adventure he was excited and alert, delighted
to be leaving town for wider fields. And just as soon,
Sally knew, he would be anxious to return. The volatile earl could never be content in one place long.

For herself, she enjoyed the rural scenery, the fresh
air, the clean breezes. The roads were in fine repair
that summer and they made good time, stopping over-

night only in Braintree. When they reached their destination, Sally saw that Fanning House was a lovely country seat, made of rosy brick and surrounded by extensive gardens. The earl had told her that two elderly great aunts of his lived there as caretakers, although they would be nowhere in sight, for they had been given orders to go and visit friends during his stay.

Sally shook her head. It seemed rather mean to order the old ladies away, simply because m'lord condescended to inspect his holding and could not be bothered with them, but as she always did she held her tongue. That was the earl's business—none of hers.

Perhaps if she had felt herself a real wife she might have remonstrated with him, she mused, but although she bore his name, his title, she was not his wife. She was only a—possession. And oh, how she wished she might be more than that!

She was helpless to change things, however, for there was no way she could tell Harry how she felt, or how she was beginning to long to be much more to him than just a beautiful doll he could dress up in finery and admire. Not when he himself seemed so content with the existing state of affairs.

They stayed at Fanning House for ten days. During that time, the earl applied himself to business—seeing his agent, inspecting the crops, talking to his farmers. But there also was time for drives and walks about the neighborhood, and one delightful day was spent roaming the shingled beach at Felixstowe.

Harry had had a picnic lunch prepared for them, and they drove to the shore in his phaeton. Once there he had left the rig in a young lad's care, and they had wandered far up the beach, away from those few people who were enjoying it near the road.

Sally's shoes were soon filled with sand. When she sat down to empty them Harry suggested she leave them off, and remove her hose as well. She smiled at him in delight as she complied, and she was surprised when he sat down beside her to take off his own shoes and stockings, and roll his breeches up.

While he spread out the rug he had brought for

them to sit on, Sally wandered down to the water. The gentle waves that came ashore were cold, and as she waded in she squealed a little, until she had grown used to the temperature. On this warm day, she decided wading was delightful. Hoisting her skirts above her knees, she ventured deeper. A larger wave than usual surprised her, and she was forced to raise her skirts even higher as she scampered back to shore.

Suddenly Harry was beside her, his arm going snug around her waist before he lifted her in his arms and carried her to safety.

Sally put her head back and laughed, as she put her own arms around his neck. What fun this was! she thought, even as she wondered she could feel so carefree.

It was then she stole a glance at her husband, and she surprised a serious, intent look on his handsome face. Her own eyes widened as he bent his head and kissed her cheek, his lips moving slowly to her jaw, her throat, in a gentle caress. Sally's heart began to pound, but before she could begin to feel uneasy at this unusual behavior of his he set her on her feet and gave her a little spank.

"I'll thank you to have a care, madam," he told her in mock reproach, although his eyes were twinkling. "I've no mind to lose you to King Neptune. You look so enchanting today, he might be plotting even now to acquire you for his watery kingdom. By the way, can you swim?"

When Sally confessed she could not, he shook his finger at her before he led her back to the blanket and their luncheon.

They spent the afternoon staring out to sea, watching the waves and seabirds, the sails on the horizon, while they talked about everything under the sun. Sally even dozed for a while. When she woke, she discovered that Harry had tipped her broad-brimmed straw hat over her nose to shield her complexion from the sun.

While she slept, Harry had been free to let down his guard and gaze at her as much as he liked. And as he did so, he wondered in amazement at his forbearance.

He knew he was not a patient man—far from it! On other occasions, if a woman he wanted had played coy, pretended she needed more time before they became lovers, he had been able to shrug and walk away without giving her another thought. There were too many other women in the world, and he was too mercurial to wait for any of them.

But now he was prepared to spend as long as it took to win Margarite, to make her care for him—want him. Was this what love was? he wondered, brushing a hovering insect away from her soft skin. He did not know. He only knew that he had to do it this way, no matter how many weeks or months must pass before he could reach his goal. For he knew how very dear, and how very important, his beautiful young wife had become to him.

Now he remembered with delight that she had not pulled away from his kiss at water's edge, nor had her body tensed in his arms, for he had been on watch for that. But even so he had not repeated that caress, or even touched her again, and he had kept his conversation light and easy. He knew he had to go slowly, that this was no time to rush his fences. This was far too important to risk frightening her, causing her to retreat even those few paces she had come toward him of her own accord. 'Ware hurry, Harry old son, he told himself. Someday she would come into his arms of her own accord. He would wait for that day.

Much later, as they drove away in the late afternoon, Sally felt light and easy—happier than she had been in a long time.

Oh yes, she would have been delighted to spend a month in residence at Fanning House. All too soon, however, they had begun their next journey, this time west to the midlands. Brentlands reminded Sally of Darlington Hall, although it was in much better condition. Here too, relatives had been displaced to give the new earl and his bride privacy. They spent two weeks at Brentlands.

In mid-August, they headed south to Reath Court in East Sussex. From the first moment she saw it, Sally could see why this estate was Harry's favorite. The old house was so lovely, so gracious—situated as it was near a wide, meandering stream, with its vast fields around it, tidy with fruit trees or rich with grains.

To her surprise, as they swept around the final approach to the house she saw a group of children being herded into a straight line near the steps. They were attended by several servants.

She turned to the earl, her brows raised.

"Yes, they are none other than my brats," he admitted. "You did say I should see more of them, did you not? Even expressed a wish to see them for yourself? Well, behold them, come to visit their dear papa and their new stepmama. Pray I have not made a most disastrous mistake. That little red-haired one looks the very devil, don't she?"

Sally took his arm and stepped from the carriage. Suddenly a deep silence fell on the assembled children, and six pairs of eyes inspected her much more critically than they had inspected their seldom-seen father. The last pair of Tredman eyes was closed, for it belonged to a baby fast asleep in a nursemaid's arms.

"Hello to you all. I think it would be wise for you to introduce yourselves to my new countess," the earl said, surveying the line from end to end. "You there, Reginald, you begin."

The oldest boy flushed, but he made a creditable bow as he gave his name. Sally saw he had his father's features and his fierce pride, and her heart went out to him.

Next to him was another boy about two years younger, who stammered as he told her he was Lawrence. It took some time and some coaxing to get all the names, and the littlest girl at the end of the row burst into tears and had to be carried away, sobbing. Sally noted that Catherine, she of the bright red hair, appeared to be scornful of her sister's cowardice. Catherine was a lovely child, with fair skin and that mass of red curls topping an enchanting face, seemingly filled by large brown eyes. Or, Sally thought, she would be lovely, if she ever stopped frowning. Idly, she wondered if her mother had been the earl's mistress, and the sleeping baby the only legitimate child of that union. She noticed then that the other children, Reginald, Lawrence, and nine-year-old Fay, stood a little apart from the rest, as if aware of their more secure station in life. It was too bad!

"Run along now, all of you," the earl said briskly. "Time enough for us to talk later."

Sally hid a smile. She could see it was a toss-up as to whether the children or the earl himself was the more relieved as they ran back into the court.

She tried very hard in the following days to make friends with them all, and to a surprising degree she succeeded. Even prickly Catherine and her gruff younger brother Trevor came to like her and trust her. But then Sally had fond memories of her own little brothers and sisters whom she would never see again, and an easy way with children. She soon discovered she had not lost her knack for telling stories, stories that not even the fourteen-year-old Reginald scorned, although he much preferred riding with his father.

Somewhat to Sally's surprise, the earl entered into family life with gusto. As he had done with so many people of all ages so many times before, he charmed the children. And if sometimes they grew boisterous, or he wearied of their company, there were always the servants to take them away until the next time he was ready to be amused by them.

As soon as the earl had sent a message saying they were in residence, Sir Thomas Avery was quick to ride over. He found Harry in his library, and after greeting each other the two settled down to exchange news. Eventually, Sir Thomas inquired for the countess.

"Oh, she's about somewhere," the earl said carelessly. "Probably with the brats. You must know,

Thomas, she cajoled me into sending for 'em. To my astonishment, it has worked out very well. Not that I'd care to see 'em en masse every day, you understand, but as brats go they are not too despicable. Margarite adores 'em. I have never been able to understand why women dote so on brats. I don't."

Sir Thomas laughed at this tepid fatherly praise for his progeny. "But somehow I cannot imagine you with children, sir," he said, shaking his head.

"Nor can I. But fatherhood seems to happen to married men with great regularity," the earl remarked wryly. He frowned suddenly. "I do beg your pardon, my friend! I forgot your wife's death in childbirth."

Sir Thomas waved a dispassionate hand. "It was a good many years ago, and Éloise and I were not a happily married couple. Strange, that. She was such a darling before we wed, and such a harridan afterwards."

"Is that why you were never tempted to matrimony again?" the earl asked idly.

"Perhaps. Who can say?" Sir Thomas said, as he rose and walked over to the window. Suddenly he leaned closer, his eyes growing keen. The countess—Margarite—sat on the grass a short distance away, under an ancient beech tree. Grouped around her was a rapt semicircle of children, all as still as mice.

"I say, Harry, what a lovely picture they make," he said over his shoulder.

His host joined him, and when he saw where Sir Thomas was pointing he chucked. "I forgot. It is the story hour. Margarite regales them each afternoon with a story before their tea. She is very good at it—all fairies and dragons and lovely ladies, secret gardens, talking rabbits, magic stones. I must admit she even caught my interest one afternoon. And look there, how intent Reginald, my oldest is, although he would die of shame if he thought anyone knew of it."

But Sir Thomas was not looking at the earl's heir. No, for he had eyes only for the beautiful Countess of Darlington. Dressed in a simple white muslin gown, and with her wide-brimmed straw hat lying on the ground beside her, she was leaning toward the children as she spoke, using her hands for emphasis as she wove her tale. How lovely she is, he thought bleakly. And what a damned fool I am to want her, when she is so unattainable.

Sir Thomas was often at Reath Court from then on, and if he found Harry out riding, seeing to his lands, he sought out the countess, perfectly content. He felt like a moth, drawn helplessly toward the bright light of her. More often than not she had a child or two in tow, and she looked happier than she ever had in all the time he had known her.

His house party assembled the following week, and he had less time to ride to Reath Court. But now, of course, the earl and countess came to him, to dine with his guests and enter into all their amusements. It tore at Sir Thomas's heart to see the countess in his home. What he wouldn't have given to have her installed there permanently.

The earl was diverted when his Margarite captured the hearts of two of the guests, only one of whom, unfortunately, was unmarried. The other gentleman's wife took umbrage in spite of Margarite's indifference to her husband, and the pair suddenly found themselves called away on urgent family business.

"It was too bad of you, you know," Sir Thomas told her the next time the Tredmans came to visit. "Mrs. Wakeford will never come here again. And poor Jack! What a miserable life he'll be leading for a few months!"

"I am sorry to hear of it," Sally told him, her eyes worried. "But you must know I do nothing to encourage them. It is all just their own . . . foolishness. I do wish Lord Canby would leave as well. He annoys me so, he is so silly!"

"Harry seems to find him a great joke," Sir Thomas said, as he helped her over a rough patch of ground. The two had lingered behind the others on a stroll by the lake.

"Yes, it amuses him," Sally said absently. She looked around, and then hastened her step. "We must hurry, sir. The rest of the party are almost out of sight around the next bend."

"Harry does trust me, you know," he said. "You may do so as well."

She turned those wide-spaced blue eyes of hers to his, looking concerned. "Of course he does; we both do. You are our friend. I . . . I did not mean I didn't trust you!"

He stared at her for a moment, then he shrugged. "I know you did not. You are only concerned about what the others would say, or think—especially the women. Is that not so?

"I tell you, countess, I wish I had never invited any of them."

Sally was going to ask why he would say such a thing about his guests, but something in his tone of voice, some little bitterness, stayed her tongue.

She liked Sir Thomas, she had always liked him, but today she was glad when they were surrounded by people again and she could seek her husband's side. She did not notice how the earl's eyes narrowed in speculation as she rejoined the group, arm-in-arm with their host.

Harry himself had escorted a certain Lady Susan Holland on the afternoon's walk, and that young woman had teased him about his beautiful wife's conquests.

"But it is too bad, m'lord, that your lady has ensnared your own good friend as well," she had concluded, her voice light and amused. "And I do assure you, I am not the only one who has noticed how often he seeks her side, nor the light in his eyes when he does so. Give you my compliments!"

"On Margarite's success, ma'am?" Harry had asked politely.

Lady Susan had shaken her head. "Of course not! Rather, on how very tolerant you are! Would that more men were like you, and not so apt to fly into a jealous rage at the sight of their wives amusing themselves with others. You are a most enlightened example to them."

Harry had returned a light answer, but when Margarite and Thomas appeared he had to admit the man did seem more than attracted, and he was sorry for it. He was not at all concerned, however, and only moments later he had put the entire incident from his mind.

A few days later Sir Thomas held a country ball, including those of his neighbors worthy of cavorting with his noble guests. The local squires, their wives, and their sons and daughters swelled the party, and it was a festive evening.

Sally was standing on the terrace, fanning herself after a vigorous schottische with a romp of a boy, when she heard someone say behind her, "Sally! Oh my love, how delightful to see you again after all this time!"

Without thinking she turned quickly, a smile on her face. She surprised a pair of ladies, greeting each other with a kiss and a fond embrace. But of course, she told herself as she turned away, trying to still her racing heart. No one here knows me by that name. Whatever was I thinking of?

"Forgive me, but I could not help noticing," she heard Sir Thomas say, and she turned again to see him approaching, bearing two glasses of punch. "Tell me, were you a 'Sally' at one time in your life?"

Sally studied his face, those kind eyes half-hidden by their sleepy lids, his air of concern. He was Harry's friend, and hers as well, she told herself. There couldn't be any harm in telling him.

"Yes, I was called Sally as a child," she admitted. "I never understood why, when I was named Margaret for my grandmother. Harry did not care for either name. It was he who decided I was to be 'Margarite.' "

"I understand you grew up in Ireland? Whereabouts?" Sir Thomas asked, as he settled down on the wall nearby. "Here, it is dry. You won't harm your gown. Sit down and talk to me, if you please."

As Sally obeyed she said, "In County Wexford."

"You have no brogue."

"Why, an' ter be shure and sairtain, I had a therrible brogue at one time, sor," she said in jest. As he chuckled she added more softly, "A very dear friend of mine helped me to lose it."

"Wexford . . ." he mused. "I myself spent some time in that county, when I served with His Majesty's troops there years ago. It is a lovely place."

"But poor. So very poor," Sally said.

He turned toward her suddenly, putting his punch glass down on the wall beside him. "Sally . . . Margaret . . ." he murmured. His voice died away for a moment and then he said, "Sally-er-Margaret Desmond! Why, it was *you*!"

"Me? What do you mean?" she asked, a little concerned at the gleam in his eyes, his broad smile, and the way he was bending toward her.

"*You* were the little girl I gave that coin to!" he told her, smiling even more broadly. "I remember that afternoon now. We had gone out for a drive to see the countryside, and there was an accident—to the harness, if I remember correctly—which forced us to wait in a tiny village until the groom could have it fixed.

"But how marvelous! And that, of course, is why I have always felt I knew you from somewhere. Do you remember that day, Sally-er-Margaret Desmond? You were playing with a group of village children, eight or nine you must have been at the time, and—"

"I was ten, and I remember it very well," Sally said, smiling now as broadly as he was. "How very strange that we should meet again after all these years! How almost miraculous, that you should have been my husband's groomsman! And do you know, I have that sovereign you gave me still?"

"You do?" he asked, taking her hands in his and squeezing them gently. "But why did you keep it? Didn't I tell you to spend it on pretty things? I am sure I remember doing so."

Sally nodded, and she was still smiling as she said, "So you did, but I couldn't do that. No, for I believed it to be a *magic* coin, meant to bring me good luck, and you, a wizard disguised in a red coat. But tell me, what happened to the beautiful lady you had with you? I can still remember how awed I was by her pink stockings, that lovely hat she wore with all the plumes."

"That was Eloise," he said, his smile gone. "She was my bride then. She has been dead for eight years. She died in childbirth."

"Oh, I am so sorry," Sally said quickly.

"We discovered we were ill suited, but still I agonized that she had to die that way," he told her. "But come! You must tell me everything that has happened to you since I saw you in that village lane. And *did* the sovereign bring you good luck? I hope so!"

To his surprise, she hung her head, and he could see she was biting her full lower lip. All the joy that had been in her face moments ago for their strange reunion was gone as if it had never been. "I—I cannot," she said at last, in a voice so soft he had to lean closer to hear it. "My life after that was not pleasant, any of it. And Harry has asked me to forget Ireland, never mention it again. I—I would obey his wishes."

"Of course. I did not mean to pry," he told her gently.

She looked up at him then, and he saw the anguish in her eyes. He wondered what could possibly have happened to her to make her look that way. Even, he wished he had been a wizard, and able to save her from it, whatever it had been.

"Thank you. You are kind. But I must return to the drawing room now. The earl will be wondering where I am, and your guests must be missing you as well."

Sir Thomas rose and held out his arm to her. As they strolled toward the terrace door, he said, "Please allow me to say before we part that I am delighted to see that you obeyed at least one of my orders, ma'am. As I recall, I foretold the beauty you would be someday, and I begged you never to grow worn and ugly. And of course you have not. You are the most beautiful woman I have ever seen."

"Ah, don't!" Sally cried, turning her head away. "This face of mine has caused me more problems than you can imagine. Sometimes I have even wished I had never possessed it."

He was confused by the bitterness in her voice, but obediently, he fell silent.

As they neared the house again, Lady Susan Holland dropped the drapery she had been holding back to observe them during their meeting, and moved gracefully away from the window. None of the other guests could know, from her pleasant smile and amusing words as she joined them, that she was seething. The lady had come on this visit fully intending to become Sir Thomas's next wife. Generally admired for her cool blond good looks, petted and spoiled, she was now furious. But she would have her revenge. Oh, yes. There could be no doubt of that.

Later, on the drive home to Reath Court, Sally thought the earl very gay. But he had spent the evening making the acquaintance of the local squires' wives, and now he regaled her with an account of the absurdities he had heard until she was convulsed. Laughing so hard she could not speak and beg him to stop, she clutched his arm with one hand, and reached up with the other to press her fingers against his lips.

Harry fell silent at once, his own hand coming to hold hers in place so he could kiss those fingers tenderly, one by one. He was tempted to put his arms around her, really kiss her, but he could see in the flickering lights of the side lanterns that she looked both confused and uneasy. He dropped her hand and moved away from her, changing the subject as he did so to give her time to recover.

Sally was confused. Confused, and warm all over. But surely she was used to Harry's kissing her hand by now, was she not? Why did she feel this way? Perhaps it had been the light in his eyes as he smiled down at her?

Briefly she considered telling him what she and Sir Thomas had discovered, for it still seemed almost a miracle. Surely the odds of such a thing happening must be infinitesimal, and how intrigued Harry would be to hear of it! But after giving it some thought, she decided not to. This coincidence involved Ireland, and Harry had been very firm when he told her she must forget that part of her life, and never speak of it again. And they were becoming so close now, she could not bear to do anything that might bring even a whisper of coolness back into their relationship.

She began to relate other anecdotes of the evening instead, but her reticence was something she would have occasion to rue in the future.

Two days later, Sally received a note from Sir Thomas Avery. The Tredmans had not seen him since the ball, for the earl had been busy with estate matters. Even today he had been preoccupied at breakfast, and moody. He had told her he must ride out, and she was not to expect him till dusk. He had gone alone, too. She remembered how disappointed Reginald had been at being left behind.

She opened her note with a little frown. Somehow she did not feel it was correct for Sir Thomas to be writing to her alone, and remembering some of his words to her on the terrace she prayed that he at least was not turning into a lovesick idiot. It would be so very uncomfortable if he did, friend of Harry's as he was.

The note was written in a strong, back-slanted hand. It begged her to meet him halfway between their two estates, and it said that he had a most important matter to discuss with her, one that must be kept private. Sally was still frowning when she read it again. She did not want to go to the wood Sir Thomas mentioned; she knew it might lead to trouble. But the note was so somber—seemed so urgent—that she felt she had little choice. Besides, there was nothing of the lover in the few lines he had penned.

Accordingly, she summoned her maid and sent a message to the stable that she would require her mare to be saddled.,

Little Catherine hung about her dressing table fingering the perfume flasks there, while her younger sister Sophie sat, admiring, on a chair, her fat little legs stuck straight out before her, as Sally was buttoned into her habit and her riding hat was adjusted on her curls.

"Now, my good girls, you must run away to your nanny," Sally told them, as she put on her gloves and took up her crop.

"You *will* be back in time for our story, *won't* you?" Catherine asked, sounding fierce.

Sally put her hands on both the little girls' shoulders as she propelled them to the door. "As if I would miss that," she said, her eyes dancing. "I quite long to know what will happen next, as much as you do!"

"You mean you don't know?" Catherine asked, her brown eyes wide.

"Don't know?" little Sophie repeated solemnly.

Suddenly, Catherine erupted in a peal of laughter. "Course you do! You are bamming us, aren't you? Bad, bad lady!"

"Bad," Sophie said with an angelic grin.

Sally watched them as they ran to the nursery, their laughter echoing in the hall, but the smile she had worn for them faded away as she went down the stairs. What could this summons from Sir Thomas mean? she wondered. Was she being wise in answering it?

She reached the wood he had named a short time later. There was a narrow bridle path that led through it, and she walked her mare along it, not even admiring the cool green shade or the soft chirping of the birds high above her.

Sir Thomas was before her, in a little glade deep in the woods. His face was stern, those lazy eyelids of his effectively masking his expression. Sally felt her heartbeat quicken.

"What is the matter?" she asked without preamble as she reached him. "Why did you send for me this way?"

At that his brows rose. "I? I was about to ask you the same thing. I did not send for you, m'lady. I came in response to your note, begging me to meet you here."

Sally patted the mare, as she sidestepped nervously at the harsh tension in his voice. "But I did no such thing," she told him. "Who did, do you suppose? And why?"

"I fear someone is making mock of us, ma'am," he told her with a frown. "Obviously, for whatever reason they might have had, someone wanted us to be together here. Should you care to hazard a guess as to who that someone might have been? I confess I am at a loss to do so, myself."

Suddenly Sally remembered one of Sir Thomas's guests, the young widow named Susan Holland. Lady Susan had not appeared to approve the amount of time her host lavished on Countess Darlington, for more than once she had sent Sally a speaking glance of scorn. Would she have been mean enough to make mischief? Sally wondered.

Not wishing to name names when she had no proof, she said, "I have no idea either. But I do not think it wise for us to remain here alone together. I give you good day, sir."

As she started to turn her mare, he reached out and grasped her bridle. "Sally! Don't be so hasty, I beg you! Please stay and talk to me for a while. We have so little time for that, just the two of us."

His voice was pleading, and as if he were suddenly aware of it he added in a lighter, more teasing tone, "After all, so much has passed between us, has it not? Surely you have not changed that much from the Irish lass I once admired! She did not run away from me; no, she held her ground, although I could see she was afraid.

"And remember the *magic* we shared? I would exact payment for that magic now. Please, Sally. Dismount and stay with me. And even if it be for a short time only, I will be content."

Sally stared at him. He looked so kind, so caring. And yes, she did remember that afternoon, and his largesse. She liked Sir Thomas so much. Surely it

couldn't hurt, just to talk to him for a few minutes—
remember Ireland and her childhood there.

She nodded, feeling a little breathless with her daring, as she unhooked her leg from the pommel. He
caught her up as she slid to the ground. Sally was
quick to step away from his arms.

"I wonder what there is about this place?" she
asked, looking around. "Somehow it appears threatening—and I can't imagine why. It seems peaceful,
and yet it is not."

Sir Thomas had been tying her mare to a branch
near his own, and as he came back to her he looked
skeptical. "I feel nothing unusual. Are you nervous,
Sally? There is no need to be. You know me. Here,
sit down, m'lady."

As Sally took a seat on the huge oak stump he
indicated, and he sat down beside her, she said, "Yes,
I am a little nervous, I suppose. How ridiculous! But
I think it is because of those mysterious notes we received. I feel someone is trying to serve us a bad turn
somehow."

"How could they?" he asked. "There is no one here
but the two of us. And I myself am grateful to whoever this letter writer is. I never thought to have the
chance to see you alone like this.

"Tell me, do you and Harry remain at the Court
much longer?"

"I have no idea of Harry's plans," Sally said absently. She hated how conscious she was of Sir Thomas's broad shoulder behind her, the way his arm was
almost touching hers. And she hated her uneven
breathing, the quickened beat of her heart. Surely her
body was behaving in the most preposterous manner!
She did not understand it at all.

Reminding herself that this was Harry's good friend,
Sir Thomas Avery, she continued, "I am sure the children will be leaving soon, however. The boys must
get back to school. How I shall miss them all!

"But tell me, do you stay, and your guests as well?"

"They leave at week's end. I would hasten the day,
if I could. I have no idea of my own plans at the

moment. While you remain here, I have no desire for London."

"Please!" Sally exclaimed, turning toward him in her distress. "Oh, please do not play the lover with me, not you, our friend!"

She saw his expression change, how he struggled with his feelings, and she was alarmed. To her relief he only said, "Very well, if you insist on it. I will obey your wishes, ma'am.

"But in return for my forbearance, I want you to explain why you will not tell me about Ireland, and what happened to you there. Harry need never know any of this; your honesty cannot affect him. And there is such a gap in my knowledge of your life. I even had trouble sleeping last night, trying to imagine what it could be that was so bad you could not tell me of it. Please, do so now."

When she did not speak, or look at him, he reached out to grasp her chin in one big hand and turn her face to his. "Come, my dear. We are private here. Is it so hard to be honest with me?"

Sally saw his expression change subtly, saw how his mouth tightened for a moment as he stared down at her and she tried to twist her chin from his grasp. He did not let her go. Instead he bent suddenly and kissed her, full on the mouth. Her hands came up to push him away, but he crushed them against his chest as he put his arms around her and held her close.

She was helpless, and she knew it. But now, strangely, she did not feel frightened, or even alarmed. His kiss was tender, even reverent. It did not threaten her in any way, nor did it demand something she could not give. But for all of that, it was a lover's kiss. Horrified, she felt herself begin to respond to it—experienced a warm, liquid feeling coursing through her traitor's body—and she was ashamed.

At last he raised his head, but she could not open her eyes. She did not dare.

"Sally, forgive me," he said, his whisper husky.

Reluctantly she looked at him, and when she saw

the light in his eyes, she gasped. They did not look lazy now.

"I know I had no right to do that," he went on. "But just once, just . . . this . . . once, I could not help myself. Forgive me that I stole that memory, for all the empty years that lie before me that I must spend without you."

Sally struggled a little, and he let her go. Quickly, she got to her feet and backed away from him. Her eyes were huge in her pale face, and she put her gloved hand to the lips he had just kissed.

He rose as well. "Sally, my dear," he said, his voice a caress. "Now you know how I feel about you, and I am not sorry you do, although I never meant for this to happen. Believe me, I did not, just as I never meant to love you. But I could not help myself, friend of Harry's though I may be. You are too lovely, too sweet. And you will never know how much I regret that you can never be *my* Sally, instead of *his* Margarite."

Sally's thoughts were chaotic. She knew she could not speak. How could he have done such a thing to her—to them both—he who called himself Harry's friend? And what was happening to her that she had felt such an answering rush of emotion, so that even now she was still experiencing the sensation of his mouth on hers, the strength of his arms, his warm, caressing hands?

She had been wrong to come here, and wrong to stay. She should have remembered that people were not to be trusted. It appeared she could not even trust herself!

She shook her head as if to clear it, then hurried to untie her mare and lead her to a smaller stump so she could mount. To her relief, Sir Thomas remained standing where she had left him. He was now as silent as she was, but he stared at her as if he were trying to memorize her features, one by one. Mounted, and with her habit settled in place, she stared back at him for a long moment.

At last she wheeled her mare. As she did so, he raised one hand in farewell.

"Remember my love for you, Sally," he called as she rode away. "Know it will never change!"

Chapter Thirteen

SALLY DID NOT RETURN to Reath Court for a long time.

When she had first left the little glade behind her she had had to concentrate on her seat, her hands were trembling so on the reins. Then, since she did not think she could face anyone at home, especially the arrogant, all-seeing earl, she had gone for a long ride about the estate. When at last she trotted up the drive she saw the children were waiting for her under the beech tree. Of all of them Catherine looked the most betrayed, and Sally forced her own problems from her mind as she gave her mare to a groom so she could hurry to them.

She begged all their pardons most humbly for forgetting the story hour, and she promised that her tale would be twice as long on the morrow to make up for her lapse. Absentminded still, she did not wait to hear their reaction to this before she turned away.

She found the house in a great uproar, with footmen and maids scurrying about bearing clothes and boxes and portmanteaus. When she questioned the butler, he told her that Lord Darlington had announced everyone's departure. The children were to return to their own homes, and he and the countess also would be taking coach first thing in the morning.

Sally did not understand, but still she nodded. "Is the earl in the library?" she asked, as she gave him her crop and her gloves.

"Yes, m'lady, but he has asked not to be disturbed, for any reason whatsoever. Quite definite about it, he was."

Sally nodded again. Whatever was going on? she wondered, as she went upstairs to change. Harry had said nothing to her about such an early departure. Was there some problem in town he had only just learned of? Had something happened on one of his other estates?

As she reached the landing, another idea occurred to her. Could it be possible that Harry had grown bored with rural life, and decided on the spur of the moment to end their stay here? But of course! she thought, shaking her head ruefully. And how very like her mercurial husband!

Still, as she hurried along the upper corridor to her room she told herself this departure was most certainly an excellent idea. For now she would not be forced to see Sir Thomas again, forced to smile and chat with him as if everything were just the same. She suspected everything would never be the same, but perhaps this time apart would help her pretend that it was when next they met.

She found Preston already hard at work packing, and all the clothes spread about the room waiting to be folded and placed in the trunks. She quickly changed to a simple muslin gown so she could help with the task.

Later, the butler brought her a message that the earl had begged to be excused from dining. He claimed such a press of work that he intended to have a tray at his desk. Sally asked for a tray as well. The packing was nowhere near accomplished, and besides, she wanted to go along to the nursery and the other children's rooms to bid them each a lengthy farewell.

When she came downstairs early the following morning she found the carriages already lined up in the drive, all the travelers milling about. It was a noisy, confusing scene.

There were more good-byes, more embraces, and there was such a lump in Sally's throat for Sophie's tears and Catherine's fierce hug, to say nothing of Reginald's hard handclasp, that until she had taken her seat in the carriage she did not notice that she was

to be in solitary splendor. It seemed the earl had
elected to ride.

Well, it was a nice morning for a ride, she thought,
as she settled her skirts and grasped the side strap as
the heavy coach lurched into motion. But still, she
regretted she had not had a chance to question Harry
about this sudden move. It was then she realized she
had not seen him since the previous morning. Even
today a groom had helped her into the coach, for the
earl had been busy settling all his offspring in theirs
and giving final instructions to their attendants and
escorts.

When they stopped for luncheon some hours later,
the earl was still nowhere to be seen. Her maid told
Sally that she had heard that his horse had lost a shoe,
and he was attending to that at the blacksmith's. He
had said they were not to wait for him, for he would
catch them up later in the afternoon.

Sally ate her luncheon with a worried little frown
on her face. It was most unlike the earl not to hand
his horse over to a groom to be seen to, and ride
another one. It occurred to her then that perhaps the
earl had somehow discovered her meeting with Sir
Thomas, and he was angry with her; even avoiding
her. But no, she told herself, that was not possible.
There had been no one in the glade or the wood but
the two of them, and they had left it in different direc-
tions and at different times. It could not be that.

Still, as the coach thundered along the roads later,
Sally wondered at the desperate pace they kept.
Something dire must have happened for Harry to de-
cree such speed! She was tired when they stopped for
the night at an inn she remembered. The childrens'
carriages had been left far behind. She would not see
them again this journey.

Of the earl there was still no sign, and her questioning of his valet gained her nothing. Griffen flushed
as he always did when he was forced to speak to her,
saying he had no idea where his master could be. He
did reassure her, however, that the coachman had his
orders, and she would be perfectly safe.

Their pace slowed when the cavalcade neared London a day later. Eventually they pulled up at an inn in Merton, and still Sally fretted, for no earl appeared. Where could he be? Had he run into trouble somewhere on the road?

After she had drunk some hot coffee in a private parlor, and gone outside again, she discovered that all her baggage, and her maid's as well, had been transferred to her coach. Miss Preston joined her for the first time as well.

Definitely alarmed now, Sally questioned her closely, but Preston had no knowledge of why such a thing had been done.

They were on their way moments later. Sally looked in vain for St. James's Square as they traveled slowly through the busy London streets. How noisy they are, she thought, how crowded, even today when a fine cold rain is falling. She missed the quiet of the country already, although she was looking forward to her own sumptuous rooms, a good meal, and finally—*finally*— an explanation from her husband.

But the coach did not go to St. James's Square, and when at last their pace quickened again Sally looked from the window and saw they had left London behind. She noticed there were no other carriages with them now—why, even the earl's sporting phaeton had disappeared—and they traveled on alone, with a groom on either side of the coach their only escort.

It was very strange, very disquieting, but she could not discuss it with Miss Preston. That would not have been seemly. Eventually Harry would tell her what it was all about. She must wait for him to do so.

As the afternoon wore on Sally began to recognize some landmarks, or she thought she did. Surely they had passed through this village on their way to Darlington Hall, had they not? she asked herself, peering through the rain-spattered window of the coach. And wasn't that the church spire in Ware she could see in the distance? Was her destination Darlington Hall? But Harry had said they would never go there again. Pray it was not an emergency! Pray there had been

no fire! Remembering the vindictive dowager countess, she would not have put such a thing past her,
even as obese as she was.

It was almost four in the afternoon when the coach
turned between the heavy iron gates Sally remembered, and she could not suppress a shudder. For if
the Hall had looked grim on the lovely June morning
when she had visited it first, today, in the gloom and
the rain of early autumn, it was three times as
ominous.

As the coach slowed before the front door and
stopped, she almost cried out to the coachman to go
on—to leave! But she forced herself to sit quietly as
the door beside her was swung open. To her astonishment, her long-absent husband stood there. He did
not look at her. Instead he beckoned impatiently to
her maid.

"Out with you, Preston," he said. "Go inside. Tell
the servants the countess is here, and start making
preparations for her comfort. She will join you in a
moment. For now, I must speak to her alone."

Obediently, Preston left the coach. The earl climbed
in and took her place, shutting the door behind him
with a decisive snap. Bewildered, Sally stared at him
where he sat across from her. His face was pale and
set and tired, but it was his eyes that drew the gasp
from her, they were so filled with fury.

"What is it, Harry?" she asked, leaning toward him.
"Why do you look at me that way? Where have you
been ever since we left the Court? And why did you
bring me here?"

"I have brought you here because this is to be your
home from now on, madam," he said coldly, those
burning eyes never leaving her face.

"I believe I told you once that I would not tolerate
deception on your part, did I not? That I expected
honesty from you at all times? But you have not been
honest with me, now have you?"

"But I have, I have!" Sally protested. "What can
you mean?"

Suddenly he leaned forward and grasped her wrists

so tightly that she cried out. "Have you indeed?" he asked, sneering at her. "And what do you call your secret meetings with Sir Thomas Avery, ma'am? Your trysts held deep in the woods? How many times did you two meet, not only there but in Ireland years ago? How long have you been lovers?"

Only conscious of the pain in her wrists, Sally moaned, "Oh please, you are hurting me! Please let me go!"

To her relief, he released her immediately. But when she saw how he took out his handkerchief and wiped his fingers where they had touched her, she felt ill, so ill she could not answer him. For even though she and Sir Thomas had never been lovers, she could not help remembering how her body had responded to his embrace, and she was ashamed.

"There is no need to make up any lies. Indeed, I see you are having trouble thinking of any. I suppose I must thank Lady Susan for sending me that note, telling me of your affair and your meeting. I might never have known, otherwise, such a little innocent as you appeared to be," he went on as he sat back, seemingly at ease. Still his eyes accused her, and Sally cringed.

"I was there, you see. I could not hear all your conversation, I was too far away for that. But I saw *my friend* caressing you, saw the kiss you shared. I even heard him call you 'Sally' as you rode away, heard him beg you to remember his undying love. Bah! I wonder you can still look me in the face, you sly, deceiving adulteress!"

"No, no, it is not what you think, Harry," she forced herself to say. "You must let me explain . . ."

"Would you still deny that kiss even now?" he asked quickly. When she could only shake her head, he went on, "It does not matter. Enough! I want no explanations from you. In fact, I never want to see you again.

"It is for that reason that I have had you brought here, madam. Unfortunately, and to my sorrow, you are now the Countess of Darlington. And since I do not care to endure the scandal that there would be if I named you in a crim. cons. case, I must allow you that title.

"But I don't want you near me—ever.

"After thinking it over, I decided to take a leaf from my father's book. I am sure you remember how he forced my mother to live here, never let her leave. So shall you live, alone—in this dark, depressing mausoleum. I wish you joy of it!

"You will not want. Mr. Bourne will see to your expenses, as before. Write to him, and to him only, for I will never communicate with you again.

"But know as well, and by my order, that you will not leave here—not even once. Indeed, the only way you will ever escape Darlington Hall is when you are buried in its graveyard. No doubt it is vindictive of me, but I hope you live to be a very old lady."

Horrified, Sally stared at him. She could feel the squabs of the upholstery behind her shoulders; every tired muscle in her body. She could hear the wind as it whistled through the narrow cypress trees, the stamp of the horses' hooves, the faint jingle of their harness. She could even smell the scent that Harry always used, and the chill, damp aroma of the earth; she could see his burning, accusing eyes. But even though all those senses were intact, she could neither move nor speak.

"Hanks! Come here and meet your new, er, *mistress*!" the earl called, as he opened the door of the coach and prepared to step down.

Sally saw a large, brutish-looking servant coming forward, and she shivered.

"Hanks is to be your guard, madam," the earl said when he stood once more on the drive. "He will always be with you, so do not even attempt an escape."

He leaned closer then, peering at her where she still sat immobile in the carriage, and he said quietly, "You were not perfect after all, were you, goddess? Nor were you the unawakened, naive little woman I considered you once, and revered. But how you must have laughed at my reluctance to demean you by mak-

ing love to you! How it must have amused you to
make the proud Earl of Darlington a cuckold!"

Thinking how carefully he had treated her in the
weeks since their wedding, how almost *reverently* in
fact, he fell silent for a moment, struggling to overcome the urge to strike her, hurt her for her perfidy.
He had wooed her so slowly, doing nothing to frighten
or disgust her, and he had been willing to wait indefi-
nitely for her love, no matter how it pained him to
have her near him, so desirable and yet so unapproachable. And all the time she had been duping him
with one of his best friends, pretending an innocence
and a fear of men that were as false as he now knew
them to be ludicrous. He told himself he would always
hate her for her deception.

Taking a deep breath to steady himself, and glaring
at her, he said slowly, "Perhaps Colonel Jenkins was
right after all. Perhaps you are indeed the devil's
handmaiden. I should have known that such beauty
as you possess could not be normal. No, for it only
serves to mask the blackest heart in Christendom!"

He turned away so abruptly that Sally had no time
to reply, even if she had been able to find the words.
Shaken by his harsh, bitter condemnation, she allowed
the large man he had called Hanks to assist her from
the carriage and up the steps of the Hall. There was
a humming in her ears now, and what little light was
left seemed to fade when she saw the Hall looming
above her, all dark and gloomy. And this was to be
her prison forever. Only hers. She would never see
Harry again.

The humming she heard became a roar, and as she
fainted the dark Hall disappeared from her sight.

When Sally regained consciousness she found she
was lying on a large bed, Preston bending over her
with a vinaigrette. As soon as that had been taken
away she became aware of the musty odor in the
room, and she moaned a little and closed her eyes.

"There now, ma'am, it will be all right," Miss Preston told her. "I'll just help you undress, and ring for

some tea. And I'll change this bed as well, put on some of the fine linen sheets we brought with us. Here now, sit up, there's a good girl."

It was not the way her maid generally spoke to her, but Sally did not notice as she obeyed the order. Miss Preston had sounded as calm as she always had, and the kindness in her voice reassured Sally. Indeed, she even found it pleasant to be told what to do for her own good. It was as if she were a little child again.

Sally drank the tea that came, and managed to eat something before she let Preston put her back to bed and pull the covers over her. Even with the fresh sheets, the room still smelled musty.

"Now you get some sleep, ma'am," the maid told her, patting her cheek. "Time enough tomorrow to decide what's best to do. I'll not disturb you. But if you need anything—anything at all—just ring the bell. A good night to you, ma'am."

Sally closed her eyes. She was not just tired, she was exhausted, and only moments later she fell into a deep slumber. As she slept she dreamed—strange, disturbing dreams that later she did not want to recall.

She woke very early, as the room was only just beginning to lighten. She lay there, staring up at the dusty, torn canopy above her head, and made herself think about what had happened. She did not want to remember any of it—how Harry had looked, the terrible, hateful things he had said—but she knew she could not run away from the truth. He loathed her now. Loathed her so much he had condemned her to live in this ghastly place, and told her he never wanted to see her again.

But how was she to bear it? she asked herself, as the tears ran down her cheeks. How could anyone live in such a way, day after day, year after year, with only death to look forward to to release her? Why, she was not even twenty yet!

But perhaps Sir Thomas would come and find her, she thought, trying to look on the bright side. Surely when he discovered she was being held a prisoner here, he would not permit it. He had said he loved her. Surely he would save her.

Sally frowned then. How strange it was, what she was feeling. For even though Sir Thomas might well be her savior, somehow she did not want him to be. Yes, her body had responded to his kiss, his embrace, but now that she was away from him he was unimportant, merely Harry's friend. She had not regretted leaving him, had not even thought of him once on the journey here. She was not in love with him, she knew she was not.

Nor am I in love with any man, she told herself, her frown deepening. She sat up and rang the bell. For even if Harry did not want her anymore she was still his wife, still countess here. She would conduct herself accordingly.

Dressed in one of her simpler gowns, Sally went down to the small morning room, escorted by her maid. To her surprise Detts was there, even smiling at her a little. But surely Harry must have let him go, she thought, as she took the chair he was holding for her. He was so old.

Careful questioning revealed that Detts had indeed been pensioned off. "But when I heard as how you was arriving, m'lady, I took it on myself to come back," he said, as he poured her a cup of coffee. "No doubt you'd prefer a younger man, but until such time as he can be engaged, you'll need a butler."

He coughed a little before he went on. "The servants what was left here are a shiftless lot. Not a lick o' work will they do without supervision. For they know, or at least they *knew*, there was no one to see or care if they stinted on their chores. But now that I'm here to harry them, if you'll forgive the pun, we'll soon have the Hall looking much more the thing!"

Sally had to smile a little at his optimism, so at odds was it with his quavering, gloomy voice. The room she was in was a perfect example of the rest of the Hall—dark, dingy, neglected. It did not look as if it could ever be improved.

Then her chin came up, and she asked the butler

to bring her some paper and a pencil. There was work to be done, a lot of work. And first of all she must write to Mr. Bourne in London, for she was going to spend a great deal of money, almost immediately.

The earl had told her she would not want, had he not? Well, since she was forced to remain here, she would see to it that the Hall was restored to whatever former grandeur it might once have possessed. Starting, she reminded herself, with a good scrubbing from top to bottom, and a large bonfire of the discarded moth-eaten carpets and draperies. Then it must be painted, and after that—

Suddenly remembering something, she turned to the hovering butler and said, "Please assign some men to cut down every cypress tree in the avenue, Detts. They must be the first to go, and the sooner the better!"

As the butler nodded and left the room, Sally tucked into her breakfast with an appetite she had never expected to have again.

That afternoon brought the dowager countess and her brother calling. Sally was firm in denying them entrance. Harry had said his mother must never step inside the Hall again, and certainly she herself had no desire to see her. Even in the library where she was drawing up some lists Sally could hear the dowager's strident voice at the front door, her angered curses as she was turned away—and she shuddered. No, not the dowager, and never her oily brother! If I have to remain here let it be alone, she told herself, as she picked up another sheet of paper. Now, where was she?

The first few weeks of her stay Sally was so busy she almost fell into bed each night, exhausted as she was. But she knew the hard work was good for her. It kept her mind from her problems, allowed her to forget Harry's rejection, and gave her a dreamless sleep every night.

She had written him a long letter, explaining everything that had happened between her and Sir Thomas, first in Ireland when she had been a little girl, and later at the Court. It took her a long time, but she need not have bothered. Her letter was returned to her, unopened. Harry had certainly meant it when he said there would be no communication between them. It saddened her, but she did not try to write again.

The servants had been set to cleaning the Hall. Those who looked glum and stinted on their work were dismissed at once. They were replaced by others, good workers eager for the position. And it seemed to Sally that Detts grew younger every day as the Hall began to change. His step was lighter, and even his voice more animated.

And Miss Preston had been a godsend. She had taken over the role of housekeeper. "At least for now, m'lady," she had said, her kind eyes twinkling. "There's little enough for me to do as a lady's maid, after all."

Sally had worried that Preston might ask to leave her employ for just that reason, but when she had ventured to question her about it the maid reassured her. She knew all about the earl's ultimatum, for Sally had told her of it almost at once to explain her changed circumstances. To her relief, Preston had accepted the situation calmly.

"Nay, I'll not be leaving you, ma'am," she had said firmly. "You need me, and to tell the truth I've always liked a challenge. I don't believe I've ever seen such a formidable one as this before. But you'll see. You can change this old place, and I'll help you.

"And even though you're not permitted to leave the grounds, I was not told *I* couldn't do so, now was I? I can serve as your personal agent in town, even in London, whenever it's necessary, and that Hanks can't stop me, brute though he is!"

Sally had nodded her thanks, swallowing a lump in her throat as she did so for the woman's loyalty and good sense.

She herself had grown used to having Hanks trailing her about. He was as unobtrusive about it as he could be, and he never spoke to her unless addressed di-

rectly. Lately Sally had noticed that he left her alone
more each day, now that he was sure she was not
going to try to escape her imprisonment. But whenever she was outside, walking or riding, he was always
right behind her.

On one occasion, she had been very glad indeed
that he was so vigilant.

She had gone out for a walk late one morning, and
had wandered farther from the Hall than she generally
did. She was about to retrace her steps when she saw
a drive ahead.

Hoping it would show her a shorter way back she
made her way to it, and saw a smaller version of Darlington Hall at its end. Obviously she had come upon
the dower house, and not wishing to see the dowager,
with her foul mind and coarse language, she turned in
the other direction.

Only moments later she heard a carriage approaching,
and she stepped to the side of the drive to give it free
passage. But the open landau did not go on. Instead
it halted beside her, and she found herself staring up
into the identically fat faces of the dowager countess
and her brother, Bartholomew Worth, who was driving the team.

"But what a pleasant surprise," that gentleman said,
leering at her. "Have you been to call on us, my dear?
What a shame that we were not at home! But come,
do climb in and return with us. It's a brisk morning,
is it not? I'm sure you would enjoy a cup of tea.

"I say, Desdemona, do scrunch over a bit and give
the gel room."

"Please don't," Sally said quickly. "I do not have
time for calls this morning. I must get back."

The dowager, who had yet to say a word, leaned
over the side of the landau, causing it to tilt
alarmingly. The horses took exception to this, and for
a moment Mr. Worth had his hands full.

"You wasn't making a call at all, was you, girl?"
the dowager asked in her high, shrill voice. "Course
not! Think you're too good to associate with the likes
of us now, I imagine."

Her face was reddening with rage, and Sally took a tiny step away.

"Such arrogance from an Irish nobody! And I must say, I thought it was damned rude of you to forbid us entrance to the Hall the other day. We're your neighbors, as well as family!"

As she glared, Sally took another step. "I cannot admit you, ma'am. You heard your son's orders," she said.

The dowager snorted. "Why are you alone here, then? Where is he? Had a spat already, have you? Well, he was never an easy one to get along with, I can tell you that!

"Here, brother, give me the reins. I fear you must get down and *persuade* my new daughter-in-law to join us. I was just thinking how grand it would be if my son were to return and find his bride with child. Serve him right, the mean bastard!"

To Sally's dismay, the hefty Mr. Worth was obeying his sister with alacrity. Deciding that flight was imperative, she picked up her skirts and prepared to make a dash for it. But the skirt caught on a bramble, and by the time she had worked it loose Worth was upon her. He took her arm in a tight grasp as he said, "Now there, don't be so hasty, my dear! Just you come along, and we'll have a nice, er, *chat*."

As he grabbed her other arm and pulled her against his large stomach, Sally suddenly remembered Hanks, and she called his name as loudly as she could.

She was tremendously relieved when Bartholomew Worth abruptly let her go, his mouth falling open in shock as Hanks's fist caught him flush on the nose. Sally saw that her bodyguard was preparing to hit him again, and she cried, "No, no, Hanks! No more! 'Tis the earl's uncle!"

"Uncle, is he?" Hanks growled as his prey staggered away, clutching his bloody nose. "From wot I heered, he weren't about ter behave like *fambly*!

"Catch ye up ter any o' yer tricks again, mate, and ye won't live ter tell about it, ye won't!" he bellowed, as the landau was driven away at a rapid clip. "Be holdin' yer 'ead in yer 'ands, ye will!"

Gravely, Sally thanked her escort for saving her, something that made him flush and reminded her of the earl's valet. As she walked back to the Hall, Hanks a respectful three paces behind, Sally decided that from now on her walks would take her in a different direction, nowhere near the dower house. Get her with child? That fat, depraved old man? It made her ill just thinking about such a thing.

The cypresses were gone, and unlamented.

Sally had interviewed the earl's agent, a Mr. Bell, and told him the improvements she expected to make come spring. Mr. Bell had agreed to each and every one. Now that the harvest was in he had even set the earl's farmers to tearing down the rotting gazebo, clearing the lake of weeds, and getting rid of the dark ivy. He had promised to hire a head gardener he knew as well, to take charge of her proposed flower beds.

Mr. Bourne, the earl's banker, had responded to Sally's first letter immediately. He had told her that whatever funds she needed were at her disposal, and he had enclosed a large bank draft for her use. Sally had sent her maid to the nearest town to open an account for her at a bank the agent recommended, and to purchase some wool for new gowns. It was late October now and there was a bite to the air, and frosty mornings when the ground was covered with rime. The gowns she had worn at Reath Court would not keep her warm through the winter months.

Preston had brought her samples of brocades, damasks, and silks as well, and the names of several tradesmen anxious to be of service to the Countess of Darlington.

As she made decision after decision, Sally felt her confidence growing. She realized that she had allowed herself to drift too long, depending on Harry to make all the decisions because he had such a forceful personality. But now she began to trust in her own good taste, and she was able to say, "No, not crimson in this room. Soft greens, and peach and cream, I think. We will have the crimson in the library."

Of course she made some mistakes. She did not think she would ever forget her error in painting one of the smaller salons a buttercup yellow. A small sample of it had been cheerful. A roomful of it was blatant. Since Miss Preston assured her the maids adored the color the paint was not wasted, for Sally used it in the servants' rooms in the attics.

She did more than just renovate the Hall. She rode over the land inspecting the farmers' cottages as well, making mental notes of the work that must be done to make them more habitable. And she made arrangements for new thatching on the village roofs, after a ride there one day. Hanks had agreed with her, when she questioned him, that he had never seen roofs so badly in need of repair.

"Leaks, yer ladyship," he had said in his terse manner. "Rats. An' then there's them drains. Bad. Very bad. Just smell 'em."

Sally was fast gaining a rapport with Hanks that the earl would have deplored if only he had known of it. The huge man, so ugly and ungainly, was growing to adore his beautiful charge, even to feel sorry for her. He considered her a fine lady, but not one at all above herself. A real worker she was, he told himself.

Once the furniture had been stripped of its moldy upholstery, Sally could see that it consisted of handsome pieces from the Queen Anne and early Georgian eras, and she decided to keep all of it that was not affected with dry rot. She set the estate carpenters to repairing it, and hired seamstresses as well for the new draperies and hangings.

Soon the smell of fresh paint filled the Hall. It did not appear to distress the countess, for Sally could often be seen taking deep, appreciative breaths as she inspected a newly painted room, one with its floor sanded and refinished to a high shine.

She did worry sometimes about the expense of all the work she was having done. It seemed a staggering amount when she added up the bills. Surely Harry would be angry when he found out about it! But then she would tilt her chin in defiance. This was her home now, and whether the earl liked it or not she was countess here. The Hall must reflect her own good taste, and her desire to live in comfort. It might be a prison, but it was one that was going to be filled with color, rich fabrics, thick carpets, and newly restored paintings, all housed in gleaming cleanliness.

Besides, she had discovered in her talks with Mr. Bell that Darlington Hall was nowhere near the profitable enterprise it should have been. Hating it as he had, the earl had not bothered to utilize that side of it. But she would make it pay, she told herself and the beaming agent. Mr. Bell was a short, rotund little man with snapping dark eyes that didn't miss a thing. It was obvious to Sally that he felt his talents had been wasted up to now; he was so eager to agree to all her schemes for fallow fields, new kinds of crops, and better livestock. Sometimes Sally remembered Ballyragh, and thought how wonderful it could have been with an agent like Mr. Bell and unlimited amounts of money. She knew she had her early childhood to thank for teaching her how important it was for the land not only to pay its own way, but turn a handsome profit as well.

"We'll have it more than returning the expense of putting it to rights, mum," Mr. Bell said, as he folded his papers one afternoon following a conference with Sally. "Take a couple of years or three, it will, but then you'll see!"

Sally stared out one of the windows in the library after the agent had left her. It was another dreary late November day, and it looked very much like snow before morning. But that did not matter. The Hall was becoming warm and welcoming under her care of it, and there was enough to do here to keep her busy all winter.

Even so she found she had a great deal of free time on her hands, especially in the evenings. Work inside was progressing apace, and she could do nothing about the outside until warmer weather came.

She had decided to line the drive with rhododendrons, and she had drawn up plans for extensive gardens planted around the Hall. She had also interviewed a young architect, who had promised her the airy gazebo she envisioned by the lake. He had even proposed certain alterations to the front of the Hall to make it less forbidding. Sally was intrigued by his idea for a terrace to soften the approach, a terrace that would contain graceful urns full of flowers and shrubs come springtime.

Winter began in earnest one afternoon a week later, when large, fat flakes of snow spun down to cover the ground. Sally watched it falling for a while, her thoughts turning to the earl's children and their well-being. She did miss them so, all of them.

Was it snowing where they were, in Oxfordshire and Berks County? she wondered. Were they impatient to run out and play, build snowmen and forts, go sliding? Did Catherine smile when she saw the snow, and little Sophie crow in delight?

Sally remembered then that she had never kept her promise to the children. No, for she had not finished the story she had been telling them before they all had left Reath Court. Excited, she went to the library, ordered the fire made up and another branch of candles brought. But of course! She must write the end of that story, then copy it all out twice in its entirety in a fair hand, and send it to them as a Christmas gift. And perhaps they would enjoy it if she wrote others for them as well.

As she pulled her paper closer, and dipped her quill in the fat silver ink pot, she smiled. What fun this would be! She only wished she had some skill in drawing, so that she might illustrate the stories as well. Perhaps if she wrote to the Sir Thomas Lawrence who had painted her portrait, he would know of some young artist willing to undertake the commission?

*   *   *

Sally worked on her stories throughout the winter. To her delight, the children wrote to thank her for them, and she began a lively correspondence with them.

She was busy, and she told herself she was content. But she knew she was not happy. No, for even when spring came, and she was able to begin her gardens and supervise all the other outdoor work, too many mornings when she woke it was to find her cheeks wet with tears.

Sally knew why she wept in her sleep. It was because she was alone—so alone—even though she was surrounded by servants. But none of them, not even Miss Preston, could fill the void she felt.

In her short lifetime she had lost her family, and then her first and dearest friend. And now she had lost her husband as well.

She wondered where Harry was and what he was doing, and whether he ever missed her. She missed him, and she admitted it. She missed his unfailing kindness, his wit, his knowledge. But even more than those things she missed the touch of his lips on her hand and her cheek, his strong arms around her the few times he had held her close, even his flashing smile.

But Harry was lost to her. The only thing she could do was remember him, and take care of the Hall in a way that would make him proud of her. Be the kind of countess he deserved.

And then she wondered why that was so important to her, when he would never know of it.

Chapter Fourteen

1816

THE EARL OF DARLINGTON returned to London from abroad in May.

He had spent most of the time traveling since he had banished his young countess to Darlington Hall almost three years before, for he had found London insipid without her, and filled with the mocking stares of his contemporaries. Some had even dared to ask why he resided in town while his beautiful countess remained in the country. He had had no trouble dealing with such impertinence, not as arrogant and scornful as he could be, but none of it had been pleasant. Nor was it pleasant living in the house he had had decorated for her. Her rooms especially were a constant reminder of her absence.

Traveling became a way for him to escape his memories, and the conjectures, the snide little smiles—even the hint of pity he felt he detected on certain of his closest friends' faces as well.

But he never saw Sir Thomas Avery, for that gentleman had remained in East Sussex.

Early in the heat of his anger at his wife, Harry Tredman had written to Sir Thomas, telling him he knew all about his love for Margarite. He had even implied that he wrote the letter at her instigation, to tell him that there was no hope for him. Margarite did not care to see him again—ever.

It was strange, he mused to himself. He did not blame Thomas for what had happened, had never even considered calling him out, for the man was only mortal. And what mortal man could avoid falling in love with her? he had asked himself, his mouth twisting with the pain he still felt. No, his anger was only directed at her, for deceiving him. On her head alone lay the guilt.

Eventually the earl heard that Sir Thomas was traveling too, and this past year word had come that he had remarried, and was busy starting a family in the country.

So much for Thomas's undying love; Harry Tredman thought with a sneer. Would that Margarite could know of it! But although it would serve her right, and might even give her pain, he held fast to his decision never to communicate with her again. He told himself she was as dead in his eyes as if she were already buried in Darlington's graveyard, although more times than he liked he wondered how she was faring, and whether she found her imprisonment as lonely as he had hoped when he had ordered it. It was then that he began to drink more heavily, although he did not connect his drinking with her absence.

At first, with Napoleon still at large and intent on regaining his empire, the earl had had to avoid Europe. Instead he had sailed to India and Burma. But when the little emperor had been banished to the island of Saint Helena in the South Atlantic, all the continent was open to him again.

He dallied for months in Paris, renewing friendships from earlier years and making new ones as well.

One of these involved a young man, the Comte Jean-Pierre de Fountaine, who had been introduced by his uncle, the elderly Duc de Jullier. Earl Darlington had been much taken by the young man, still barely in his twenties. As handsome as Adonis, witty and amusing, and always elegantly dressed, the count was a superb horseman. It appeared to be his only real accomplishment, for like others of the nobility he spent his days and nights in idle amusement. Since Harry Tredman did so as well, they were instantly compatible.

But after several weeks, when the earl invited de Fountaine to join him on his travels, the count had raised his brows, looking most suspicious. The earl only chuckled and shook his head.

"*Non, non, mon ami*, my tastes do not lie in *that* direction. You may be easy," he had assured him. "Only consider the lovely Madame Bonheur who is currently in my keeping—and all the women before her. I ask you simply because I find you amusing, good company. And you are handsome. I have ever been a lover of beauty, and yours is outstanding."

Always in need of money, the count had agreed with a languid air that belied his relief. He knew the earl for a wealthy man, and his debts were piling up in an alarming manner. Certainly it would be wise for him to avoid Paris for a long time.

For many months the two had traveled together throughout the continent, even going as far as Greece and Turkey. It cost a great deal of money, for the young de Fountaine was an expensive companion. He would settle for nothing but the best, and since the earl agreed with him that anything less would not do for either of them, their travels required a small fortune. It required a large entourage as well, which came to be known as the Darlington Circus, half in mockery and half in envy.

But now, at last, in the spring of 1816, the two of them stood on the deck of the ship that had brought them to England, watching London come ever closer as it sailed up the Thames. They were there because Harry Tredman had grown jaded with traveling, his dilettante friends, his restless life. He had suddenly had a desire to see England again, to visit his estates and do some hard work for a change.

He installed the count in a suite of his own in the townhouse in St. James's Square, and he introduced him to the ton—and more importantly, to his tailor, his jeweler, and his bootmaker. Jean-Pierre was soon a welcome guest at any party, for he was universally admired. Young, tall, and slim as he was, with romantic dark curls that surpassed Byron's, he captivated the ladies. They found his handsome face and French accent impossible to resist. And he had only to appear

in public sporting a new style of cravat, or a coat with
a different lapel, to send all the gentlemen scrambling
to emulate him. Harry Tredman watched it all, and
he chuckled in amusement. He told himself that whatever the cost, Jean-Pierre was worth it.

By now he was well aware that the count was all
flash and no substance; greedy, amoral, and completely selfish. But what did that matter? he asked
himself. The boy was entertaining, and the earl knew
he needed to be entertained in order to take his mind
from his biggest failure—his countess.

He was sitting in his club early one afternoon, waiting for the count to join him after an appointment
with the tailor, when he overheard a conversation that
stunned him. Stunned, and angered him as well.

He was seated in a high-backed wing chair before
the fireplace at the time, hidden from the two gentlemen who had entered the room in animated conversation. He did not make his presence known, first
because he was nursing a terrible headache from too
much brandy the night before and did not want to talk
to anyone, and second because he heard his countess's
name mentioned almost at once.

"But how does one get an invitation to Darlington
Hall?" one young man asked, his voice eager.

The other's laugh was smug. "It is not easy. The
divine countess only invites a select few to her salons.
I understand she considers a man's knowledge and wit
more important than his rank. M'lord Brinks introduced me some months ago. I am forever in his debt.

"But an introduction is no guarantee that further
ones will be extended. All is merit.

"I understand she intends to have the Wizard of the
North at her salon tomorrow. What a treat it will be
to hear him read from his own works!"

"Walter Scott will be there? My word, what I would
not give to hear him!"

"Not only Scott. John Stevenson is to play for us—
the Irish melodies he wrote for Moore's verses. And
then there will be the glorious soprano, Señorita
Maria Alvarez."

"How I envy you! But tell me, is the countess as beautiful and talented as they say? I have heard such things I cannot believe them. It makes me anxious to see for myself."

"She is the most beautiful woman I have ever met, and the most unapproachable," his friend answered reverently. "One wonders why she remains in Hertfordshire, when she might have London at her feet. But no matter how she is implored, she will not leave Darlington Hall. She claims to dislike London, says that there is no need for her to bestir herself since all the interesting people come to her. Besides, she says, this way she is able to avoid the bores, the uneducated, the superficial.

"The countess is known for her honesty and her sharp wit, you see.

"But still it's strange, her situation," he went on. "And no one seems to know why she and the earl separated. She never mentions it. I understand he's been abroad for some years."

"Not the sort of thing one could ask either of them," the other gentleman said wryly.

His companion agreed. "But you may see her for yourself, even if you are not invited to the Hall," he said. "Sir Thomas Lawrence has painted her several times. His newest portrait will be shown at this year's Royal Exhibition.

"Have you read the countess's work? She wrote the most delightful book of stories for children, fables if you like. There are those who say they are as entertaining for adults as they are for the infantry. Parris illustrated them for her. Now she is at work on another book, for the first one was such a resounding success."

"Yes, I did read it. It was excellent. Still, I find it hard to imagine all those people driving out to Hertfordshire just to attend a salon, no matter how lovely and talented the countess is. You must agree it is most unusual."

"We do it in order to be able to enjoy her company, of course. And it is a pleasant drive, well under four hours. The guests are summoned for noon. After a repast, and a stroll through the grounds, the afternoon concert begins, sometimes by the gazebo near the lake, sometimes in the drawing room. Then there is some literary talk, and a lively discussion before dinner. There are some comfortable inns in the neighborhood, for no one is invited to stay at the Hall. A shame, that. The Hall is outstanding! Such lovely rooms, such beautiful things! Her gardens have to be seen to be appreciated, especially the rose garden."

"I must find a way to attend! I say, Charles, can't you do something? I'm sure I'm as literate as you are, as learned and musical—you must help me! After all, you claim to be my friend."

"I'll do what I can—not for tomorrow, of course, but next time.

"Oh, there's Gareth Fielding just come in. I must speak to him about his plans to go to the Hall tomorrow. Perhaps we can travel . . ."

The Earl of Darlington straightened in his chair as the two quit the room and their voices died away. His eyes were very cold as he did so. Could what he had just heard be true? Was Margarite extoled as a premier hostess—a *literary* figure—one whose salons were attended by the brightest and best? How had she accomplished such a thing in less than three years? She was so young—why, she was not even twenty-three years old.

It angered him to think that she was not suffering at all, that life at Darlington Hall agreed with her so, and the Hall was not the prison he had intended.

But surely he could not have heard correctly. The young man who had visited the Hall had called it beautiful, with lovely rooms, spacious and outstanding gardens. How could that be? he asked himself, mentally picturing the dark, ugly pile of stone he had exiled her to, the somber, neglected grounds, the depressing ambiance.

He was frowning as he rose and went to write the count a note. He would forgo their appointment. He knew Jean-Pierre would not mind. He had a most important call to make, for he intended to go to the city and question Mr. Bourne. If anyone knew what Margarite had been up to, it was sure to be his banker.

An hour later the earl's face was rigid with anger, and his frown even more pronounced. "*You* authorized all these expenditures, sir? *You?*" he asked a pale and nervous Mr. Bourne. "For thousands and thousands of pounds?"

"But—but you told me the countess was never to want, m'lord," the banker protested, trying to forget the earl's own massive expenses these past three years.

Harry turned over another bill, and his brows rose. "I do not believe I told you, however, that she was to live like royalty!" he snapped. "How much money has she spent in all?"

"Some forty thousand pounds—er, or a bit more, m'lord," Mr. Bourne admitted. As his noble client appeared to have been struck dumb by this information, he hastened to add, "Of course, the Hall is turning a good profit now. The countess, and your agent there, have been excellent overseers. I am confident we shall realize well over four thousand pounds this year alone against the debt."

Harry Tredman was not listening. Instead, he rose abruptly. "You are not to authorize any more money for Darlington Hall, do you understand? Not a penny, without checking first with me. I bid you good day, sir!"

He left his banker much bewildered. Taking a hackney back to the Square, he stopped at a bookseller's on the way. The count was not at home, nor had he expected him to be. He would talk to Jean-Pierre later, for he intended to travel early into Hertfordshire. So, Countess Darlington was giving one of her salons tomorrow, was she? As her husband, he was sure he need not be concerned that he lacked an invitation. He reminded himself that he must cancel his dinner engagement. He had a very interesting book to read instead, and a great many plans to make as well.

"*Mon cher* Harry, you know I would do anything for you, positively *anything*, but was it really necessary to drag me away from town only to attend a *literary* salon?" Count de Fountaine asked the following morning. He was not feeling at all in accord with his benefactor. No indeed, for had he not had to suffer being called at an ungodly hour of the morning, and forced to hurry his all-important toilette, just so that the earl could rush to his estate to see his long-forgotten wife? It was all most unfair!

"But you may find it amusing, dear boy," Harry Tredman said, his mouth grim. He was tooling his phaeton along the country roads at a rapid clip. Even so, and although it was still early, there was a lot of traffic, and often he was forced to slow the pace for a herd of cows, or a countryman's dray loaded with manure. He could tell from Jean-Pierre's sniff, the ostentatious way he waved his scented handkerchief before his nose, that he thought the entire expedition a disaster, but he did not care.

"Ah, we are approaching Darlington land now," he said, slowing his team so that he might more carefully inspect the fields and farms of his principal seat. His brows rose as they drove along. Surely he had never seen the place so prosperous, so busy, he thought, a little frown appearing on his face.

The count observed this sign of Harry's displeasure, and he wisely decided to hold his tongue.

To his regret, the earl did not go at once to his Hall. Instead he drove past several farms, turned off into small lanes, even stopped occasionally to converse with the yokels. Jean-Pierre shuddered at their dirty hands and humble dress, their uneducated voices.

"A most impressive herd, wouldn't you say?" the earl asked, stopping again to inspect some cattle grazing nearby. "It is all truly astounding, and whoever would have thought Margarite had it in her? And why ever does she bother, I wonder?"

"*I* have no idea," the count said, his voice testy. "Why don't you go to the Hall and ask *her*?"

The earl nodded in an absentminded way, as he gave his horses the office to start.

Some time later he turned between a pair of large ornate gates, and Jean-Pierre began to look more cheerful. As he was driven up a well-kept avenue bordered by magnificent rhododendrons in full flower, he felt even better. Farms and herds and peasants were a necessity for wealth, he knew, but the less he had to with them all the better. This was more like it, for it appeared they had returned to civilization again, and not a moment too soon for him.

"But how very impressive, m'lord," he said in genuine admiration as the phaeton rounded the last curve, and Darlington Hall appeared before them. "What a noble place!"

The earl did not reply. He was busy inspecting his seat—the soft, green, well-scythed lawns around it, and the gracious terrace with its flowering shrubs. He could see the gardens he had heard about stretched out on either side of the Hall. It was all so impressive and lovely, and he couldn't believe his eyes.

A groom came running to take charge of the team, his eyes popping in astonishment when he recognized his long-gone master.

The earl ignored the groom as well. It appeared to the count that he had retreated to some private world of his own. And after he had stepped down, he even strode to the terrace steps as if he were alone.

The loud clang he gave the knocker had barely stopped reverberating when the door was opened for them.

To Harry Tredman's surprise his old butler stood there, preparing to bow. But when he saw who the caller was, Detts gave a strangled cry, and his eyes rolled up in his head as he fainted and fell to the floor.

"*Mon dieu!* What an effect you have on your servants, Harry," the count remarked. "Now I am glad I came. I am sure to be entertained in royal fashion. Do you expect your countess will swoon as well?"

Once again, he was ignored. "You there, attend to Detts," the earl ordered one of the footmen in the hall. "There is no need for anyone to announce me. I am Earl Darlington."

"M'lord!" the footmen said in unison, as they bowed low.

Harry stepped inside, giving only a cursory glance to the recumbent figure of his old butler. He could see Detts was recovering consciousness and moaning a little, so he was not concerned for him. Instead he looked around, and as he did so his eyes narrowed. The gloomy hall he remembered was no more. Instead, light streamed in through a huge oriel window at the back. It revealed shining marble floors, graceful furniture, and rich hangings. On one wall he could see a portrait of his countess that he had never commissioned. Beneath it, on a side table, was a huge bouquet of roses in a silver vase. Their perfume scented the air.

"M'lord, oh, m'lord, that such a thing should happen!" he heard Detts say in his quavering voice, as a footman helped him to his feet. "I am so ashamed! It is just that I was not expecting you, sir—er, that is, the countess did not mention . . . I mean . . ."

"It's all right, Detts," the earl said over his shoulder. "I am only glad that you did not expire with the shock. Where is the countess?"

"She—she is still above stairs, m'lord. Today is her salon day, but the guests are not expected for an hour yet."

"The count and I will wait for her in the library," Harry Tredman said. "A glass of wine, *mon ami*? See to it, Detts! Or better yet, send one of the others. I would have you rest after your alarm. And you'd better have some wine as well."

Upstairs, Sally had just reached the stairs, and was preparing to come down. But when she heard that well-remembered voice below, she stiffened. Harry was back! He had come to the Hall after all! But why had he done so? He had told her he would never come here, never see her again.

Bewildered, and a little frightened, she went back into her room and closed the door behind her to lean against it, almost as if she were trying to keep someone, or something, out.

"Is there anything wrong, ma'am?" Miss Preston asked, her face concerned. She was tidying the dressing table, for she had been helping the countess, as she always did on these important occasions. Housekeeper or no now, her expertise was necessary, for the countess's country maid did not have the skill.

"The earl's come back," Sally whispered, her eyes huge in her pale face. "Harry has come *back*!"

Miss Preston thought for a moment before she came and took her mistress's arm. "There now, just you sit down for a moment, ma'am," she said in her calm, steadying way. "Yes, it must have been a shock to you, but there was always the possibility that he might return, was there not? Indeed," she went on, as she pushed Sally gently down into a chair, "I am only surprised that is has taken him so long."

"You are?" Sally asked.

The servant nodded. "But of course, ma'am. You are so beautiful, and he was so in love with you. How could he bear to stay away, no matter what he claimed?"

Sally decided there was no point in telling Preston the earl did not love her at all, that she was mistaken. But she knew Harry had not come because he could not help it. No, there was some other reason. But what could it be?

And today, of all days, she had guests arriving in less than an hour! Had anything been more unfortunate?

Her eyes grew thoughtful then. Perhaps Harry had heard of the salon? She knew how they were talked of in London, for many people had told her so. Some of the ton who were strangers to her had even written to her, begging an invitation. Had Harry come to see what she was up to? Or had he interviewed Mr. Bourne and learned of her expenditures? Was he angry at the amount?

Her chin came up then. If he was angry that was too bad, of course, but she would not regard it. She was the Countess Darlington, and here, in his place, she reigned supreme. After all, it was he himself who had decreed that she do so.

She rose then and straightened her skirts. "How silly of me to be so timid," she said to the hovering Preston. "I shall go down and welcome him at once. Thank you, Preston. The new gown looks splendid, does it not?"

"You are a picture," Preston assured her, smiling now. "You always appear to advantage in that shade of blue, and the lace Madame Clotilde insisted on is the perfect finishing touch.

"Er, will be the earl be remaining here, ma'am? Shall I see to having his rooms readied for him?"

Sally's hands flew to her cheeks. "I—I do not know," she said. "Best wait. I'll tell you of Harry's plans as soon as I hear them. But at least set one of the maids to airing his rooms, just in case."

Miss Preston curtsied as her young mistress left, her head high. As the door closed behind her, she said a prayer for her and wished her well. She had grown very fond of Margarite Tredman.

When Sally entered the library her heart was beating fast, but she had schooled her expression to one of only a polite coolness. To her surprise she found that Harry was accompanied by another much younger gentleman, who was as handsome as any man she had ever seen. And he was so beautifully dressed, so impeccably turned out, too. Who is he? she wondered. What hold has he on Harry?

But she did not wonder long, for her gaze was drawn to her husband's high-cheekboned face, that face she had not seen for almost three years. He was serious, but she could read nothing else in his expression. She did notice a muscle beside his mouth move for a moment, and the intentness of his stare as she curtsied to him.

"Why, m'lord, what a surprise," she said, as he

drew her to her feet. Her fingers tingled even after he had released them.

"May I present the Comte de Fountaine, madam?" Harry asked, his voice stiff. "Jean-Pierre is a friend of mine. I trust you do not object to my bringing him with me?"

Sally raised her brows. "Object? But this is your home, m'lord. Who am I to object to whomever you bring? You are most welcome, count."

Again she curtsied. As she rose the young man murmured, *"Enchanté, madame. Harry, mon ami, mais belle! Très, très belle!"*

Before the earl could respond Sally thanked the count for his compliment in fluent French, and with a perfect accent. Jean-Pierre's brows rose.

"I see you have been served some wine," she said in English, as she faced her husband again. "And perhaps you have also been informed that I am giving a salon today? May I count on you both to attend?"

"Yes. We will certainly be here," Harry told her.

Sally was very conscious of his stare, for he had not taken his eyes from her face since she had entered the room, and she was beginning to feel uneasy under such close scrutiny.

"How delightful that will be. But I must ask you to excuse me now, sirs. There are several last-minute details that I, as hostess, must attend to. Might I suggest you stroll about the grounds, or inspect the Hall while I am thus engaged?

"I hope you will approve the changes I have made, m'lord," she could not resist adding as she walked to the door. "It has been such a pleasure to set the Hall to rights, restore it to its former grandeur; and in some cases, improve on that.

"And now I must leave you for a little while. Till later?"

When she was gone, Harry Tredman sat down abruptly in a large leather chair. The count eyed him, wondering what was happening here. For even if these two had quarreled at one time, as he rather suspected they must have, surely after almost three years of separation their meeting had been excessively formal. And somehow he was sure it had nothing to do with his having been there to witness it.

But he would find out what it was all about, he told himself. He had not liked the look in Harry's eyes as he watched his young countess, nor did he like the way he was being ignored by him now. It was something he rarely had to deal with, and it bruised his massive ego. Accordingly, he set about to chatter of various things, until Harry was forced to abandon his abstraction and respond.

After they had finished their wine, the two wandered about the lower floor of the Hall. The count thought it all very grand, and yet somehow home-like in a way he had never experienced in formal settings before. The countess had remarkable taste. He was especially taken by one of the larger salons, where the wainscoting had been painted a dark forest green instead of the usual cream or white. Above it, the walls were covered in a brilliant green-and-gold brocade. It was a conceit he had never seen before, and it was stunning. Yet the more he exclaimed and complimented the countess, the quieter Harry became.

The last room they inspected was the smaller morning room, where Sally generally had breakfast. Here again de Fountaine was lavish with his praise, especially for the long windows that opened to a terrace overlooking the lawns and gardens, and in the distance, the lake. Part of the terrace was covered by an awning, and a wicker table and chairs had been set there for al fresco dining.

"I say, Harry, I might just as well be talking to myself!" the count said, exasperated by his host's continued silence. "What is the matter with you? Have you been struck dumb?"

The earl turned and faced him, and Jean-Pierre's merry smile disappeared at the pain he saw on the man's lean face.

"Shall I tell you what this room used to look like, my friend?" Harry asked, his voice quiet.

He wandered over to the window then, and with his

back turned he said, "It was dark and dingy—no, it was filthy. The hangings were rotting on their rods, and the upholstery and carpets were full of moth. There was no terrace then, no doors, no sunlight. And that was the way this room—all the rooms—looked all the time I was growing up. I hated the whole place.

"But of course it is different now, and not just because Margarite has spent a small fortune on it. Yes, she has changed all that ugliness, but it is also as if she has managed to erase the pain, the degradation—even the hatred—that was here, so thick you could feel it like a living presence.

"Yes, Darlington Hall is lovely now, isn't it? It is because she has made it so."

"She is a lovely woman," the count said, his voice easy. "I wonder you could bear to leave her all this time."

The earl's face grew cold, shuttered. "I will not discuss my wife with you, Jean-Pierre," he said.

"*Bien entendu*, as you prefer," the count replied with a very Gallic shrug. "I believe I hear the others coming. Shall we join them? I am hungry, after our early start."

There were some thirty guests who attended the countess's salon that afternoon. Harry knew most of them, and if anyone was surprised to see him there with his estranged countess no one was gauche enough to mention it, at least not within his hearing.

When everyone had assembled, luncheon was served at tables set in the rose garden. Those ladies who were present exclaimed in delight, but still, not a few of them wondered aloud about bees. Sally assured them there was no need to be concerned, for the gardener had filled the hives with smoke to quiet the bees only a short time ago.

"But," she added with a little smile, "you do see how clever I have been? I have made sure the afternoon's schedule will not be delayed, for no one will linger here. Smoke only lasts so long!"

As everyone laughed, she signaled Detts and the footmen to begin serving.

After luncheon—served with the best wines, Harry noted with a sardonic little smile—the guests dispersed to wander through the grounds. Jean-Pierre was captured by two middle-aged ladies to serve as their escort, and Harry went to seek his wife. He found her accepting Walter Scott's arm, and he had to make do with some of the other gentlemen, all loud in their praise for his Hall and its surroundings.

The guests gathered in the drawing room an hour later. Harry was pleased when Margarite took the seat beside his, in a prominent place.

John Stevenson performed first. A young tenor had been pressed into service to sing Moore's verses. The songs were familiar to Harry, for he had heard them any number of times. He was stoic through "The Harp that Once in Tara's Halls" and "The Minstrel Boy" but when the two began "Believe Me, If All Those Endearing Young Charms," he began to feel restless. It was such a poignant song. And so very *Irish*, he realized, turning his head so that he could observe his wife's profile. As he did so he saw the flush that started at the top of her low, round neckline and rose rapidly to her cheeks, and he turned his attention back to the performers. He had not come with the intention of humiliating Margarite in public.

Stevenson and the tenor were much applauded, and gave several encores before Señorita Alvarez entered the room. She was a short lady with a very large bosom and hips, and she was addicted to the most unbecoming clothes—all bright red satin, gaudy shawls, and high-flashing combs to hold her black lace mantilla—but there was no denying she could sing like an angel.

Following a short intermission, Walter Scott read several verses from his long lyric poem, *The Lady of The Lake*. Harry knew the man was fast being eclipsed in fame by the sixth baron Rochdale, George, Lord Byron. Still, the verses were stirring, and especially so when read by the poet himself. After Scott had concluded, he was asked a number of questions about this work and some of his others.

At last, one of the younger guests spoke up. "I have heard it said, Mr. Scott, that the author of the acclaimed novel *Waverly*, who has chosen to publish anonymously, appears to speak with your voice. Would you care to comment on this, sir?"

"People will see—and hear—whatever they like," Scott said, a little testily. "I cannot help that.

"I have read this work. I see no similarity to my verses."

"Well, perhaps not, but isn't that because it is prose as opposed to poetry, sir?" the young man persisted.

Harry recognized the voice. It was the same one he had heard in his club. Poor young man, he thought. Was he hoping to stir up a controversy here? Perhaps to show off how clever he was, and thus ensure his next invitation?

"There is a certain likeness in the imagery, I will grant you, Mr. Danvers, but surely there can be no comparison," Margarite said. "Mr. Scott, do tell us what you are working on now."

As the conversation changed, grew more general, Harry Tredman thought how neatly Margarite had managed that. Not snubbing the young man, but moving Scott gently away from a topic she must have seen was making him uneasy. How very adroit and sophisticated Margarite has become in the years we have spent apart, he thought.

But then he wondered why he found that so disturbing?

By the time an early dinner had been served, the earl was growing impatient with his wife's guests. He knew he would have enjoyed them at another time, and the witty, sparkling conversations that abounded, but now, wanting to talk to his countess as he did, they were just an aggravation.

It was only nine in the evening when the carriages were called for at last, but it seemed much later to the earl. He had told Margarite, when she had inquired earlier, that he and the count would be staying overnight, reminding her that it would be much re-

marked if they did not. He recalled how bitter he had
felt when he saw what he took for relief in her eyes
at the shortness of his stay.

The count excused himself almost at once, claiming
that his early rising and the country air had made him
languid. Alone at last, the earl allowed Margarite to
lead the way to one of the smaller salons.

After he had accepted a brandy—one she privately
thought he did not need, after the amount of wine he
had drunk with dinner—she said as she took the seat
opposite his, "I can see there is something you wish
to discuss with me, sir. Do you care to begin?"

"I remember asking you that once," he said a little
absently, as he twirled his snifter between his hands.
"Yes, I will admit I came down here to give you a
tongue-lashing, for which, if you remember, I am considered famous. At least in some quarters. But now
that I have seen the Hall, observed you moving among
your guests—what can I say? The money you have
expended was used well. For the first time in my life,
the Hall is a noble home. My compliments.

"But why did you even bother to set it to rights? It
must have been a great deal of work."

"I did not care to live here in filth and decay, and
I saw no reason why I should," she told him. "And
yes, it was a lot of work, but I had the time to see to
it, and little else to occupy myself. And I must say it
was a pleasure to watch the place change. No doubt
you will think me fanciful, but I felt that even the Hall
itself approved."

She blushed a little and fell silent.

"Have you had much to do with my mother, my
uncle?" he asked.

"Very little, thank heavens. They tried to get back
in here right away, but I would not have them admitted, as you ordered. Then once, when I was out walking, they came up to me in their carriage and tried to
force me to return to the dower house with them. I
was never so glad that Hanks was there! He . . . er,
he hit your uncle, and I was hard put not to cheer."

"Why ever would he do that?" the earl asked, leaning toward her. "Was that old satyr coercing you?"

Sally debated only for a moment. "Yes," she said. "Your mother had conceived a charming scheme to pay you back for what you had done to her. It entailed Mr. Worth's getting me with child while you were away, thus creating a scandal she hoped you could not live down."

"What?" the earl demanded, rising quickly to his feet.

Sally raised her hands. "Hanks saved me, m'lord, and I think his threats afterwards had a great deal to do with curbing the gentleman's ardor for the project."

"This is intolerable!" Harry Tredman exclaimed. "Know he will be gone tomorrow, and not unbruised, either!"

"There is no need to stride about so, sir. He has left Darlington land, and your mother has gone with him. They decided a year ago that remaining here had grown boring beyond belief, so they packed up and went to their childhood home near Liverpool. I was delighted to see them leave. The dower house is once again empty."

He nodded as he took his seat again, and Sally saw he was making a great effort to regain his coolness.

"You remind me, countess, that there is no longer any need to employ Hanks. Obviously you have no plans to run away, for if you had I am sure there must have been several occasions when it would have been easy for you to make your escape."

"I never had any intention of doing so, Hanks or no," Sally told him, her eyes never leaving his. "And if you dismiss him, I am afraid I shall simply hire him back. He is invaluable to me, and to Mr. Bell."

"As you wish," the earl said carelessly. "I notice Miss Preston is still with you, as housekeeper now."

"She is a wonderful woman. I am very grateful for her competence and her care."

"I must say I was almost as stunned as Detts was this morning, when I saw him at the door, for my orders were that he was to be pensioned off."

"He came back to help me, just until I could engage another butler. He was so happy to be here, however, that somehow I could never bring myself to do so. But he is beyond the work now, even though we all try to spare him. It is just that I cannot find the words to tell him he must leave. And I would you do not do so either, m'lord," she added, a little tartly. "It would hurt him so much."

"I doubt that will be necessary," he said. "He was humiliated today, to have fainted as he did. He'll give his notice tomorrow."

There was a little silence then, and the earl rose to replenish his snifter. Over his shoulder he said, "Your salon was a great success. My compliments."

As Sally thanked him, her voice composed, he took his seat again and asked, "But how did you meet all these people, isolated as you have been down here in the country? And how are you able to persuade lions like Stevenson, the Señorita, and especially Scott to come?"

"I suppose it all began when I first wrote to Sir Thomas Lawrence, asking if he knew some young artist I could commission to illustrate the stories I was writing for the children's Christmas gift.

"He very kindly recommended Parris. As for Walter Scott, I wrote him to thank him for all the enjoyment his verses had given me, and to ask him to clarify some points that had confused me. He replied, we started a correspondence, and eventually he asked me to send him my own work. He was the one who made arrangements to have it published."

"I have read it," the earl said. "It is excellent. I see it was dedicated to my brats, each and every one of them. That was kind of you."

"Well, the fables were written for them first. And they were so pleased," she told them, smiling for the first time. "Even Reginald wrote to tell me how puffed up he felt, for none of the other chaps at school had ever had a book dedicated to them." She chuckled. "He said he was cock of the walk!

"Have you seen him? At seventeen he has a great

look of you, and Lawrence is fast becoming more like you every day as well."

"Poor fellows," the earl murmured, as he raised the snifter to his lips.

"To answer your question, no, I have not seen them. I don't care to have any of them in London—it would not be suitable. I know how they are, and what they do, and that is quite sufficient."

He saw his wife's mouth open and then close firmly, and he was delighted she had thought better of whatever it was she had been going to say. Not that he had any doubt what it would have been, however.

"But what you have told me still does not explain how you have gained such a large circle of friends," he went on quickly, to change the subject.

"It was not done deliberately; I did not set out to acquire them," she assured him. "And they are not friends. They are only acquaintances. I do not have friends. I—I don't want any.

"But I think it was your neighbor here, Lord Brinks and his lady, who were instrumental in introducing me. They came to call on me early on. And when Mr. Scott wrote and said he was coming to London, and might be persuaded to journey to Darlington Hall for he wished to meet me, I conferred with them. Being older, and wise in the ways of the world, I trusted them to guide me. Lord Brinks helped me plan a small party, and Lady Brinks advised me on arrangements. After my book was published and had its small success, many were anxious to come. And thus the salon became an established thing."

"I notice Sir Thomas has painted you again. It is a lovely pose, with the lake in the background."

"Yes, he asked me if he might do it for the Royal Exhibition held a year ago, and he gave it to me when that was over. Lady Brinks assured me it was quite all right, why, she even insisted on housing him while he was painting it, for no one stays here."

"You are careful of your reputation, Margarite," he remarked. "How fortunate, even if it is rather late in the day for that."

Her face paled a little, but she did not lower her eyes. "But of course, m'lord. I am Countess Darlington. I want no scandal to attach to my name—or to yours."

He nodded in acknowledgment, but he did not speak.

"Harry, will you let me tell you something?" she asked, leaning forward and holding out her hand to him. He did not take it. Instead, his expression hardening, he put his empty snifter down on the table beside him and rose.

"I think not," he said curtly. "I can see you are burning to explain what happened at Reath Court, but I have no desire to hear anything you might have to say on that subject. That kiss you shared with Sir Thomas—your affair with him—can never be justified. It happened."

Sally heard in his voice the bitterness he still felt, and she bowed her head so he could not see the tears that had sprung to her eyes. She heard him move away, but she did not look up.

"It may interest you to know, Margarite, that your lover, in spite of his *undying* devotion for you, has married again. He has a child now, and another is expected. How unfortunate he was so fickle. But out of sight, out of mind, you know."

Chapter Fifteen

THE EARL OF DARLINGTON and his companion returned to London the following morning. Harry had not seen his wife, although he learned from Miss Preston that she was ever an early riser, and had already gone out to meet the agent at one of the outlying farms, attended as always by the faithful Hanks.

As he drove along the country roads later, Harry Tredman wondered why, when he himself had told her not to bother, he was so disappointed she had not been there to see them off.

London seemed stale to him after the country. It was warm for this time of year, and the loud noise and confusion, the ever-present stench, far outweighed its attractions. The count, of course, was welcomed back with great delight, and he reveled in it, but Harry Tredman spent more and more evenings alone in the library of Darlington House in St. James's Square, drinking far too much and brooding over a book he did not bother to read.

By early July, he had made up his mind. After all, Darlington Hall was his seat, was it not? He would go there and enjoy it, and if Jean-Pierre did not care to accompany him he would be not at all sorry to part company with the boy. True, his bills had been staggering lately, but it was not that. It was that the count had in some way ceased to amuse him. And his massive conceit, his complete selfishness, were beginning to be an annoyance rather than a jest.

When apprised of the plan, however, Jean-Pierre pronounced himself delighted to retire to a rural location, much to the earl's surprise. He took himself off to order new clothes more suitable for the country, and a complete supply of oils and brushes and canvas so he might dabble once again at painting. He was full of enthusiasm for the fresh air they would enjoy, the bucolic scenery just waiting to be captured by his talent, the marvelous gallops to be had on the earl's lands.

Harry Tredman was not to know that his enthusiasm masked a real desire to escape London, for his prodigy had gotten himself deep into debt by gambling—a debt he did not care to divulge to the earl as yet. The gentlemen he owed had assured him they were in no hurry to be repaid, and Jean-Pierre felt that perhaps if he lived quietly in the country, and spent no money, Harry would be more amenable to paying that debt in the autumn. He did, however, suggest they plan a house party for some convivial friends, for he knew he had to have others to admire him, lest he go mad. And even in the short time he had spent with Countess Darlington, he had been aware that she would never make one of his adoring court. Her gaze had been too level, too serious. She had not been impressed at all by his handsome face, his impeccable attire, or his beautiful manners.

The earl did not surprise his countess this time. Instead he wrote her a curt note announcing the date of their arrival, and he asked her to be prepared to receive them for an indefinite time, as well as the large house party he had invited for later.

On this occasion, his arrival was much more in keeping with the way he generally traveled. Sally was watching from one of the library windows as the entourage swept up the drive, the earl's sporting phaeton leading the way. It was followed by two large traveling coaches containing the gentlemen's valets, and mountains of baggage. Behind those, grooms on horseback led four riding horses. Sally had heard of the Darlington Circus—who had not?—and it amused her to see it for herself.

Or it would have, if she had not been so preoccupied—even nervous—about this visit. Like Harry, she reminded herself that this was his house, and it was certainly his right to visit it any time he liked. And as his wife and hostess, it was her duty to make his stay as pleasant as possible. But still, she wished it was not taking place, for she knew Harry had not forgiven her.

She remembered how she had wept the night after the salon, when he had left her again. How stubborn he was! she had told herself. How proud! And if he would not let her explain, he would always hate her. Just thinking of living—even in such a vast mansion as the Hall—in concert with someone who despised you was not a pleasant prospect. Nor would it be one for him. Indeed, she was at a loss to understand why he had even bothered to come.

She watched the earl as he stepped down from his phaeton. She did not notice James, her new butler, on the steps to welcome him, or the handsome count, for all her attention was riveted on her husband's fine profile: that strong jaw, those high, lean cheekbones, his firm mouth. He was frowning a little, and she shivered.

As the earl turned to look up at the Hall, she drew back from the window in some confusion.

Harry Tredman stepped into his elegant Hall moments later. He was looking around in appreciation as the footmen surged around him, bringing in the baggage, when an impetuous figure came running down the stairs. It was followed closely by another, much smaller one.

The two girls skidded to a halt when they saw the arrivals, and the littlest one's mouth fell open.

"Who are you?" the earl asked bluntly.

"Why, I'm Catherine, father. Don't you recognize me?" the eldest asked, frowning.

"Now I do, since you frown. And this must be your sister, er . . ."

"I'm Sophie," the little one said, giving him a curtsy and an enchanting gap-tooth smile.

She was a pretty little girl of about six, with dark chestnut curls and brown eyes. Her sister Catherine was not pretty. No, he admitted, not pretty at all.

Rather she was handsome, with that fiery head of hair of hers, those direct dark eyes. She looked so much like his late mistress he had to catch his breath.

"Why are you here?" he asked abruptly.

Both pair of eyes widened. "Why, to visit, o' course," little Sophie said, as if explaining something to the village idiot.

"We always come every summer," Catherine added. "Sally has asked us to do so."

"Sally?" he repeated, his voice cold.

"I mean, uh, Lady Darlington."

"Yes, well, run along now. You are just in the way here. And why aren't you with your nanny or your governess, by the way?"

"Sally—er, m'lady—is going to take us out in the dogcart. She promised!" Sophie volunteered. Unlike her frowning sister, she did not seem to feel any undercurrents here, for she was still smiling at her long-gone father in complete trust.

He made a shooing motion with his hands, and they beat a hasty retreat.

"Yours, of course," the count remarked behind him. The earl turned to see Jean-Pierre removing his gloves and shining top hat and handing them to his hovering valet. "Charming children. Charming. Er, one hopes, however, that they will not be much in evidence. I am not fond of children. So fatiguing, are they not?"

The earl ignored his petulance. Really, the boy was too much, pouting because he might be upstaged by a pair of moppets. "Where is the countess, James?" he asked the butler instead.

"I have sent to tell her that you have arrived, m'lord," that man said with a bow.

"Father! Is it you? *Really* you?" an adolescent voice exclaimed from the door. Harry turned to see another of his children running in, his dark hair wildly disarranged and a wide grin on his face. Now who is this? he wondered.

"I saw you approaching just as I was going to the stables," the boy continued, giving a sketchy bow.

"And won't Reggie be cross as crabs that I saw you first! He's out riding this morning, and he wouldn't let me come with him. Serves him right, don't you think? 'Sides, I ride just as well as he does now. Wait till you see me, Father! Sally says I have a very good seat, and—"

"Lawrence," the earl said, bringing to a halt the boy's burbled enthusiasm. "Yes, Lawrence. Do contain your delight, my son, and make your bow to our guest. This is the Comte Jean-Pierre de Fountaine. When you see him ride, you will cease to brag of your own prowess."

Lawrence bowed again, but he seemed singularly unimpressed by his father's friend, for he turned away from him almost at once.

"I say, it is just famous that you are here, sir!" he exclaimed. The earl studied his lean face, those high cheekbones, the clear hazel eyes. Was I ever so young? he wondered.

"Tell me, Lawrence, are you *all* here, every one of you?" he asked.

"Why, of course," the boy told him, keeping close to his father as he walked toward the drawing room. "Sally invites us every year to spend the summer months, all seven of us."

"Do you mean to tell me that even the baby is here?" the earl asked, trying not to sound appalled.

"Yes, he is," Lawrence told him with a gusty sigh. "He's such a nuisance! He tries to follow us around, and he cries a lot. But then, he's only three."

"*Trois? Un bébé? Dégoûtant!*" the earl heard the count mutter behind him, and his lips curved in a little smile.

"Oh, hardly that, dear boy," he said. "As brats go they are not too deplorable, I do assure you. And they will be in the nurseries most of the time."

"I won't!" Lawrence said stoutly. "Nor Reginald, nor Fay—why, certainly not Catherine or Trevor either. They're too old for that! Only babies stay in the nursery, and Catherine's thirteen now, and Trevor, eleven. He's a pest, too," he confided.

"As you are becoming," the earl told him. When Lawrence flushed dark red he relented, and put an arm around his son's shoulders. "Come now, go out for your ride. I will see you later, after we have had a chance to settle in here. We'll talk then, I promise."

Still red-faced and embarrassed at his gaffe, Lawrence was only too eager to make his escape.

As he passed Sally entering the room, she noticed his shame-faced expression, the unhappiness in his eyes. Now, what had Harry been saying to upset him? she wondered, as she curtsied to her husband and his guest. Really, it was too bad! Not even in the house five minutes, and after an absence of three years too, and the first thing he did was discompose his son. Sally was well aware that at age fifteen, hovering between youth and adulthood, Lawrence was easily thrown into confusion. She was quite put out with Harry.

Not a hint of her feelings showed on her face or in her eyes, however, as she greeted the two men and asked if they cared for refreshments. Nor did she say anything after the wine and biscuits had been served, and they were all sitting together near the empty fireplace.

"I was surprised to see that the children are here," Harry said, frowning now. "I understand from, er, Lawrence, that you invite them all every summer? I wonder my first wife's parents agreed to such a thing, when my mistress's children are also present. They are such proud people, such sticklers."

"They do not know of it," Sally told him. "I did not consider it at all their affair. But why should it upset them? These are *all* your children, even those three of them who are illegitimate. Why should they be treated any differently?"

The count lowered his glass, looking astounded. As well he might, the earl thought grimly.

"Why did you do it, Margarite?" he persisted. "It is not at all the thing, as I am sure you are aware."

Sally tilted her chin in unfamiliar defiance. "I could

tell from their letters that they were feeling lonely—neglected, even."

She ignored the slight flush along her husband's high cheekbones as she continued. "You were away, and had been for some time. It occurred to me that someone must show attention to the children—someone beyond elderly grandparents on the one hand and paid attendants on the other. That someone should love them, as they deserve to be loved. They are wonderful children, m'lord, bright and spirited. And wait till you see the baby, Alistair! What a darling little boy he is!"

"*Incroyable!*" the count muttered, and then he pretended to cough as Sally turned large dark blue eyes in his direction, her expression cool.

"You yourself have never known the joys of a large family, m'lord?" she asked politely. "Well, let me reassure you. In a place as huge as Darlington Hall, there will be no need for you to be bothered by the earl's offspring. Indeed, I daresay you won't even see them more than once or twice a day. They are, like all healthy children, very busy with their own concerns, and I doubt very much if the pursuits you engage in would be of any interest to them at all."

The earl chuckled a little. "*Touché*, my boy," he murmured. As the count nodded distantly he added, "I wonder if you would excuse the countess and me now, Jean-Pierre? We have some tiresome family business to discuss."

The count was quick to excuse himself, bowing over Sally's hand with infinite grace as he did so.

There was silence in the large room for several moments after he had left it. Sally folded her hands in her lap, determined to outwait the earl. She need not have bothered.

He turned from contemplating a large bouquet of roses on a side table and said, "Why do you permit the children to call you Sally?"

Her eyes widened. "Why, because 'm'lady' was too formal, and I cannot be considered in any way their mother. It seemed easier. And after all, at seventeen,

Reginald is not that much younger than I am myself at twenty-three."

"I did not mean that," her husband said, waving an impatient hand. "Why Sally? You are Margarite Tredman now—or had you forgotten?"

"I am hardly likely to be able to, now am I?" she said. "But even though you insisted I be called Margarite, I have never been Margarite to myself. I am still Sally, in my head and in my heart."

"I shall have the children call you 'm'lady' then, since you have taken such a dislike to the name I chose for you," he said, his mouth tightening. Sally would have liked to protest, but she bit her lip and remained silent.

"I shall have to impress it on them in short order, for my guests arrive the end of next week," he went on, putting down his empty glass and rising to pace the room. "As my wife, and my countess, I do not care to have you called by a milkmaid's name. Do you understand, Margarite?"

She nodded, even though she was still rebellious. You can call me whatever you wish, my arrogant lord, she thought. But inside, I will always be Sally.

"How many guests should we expect, sir?" she asked, to change the subject. "I would be prepared for them."

"There will be two dozen or so—I'm not sure," he said absently, as he picked up a small needlepoint of a bowl of flowers done in delicate pastels. "Your work?" he asked, gesturing toward it.

"No, Catherine did it for me as a Christmas gift. She is wonderful with her needle, and her designs are lovely. She is so talented."

"Just as well," he said absently, as he put the frame down. "As I recall, she is thirteen now? It will be well for her to have something to fall back on, if I cannot find her a husband willing to overlook her background. Not all men look kindly on bastards."

"That is something you should have considered fourteen years ago, m'lord," Sally told him evenly as she rose.

Before he could reply she went on, "You remind me, however, that the girls are waiting for me. I promised Sophie a ride in the dogcart today, and she has been so angelic in anticipation that I may even let her try the reins. Catherine, of course, considers the dogcart very tame. Perhaps you might take her out in your phaeton someday soon? And Fay, of course, as well. You cannot play favorites, you know, although it is hard not to. Catherine is so vibrant, such a darling."

"And Fay is not?" he asked, brows raised.

Sally sighed. "It is difficult for me to like Fay," she admitted. "Somehow or other she has come to think of herself as being above the others, and she twits them about their illegitimacy. In fact, this year she tried to insist that they call her 'Lady Fay,' as the servants do."

"And do they?"

Sally's lips curved a little, and he stared at them, mesmerized. "No, they do not. Fay decided she would rather not be a lady here, after all. I suspect Sophie's giving her a bloody nose influenced her decision. It was not just that I told her that if she continued haughty, I would send her right back to her grandparents.

"You must excuse me now. I have arranged for a luncheon to be served to you and the count, since I will not be back in time. We are taking a picnic with us to eat in the woods."

After he nodded she went away, quietly closing the door behind her. The earl poured himself another glass of wine before he wandered over to the window that fronted the drive. He was there when the three came out to the dogcart, Sophie chattering as she swung Margarite's hand and skipped along beside her, and Catherine smiling as she stowed the picnic basket in the cart. All three were dressed in simple white muslin gowns and broad-brimmed hats, but he had eyes only for his countess. What a picture she was in the sunlight. So graceful, so lithe.

As the dogcart moved away down the drive, the

pony at a fast trot, the earl sighed and left his vantage point. He felt left out somehow, and it rankled.

The earl's guests arrived the following week. By then, a kind of unspoken accord had been reached. Sally kept the children as far from their father as possible, lest they annoy him. She could not keep his heir or second son away from him, however, and many mornings the boys rode out with him and his guest.

Reginald was in awe of the count, and in a fair way of hero-worshiping him, something Sally deplored. She was very fond of Reginald, and hated to see him take the conceited popinjay who was Jean-Pierre de Fountaine as a model. Lawrence, she was pleased to see, seemed to dislike the count more and more.

The earl, however, insisted that all his family be present at tea every day, right down to baby Alistair. The count endured only one such gathering before he declined further attendance, claiming he did not like to intrude on the happy family group. Harry, watching his youngest smear icing all over his face and spill his milk, did not have to wonder why Jean-Pierre was so quick to excuse himself.

With the advent of his guests, however, he was too busy to continue the tea parties. Now he was involved in seeing to his guests' amusements, arranging sight-seeing trips for the ladies, and fishing and riding expeditions for the men. Sally tried her best to entertain them as well, while keeping her distance from those susceptible gentlemen who fell in love with her at first sight. She discovered that Alistair, with his always sticky fingers, or Sophie, who often asked embarrassing, ingenuous questions, both made perfect chaperones.

The children were not present at dinner, though, and she was forced to endure several distasteful evenings, parrying lewd suggestions and pretending she did not understand the jokes that were told. But she was dismayed by these new friends of her husband's. Even the women could not be considered ladies in her eyes, for they were as bold and unprincipled as the men. Old Lady Sybil, the Dowager Duchess of Wey, was positively crude in some of her comments, and her curses would have astounded a hardened soldier. Still, Sally smiled and was pleasant, and tried to avoid looking to the other end of the table, where Harry sat and brooded over his ever full wine glass, his eyes often on her face.

The young French count was much admired and petted by both sexes, and Sally could see how he reveled in the attention. She had also seen how his lips would thin whenever one of the gentlemen admired her instead. She thought the count would make a formidable enemy, and she was determined never to place herself in his power. She knew he didn't like her any more than she liked him, although he pretended he was as smitten with her as all the rest, and was all smiles and gracious courtesies in company. But she knew instinctively that he was not a good man, and she wondered that Harry had kept him close for such a long time, even if he was so handsome.

When she finally saw the count's first painting, one he had done of the gazebo and the lake, she thought it insipid.

The earl, noticing her reticence in praising it, came to her side as the other guests crowded around it to exclaim.

"No, Jean-Pierre is not an original, is he?" he murmured in her ear. "Nor are landscapes his forte. He is, however, a superb copyist. There was one Italian painting of a young nobleman that I wanted to purchase for my collection. It was not for sale, but Jean-Pierre copied it for me, and I swear it is almost impossible to tell it from the original. Some people are only gifted that way, you know."

Sally shrugged. "I suppose so," she said. "But not having any talent in drawing, I am not one to judge."

She turned away to reposition some roses in a large bouquet nearby, and as she drew them from the vase she dropped one of them. Quickly, the count was beside her to kneel and pick it up for her. Still on bended knee, he offered the rose to her, an intimate smile on his handsome face. Sally knew he did so only for effect, and she was hard put to thank him in an even voice.

"Charmin'! Demmed charmin'!" the dowager duchess crowed in her harsh, cracked voice. "By God, you should have them painted like that—immortalized, Harry! They are a picture together, your lovely young countess and our handsome French count."

The earl stepped back, motioning for Jean-Pierre to hold the pose. He caressed his jaw for a moment before he said, "My thanks, ma'am. I quite agree with your idea. I shall write to London tomorrow and engage an artist. That is, I shall if I can implore Margarite and Jean-Pierre to humor me in this."

As the count rose to his feet and dusted off his knee, he smiled easily, "But of course, *mon cher* Harry," he said. "I should be honored. For what man would not be delighted to kneel at such a lovely lady's feet, able to stare for hours into her beautiful face, and with her husband's blessing at that? I am sure the other gentlemen must envy me."

"Well, I certainly do," Lord Haverford said, clutching his heart and groaning in pretended agony.

Sally forced herself to keep smiling. She could think of nothing she would care for less, but she knew there was no way she could avoid the sittings if Harry insisted on them. As the guests began a spirited discussion of which artist should be chosen for the commission, she excused herself. She had a headache, as she so often did these days, and she intended to go to her rooms after she had said good night to the children.

The earl watched her from under lowered lids as she left the room. He could tell Margarite did not like his friends—indeed, he himself sometimes wondered why he had invited this particular set. They were crude, unmannered, lecherous, and not a one of them had ever had a serious thought.

Had he asked them in order to punish his wife further? he wondered. Had he brought them here because they would be the complete antithesis to the guests she usually entertained, and whose company she enjoyed?

The earl shook his head as Mrs. Fletcher climbed up on a chair, shrilling Joseph Turner's name over and over while she waved a full glass of wine. Distracted, he moved closer. As drunk as she was to be choosing that slovenly landscape artist for the portrait, she was sure to fall, and he didn't want her laid up here for weeks with a broken bone.

Later, he had card tables set out in the drawing room for some serious gambling. He knew that if his guests were thus involved, they would not remark Margarite's absence.

Upstairs, Sally spent a lot of time with Catherine after she had kissed the younger children good night. She had noticed that the girl had been upset about something these past few days, and she was determined, headache or no, to discover what it was. She was delighted when Catherine brought it up herself, almost at once.

"Do you like Lord Winston, Sally?" Catherine asked, her dark eyes lowered to her clasped hands. She was sitting up in bed, propped against her pillows, and in her modest white night robe she looked even younger than she was.

"No, not particularly," Sally answered, as she smoothed the covers. "Why do you ask?"

"I hate him!" Catherine said, her voice so vehement Sally felt the hairs on the back of her neck rise in warning.

"What has he done?" she asked, trying to sound easy. As she took the girl's hands in hers and squeezed them she added, "Please, you can tell me, my dear."

"It isn't so much what he has done, exactly," Catherine told her, a frown on her brow. "It's what he *says*, and how he looks when he says it. He keeps staring at me, *measuring* me almost. And today he told me that in a year or so, I would be as tempting as my mother. And . . . and he said I would be sure to engage in her profession, for my hair gave my heat away. He . . . he said he'd give anything to be first."

She raised her eyes then and stared at Sally, her expression anguished. "I . . . I knew what he meant, Sally, but I'm never, *ever* going to be any man's mistress!"

"Of course you are not," Sally said indignantly. "The very idea! Lord Winston is much at fault—you are only a child. And to be saying such things to you, why—"

"But I'm thirteen now," Catherine interrupted. "And have you noticed, I'm getting a shape? Oh, Sally, I don't want to have breasts. I don't, I don't!"

Bending, Sally gathered Catherine's still slight figure into her arms so she could hug her close. "I know. Sometimes growing up is not much fun, is it? But trust me. I'll speak to your father, and he'll take care of m'lord lecher. And if he doesn't, I shall. I beg you not to worry about such things, love. I'll see you safe, and nothing bad will happen to you, I promise."

As Catherine sniffled against her sleeve, Sally stared down at the top of her fiery head. And as she did so she remembered how she herself had been sold into marriage when she was only two years older than this girl, and how distressing that marriage had been. No, she vowed, setting her lips. Nothing like that was going to happen to her beloved Catherine—not if she had anything to say about it.

The house party was not over until the third week of August, but by that time Sally felt as if it had gone on for months.

She had spoken to Harry early in the morning after her conversation with Catherine, and she had been relieved when he had not taken what she had to tell him lightly. Indeed, she was sure he had been instrumental in speeding the guests' departure, for she had been expecting them to stay longer. She never learned what the earl said to Lord Winston, but Catherine assured her that the gentleman had not bothered her again.

An Alfred Chalon, newly elected to the Royal Academy, had come from London as soon as he'd received the earl's summons, and he had been hard at work since on the combined portrait. He had chosen to pose Sally reclining on a chaise lounge, the count kneeling at her feet. They were both in profile, Sally's face turned away as if she were too demure to accept the tribute the count held out to her. She had been relieved when that particular pose had been decided, for she knew she was not a good enough actress to smile down into Jean-Pierre's conceited eyes and play the lover, not with any degree of composure. The count, of course, looked completely smitten and eager—even a bit heroic. Chalon was so pleased with his handsome subjects, and the pose, that Sally tried to stifle her own misgivings about the work.

Harry often visited the salon where the Swiss artist had set up his easel and his equipment, but he never interrupted, only took a seat quietly to one side so that he could study the subjects, and the painting that was taking shape on the canvas.

Try as he might, Harry could not forgo these visits. They were the only time he could really look at Margarite without discomposing her, and he had to look at her. She drew him toward her like a lodestone, and he was helpless to resist. Knowing now how devious she was he hated this weak dependency of his, but although he scoffed at himself he could not stop coming to the sittings so that he might devour her with his eyes.

Made uneasy by his scrutiny, Sally was quick to excuse herself as soon as a sitting was concluded, to see to her household, ride out with Hanks, or busy herself with the children.

Even so, there were times when she and the earl were alone together, although it was always by chance. Sally still felt a little stab of sadness when she looked at him, for she knew he had not forgiven her, and indeed, probably never would. Sometimes she was tempted to try to tell him again what had happened at Reath Court, but remembering his last rejection, she held her tongue. She was shy with Harry now. What little rapport they had had in their short married life together was gone, as completely as if it had never been. And she had only to look into his hazel eyes, see how shuttered and wintry they were, to know that nothing had changed.

It was very difficult for her, for in or out of company Harry was unfailingly polite, always asking after her wishes, helping her to a seat, or complimenting her on a gown or a meal. But he rarely smiled at her. She wondered if any of the guests had noticed, and were whispering among themselves.

She knew there were all kinds of liaisons going on at the Hall, and secret midnight trysts, for once, summoned to the nursery late at night when the baby had taken sick, she had surprised Mr. Fletcher coming out of Lady Ander's bedroom. He had colored up, his mouth opening and closing like a landed trout, before he hurried away to his own room without a word. What *Mrs.* Fletcher and *Lord* Ander were up to, Sally did not care to contemplate. But as she hurried to the baby, she could not help but wonder if Harry had a mistress here. Lady Ellen, with her blond curls and limpid blue eyes, was tempting, and Mrs. Caine certainly was voluptuous. Sally prayed it was neither, prayed Harry would not embarrass her in that way at least.

One morning, as she wandered through the gardens selecting blooms for a bouquet, he found her there, and he insisted on carrying her basket for her. As usual Sally was uncomfortable in his presence, and her breathing became shallow as she cut a long-stemmed red rose.

"I recall strolling in a garden with you once before," Harry mused, as he took the rose and put it with its fellows. "At Beechlands. Do you remember that day, Margarite?"

Sally nodded, unable to speak.

"Have you ever heard from Anne Jenkins?" he asked next.

She turned to stare at him then, noting the firm set of his lips, his serious expression.

"No, never," she said. "I have not tried to write to

her, but I do wonder how she is sometimes, and hope she has forgotten me."

"I would be willing to wager any amount that she has not," he said quietly. "Do snip some of the lark-spur, ma'am. It will complement the roses, don't you think?"

As Sally obeyed he went on, "I myself have found you are not an easy person to forget. No, not easy at all."

Startled, Sally dropped her shears, and he knelt to get them for her. As he held them out he said, "Some of the white phlox, perhaps? What a patriotic display these will make in the drawing room!"

"Yes, of course," she made herself say, as she walked toward those flowers. "I intended to pick some, for their scent."

To her relief he did not say anything personal again, but even later, when she was alone in the garden room arranging her flowers, she pondered his remarks. And then, once more, she wondered why he had come back here, to a place he had said he would never return to again.

Harry himself was wondering just the same thing. But when he had returned to London after his first visit, he had not been able to put her from his mind. The time he had spent admiring the portrait of her, dressed in her ball gown and jewels! The hours he had sat quietly alone in her rooms, touching the things she had touched, admiring all the lovely objects he had bought for her, his bride. His cool, untouchable bride.

And then his mouth would twist with anger, and he would put down the delicate carving of the ancient Chinese empress, the silver hand mirror, the gilded porcelain box, and he would take himself to the li-brary, where the brandy decanter that his butler kept so discreetly filled for him awaited.

He hated himself for his weakness, hated knowing he was still drawn to her beauty, but he admitted he had a grudging admiration for her in spite of his dis-gust at her having deceived him with one of his friends. Margarite had conducted herself like a true lady ever since she had taken up residence in the Hall. And she had made it a noble seat, befriended his children, assured her own reputation as a literary figure—all without disobeying his order that she never leave the place. It was amazing.

There had been no one since Thomas Avery. He had made a point of questioning Hanks most particularly on that possibility. Even now he could remember the man's astonishment; how angry he had been at the mere suggestion that his beloved mistress might have had a lover. For a moment, before he had remembered whom it was he was speaking to, the huge Hanks had looked furious enough to do Harry Tredman harm.

But, the earl reminded himself, whether there had been another man or not, it did not matter now. She had betrayed him once, and once was all it took. And it was not as if he had not warned her that he would stand for no deception on her part, for he had.

When he remembered how sure he had been of her—how positive that she was still unawakened, in spite of her disastrous early marriage—he felt hot anger flare anew. It was galling to think he had been fooled so, that he, Harry Tredman, Earl Darlington, had been *wrong*. That was quite the worst part of it all.

So why do I remain here? the earl asked himself. There were his other estates to see to, and he had had invitations to parties in Scotland and the Lake District. But he had refused those invitations, and he had only sent his instructions to his agents at Fanning House, Brentlands, and Reath Court. He could not bring himself to leave the Hall.

Not yet.

Chapter Sixteen

EVEN WITH SEVEN young Tredman offspring in residence, the Hall seemed very quiet after the guests had driven away. Monsieur Chalon had gone as well, saying that those few touches that were necessary to finish the painting of the countess and m'lord's handsome young friend could just as easily be done in his studio in London. The earl suspected Chalon had another commission he was anxious to begin, but he was so pleased with the double portrait he did not attempt to stop him, even though he knew those "finishing touches" would probably be done by one of the artist's students. It was ever thus, with the famous ones.

Jean-Pierre tried to take up his own painting again as a way to pass the time, but after having watched a master at work he grew disgusted with his efforts and abandoned them. He took to riding most days, but he often wore a discontented frown, for Reginald's sole admiration was not enough to soothe his ego or keep him happy.

Eventually, he announced that he rather thought he would go and visit a friend for a few weeks. There was a large house party gathering for the races, and it was sure to be amusing. That is, if *cher* Harry did not object? *Cher* Harry was indifferent to the scheme, and waved a careless assent.

Feeling a good bit more cheerful, the count went away to order his valet to start packing. It was true he was bored here now and hoped to relieve that boredom, but he also hoped that Harry would miss him when he had gone. Miss him so much he would not refuse to pay his gambling debts. For Jean-Pierre was worried. The countess did not like him—he couldn't imagine why, unless she was jealous of him. And perhaps she would find a way to poison Harry's mind against him. Then where would he be?

But if he played least in sight for a while, she might forget him. He knew, as all such creatures do, that Harry was still at odds with his lady, and he told himself that as long as that state of affairs continued he was quite, quite safe. And only a few weeks from now the Little Season would begin in London, and he and Harry would be back there, far from the countess's influence.

Much as she disliked de Fountaine, Sally was almost sorry when he drove away one warm August morning. Now she and Harry would be alone here, and she was not looking forward to that at all. There was only so much for them to discuss about the estate, the children, her writing.

She had begun another book, and she spent hours working on it in the evenings as a way of evading his company. For the evenings were the worst. The younger children all disappeared after teatime, and only Reginald and Lawrence ate dinner with them. Lady Fay had been miffed about that, for she was sure she should have been present, too. But Sally had no intention of asking Lady Fay, for if she did it would mean snubbing Catherine, who was a full year older. And somehow she did not think the earl would welcome Catherine at his table. Sally worried a great deal about what was to become of the girl, and of Trevor and Sophie as well, for only their little brother Alistair was legitimate. But she could not discuss any of this with the earl. It was impossible, and she knew it.

Harry had noticed how uncomfortable Margarite was, now that she was alone with him, and it annoyed him. Surely she was not afraid of him, was she? He had never treated her with anything but perfect courtesy; had never even raised his voice to her. And he did not like this new habit she had of leaving him right after dinner, supposedly to work on her book. She had done so again tonight. Surely she can find the time to write during the day, he told himself. It was obvious to him that she was doing it for one reason and one reason only. To avoid him. To keep from spending a second more in his company than she had to. It was an insult that could not be endured.

He was sitting late that evening at table, finishing a bottle of port and brooding over the situation, when his anger came to a head. How dare she treat him this way? How dare she run away from him, prefer ficticious characters and invented conversations to *his* company? Well, he would not stand for it!

Intending to go to her and have it out, he rose from the table, swaying slightly for a moment. Perhaps he had better take a walk first, he told himself, as he made his unsteady way to a side door. It was full moonlight, and the fresh air would do him good.

He walked slowly down to the gazebo, taking deep breaths of the soft, scented air. After he had seated himself on one of the benches that lined the sides of it, he thought hard as he stared out at the quiet sheet of water that was the lake. The moon had painted a silver path across it, one that beckoned him closer and distracted him. He was tempted to swim in its light, as he had done once as a boy. He had heard some of the children here this same afternoon, having a wonderful time. Even little Alistair had paddled at the edge, managing to cover both himself and his nursemaid's white apron with mud, or so Lawrence had told them at dinner.

Harry stood up then and stripped off his clothes. Only a moment later he was diving in. The shock of the water was refreshing, and it cooled his anger.

When he came ashore afterwards he felt better, and his head was clearer. He dried himself off with his shirt, and then sat down wearing only his breeches.

As he sat there he knew suddenly why he stayed at Darlington Hall, and why he had come here in the first place. It was because he still wanted Margarite, as he had ever since he had met her.

And why shouldn't I have her? he asked himself, his eyes growing keen. I always knew she was not the "goddess" I named her. And I am her husband. Why shouldn't I enjoy her, just as Thomas did? Then perhaps this spell she has cast over me will be broken.

Harry rose to pace the gazebo, too restless to remain still any longer.

Of course! That was the problem, the *only* problem! He had been in her thrall all this time, and he hated to think that one such as she, an unfaithful wife, had bound him to her in such a way. Well, she would do so no longer. He would use her as he had used many other women, and eventually, when he grew tired of her, he would be able to leave her, as he had always left those others.

He started down the steps, scanning the sky. The moon was low. It was late—very late. She would not be writing now. No, she would be in bed.

As he hurried back to the Hall, completely forgetting the rest of his clothes, he pictured her there. Did she sleep on her side or her back? Was that glorious hair of hers spread out in an ebony curtain across the white of the pillowcases? Or did she wear it braided under a dainty night cap? He grinned, thinking she would not do so much longer, nor would she keep on whatever pretty night robe she favored for many more minutes.

As he passed the butler James stepped back in amazement, even forgetting to bow. The earl ignored him, as he took the steps two at a time. Naked to the waist and barefoot, his clinging breeches damp, he moved impatiently, the long smooth muscles of his back and his thighs clearly delineated as he climbed.

As the earl had thought, Margarite's room was dark as he entered it. Holding high the candle he had brought with him from his own room, he looked around. He had never been here before, and he was surprised at how plainly it was furnished. Obviously Margarite had not spent much money on her own comfort, for the room was almost spartan. He set his candle down on the dressing table and moved closer to her bed.

For long moments he stood there, staring down at

her. The faint moonlight revealed that she was fast
asleep, her dark lashes a striking contrast to her ivory
cheeks. He realized that he had never before seen her
sleeping in her bed at night. She lay on her side facing
him, one hand under her pillows and the other resting
on the light coverlet, its fingers curled slightly in re-
pose. She was beautiful—so beautiful.

His throat felt tight, and he trembled as he sat down
beside her. Lord, he was as uncertain as a schoolboy,
he thought. Anyone would think he had never had a
woman before!

Disgusted with himself, he reached out abruptly and
grasped her shoulders so that he could take her in his
arms. As he did so, Sally woke. She had been dreaming, and she was confused and frightened, and not at
all sure she was not dreaming still. She forced herself
to open her eyes, but she could not make out anything
but the dark, naked bulk of a large male figure bending over her. When she smelled the liquor on the
man's breath she choked back a scream and closed
her eyes tight, as if by doing so she could make him
disappear by sheer force of will.

Still more than half-asleep, and now bewildered and
terrified, she twisted away from the powerful hands
that held her, cringing as she curled up in a small ball,
her back to the threat he posed.

"Please, oh please, don't hurt me!" she cried, trying
as she did so to cover her head, her breasts, and her
abdomen.

Harry Tredman was startled as well. Why was she
sobbing? Why did she cower like that? he wondered.
And what did she mean, crying "Don't hurt me!"? He
had not been going to hurt her. He was not a beast!

Suddenly he knew, and his eyes grew bleak. Margarite was *afraid* of him. She thought he was just as
much a brute as that first husband of hers had been.

He reached out and touched her again, as he tried
to find the words to tell her it would be all right. But
at his touch she cringed away, and he could hear her
disjointed, hurried pleas. "Don't hit me! Don't kick me,
I beg you! No, no, not again, oh please, don't . . . !"

He felt the hot bile rise in his throat, and he stood up unsteadily and backed away from the bed. More than anything now he wanted to leave quickly without speaking to her, but he could not. That was the coward's way, and he was not a coward. Instead, he remained standing there until her broken little words had died away, and she had turned cautiously to face him. He saw that she still held her hands protectively before her, and he grimaced with actual pain. Her eyes widened in shock when she saw who had invaded her room, and one hand crept, trembling, to her throat.

"I beg your pardon, Margarite," he said. He had to force the words out, and they sounded stiff and cold. "I did not realize . . . Go back to sleep—I will not trouble you again."

As Sally raised herself on one elbow she tried to think of something—anything—to say, but she was still in shock, and the words would not come.

A moment later Harry had taken up his candle and closed the door between their rooms with a gentle, final click, and she was left alone in the darkness.

It was a long time before Sally could fall asleep again.

At first she merely lay back on her pillows and closed her eyes, waiting for her heart to stop pounding and her breathing to return to normal. Eventually, she forced herself to think back on what had just happened.

Harry had come to her, and almost naked too, and he had touched her as she slept.

But I didn't know who it was! she protested silently. How could I? He has never come to me at night before!

No, but then she knew very well who she had thought that threatening figure had been. She had been dreaming of Ireland and, half-asleep as she was, she had reacted instinctively, as she would have with Leo Mannion. And Harry had been drinking, too. She had smelled it on his breath. No wonder she had made the mistake. Why, even now she could remember how liquor fumes on her husband's breath had been enough to trigger panic in her heart during those three endless months of her first marriage.

I'll explain it to him tomorrow, she promised herself. Surely he will understand why I made such an error. And he will not blame me, for he knows what Leo did to me. And then perhaps Harry would come to her again, when she was wide awake and prepared. It would be better that way, and she would try very hard not to let him know how repulsive the physical side of marriage was to her. She was sure she would be able to pretend—

Suddenly Sally's eyes widened.

Why? she asked herself. *Why* had he come? He had never done so before; indeed, he had called her a "goddess" and told her that lovemaking would demean her.

And she remembered she had thought him mad, for she knew she was only human, even as she had been grateful for the reprieve.

Tears came to her eyes then, and she whimpered a little, her fist tight against her mouth lest he should hear her. It was suddenly very clear to her. Harry had come because he believed she wasn't perfect. Not now. Not any more. No, for he thought she had already betrayed him with Thomas Avery. No doubt he had convinced himself that there was no need for such niceties as affection and gentleness, not with an adulteress. And he had come because he saw no reason why he should not have her, too.

This foray to her room in the early hours of the morning had had nothing to do with love. No, rather it had had to do with hate. For Harry could not have told her of his hatred for her in words, any more plainly than he just had done by his actions. She shuddered. He hated her still. Perhaps he even considered this aggression he had planned a just punishment for her, intending to use her as men so casually used the young prostitutes in London, tossing them a coin afterwards for their trouble and strolling away, to forget them before the next corner was turned.

Sally felt degraded, as degraded as she ever had at Leo Mannion's hands. What could she say? What could she do to prove she was not the woman Harry thought her? And would he even listen to her, if she tried?

The next morning Sally woke much later than was her custom. Bright sunlight was streaming in through the curtains, and she could hear the birds singing in the beech tree outside her window, even smell the scent of flowers in the gardens below. On such a lovely summer morning, she wondered why she felt so despondent and unsettled.

When she remembered, she was tempted to slide back down and pull the covers over her head. Scorning such cowardice, she rang for her maid before she padded to the dressing room to wash her face and clean her teeth.

When her breakfast chocolate arrived, there was a note on the tray from the earl. Sally waited until the maid had left the room before she opened it with trembling fingers. But the note only informed her that he would be out riding for most of the day, and that he intended to dine with friends in the neighborhood that evening. She was not to be concerned. When they met again, he promised her everything would be just as it always had been.

Sally traced the black letters of his name. How abrupt he sounded, how cold, she thought. Or was he feeling a little ashamed of himself, perhaps? She hoped it was that.

She sipped her chocolate as she planned her day. She wanted to visit one of Harry's old pensioners in the village who had not been well lately, and this afternoon she intended to take the three girls for a row on the lake. No doubt Trevor would go fishing. He was fascinated with the sport. Reginald and Lawrence would be busy with their own pursuits—she need not consider them.

She was just about to rise and summon the maid to help her dress, when Miss Preston knocked on the door to ask if she might have a few minutes of her time.

Sally smiled as she bade her take a seat.

"I'll not keep you long, ma'am. Griffen, m'lord's valet, spoke to me a little while ago, and I thought I should tell you about it."

"Tell me about what?" Sally asked, trying for a casual tone.

"Griffen said he wished that he could speak to you himself, but he did not dare, for he knew he would never be able to get the words out," Preston told her with a twinkle in her eye. "Poor man, that infatuated with you he is! I notice he blushes like a girl whenever he sees you. So instead he told me his story, and he begged me to tell it to you. Have you the time to listen?"

"Of course," Sally said, pretending to be busy fluffing up her pillows. She prayed that the heat she felt on her cheeks was not too obvious.

"Griffen is aware that there is something wrong between you and his master," Preston began, folding her hands in her lap. "He has known for some time, although he has no idea what it could be. But he says that Earl Darlington has been most unhappy all the time he has spent away from you. And he is worried about the earl, for he is even moodier now, much more so than he ever was before. He has been drinking heavily, too.

"Griffen feels he must speak of this now, because only this morning one of the gardeners brought him most of the earl's discarded evening clothes. He found them in the gazebo. Griffen is afraid that if the master swims there at night when he is, er, in his cups, he might drown."

She paused, and Sally drew a deep breath, the first she had taken since Preston had begun to speak. "Yes, I am aware of his drinking," she said. "But why does Griffen think I can do anything about it? I do assure you, Preston, I have no influence over the earl."

"Perhaps you have more than you know, ma'am,"

the housekeeper replied. "Griffen has asked for your help because he is fond of Harry Tredman. They have been together for almost twenty years. He wants him to be happy again, as happy as he was when he first married you."

She paused, but when Sally would not look at her, or speak, she continued, "Won't you at least try and help, ma'am? He is your husband, and I do not think you are indifferent to him."

Sally looked up, and her dark blue eyes were troubled as she gazed at her housekeeper. "No, I am not indifferent. I do not want anything to happen to Harry," she whispered. "I am very sorry for him. Sorry for myself too, if you want the truth.

"Very well. Tell Griffen that I will do what I can, although what that could be I have no idea."

Miss Preston rose, smoothing her white apron over her sedate dark dress. "No one can do more than that, m'lady," she said as she curtsied.

As she started to leave she remembered something, and she said, "Cook has asked me to inquire if she must make roly-poly pudding for the nursery today. She says the children want it every day, and she would prefer to do something different. But Miss Sophie has been pestering her. . . ."

Her mistress managed a little smile. "Tell Cook she may serve whatever she likes. I shall deal with Miss Sophie."

When she was alone again, Sally sank back on her pillows and frowned. Yes, she thought. That is one problem I can handle nicely. But what am I to do about the earl?

All the while she was being dressed she thought of it, but it was not until she went down the stairs that an idea occurred to her. Her step grew lighter as she hurried to the library, telling the butler over her shoulder that she did not care to be disturbed. The children and the old pensioner would have to fend for themselves today. She had something much more important to do.

*   *   *

The next morning, she came down to the small salon at a time when she knew Harry generally had breakfast. She found him seated on the terrace under the awning, James hovering solicitously in case he should be needed. She dismissed the butler as she took her seat, for she preferred to speak to Harry alone.

Before she could do so he said, in the same cool voice he always used these days, "Lady Brinks sends her affection, Margarite."

His eyes were lowered as he buttered a scone, and he continued, "She says she understands how busy you are with the children, but she begs you to bring the girls to tea someday soon. Just the girls. She was quick to admit she is not fond of young males."

Sally nodded as she stirred cream into her coffee, proud her hand did not shake. "I know. She has told me so before. It is just as well she never had any, although it is unfortunate for Lord Brinks. Now there is only his nephew to succeed him.

"Harry," she continued, looking at him squarely for the first time. She waited until he had given her his complete attention, those hazel eyes of his shuttered and wary, before she asked, "I wonder if you would do me a great kindness?"

She stole a quick glance at the front of her muslin gown, for she was sure that the way her heart was leaping in her breast must be plainly visible. To her relief it was not.

"Of course. Anything," he said.

"Then I would like you to read this latest fable I have written," she went on, drawing some sheets of paper from the pocket of her gown. "I would have your opinion of it, if you would be so good."

"I should be delighted," he said, stretching out his hand for the sheets. Sally thought he sounded much easier, and she knew why that was so. He had been afraid she was going to bring up his disastrous visit to her room the other night, when he had no wish to discuss it.

"Thank you," she said, before she pushed her cof-

fee away and rose. "Please excuse me. I must see
Cook about the menus for today."

The earl nodded, a frown across his brow as she
curtsied and went away. Sally's heart was still pounding, and she had to force herself not to run. Well, it
was done. Pray God her plan succeeded!

Harry unfolded the sheets she had given him, and
smoothed them flat. Taking up the top one, he began
to read.

> *Once upon a time, for that is how all the best
> stories begin, you know, there was a little girl who
> lived across the deep and restless sea on an emer-
> ald island.*

A little smile curved his lips, but by the time he had
put that sheet aside and taken up the next, he was
smiling no more. He read on however—about a wizard in a red coat, the magic sovereign he had given
the little girl, and all the things that had happened to
her as she grew up, before the Prince of the West
Wind had come. The prince wanted to marry the girl
and make her his princess. As, of course, he did, this
being a fairy tale.

Harry read on:

> *The Prince took her away to his castle. It was
> the most beautiful place the Princess had ever
> seen, and it was filled with beautiful things. And
> there she had no worries anymore, for the Prince
> showered her with gowns and jewels and every-
> thing her heart desired. There was even a coach
> made all of pure silver for her to ride in, drawn
> by sixteen perfectly matched black horses.*
> *But the Princess was not happy. No, for she
> had nothing to do all day but amuse herself. I
> suppose you think it would be wonderful to live
> such a life? Why, just imagine, you could eat
> cakes and ices and roly-poly pudding all day
> long, and never, ever have to see a vegetable
> again! And there wouldn't be any lessons to learn,*

*or chores to do. But perhaps, like the Princess, you
would grow weary of such luxury after a while?*

*The Princess tried to tell the Prince how she
felt, but he would not listen. He told her that all
she had to do was to be beautiful, and never lift
her hand to anything, and she was sad, so sad.*

*Now the Prince had another castle, and they
went to visit it. And there, the Princess met a man
who called her by her childhood name. And lo
and behold, do you know who he was? Why, he
was none other than the wizard who had given
her the magic sovereign all those years ago when
she had been a little girl!*

The earl was frowning mightily now, his eyebrows
a solid bar across his forehead. He wanted to stop
reading, but somehow he was drawn on. He read how
a meeting had been arranged between the princess
and the wizard by a jealous woman, and how that
woman had informed the prince of it, even how the
wizard had kissed the princess; how she had run away,
confused, for she did not love the wizard as he claimed
to love her.

Harry Tredman's eyes were bleak as he took up the
last page. On it the princess tried to tell the prince
what had happened, but he would not listen, or believe her. Instead, he read,

*He took her to yet another of his castles, a dark
and gloomy, lonesome place, and he left her there
all alone, telling her she would never be allowed
to leave because she had deceived him. No, not
ever again.*

Harry's mouth twisted as he read the last line of the
story:

How the Princess cried!

He crushed the sheets, still frowning. And then he
remembered he would have to return them, and he

smoothed them with an unsteady hand. Could it be true? he asked himself. Could it have happened that way? If it had, Harry knew he had made a grave mistake three years ago.

He looked out at gardens he did not see, for he was thinking hard. He knew Thomas had been stationed in Ireland right after his first marriage to the pretty but shrewish Eloise, and before she had insisted on his selling out, not liking the life of an army wife. Thomas could have met Margarite there, at Ballyragh—stranger things had happened. And he could believe Thomas had given the pretty little girl she must have been a coin, smiling as he did so. Thomas liked children—he always had. Harry himself had seen him give them money many times in London, and no amount of scoffing at his tender heart, or telling him the impossibility of a penny's making any difference in the unfortunate child's life had ever dissuaded Thomas from his charity.

When had Thomas returned from abroad? he wondered. He could not recall. He had been traveling then, and they had lost touch with each other for some years.

But the earl did know his wife's history, knew it well. She had lived with her husband for only three months before she had run away back to her childhood home. And she had remained there for a year until her father was arrested for murder, the family dispersed, and she left for England with Colonel Jenkins. If she and Thomas had had an affair, it had to have been during that year. And somehow, in thinking about it now, he found he could no longer believe it.

He rose and walked to the edge of the terrace, to lean against the wall there. What have I done? he asked himself, despair washing over him. What have I done to my lovely wife by not trusting her, treating her so harshly?

He remembered the fairy tale she had written then, and he grimaced. The only good thing that had happened was that she had not had to sit about being beautiful and bored these past three years! Hardly enough to cancel out the evil he had done to her.

He strolled down the terrace steps and entered the gardens. He knew why she had written that fable—so he would learn the truth, since he would not let her tell it to him in any other way. But why had she done so now? Had it anything to do with his invasion of her room the other evening—the fright he had given her?

He was ashamed of himself, mortally ashamed that he had even thought of using her that way, without love. But he could see no way to redeem himself in her eyes. It was past time for that.

The earl did not see his countess again until late that same afternoon. He had gone riding that day with his two eldest sons, but he had been in such a brooding, abstracted mood, that even the bickering and rivalry that occurred between Reginald and Lawrence with such great regularity did not draw the usual reprimand.

After the family tea, however, he asked Margarite if he might see her alone, and he took her arm and led her to the gardens for privacy.

"I have read your story, Margarite," he said, as soon as they were out of earshot of the children and the servants. "It is well written, but I must say I do not care for the ending. I doubt children will like it, either. Fairy tales must always have a happy ending, you know."

"The ending of the story has yet to be written," she told him, turning away a little so all he could see was her glowing cheek, framed by the curls of her dark hair. "I hope it *will* have a happy ending," she added, so softly he had to bend closer to hear her.

"And that is important to you?" he asked.

He waited for what seemed like endless moments before she said, "Yes. Yes, it is."

She turned toward him then, and he saw the trouble deep in her eyes as she abandoned the effort of pre-

tending that her fairy tale had been only make-believe
after all.

"I have not been happy these past three years,
Harry. And somehow I sense you have not been
happy either. Have you?"

"No, I have not," he told her, never taking his eyes
from her face. "It has been a long and aimless time for
me, full of amusements that did not amuse, activities I
had been better not to have indulged in, so-called
friends I would have been wiser not to have made."

He paused for a moment and turned away, as if he
could not bear to look longer into her eyes as he said,
"I am ashamed of myself, Margarite. Ashamed of how
I banished you, how I would not even listen to you
and refused to trust your goodness. But I was so
angry! There was no forgiveness in me, and the anger
has festered all this time."

"Do you believe what I told you in my fable?" she
asked, holding her breath.

He turned back and took her hands in his. "Yes, I
do believe it—and you. But come, let us go to the
gazebo while you tell me about it. I am most anxious
to hear why you never mentioned you had met
Thomas all those years ago when you were a little girl.
If I had known that, it might have been different."

As they strolled toward the lake Sally said, "Yes, I
was at fault there in not telling you, but I did not
dare.

"I discovered he was none other than my wizard
the night of his ball. He heard one woman greet another as 'Sally', and when I turned with a smile I gave
myself away."

As he helped her up the steps of the gazebo, his
hand cupping her elbow, she went on, "He made the
connection then. I wanted to tell you about it on the
way back to Reath Court, but I remembered how adamant you had been when you told me I must forget
Ireland, and never speak of it to you again. So I held
my tongue."

"Would that I had never given you such a stupid

order!" he muttered, as he led her to one of the benches and sat down beside her.

She waved her hand a little and shook her head. "It is over now," she said. "Do you know, I really did think Sir Thomas was a wizard when I was ten? And I still have that sovereign, even now. Of course I know it is not magic. It is only a coin, but I have kept it by me all these years, just in case."

"Much good luck it has brought you!" he said, still sounding disgusted with himself.

She picked up his hand and pressed it. "Do not blame yourself so, Harry. I realize how it must have looked to you, that meeting in the woods, that kiss. What else were you to think?"

"Why didn't you insist on denying it, when I brought you to the Hall and accused you of being his mistress?" he asked.

She did not look away from his intent hazel eyes, even though she was pale now. This was the hard part, and she had to steel herself to say, "I was so shocked by your ultimatum, I could not. Then too, I was feeling guilty, for I knew how I had responded to him that afternoon."

She saw a dark shadow cross Harry's face, and she added quickly, "It was the first lover's kiss I had ever known, you see. And it was tender, caring. It did not hurt or disgust me, as Leo Mannion's kisses had done."

He stared down at her hand holding his, and he squeezed it a little. "If only there were some way I could undo this evil I have brought to us."

"Well, it wasn't all evil. After all, Darlington Hall has been restored to its former grandeur, and its demons banished. Besides, it is paying a profit now. And I learned I could write. I learned something else as well: how to be independent, to make my own decisions. I think I finally grew up these past three years. For that I am grateful."

They fell silent then, but Sally was glad when Harry did not release her hand. The slanting sun of late afternoon cast shadows across the far side of the lake, and she could already see the faint globe that would be the full moon in the sky above the trees.

"May I tell you something else?" she asked.

He nodded, unable to speak just then.

"The reason I behaved as I did the other night when you came to my room, was that I had been dreaming of Ireland. And when you touched me without warning, just as Leo used to when he came home from his carousing, so angry and bitter at me because I could not love him, I reacted instinctively. I think it was the liquor on your breath that frightened me. That . . . that was how he always smelled when he was going to beat me, you see.

"I . . . I am very sorry I did not realize it was you."

Harry rose abruptly, and she caught her breath. Had she said too much? Gone too far? she wondered, as he walked away to stand with his back to her.

Over his shoulder he said, "My dear Margarite, once again I must apologize. I am ashamed of myself. I pray you will find it in your heart to forgive me some day. You may believe I will never frighten you that way again."

He came back to her then and raised her to her feet, before he took her hands and kissed them as he had been so wont to do when they were first married.

Sally wanted to say something more, but wisely she did not. They had come a long way, the two of them, these past few minutes. She would not press him for more at this time. It was too soon, and their new rapport was too fragile for that.

As she smiled up at him, she told herself there would be plenty of time for further confidences in the days that lay ahead.

Chapter Seventeen

DINNER THAT EVENING was a pleasant meal, even though the earl seemed abstracted and was often silent. But Sally conversed with his sons, feeling, in spite of her emotional exhaustion, as if she had found her way out of a dark labyrinth into the sunlight.

She noticed that Harry drank sparingly, and she was delighted when he joined them in the drawing room so quickly after dinner that he could only have had time for one glass of port. It seemed she did have some influence over her husband, after all.

She knew he was feeling uneasy with her still, and rueful, but she would not allow him to lapse into brooding again. Instead she sent for Fay and Catherine, and then she proposed any number of old parlor games, to pass the time. Reginald would have scorned such amusements as Blind Man's Buff, Hunt the Slipper, and jackstraws, but when his father said he would play he was forced to do so as well. And by bedtime he was having such a famous time of it, he crowed every time he won.

Alone with Harry at last, Sally was nervous, until he began to discuss experimenting with an early strawberry crop come spring, and the condition of the village street.

They parted with smiles that evening, and Sally fell asleep smiling still.

In the days that followed, it was no different. Harry suggested they resume their early morning rides before breakfast once more, and he became much more interested in his children and their doings. Sally noticed he kissed her hand often, and once, helping her dismount, he hugged her to him briefly. He let her go at once, before she began to feel uneasy, but now she found she was waiting for that hug to be repeated every time he touched her. One evening he had even dropped a kiss on her hair, and only last night he had kissed her cheek when he had bade her to sleep well.

She did not know it, but once again the earl was wooing her, slowly and with infinite care.

Harry knew now that, as a result of her earlier marriage, his wife feared all men. Even when he had first married her he had been aware that she had never been in love, and he had tried to woo her then. For contrary to everything he had told her, he did not consider her a goddess—far from it. No, that had been only a ploy he had used, until someday she might come to love him as he loved her. He remembered how he had wanted a woman for wife, and how he had seen how impossible that would be, her mind and heart being what they were then.

Even now, when he knew he could gain her consent to lovemaking, he did not want to settle for a wife who was merely fulfilling her marriage contract. No, he wanted her to desire him as much as he desired her, and always had. He told himself that once again he must be patient for as long a time as that took, because it would be worth the wait to gain Margarite.

Of course, the debacle at Reath Court had put paid to all his good intentions, that tentative, early courting. Now he was forced to begin again.

When he remembered how he had treated his first two wives, how arrogantly he had claimed his rights, he was amazed at his continued forbearance. But he knew that what he had told Margarite so long ago was only too true. He had never loved before, not really. It had been all desire and expediency. He had not even mourned them when they died as they'd deserved. He shook his head in regret. The gods were exacting payment for such insolence now, making him struggle so to gain Margarite's regard, making him wait as he had never waited for anything. A humbling lesson, and he admitted it. Perhaps he even deserved it?

He was not at all displeased when the children were bundled into their carriages a few days later for the journey to their homes in other counties. It was September, and although it was true he had enjoyed their company and, in a way, they had even eased his path with Margarite, for some time now he had been anxious to be alone with her. So often it seemed that just when he was about to touch her, or say something provocative, the baby's condition would require her attention, or little Sophie would appear with her big, all-seeing brown eyes, and a million questions to be answered. Sophie, he had discovered, was not an easy little girl to dismiss or ignore.

Now, however, he stood beside Margarite on the terrace steps that fronted the Hall, and waved as the carriages started down the drive. He had put his arm snug around his wife's slim waist a moment earlier, and he had been elated when she had not tried to escape.

"Good-bye, my dears! Write often!" she called, blowing kisses to them.

When the carriages had disappeared from sight, she sighed before she looked at her husband a little shyly.

"How quiet it will seem at the Hall, don't you agree, sir?" she asked.

She sounded breathless, and inwardly the earl smiled to himself before he gave her waist a final squeeze and released her.

"Yes, but restful as well. And now perhaps we may have time for more, er, important things," he said.

"What?" she asked, looking confused and a little apprehensive.

"But of course! How could I have been so remiss?" he asked, as they strolled to the front door. "For I never did provide you with a coach made all of pure silver, did I, and I must see to it. Naturally it will require constant polishing, but we will not regard that, and one only hopes that it can avoid contact with other vehicles. I am afraid it would dent badly. But since you obviously want such a showy mode of transportation, I must procure it for you at once. Er, violet satin cushions, do you think? Or do you prefer rose silk? Neither is practical, but in this case . . ."

As he held the door for her, he saw her smile, the way her lips had parted, as if she were about to speak, and he added, "However, much as it desolates me to disappoint you, I do think sixteen horses would be excessive, unless they were all decrepit. Do you think you might be able to settle for four in their prime? Perfectly matched blacks, with silver-studded harness, of course."

"Oh, Harry, you know I never intended any such thing! You are teasing me," she said, chuckling as she did so. "That was just part of the story, for it appears to me that every princess worthy of the name has something of the sort. And after all, you can't write of one climbing into just any old fusty coach with bad springs," she added. "It wouldn't be a fairy tale if you did!"

He held her hand for a moment, ignoring his butler and the footmen on duty. "Why did you name me the Prince of the West Wind? Although it has a very poetic sound to it, I must admit I do not know why you chose it."

She drew away to curtsy. "Oh, because you are like the west wind, I suppose. It can be very forceful on occasion, can it not? And it is well known to be volatile and capricious, even restless, if you like."

He pretended to frown, and she laughed at him as she went toward the stairs. "Do we ride this morning, sir?" she asked. "The children left so early, we have not had the chance."

"Yes, let's," he said. "It will give us an appetite for breakfast."

Sally nodded and hurried upstairs to don her habit, while the earl gave orders for their horses to be brought round.

As she ran lightly to her room Sally found she was humming a little Irish melody, and she wondered that she felt so lighthearted. Generally, she was depressed, melancholy, when the children left her in September, for she knew how many months she had to spend alone before they returned. This year it was different. Very different.

Still, as her maid buttoned her into her habit, and she drew on her gloves and settled her riding hat, she wondered how long Harry intended to remain at the Hall. It was most unlike him to linger so long in one place. He *was* like the west wind, she thought. That was a truer name for him than she had imagined.

The next afternoon, the post brought Sally a small package and a letter. She was alone in the library at the time, and she stared at the handwriting of the address for long moments. She had not seen that handwriting for three years, but she knew it for Anne's.

Her fingers were trembling as she broke the seal of the letter. It was bulky—she could tell there were several sheets enclosed.

By the time she had finished reading it her eyes were full of tears, and she had to choke back a sob. Dashing those tears away, she opened the package that had accompanied the letter. Inside, carefully wrapped in a velvet cloth, was a miniature of her dear friend, enclosed in a delicate gold locket.

As she stared down at Anne's likeness, saw her honest eyes, her pretty face and eager smile, the tears welled up and she began to cry in earnest. She had not cried over Anne for a long time, but she could not help but do so now. Her throat ached with her sobs.

"My dear Margarite! What is the matter?" she heard Harry ask, and she raised her head to see him entering the library and hurrying toward her. Her eyes were so full of tears it was like looking through a misty window pane, but even so she could see the concern for her in his hazel eyes as he bent over her and pulled her up to take her in his arms.

"Shh, my dear," he said, holding her close. "Whatever it is, it cannot be that bad!

"No, don't try to tell me yet. Just cry until you feel
more the thing. There is plenty of time."

Sally reached up to grasp his lapel with her free
hand. As she buried her face in his shirt, she thought a
little irrelevantly that Harry always smelled wonderful.
There was just the faintest scent of his favorite lotion,
so faint it did not mask the comforting warm, living
essence of the man himself. She would have known
him anywhere now, blindfolded or in the dark.

After a few moments her sobs died away, and she
let go of him to wipe her eyes on her handkerchief.
Harry pushed it away so that he could use his own
large, snowy square to perform the chore.

"I have never, no, never, been able to understand
why you ladies think that a mere two inches, made up
mostly of lace, will be at all practical," he muttered
as he did so. "Women!"

Sally managed a weak smile.

"Here, blow your nose," he ordered. She obeyed.

He put his handkerchief away then, and reached
out with a gentle finger to collect the last shining tear
that gleamed on her dark lashes.

"What made you cry like that, Margarite?" he
asked, serious now.

She motioned to the sheets of paper she had placed
on the table, and opened her clenched fist to give him
the gold locket she was holding.

Not releasing her, he took it in one hand and flicked
it open.

"Anne Jenkins," he said, as he stared down at it.
"After all this time, Anne Jenkins."

"Yes, she sent me the locket and letter. I am sorry.
It was so very sad, I could not help but weep for her."

"There has been trouble at Beechlands?" he asked,
bending closer to lay his cheek against her hair for a
moment.

"You—you had better read it for yourself," she told
him. "I—I cannot speak of it just yet."

She pulled away from him then, to walk over to the
window and stare out into the gardens, her back to
him.

The earl gazed at her bowed shoulders for a moment before he picked up the sheets she had indicated.

The letter was indeed sad. Even after she had recovered her health Anne had not stopped loving her friend, and she had been very unhappy. She wrote of how her father had tried to force her into marriage with this man and that, and how she had always refused. But now the colonel was dead. He had hurt his head in a riding accident last winter, and he had lingered for months in a coma before death released him. He had left Beechlands to his daughter, with the provision that she care for her aunt Honour until her death. As, of course, Anne wrote, she had every intention of doing.

Then the letter became more personal, and Harry hesitated to go on until he remembered that Margarite herself had asked him to read it.

"I have heard of your marriage to the once viscount who is now Earl D———", she wrote. "I can even pray that you are happy, my dearest Sally. Indeed, I do hope you are.

"But if for some reason—any reason—you are not, know that you would be welcomed back to Beechlands at any time, now I am mistress here.

"I know you do not love me, not as I love you, but that does not concern me anymore. I would be more than happy to live with whatever affection you might still have in your heart for me, and if it can be no more than friendship then I shall be content with that. And I do assure you, my dearest Sally, I will never try to sway you to my way of thinking, or attempt to become more to you than you are willing to accept. You have my word on it, my friend—my dearest friend.

"I enclose a miniature of me, done some years ago, that my father always carried, hoping it will remind you of me, and of happier times.

"Please write to me, even if you cannot come. And know I would treasure a keepsake from you as well. And know, too, that as long as I draw breath, there is someone in this world who loves you."

The letter was signed, simply, "Anne."

Thoughtfully, Harry put the sheets down, a frown on his face. After a moment he went to his wife, to put his arms around her and pull her tight against him. He was careful to do so slowly, and he was delighted when she sighed and relaxed in his embrace. He bent to rest his chin on top of her shining curls.

"I can see why you cried, my dear," he forced himself to say, although deep inside he felt only despair. "It was very touching. Will you write to her?"

Even as he spoke, the question he really wanted to ask hung in the air between them, unheard, except by the heart.

"Yes, I think I must," she said. "That is, if you have no objection, sir?"

"Of course not. You must tell her the miniature arrived safely." He paused for a moment before he added, his voice stiff, "You must also tell her how sorry you are that you cannot come to Beechlands. I know, after what I have done to you, you may well want to leave me, but I cannot let you do that. You see, I do not want to lose you, not ever. You are my wife, and I want you with me."

Wondering, he watched the way her sad face brightened, how a look of—could it be relief?—appeared in her eyes, and he reached out to gather her in his arms again.

"Margarite," he whispered, his lips a scant inch from hers. "I cannot let you go."

She closed her eyes as he kissed her. Moments later, her arms crept up around his neck and she held him tight, for she was sure she would crumple to the carpet if he released her. And still his lips were on hers, still his hands moved gently on her back, exploring, caressing. Still she could feel his hard thighs pressed against her own, and she sighed into his mouth. How very strange it was, what she was feeling! she thought. Like a wisp of smoke . . . the melting softness of silk sliding through the hand . . . the warmth of an August sun. And even though her heart was pounding she knew full well it was not from terror, for if it had been she would not have wanted to be closer to him still.

"You will not leave me, ever," he told her when that kiss had ended, shaking her a little for emphasis.

Sally opened her eyes to stare at him. He was still so close to her—she could see the amber flecks in his intent hazel eyes, those firm lips that had just kissed her. She felt an insane desire to trace them with her fingertips, but she forced herself to say, "Of course I won't leave you. In some ways I shall always miss Anne, but I could not live with her again, even in friendship. That . . . other . . . would always be between us."

"Should you like to send her a miniature of yourself?"

Sally shook her head. "No, that wouldn't be wise. Anne believes she will never forget me, but she must eventually, especially if she does not have my likeness at hand to remind her of me. Someday I will be no more than a distant memory, like a rose you find in an old book, pressed between the pages."

She felt breathless and unsteady, still held so close to him, and she knew she was talking too much. She grew uneasy then, and she made a little movement. He let her go.

As she walked away from him to take a seat she said, "I shall send her something else. My new book, perhaps."

"Then, if you are quite recovered, I shall go away so you can write that letter, my dear," Harry said as he bowed. "I must see Lord Brinks this afternoon. Some local business about the toll road."

Sally did not know whether she was relieved or disappointed that Harry was leaving her. Both emotions seemed to war in her breast, but she made herself say calmly, "Do remember me to him, and to his wife. We really should have them to dine soon. They have always been so kind to me."

Before he left her Harry agreed to extend the invitation.

Still feeling a little breathless, Sally sat quietly for a long time. She supposed she should be thinking about what she was going to write to Anne, but she found that all her thoughts were of her husband and that startling, wonderful kiss they had just shared. She wondered if he would ever repeat it, and she admitted to herself that she hoped he would. And soon.

But the earl did not rush his fences. He was too experienced for that. Instead he returned to his former courtesy, treating her to light conversation that made her laugh. Sally was as amused as he had intended, but always she felt that she was waiting—for what, she wasn't quite sure.

Lord and Lady Brinks, and the vicar and his wife came to dine, and Sally became involved again in estate business and the harvest to come.

One rainy morning, when she came down to breakfast, she found Harry lingering at the table, reading a newspaper. He rose to help her to her seat, dropping a light kiss on her cheek and squeezing her shoulders briefly as he did so. Sally felt a warmth deep inside her, but she tried hard to keep her face expressionless.

"Do you, as I, begin to find the Hall tiresome, my dear?" Harry asked, as he took his seat again.

"Why—why no," she said. "What can you mean?"

"I have been thinking that perhaps we should return to London. The ton will be gathering again, there will be new plays and concerts to attend, you must need new gowns. And surely, after such a long time spent in the country, incarcerated there by the wicked Prince of the West Wind, you could use a change."

Sally was flustered. She had not considered going to London, but she had to admit that when the autumn rains came, followed by the winter storms, she did dislike the country. She always felt so isolated then. And of course Harry was growing bored, looking forward to seeing his friends again. But at least he was asking her to go with him—it was such a relief!

"Why, if you would care for it, of course," she said. "But how strange it will be for me, leaving here, when I never thought to do so again."

"Do not be so constantly reminding me of my iniquity, madam," he told her, trying for a stern tone. "I am doing my level best to atone."

"And perhaps in twenty years or so, you might do just that," she told him cordially. "Or thirty? I am not quite sure how long it will take."

She laughed out loud at his raised brow, the astounded look he assumed, as she took a muffin and buttered it. For some time they discussed their departure, until Sally remembered de Fountaine.

"But have you forgotten Monsieur le Comte, sir?" she asked. "What of him? I believe I did hear that he would be returning to the Hall? How impolite if he should find us gone."

The earl frowned. He had forgotten Jean-Pierre; indeed, now that he was reminded of him, he wished him at the devil. He promised himself that as soon as they reached London he would see about severing the connection. He would give the boy enough money so he would not want, of course, until he found another bored nobleman to foot his bills. Although he was no longer of their number, Harry knew there were sure to be several eager for the privilege.

"If he has not returned by the time we take coach, we can leave a message for him," he said carelessly. "I find I have wearied of his company, and his extravagance and selfishness have ceased to amuse. And somehow I have always sensed that you don't like him, do you?"

"No, I don't," Sally said, as honest as ever. "I think it is because it is so obvious he has never learned more than the third note of the scale."

The earl thought for only a moment. "Do-re-mi? Me-me-me-me, you mean?"

As he chuckled at her wit, Sally finished her coffee and rose. At once, he was beside her to take her hand in his and kiss it. Sally stared down at his dark head, and when he straightened she reached out impulsively to hug him close for a moment.

He looked at her questioningly, but she could not speak. Instead she smiled tremulously and hurried away, praying Harry would not remark her blush. The earl stared after her for a long moment, a little smile curving the corners of his mouth.

That night, when he escorted her to her room, he did not leave her at the door. Instead, he came in behind her to look around. "How very plain your bedchamber is, Margarite," he said, frowning. "It is not fitting for one of your beauty. And why didn't you have it decorated, as you did the rest of the Hall?"

Flustered, and hoping she did not look as unsteady as she felt, Sally went to her dressing table. It seemed her knees had turned to water. Wanting something to do, she reached up to unclasp her pearls. The earl stepped close and brushed her curls aside so that he might do it for her.

"Well, Margarite?" he asked, his fingers lingering on the nape of her neck to caress it.

"Hmmm?" she asked, enjoying the shivery feeling those fingers conjured up, as she leaned back against the tall, hard column of his body.

"I asked you a question," he said, his voice husky. "Don't you remember what it was?"

He turned her around then, and with one arm holding her tight he tipped up her chin with his other hand. "Never mind," he whispered. "I find I really don't care for any conversation just now, my dear."

Sally closed her eyes as he kissed her. At last, she thought. She wished she knew more about kissing. She did not feel she was very good at it, although Harry didn't seem to mind. I just need more practice, she told herself. His lips became demanding then, and she parted her lips and stopped thinking about anything but him—how he felt in her arms . . . what his hands were doing . . . how thrilling his mouth felt joined with hers. . . .

How they both got undressed Sally never knew, nor did she know how she ended up naked in his arms in her bed. To her surprise she had not been afraid, had not even felt awkward or tentative. It seemed so right, so inevitable, and with Harry to guide her she was able to forget her doubts and her fears, and let him take her where he would.

Where he took her was a revelation. His tender, slow lovemaking could in no way be compared to Leo Mannion's crude, abrupt fumbling, and instead of feeling abused and degraded Sally felt cherished, wanted, adored. And although she tried to steel herself for the pain she was sure would come, her body would not cooperate. It welcomed him. It was as if she had been made for this one man alone, they fit together so perfectly. And, she realized, it did not hurt—unless longing hurt. There was no pain, unless wanting more, always more, was painful. And there was no danger, unless sliding into something very like oblivion was dangerous.

He held her cradled in his arms afterwards, dropping little kisses on her face, her throat. And as he did so he talked to her in a husky whisper, telling her how he worshiped her, how long he had waited for her, how happy she had made him. She opened her eyes then.

She had kept them closed throughout their lovemaking, not wanting to see what was happening to her, or daring to look at him. But now, somehow, she wanted to see him. Had he changed? she wondered. Surely they must both have changed, in some miraculous way.

He gave her a lazy smile of contentment. His dark hair lay tumbled over his brow, and as she reached up to smooth it back she said breathlessly, "So, I am not a goddess after all, am I? I am so glad you discovered it."

"But of course you are," he said, his fingers trailing from her shoulders to her breasts. "A living, breathing goddess—all woman. I knew you could be, given half the chance."

She clung to him, startled by what was happening to her. She was all aglow again, and she gasped as his hands moved lower and he bent to kiss her breasts.

*　　*　　*

"It must be very late."

"Late enough. Does it matter?"

"No, oh no. But I . . . I was just wondering what my maid must be thinking. I always call her to help me undress long before this."

"You're already undressed."

"But she will *know*—oh, however am I to face her tomorrow?"

"As you always do. You are a married woman. And do you think she will be able to guess that tonight was the first time for us?"

"How could she not? I feel so different. I must *look* different, too."

"No. Only lovelier."

"Really? But—but Harry, I—oh. Oh, my . . ."

"I am so sorry I'm not better at making love."

"Aren't you? I hadn't noticed."

"No, for I never knew it could be like this; that is, it is all so very unlike—"

"Don't mention him. Don't even think of him."

"I won't. Not again, I promise."

"Good."

"But perhaps I only need more experience? What do you think?"

"We'll have to see."

"Will we?"

"But of course. And if practice does make perfect, my beauty, I expect you will be an expert in a very short time. You already drive me wild."

"I do? *Me?* Why, just think of that!"

"Do you suppose I might have a baby after tonight?"

"Good heavens, how could I know? Perhaps."

"Will you be sorry if I do?"

"Only if you are."

"I used to think I didn't want babies. But now . . . well, it's different somehow. I—I think I'd like to have *your* baby."

"Sweetheart."

* * *

"Harry?"

"Mmmm?"

"Are you awake?"

"Mmmm. Yes, I think so."

"Let's not go to London for a while."

"No, we won't go. Not just yet. We're going to be much too, er, busy here."

"I'm glad."

"Margarite, dear one. It is almost dawn. I have to sleep now. Men need their sleep, if they are to make love to their wives often."

"Oh, I didn't know that. I won't say another word . . . except it really is too bad you're not the Prince of the West Wind, isn't it? I'd wager anything you like *he* wouldn't need much rest."

Harry snorted a little, and she smiled as she cuddled close to him. He felt so good.

"Alas, I am only mortal, ma'am," he said in a sleepy voice.

"Harry?"

"Mmmm?"

"I'm awfully glad you are—too."

Chapter Eighteen

WHEN HE RETURNED a few days later, it did not take five minutes in the Earl and Countess of Darlington's presence for Comte Jean-Pierre de Fountaine to discover that whatever had estranged the couple had been happily resolved. It was all too obvious—from the countess's lingering smiles and blushes, the way the earl did not seem able to keep from touching her, and the private jokes they exchanged. And only a blind man could not have seen what was going on whenever their eyes met.

Jean-Pierre was more than annoyed, he was angry. He knew what would happen, for already Harry was talking of taking the countess to London with him, and last evening, as the two men had sat over their port, he had even suggested that perhaps it was time for the count to look for another sponsor.

It was so unfair, Jean-Pierre fumed, as he got ready for bed later. And at such a time, too! For he had not prospered, either at the races or at the gambling tables his host had provided for his guests. And where he had thought to recoup some of his losses, he was now much deeper in debt than before. And somehow he was sure that although Harry would be generous with a parting gift, he would not be at all willing to assume those debts. They were, the count mused, even from his extravagant viewpoint, enormous.

Jean-Pierre thought hard as he rode the earl's lands alone the next morning. He told himself he must be clever if he was to win through. But in order to do so, he must find some way to turn this situation to his own advantage.

He had concluded it was all the countess's fault. He knew well she had never liked him. No more than I have liked you, *madame*, he scoffed inwardly, as he urged his mount over a hedge. Before you came onto the stage again I had all of Harry's attention, all his kindness. And the only person he looked at with admiration was *me*. It is because of *you* that he has decided to cast me off. Me, Jean-Pierre de Fountaine! To think of it!

The count had never been dismissed before. Far from it. It had always been he himself who had severed a relationship he felt was becoming tedious, or in danger of turning unprofitable.

And what could he do when he left Harry Tredman's patronage?

Well, he knew he could always find a haven with the elderly William March, Viscount Lockwood. The man had suggested it to him last spring. And he knew Lockwood was wealthy beyond belief. But he suspected the viscount wanted more than a pleasant companion, and he was loath to agree to such a thing. Sexual intercourse between males was illegal in England, punishable by death. Even if he had been inclined that way it would have been too dangerous, for he knew he was not the only one who suspected the viscount's depravity. The man's footmen and grooms were always so young, so good-looking, and they left his employ with such regularity. Besides, Jean-Pierre had a reputation with the ladies, all of whom believed he was a great lover. He could not bear to forfeit that reputation.

But there was the Marchioness of Gower. He knew she would be delighted to have him in her train. If only she were not so ugly, Jean-Pierre thought with a shudder.

He toyed with the idea that that ugliness might be the perfect foil for his own handsome face and form, but he could not bring himself to the experiment. One had one's standards, after all, he reminded himself as he slowed his horse to a trot to rest him. He could not compromise them, but perhaps the lady would be good for a loan, with a promise from him as bond, if things got out of hand? Of course he had no intention of honoring any such bond, but the marchioness wouldn't know that.

In the meantime, the count knew he must somehow contrive to remain with Harry and his countess until he had secured some kind of future for himself. The lovebirds, he sneered, whipping his horse to a gallop again.

Sally had been disappointed that the count had returned to the Hall so soon. She was shy with Harry still, unsure. She had hoped to have more time alone with him, for every day they spent together was a revelation to her. She suspected she had even come to love him, and this after she had claimed she could never love anyone. And she told herself that perhaps now she could even trust him. But she had noticed—for all the sweet things he whispered to her, all the dear names he called her when they were together in bed—that he had never told her he loved her. This made it impossible for her to speak of her own love for him.

She remembered that once, long ago, he had mentioned that he did not know what love was; that he too had never loved. But how could he behave as he does and not love me? she wondered. Was he that good an actor? Sally did not know, but she was determined to do everything she could to earn that love, and the trust she suspected he, like she, was afraid to give.

We are flawed, both of us, she thought sadly. Flawed by what happened to us when we were younger. I wonder if it is ever possible to erase the past so thoroughly that it ceases to matter, or affect one? And if it is, can *we* do it?

That evening at dinner she sat quietly, letting the count amuse Harry with some gossip he had gleaned while visiting. He is a witty companion when he wants to be, she thought, as she took some Dover sole from the platter the butler was presenting.

"Lady Agnes was there as well," the count was saying, and she tried to concentrate. "I do not believe I have ever seen a woman so tiny and thin. She looks as if she has not eaten for months. In fact, *cher* Harry, the only large thing about her is her temper. She reminds me of a particularly virulent little shrew.

"She managed to quarrel with almost everyone present, and about the stupidest things, too. Once another lady wore the same color gown—off with her head! Another time, a gentleman failed to notice she had dropped her fan—to the dungeons with him! She even took *me* to task for begging to differ with her about which was the best of Sheridan's plays!"

As Harry chuckled he went on, "One must feel most sincerely for her long-suffering husband. Poor man, to be cursed so! I wonder he dares close his eyes and sleep beside her. Perhaps he does not?

"Oh, by the way, several people asked me about the portrait you had painted of me and your countess. Word of it has spread, and for some reason everyone is anxious to see it."

"You remind me," the earl said, covering his wine glass when his butler would have refilled it, "I must write to Chalon about the framing. I forgot to tell him to have it done."

Jean Pierre smiled warmly. "But you must allow me to see to it for you, *mon cher ami*. You will agree my taste is superior to his in such a matter?"

The earl nodded. "I would be agreeable, if you would care to undertake it," he said carelessly.

"I shall take coach for London tomorrow in order to do so," the count assured him.

Sally tried not to look too pleased.

"And I will have the painting not only framed but hung when you return. Er, when do you think that will be?"

The earl looked down the table to where his countess sat and gave her a slow, intimate smile. The count's hand tightened on the stem of his wine glass.

"Perhaps in two weeks or so? I am not quite sure.

There are some pressing matters here that must be resolved first," the earl said.

"Of course," the count agreed easily, stifling his anger. "I shall make sure all is in readiness in St. James's Square for you both. *Madame?* Do you have any commissions for me?"

Sally forced herself to look away from Harry's hypnotizing eyes. "Why, how kind of you to ask, sir," she said. "But no, there is nothing."

To her surprise, the count rose and bowed to them in turn. "Then if you will excuse me, I shall go and give the necessary orders. It will take quite a while for my man to pack, and I would make an early start."

Neither the earl nor the countess tried to dissuade him, and he was aware they had forgotten him before he had even closed the doors of the dining salon behind him. To think of it, he fumed. He, the handsomest, most courted man in England and France— ignored! Well, they would pay for it, both of them. And now, since he knew exactly how he would exact that payment, the count smiled as he climbed the stairs.

Alone again, the Tredmans most certainly did not miss Jean-Pierre. Instead they reveled in their new solitude, and spent every moment they could together. They went riding most mornings, and breakfast often had to be delayed when they failed to return at the normal time. One rainy afternoon they spent closeted in the countess's room, after the earl gave orders that they were not to be disturbed for any reason. On pleasant days they drove out, taking a picnic luncheon with them. Miss Preston smiled when she saw how little was missing from that basket when it was returned. Obviously the earl and his countess fed on other food these days, and she was glad for both of them, most especially her mistress, radiant in her new happiness.

All the servants were talking, and some of the younger maids sighed in envy at the happy couple who were so oblivious to the world. And the earl's valet,

Griffen, walked with a lighter step, for his master drank sparingly now.

One warm evening, the earl even coaxed Sally into going for a dip in the lake. She insisted on wearing her shift, for she was still very much aware that they were not alone here. She had marveled before at how easily Harry could forget the servants, when she could not. But he acted as if they were invisible. She envied him his nonchalance.

That evening she was able to forget other people, however. The water was delightful, and she felt almost as she had as a young girl—carefree and easy. She did not even protest when Harry took her shift off, telling her as he did so that he could not bear to have even that flimsy barrier between them. And how gentle he was when he dried her off later, how tender when he laid her down on the cushions of one of the benches, how beautifully he loved her. Sally found herself weeping a little from joy as she held all the lean, long muscled length of him close.

Much later, after they had bathed again and dressed, they walked up to the Hall through the gardens, arms about each other's waists.

"Do you know, I do believe I shall miss the Hall when we go to London," the earl said, looking up to where it loomed over them. "How very strange to hear myself say such a thing; I, who have always hated the place so!"

"But what you hated is no more, Harry," Sally reminded him, turning a little so she could rub her cheek against his sleeve.

"Yes, that is true, all thanks to you, dear heart," he said, smiling down at her. He thought she looked like a contented kitten, and he wouldn't have been surprised if she had begun to purr. He hugged her closer.

"I'll miss it, too," she confided. "Oh, I know London is very grand, and there is so much to do there, but it is . . . busy, crowded. There are just too many people. And I find I don't want to be surrounded by people. I only want to be with you."

He stopped and turned her so that he could draw her into his arms. "We shall still be together, even in town. You'll see," he told her, before he kissed her lightly.

Sally nodded, but there was a little frown on her brow. Of course Harry was right, but when they were in London she knew she would have to share him with the world, and she was not ready for that. Then too, the odiously conceited count would be there, making a most annoying *ménage à trois* again. She sighed.

The earl heard the little sigh, saw her frown, and to divert her he said, "How I shall enjoy seeing you give one of your famous salons, madam. But I think it would be wise to keep them exclusive. No need to have all the ton crowding in. And that way an invitation will be quite a cachet, something to be boasted about and prized.

"You must have some stunning new gowns made for the occasion. Let me see. . . . Perhaps a figured silk in royal blue? And I would like to see you in creamy white, with a low neckline and soft, floating sleeves, with only your pearls as adornment."

"I shall choose my own gowns from now on, Harry," she warned him. "Remember, I am not a doll for you to dress."

His dark brows rose. They had just reached the terrace off the small morning room, and as they went up the shallow steps he said, "And so you shall. But just occasionally, *very* occasionally, might I have the honor of approving your choice? Er, even if it is only once or twice a year?"

His meek pleading did not fool his countess, and she shook her head and chuckled. "*You*," she said. "I very much fear you will never change!"

The following afternoon it rained again, a steady, cold downpour, and they took tea in the library. A small fire burned in the grate to take away the damp chill that told them autumn was coming.

As she handed him his cup the earl thanked her and said, "What a picture you make, no matter what mundane chore you are performing! Do you know, I find I still catch my breath at your beauty, my Margarite?"

"Have you ever thought how very unfair you are?" Sally asked, as she picked up her own cup and settled back against the cushions of her chair.

"Unfair to call you a beauty?" he asked, perplexed.

"No, unfair because you changed my name, and without so much as a by-your-leave either. It was very arrogant of you, you know. And yet I have never suggested you change *yours*. What if I don't like it? Have you considered that? To tell the truth, I don't. Harry reminds me of a footman, or perhaps a cowman."

"I'll have you know I was named for an English king!" he said indignantly.

"What of that? I don't like George or John or Charles either."

His brows rose as she sipped her tea. "No? How very unusual of you. They are all such well-liked names."

"Not by me," she said firmly. "But I do seem to remember that you have other names as well, although I must admit I was not attending closely on the only occasion I heard them—our wedding. What are they? You must refresh my memory."

He did not speak for a moment, and he looked so wary that Sally had to swallow a giggle.

"Come now, sir, confess!"

He shook his head before he relented. "Very well, since you insist. I am Henry Augustus Vivian Brentwood Tredman." He laughed briefly. "What a mouthful that is! And do you know, it has convinced me that only solemn, staid men are suited for the clergy."

She looked a question, and he went on. "Why, faced with a tiny infant of only a few pounds, no doubt red-faced and squalling and ugly, how could anyone bestow that sonorous string of names without laughing right out loud? Obviously, only a man completely devoid of humor could have done it."

"Oh, I can just picture it. In some dank, murky church . . ."

"Cathedral, my dear. Remember my status, if you please!"

". . . with the acrid odor of smoking candles poisoning the air . . ."

"I wish you would stop placing me in some dreary chapel! The candles were beeswax, of course."

". . . you, dressed in an ancient, yellowed christening gown, and attended by weeping relatives on both sides of the family."

"It was brand-new, and I rather imagine they must have glared at each other, don't you?"

"No doubt—Augustus."

"Oh no, you shall not call me Augustus, madam! Nor Gus either. I absolutely forbid it!"

"But you call me 'Margarite' when my name is Sally. Furthermore, I will *always* be Sally to myself."

She saw he was looking displeased, but she hastened to add, "Besides, I think Harry and Sally sound as if they belong together, much as Margarite and Augustus do. Very grand, those two names, don't you think?"

"Perhaps, but I still refuse to let you saddle me with such a title. 'Augustus,' indeed! Bah!"

"As you wish, sir," she said meekly, and he looked at her suspiciously. He saw the light that danced in her eyes, the way her lips quivered as she tried to contain a smile, and he shook his head. Putting down his cup, he came to stand over her, bending to place his hands on the arms of her chair.

"Margarite," he said, his voice soft but still a warning, "you are not to call me Augustus—no, not even in your head. Do you understand?"

Sally only laughed at him, and he took her cup away and pulled her into his arms to kiss her thoroughly.

"I cannot promise that," she said when he let her speak again. She was breathing fast, and she closed her eyes as his hand caressed her breast. "And I do hope that someday you will be able to call me Sally."

His hand became more persistent, and she fell silent for a moment, lost in sensation.

"We must finish tea," she protested, although he noticed she did not try to pull away from him.

"Why?" he asked. "Are you hungry? No? Neither am I. Not for tea, at any rate."

The Earl and Countess of Darlington were at home in St. James's Square in London ten days later. Sally wondered if the count would mention how long it had taken them to get there, for they had twice delayed their departure from the country. To her relief, he said nothing. Indeed, he appeared to be on his most caressing behavior: eager to amuse, conciliatory, and even, on occasion, absent.

She had to admit the house looked marvelous. It was as clean as a new penny, and the count had had it filled with flowers to welcome them. There were even some roses in her own suite.

She admired anew those rooms, which she had not seen for three long years. They looked as fresh as when she had first come here, a most apprehensive bride. Her little country maid was round-eyed as she inspected the beautiful sitting room, the luxurious bedchamber, the well-appointed dressing room, whispering that she was sure she would never be able to bring herself to touch a thing lest she break something.

Sally knew Nancy would have to be replaced. She would not be happy here so far from home, and to be truthful, she had yet to acquire the skill necessary for a lady's maid.

Sally regretted that Miss Preston had not returned with her, but when she had discussed it with the older woman, Preston had told her she would prefer to remain as housekeeper at the Hall. Reluctantly, Sally had agreed. It was the better position, and Preston was so competent at it that she knew she could not insist. She reminded herself that one of her first orders of business must be to hire another dresser, before she and Harry went out in company again.

The count had shown them the double portrait with a great deal of satisfaction. He had had it hung in the entrance hall, in a prominent central place beneath

the gallery. It did look well there, Sally admitted, even
as she wondered at the count's unusual ebullience.

Both she and the earl were very busy in the days
that followed their return, but Sally was glad that
there was still time for them to spend alone. And of
course, it was a rare night that Harry did not come to
her before they slept. And somehow, because they
were not free to be with each other exclusively, she
found that the time they did spend alone became all
the more precious, and their lovemaking more passionate and consuming.

When they began to go about again she discovered
that the acquaintances she had made at her salons
stood her in good stead now, for there was always
someone interesting for her to talk to at any party
they attended. She was amused also by how eagerly
she was courted by men and women alike. Harry told
her that they did so in order to gain an invitation to
one of her salons, and Sally suspected he was right.
All unbeknownst to her in the country, she had become a *cause célèbre*. However unwarranted that
might have been, it certainly eased her way in the ton.

Of course there were still some who looked at her
askance, questioning the Irish background that no one
seemed to know anything about, and wondering if
there had ever been a first husband at all. Rumors
flew that she was no better than she should be, and a
great deal worse if the truth were known. Some of the
older ladies sneered at her, and could be seen whispering among themselves about the advantages of a beautiful face and how taken in Harry Tredman had been.

No one was more scornful than Grace, the Lady
Rolls. This formidable, elderly dame had held successful salons for years, and she did not welcome any
competition. Furthermore, she had heard how well received Sally's salons had been in the country, and she
knew society was agog to learn that she intended to
continue them in town. Indignant, Lady Rolls was in-
sufferably rude to Sally, when she did not cut her
directly. It did no good at all. Sally ignored her, the

earl laughed at her, and even Jean-Pierre was indifferent to her slights.

Lady Rolls fumed, for she suspected she could not compete with the beautiful young countess, and as time passed her fears proved correct. All of the nobility in London followed the men of genius to St. James's Square, and those who were not fortunate enough to be invited redoubled their efforts to gain that most important little rectangle, edged in gilt, that was an invitation.

Everyone who saw the double portrait proclaimed its beauty, and Chalon had many new commissions. For herself Sally hated that painting, and she especially loathed the way Jean-Pierre would gaze into her eyes as others admired it, smiling down at her so intimately and taking her hand in his to kiss it in lingering tribute. He appeared the eager lover, and she wondered Harry did nothing to stop him. He had been jealous enough of Sir Thomas, after all. But then, she told herself, sometimes Harry was as unfathomable as he had ever been.

Naturally the earl had noticed Jean-Pierre's attentions to his wife, but he only smiled to himself. The boy would do no harm, and it still pleased him to see the two of them, so perfect in face and form, together. However, he did not forget that he now wanted Jean-Pierre gone. He had heard some rumors of enormous debt, rumors that quickly became reality when the bills were presented.

He called the count into his study one morning and had it out with him. Even he was staggered at the amount of obligation the young man confessed to, and he was furious that he had been taken advantage of in such a way. He ordered the count to leave his house, and told him further that he had no intention of paying all his debts.

"I do assure you, Jean-Pierre, that as your patron I at no time intended to be made a dupe. And I do believe that is what you have tried to do. Why did you not confess all this to me sooner? Some of these bills date back to early spring! And then there is the

matter of your gambling debts, which relate directly
to your honor. Have you no pride?" he added, looking grim although his voice was even.

Jean-Pierre shrugged. "You are angry with me, *mon
cher ami*. I am so sorry. But I do not understand how
it happened, truly I do not," he said, trying a winsome
smile. He saw the earl was not amused, and he hastened to add, "You know how it is with runs of bad
luck. And you have never complained of my expenses
before."

"A few hundred pounds here and there is one thing.
Thousands are another," Harry said coldly. "I shall
expect you to leave Darlington House by the end of
the week. I shall settle enough on you so you may
pay your most pressing debts and still have enough to
live in comfort, but I shall not frank you further. And
if any more tradesmen or even gentlemen come, waving unpaid bills and vouchers at me, I shall of course
inform them that I am in no way responsible for you
any longer. We have had a pleasant time of it these
past few years, but that time is over now."

He noticed that the count's handsome face was pale,
and that there was an angry gleam in his eyes. Harry
raised his brows. "Surely you cannot think me unreasonable. How could you?" he drawled. "For even
such as I can grow weary of . . . er, being plucked,
you know. Admit it: You have lived for almost three
years entirely at my expense. Enough is enough."

He rose from behind his desk then, and came to
put a hand on the count's shoulder. "Come, Jean-
Pierre! Acknowledge that I am right, and let us part
friends. I wish you good fortune. I am sure you will
find another . . . mmm . . . patron before long."

"I do assure you that will be no problem," the count
said stiffly. "But perhaps I may not have to do such
a thing, after all. You shall see. I beg you excuse me,
sir."

Harry waved a careless hand and went back to the
papers he had been studying when the count had been
announced. As he picked up another sheet, he thought
how happy Margarite would be to hear the news. She

had never liked Jean-Pierre. How delighted she would be to learn he was quitting the house at last.

The count went up to his own suite of rooms and called for his valet to bring him his hat, gloves, and cane. As his man set the hat reverently on his carefully tousled curls, he told him that they would be leaving Darlington House before week's end.

"I shall see to the moving of my canvases myself, Henri. Be sure there is an ample supply of heavy paper, twine, and padding. You will pack my clothes and accessories."

The thin, dark Frenchman who had been with him for years nodded, his sallow face giving no hint of his feelings in the matter. Jean-Pierre ignored him as he strode to the stairs, for he was thinking hard.

Reggie Hadley had spoken to him only yesterday. He had been called into the country because of his father's illness, and he had mentioned that he was giving up his rooms. No doubt he would be delighted to let his friend use them for a few weeks, and it would be at no cost to the count. Mr. Hadley was one of his most fervent admirers. As he strolled around the square, Jean-Pierre was busy reviewing the names of others who might be helpful to him. Fortunately, there were any number of them. He did not think he would have much trouble—not he, the Comte Jean-Pierre de Fountaine!

In his arrogance, he did not foresee how insurmountable a problem those unpaid debts of his would be. Somehow he had convinced himself that they would all disappear, or be forgiven, or forgotten. Spoiled and petted all his life for his handsome good looks, his wit, and his style, Jean-Pierre had no honor, and certainly no clear grasp of reality. He considered himself above other human beings and their obligations—one beloved of the gods.

In the next two weeks, he was to realize his error.

It was true Reggie Hadley had stammered in delight at the opportunity of doing him a favor, and some of the other more impressionable young men had been quick to lend him a few hundred, but the older men—

those with the greatest wealth—seemed most reluctant to part with any. The count wondered if Harry had spoken to them, warning them away, and his anger at the earl and his countess became a consuming thing.

He took to remaining indoors most of the time lest he be hounded by creditors, only emerging after sunset and on Sundays, when he would go riding with friends. He even instructed the man who let the rooms that no one was to be admitted to his presence before he himself had established the visitor's identity. That man, used to the peculiar ways of the nobility, had agreed.

One day, however, when the landlord was out, a young housemaid answered the front door, and allowed a Mr. Alfred Dunne to enter. Mr. Dunne gave her a small coin for her trouble, and pinched her cheek, saying he would not need an escort to the count's rooms.

It was precisely three o'clock in the afternoon when he pushed his way inside those rooms, waving papers and proclaiming the count's arrest for debt. Jean-Pierre was horrified, but he blustered, saying that whatever the man's business was he would have to wait.

"I am not dressed for the street, sir, and I have my reputation to consider," he said grandly. "I suggest you take a chair. This may take awhile.

"*Henri!* Henri, my bath water, if you please," he called.

His manservant entered the room, a question on his lips. The count had bathed not an hour ago, and Henri was still weary from carrying all those copper cans of hot water up the stairs. But when he saw the red-faced commoner sitting stiffly on a chair against the wall, clutching his hat and various papers in his hands, he understood the situation even before his master explained it to him in rapid French.

"But of a certainty, Monsieur le Comte," he said with a deep bow. "Your bath will be delayed only a few minutes. *Je regretes.* It is the maid's fault there is no hot water."

"No matter," Jean-Pierre said airily. "This gentleman can wait."

After almost half an hour, the bath had been duly prepared. Stripped, the count lowered himself into the hot water gracefully, and proceeded to soak with his eyes closed for some time. Then his valet scrubbed his back for him, and washed his hair. This operation required more hot water, and a special rinse which, the valet kindly explained to their fascinated observer, preserved the color and sheen of Monsieur le Comte's dark curls.

After his bath the count was rubbed thoroughly dry, given a lengthy massage, and then anointed with perfumed lotion. Only then did he don his dressing gown.

"A shave, do you think, Henri?" he asked anxiously, as he peered into his hand mirror.

"*Mais oui, Comte*," the valet agreed. "There is a faint shadow. . . ."

"*Atroce!* Hone my razor at once!" Jean-Pierre exclaimed.

After he had been shaved, and more lotion stroked onto his face, the count's nails and cuticles required lengthy attention. And as his hair dried it was brushed and curled and pomaded, before it was arranged in a time-consuming but elegant style.

Mr. Dunne thought the final effect much the same as if the young man had only run his fingers through it carelessly, but he made no comment. Lordy, wot a fop we got 'ere! he thought to himself, shifting a bit in his chair. Silly Frenchies! No wonder they're no match for a 'onest Englishman, and never wuz.

The count's clothing was discussed next. The valet brought out what seemed an enormous assortment of shirts, coats, waistcoats, and breeches to a sheriff's deputy who had but one other pair of pants to his name. The count decided on his outfit only after a long, excited conversation in French with his valet about the merits of each and every article produced.

Mr. Dunne rose to stretch his legs and yawn. To tell truth he was becoming very bored, and he only hoped he would not fall asleep.

"No, I think I prefer the pale gray waistcoat after all, Henri," the count said a long time later, as he studied the patterned ecru one he sported in the full-length pier glass.

The valet protested in a spate of French, and a great many minutes elapsed before the matter was decided. Next came the count's cravat. Mr. Dunne's eyes were popping as he counted. Fourteen, no *sixteen* large snowy rectangles, heavy with starch, were attempted before the count declared himself satisfied. A further amount of time was spent waiting for the valet to re-polish the count's pumps, and brush his top hat. Jean-Pierre had seen a dull place on the former, and a spot on the latter. And as he waited, he sipped a glass of wine that Mr. Dunne eyed longingly. He was not offered any. Indeed, the count acted as if he were here alone.

Choosing the correct fob, chain, and stickpin took almost as long, and for some reason the count suddenly seemed unable to abide any of his large collection of canes. And then nothing would do but for the valet to go out and fetch him a boutonnier.

"Do bring a selection, Henri. And hurry! It grows late!" the count called after his man, as he went down the stairs at a slow, measured pace.

Eventually a small white carnation was positioned in the count's lapel, and his shining top hat adjusted on those gleaming curls of his. Mr. Dunne stirred in anticipation, sitting up straighter in his chair. On being handed his gloves, Jean-Pierre wandered over to the window and stood there for several minutes, smoothing them slowly onto his hands, finger by finger, until not a wrinkle could be seen.

When he turned at last, impeccable and urbane, he was smiling. "And now I fear I must bid you farewell, sir," he said to the startled Mr. Dunne.

" 'Ere, now, wot's all this then? I've been waitin' about fer ye fer hours, and you can just come with me, me foine sir! I'm 'ere ter arrest ye, ye know!"

The count shrugged, his dark eyes gleaming in amusement. "But how can that be, *mon ami*?" he asked. "Do look out the window. It is dusk. You cannot serve those papers and arrest me now. Surely you remember that such papers can be served only between sunrise and sunset on weekdays, and never on Sundays. A most peculiar English law, wouldn't you agree? But one most beneficial to me.

"I give you good evening. Henri. Show this, er, person to the door. At once."

Chapter Nineteen

SALLY'S LATEST SALON had been her most stunning success, and she was still receiving congratulatory notes and letters from the attendees days later. One morning at the breakfast table Harry watched her fondly as she read her post, admiring the little smile she wore and, occasionally, the slight blush that tinged her cheeks. When he asked her to read aloud some of her notes, she refused.

"You may read them for yourself, sir," she said, rising to bring them to him where he sat at the other end of the table. "They are much too effusive. And surely you deserve some of the credit, anyway. I do not believe I could ever have persuaded Mrs. Siddons out of retirement to read to us from her most famous roles, had you not taken a hand there."

Harry waved that hand. "Ah, but I was not the one who coaxed the young tenor who is being lionized at the moment into honoring us. What a pure, true voice he has! What range!

"But the *pièce de résistance*, of course, was the Prince Regent's appearance as cellist in the string quartet. For securing his royal performance you will be talked about for years, Margarite my beauty."

He blew her a kiss, and she smiled at him.

"However, I find I do take exception to this note from Mr. Danvers," he said a few minutes later. His voice was so cold Sally felt a tremor of alarm, and she put her coffee cup down.

"Granted that the young man is impressionable, and—dare I say it?—exceedingly silly, but even so to compare you to a saint who is beloved of the angels and, he implies, himself as well, is a bit much. Perhaps Mr. Danvers should be required to admire you from afar for a while?"

Sally chuckled, relieved by his sarcasm. "Somehow I doubt you are serious, Harry," she said. "Jealous of that poor young man? Surely not you."

"You're right, of course," he agreed. "I was teasing you. And truly I do feel for him, for it is obvious he adores you."

"Harry . . ." she said slowly, as he dropped Mr. Danvers's note and picked up another.

He looked up and saw her little frown. "What is it, my dear?" he asked. "What is troubling you?"

"I must admit I am concerned about the gossip that is going around about me," she confessed softly. "I have heard the whispers, and they seem to be growing, even now that the count has left the house."

"What whispers?" he asked. "Be plain with me, if you please."

She raised her eyes to his, and he could see the worry in them.

"People are saying that Jean-Pierre and I are . . . are more than acquaintances."

"I am sure they are, but you must not be troubled by that," he told her. "The ton loves to talk. And since the double portrait of the two of you in that romantic pose has been admired and discussed by so many, it is only normal for them to do so. Never listen to gossip, Margarite. It means nothing."

"But—but there is so much of it about," she protested. "Is there no way we can stop it?"

"How? By denying it? Who would believe you? And if you did such a thing, they would think it a sign of your guilt. No, no. Much better to ignore it as something beneath your consideration.

"I have heard the whispers, too. I only smile. And surely I would not do that, would I, if the gossip had any basis in fact?"

"I think it is Lady Rolls who has been the most assiduous in keeping the talk going," Sally told him.

"Grace Rolls is a vicious old woman. A damned

foolish one, too, for her delight in trying to blacken
your name only gives her away, to anyone with any
brains and discrimination."

"It does? How?" Sally asked, fascinated.

"One: She dislikes you for having taken her place
as London's premier salon hostess. Everyone knows
that. Don't you agree?"

Sally nodded.

"Two: By spreading this gossip, she acknowledges
her defeat. And three, by doing so she only sounds
the backbiter she is. Before long the ton will be laughing at her, and she may well find it necessary to retire
to her country estate. Trust me in this, Margarite."

Sally nodded again, but she still looked troubled.

"Do you remember my saying once that I never pay
attention to what others think of me?" Harry asked.
Not waiting for her reply, he went on, "I would that
you would adopt the same attitude. I don't care. Why
should you? Forget it, I beg you."

"That is very easy for you to say, Harry, but it is
different for me. You were born to this society. I was
not. And I know people are still talking about my
Irish background, my family, my . . . my complete
unworthiness to be one of them. Don't you think I
can interpret the scornful looks, those little sniffs, the
snide remarks about the poor little Irish nobody who
trapped a noble lord with her pretty face and nothing
else to commend her? You tell me to ignore it, forget
it, but I can't! I—I am not like you. I doubt I ever
will be. And Harry, I cannot tell you how it hurts."

The earl rose swiftly and came to kneel beside her
chair. His hazel eyes were blazing. "Stop this at
once!" he ordered. Then he took her unresisting
hands in his and said more quietly, "You are never
to denigrate yourself in that way again. You are a
wonderful woman, with a great deal more than just a
pretty face. And I was not trapped. The very idea! I?
You insult me!"

Sally tried a little smile, but her throat was so tight
she could not speak. Oh, Harry, she thought, you
don't understand at all, but I will try, for your sake,

to put the insults behind me, be the kind of countess you require.

He kissed her hands and rose. As he went back to his chair he said, "Now, I think you still have some letters to read, do you not?"

Obediently she turned over a few cards of invitation, but her face did not brighten until she spotted a letter from Catherine. She picked it up eagerly and broke the seal.

Of all the earl's children the red-headed Catherine was her favorite, and her most faithful correspondent. Sally knew it was probably because the girl felt isolated in the country, with only those paid attendants to care for her and her sister and brothers. And she was older than they were, and going through a difficult time in this, her early teens. Sally knew only too well how tumultuous the period between childhood and girlhood could be, how confusing and sometimes even frightening, for at that age you didn't know who you were. You only knew that the childhood you were leaving had become something safe and precious, and hard to give up. And Catherine also had to contend with the stigma of illegitimacy, poor girl!

Shaking her head a little, she read Catherine's letter. The girl told her the news of the family, spoke of her own pursuits, mentioned a book that Sally had sent her to read, and asked a great many questions about London and her father, and Sally's activities in town. In every line Sally could sense the longing and loneliness, and by the time she had finished the letter she was frowning.

His breakfast completed, Harry rose and came to her, to put his hands on her shoulders and bend to kiss her hair. "What is it now that makes you so pensive, my dear?" he asked softly, one hand moving to caress the soft skin above the neck of her morning gown. "What a difficult time of it we are having today. One problem after another! I wish someone had sent you a funny letter, full of jests to make you laugh."

"It is this letter from Catherine," Sally admitted,

putting it down with a sigh. "She is such a dear, and I am worried about her.

"No, Harry, stop that!" she ordered, as his hand went lower.

Obediently he took the seat beside her, folding his hands virtuously on the table before him.

"Very well. Tell me. But when you have finished doing so, know I shall resume where I, er, left off," he threatened.

"It is obvious that Catherine is not happy," Sally said, ignoring his provocative statement. "Harry, isn't there some way the children could come and live with us? All of them?"

His brows rose, and that haughty look she knew so well returned to his face. Sally had come to hate that look, and now she steeled herself.

"No, they cannot," he said brusquely. "I do not care to have any of them about. Furthermore, Catherine—all my bastards—can never be accepted by society, and they should not be raised with my legitimate children. I've told you this before."

"But you say you don't care what people think, how they gossip," Sally protested. "Why should this particular matter be of concern?"

"Because, my dear innocent countess, it does not affect only you and me, it affects all the children. My heirs, and Fay, would be pitied, made mock of. And the bastards would be scorned. And whatever Catherine is feeling now would be more than trebled if she were under my roof. Many of the nobility have illegitimate children, but they do not flaunt them."

"It seems such a shame, such a shame." Sally mourned.

"It is the way of the world," he told her, his voice still cold.

He rose then and went to the door. "Please, forget it. The children do well where they are. Eventually, of course, Reginald and Lawrence and Fay—even baby Alistair, someday—will take their place beside us. The others will not, because they cannot. And that is my final word on the subject."

As he left the room, quite forgetting his amorous intent of only moments earlier, Sally bit her lip. She held her tongue—she knew that tone in Harry's voice—but she did not forget.

Sometime later she summoned the housekeeper, to go over the daily menus with her and to discuss any special chores to be done by the maids. She reminded herself, as she waited for the woman to appear, that she must be sure the butler set the footmen to polishing the plate. She had noticed at dinner last evening that it was becoming dull.

Then, in spite of the ache in her heart still, she smiled to herself. She had taken over the running of the house only the day after her arrival a few weeks ago. Harry had been astounded to discover from his butler that she had done so. He had called her to his study to remonstrate with her. But somehow, although he had meant to take her to task for getting involved in something he was quite capable of handling himself—something he had specifically told her he did not wish her to interfere in—his lecture was never given.

Instead, after hearing only his first few sentences, Sally had gone into battle, all guns blazing. She had taken care of Darlington Hall for three years, had she not? she asked. Restored it, maintained it, made it again a happy place in which to live? And she had brought the land to profit as well? How then could Harry think her incapable of seeing to his townhouse? It was a chore that took only a few minutes a day, and she insisted on performing that chore. And was there anything else he wished to see her about? If not, she had an appointment with the modiste.

Shrugging in the face of her indignant argument, and remembering how the princess in her fairy tale had felt, he had struck his colors and agreed.

As he did so her face had lit up, and she had run to kiss him. "Thank you," she had whispered. "It is important to me, you see. It makes me feel your wife, not just a possession. For I was never that, Harry, and I never will be. But I will be your wife, if you'll let me."

Later that morning, Sally had had to make her excuses to Madame Clotilde for being over an hour late for her appointment. Now she smiled, remembering what had happened next in the study.

After interviewing the housekeeper, Sally had a busy day. She did some shopping with her new abigail, attended a luncheon, and wrote for most of the afternoon before joining Harry for a drive in the park at five. They were to attend a play that evening, after dining out with friends.

As she took her seat in the theater later, Sally was distressed to see Jean-Pierre de Fountaine in the box immediately opposite theirs. She noticed that he was one of the Marchioness of Gower's party.

She would have pretended she hadn't seen him, but he looked across the theater then and their eyes met. Immediately, he bowed low to her. Sally could hear the comments and conjectures in the neighboring boxes and she knew he had been observed, that the long time he had held his right hand to his heart had been noted, as had his amorous, burning gaze, so intent on her face. Furious with his playacting, Sally lowered her eyes to her lap and pretended to be searching in her reticule for a handkerchief.

She heard very little of the performance that night. True, she kept her eyes on the stage, and she laughed and applauded and exclaimed at all the appropriate times, but her mind was elsewhere.

Jean-Pierre de Fountaine, that formidable enemy of hers, was up to no good, and she knew it. And even though there was nothing between them, and never had been no matter how he acted now, surely Harry would begin to wonder why his former protégé was so obviously enamored of his wife. Would he begin to think that where there's smoke, there's fire? Sally wondered. She was worried. She suspected Harry did not really trust her even now that they were intimate, for after all, he had yet to tell her that he loved her. Oh, they were close now, physically, but she could never forget how quick he had been to believe the worst about her and Thomas Avery. Why should he be any different now? He was still the same man, still arrogant, aristocratic, demanding, and volatile. Still difficult.

As the first act curtain came down, and the orange sellers again began to call their wares, she wondered that she could love her husband so completely, for no one knew better than she did that Harry was far from perfect. *Very* far.

But love him she did, and she would not let this odious count ruin their newfound happiness. She promised herself, before she turned to the others and joined their conversation, that she would do whatever it took to stop him. No conceited, worthless sponger was going to come between her and Harry. She would make sure of that!

The count had been delighted to have the opportunity to bow to the beautiful Countess of Darlington and pretend he was stricken with love for her, for it reinforced the lies he had been telling about town.

Ever since he had left the Tredman house to move into rooms, he had been questioned closely for the reason. Not caring to admit his debts, which he felt he had kept from almost everyone thus far, he had implied that the earl had asked him to leave because he had discovered that his protégé and his wife were lovers.

"I have been forbidden ever to approach her again," he would say, staring broodingly into some distance over his questioner's shoulder. "I cannot tell you of the pain that this banishment has brought to me. Because, my friend, although she is not accepting my tribute in that painting the earl had done of us together, I can assure you she was most happy to accept it, and me as well—ah, yes!—when we were alone.

"Ah, those passionate hours we spent in each other's arms! There is no woman who can compare to her—my wild, lovely Margarite!

"Do you know, I have found that in general English women make poor lovers, but Margarite is different.

So giving she is, so accomplished, so abandoned! I am distraught! How shall I live without her, she, who brought me so much joy?"

Here he would clench his fists and frown, or perhaps run a frenzied hand through his hair for emphasis.

His friends always patted him awkwardly on the back, uttered a few disjointed, sympathetic phrases, and excused themselves to hurry away and pass on the news, just as he had hoped they would.

Even the Marchioness of Gower had had to wipe her eyes with her handkerchief, so affected had she been by his tale of lovers cruelly separated. She had been good for a loan as well, even though Jean-Pierre had told her he could not move into her house and her bed, not heartbroken as he was. He could hear her sigh of regret even now.

"Perhaps someday, dear boy," she had said, stroking his pale cheek. "Perhaps you will be able to forget her someday."

The count had shaken his head sadly. But when he also remembered how she had offered to arrange a tryst in her own house for the lovers, hinting of the large sum she was willing to part with if he would allow her to observe his lovemaking with Countess Darlington, he grimaced. Horrible woman, he thought. Just horrible. Some people are too disgusting to live.

And when a few of the more astute nobles mentioned that it did not appear that the countess also was suffering, he only shrugged.

"The poor darling," he would say, shaking his head in remorse. "What choice does she have? *Mon cher* Harry is insanely jealous. He has threatened her with bodily harm. I told her, for her own safety, that she must pretend that nothing happened between us. She does not even dare to meet my eyes, lest she be overcome and give us away. Alas, that we are so ill fated!"

Like Sally, the count heard very little of the play that evening. He was busy making plans, perfecting the elaborate plan he intended to use for his revenge. For things were not going well for him, and he was getting worried. Although several gentlemen had suggested he join their households, he could sense that none of them would be willing to settle any former debts. Besides, he was getting tired of skulking about after dark, and tired of being dunned. But now things would be different. All was in train.

When he had first come up to town from Darlington Hall, he had called on the artist Chalon to pick up the portrait. He had chatted briefly with the master, even admired some of his students' work, for a class was in session. He had also carefully noted the name of a young artist who seemed more than competent.

The next day he arranged to meet the man in a shabby coffeehouse not frequented by the ton. Knowing as he did how precariously most artists lived, he had mentioned a large sum for the commission he had in mind. The artist's eyes lit up as he did so.

"But it will be yours, you understand, only if the painting I desire is completed within the week," he had said. Mr. Sarles had nodded.

"I see no problem, sir," he said, his voice betraying his eagerness.

"You will not be required to paint the heads," the count told him. "I will sketch them in lightly, as well as the pose necessary, for, you understand, this is a matter of some delicacy. You will be responsible only for the figures and the background, all to be done in Chalon's style. The painting is to be a surprise for the lady to be portrayed. I'm only her husband's emissary. How sad it is for you that he does not intend to exhibit it—except for his wife's titillation, and of course his own."

Mr. Sarles had nodded again, his fingers moving so restlessly on the scarred tabletop between them it was obvious he could hardly wait to begin.

Queer do, Sarles thought to himself later, as he walked home to await delivery of the prepared canvas. But then, the nobility had funny ways. And it was not the first time some lord had asked him to do an obscene painting. Such paintings were popular with the better brothels as well, and the commissions from them had gone a long way toward feeding his wife and babies through these difficult years.

Turning up his thin coat collar against the chill, damp evening air, Mr. Sarles told himself that when he was famous, however, he'd be damned if he ever did another of 'em.

His work, still wet, was delivered to Darlington House in five days. The count had made arrangements for it to be brought to a side door after most of the servants were in bed. His valet had accepted it, telling the disappointed artist he was to send his bill. Mr. Sarles had hoped for an immediate payment, but he could do nothing but agree.

Jean-Pierre had then closeted himself in his rooms for a week. Trays were brought to his door, fresh candles, and hods of coal—to be left there, for no one was allowed inside. His valet was the only one who saw him. The earl's servants discussed this strange behavior among themselves, only accepting it after the butler, in his plummy voice, pointed out one night at supper that it was well known that all foreigners were peculiar, them not having the advantage of being English. They couldn't help it, poor souls.

The day the count finally left his rooms he took Chalon's painting to be framed, once again promising the artisan a large sum to finish the job quickly. He had no real idea when Harry and his countess would be in town, but he wanted to be ready for them. This time, he ordered the man to present his bill to the earl. He made arrangements to have the other painting framed, just as soon as it was dry enough, in another shop on the other side of London.

Now, a few evenings after he had seen the Tredmans at the theater, he called at the familiar house in St. James's Square. He had overheard Lord Pritchard mention at White's Club earlier in the day that the earl was promised to him that evening, so he knew he would find Harry's countess alone.

Wayland the butler had no qualms about admitting him, for although he did not know why the young Frenchman had quit the house he knew him for m'lord's friend. He did not even protest when Jean-Pierre waved a careless hand and told him there was no need to announce him to the lady, such old friends as they were.

As the butler bowed, and the count strolled to the drawing room, Wayland sniffed. It was just as he had said. They were peculiar, foreigners, each and every one of them.

Sally was seated before a cozy fire, reading, when Jean-Pierre stepped inside to coolly close the door behind him and bow to her. Startled, she dropped her book.

"You!" she exclaimed. "What are you doing here?"

"As always, you look enchanting, madame," he said, as he took the seat opposite hers without even asking permission to do so. Sally's heart began to beat more rapidly, and her eyes narrowed slightly. Why had he come, and when Harry was not here? What did he want? Nothing good, she was sure of that.

"I am here for a very good reason, as you will discover presently. No, do not ring the bell, if you please. Hear me out, or it will be disastrous both for you and for my *cher ami*, Harry."

"Whatever can you mean?" Sally asked, trying to keep her voice from betraying her nervousness. When she saw the count's little smile, she doubted she had been successful.

"I must tell you, *cher madame*, that unfortunately there is another painting of us in existence. It is very similar to the one Monsieur Chalon did, but it does differ in one very important regard."

Sally merely stared at him. She told herself she would say nothing yet. No, she would wait and see first what this was all about.

"You are not at all curious, madame? How very unusual," her unwelcome visitor murmured, as he leaned back at his ease and crossed one beautifully tailored leg over the other.

"It has been my experience that women are invariably inquisitive creatures, much more so than any man. How refreshing that you are different! I see you have hidden depths, as well as great beauty. My compliments."

Sally could remain silent no longer. "I find it hard to believe that there is another painting in existence. Are you saying that Chalon did one? But what reason would he have had?"

"No, it is not by his hand, although I doubt many people could tell. It is most faithful to his style."

Sally recalled that Harry had told her what an expert copyist Jean-Pierre was, and her hands formed two fists beneath the folds of her skirt. "Am I to assume you are the artist, sir?" she asked, her voice haughty.

"The artist desires to remain anonymous. Because of the . . . mmm . . . delicate nature of the work."

Sally rose then and walked away from the fireplace. The count remained seated, quizzically regarding her, and still with that little smile on his face.

"Enough sparring, Monsieur le Comte," she said as she turned toward him again. "I do not care for you to remain here longer. State your business, and then leave me."

"Such arrogance," he murmured. "But I live to obey you, *madame*, so I shall be more than happy to do so.

"The second painting is of course of you and me, and the pose is somewhat similar, although, shall we say, much more explicit? In this new version I am not offering you a rose, *madame*, but something else. It is obvious I have gone beyond the point of begging for your attention, and as you are portrayed you appear more than willing to have it so."

"Indeed?" Sally asked, her mind working furiously.

As she came and took her seat again, he added carelessly, "Did I mention that we are both nude? No, I can tell from your expression that I did not. It is most revealing, and in a way—although of course, obscene—it is touching. I mean no pun. No, indeed. Two lovers, lost in passion. Would you care to see that painting, *mon cher madame*?"

"Certainly not!" Sally said quickly.

"Unfortunately, a great many other people will see it, if you and I cannot come to . . . mmm . . . an arrangement."

Sally eyed his confident young face. It was as handsome as any angel's. His body was perfectly formed and his eyes lucid and innocent, without a shadow of sin. And his voice had been calm—and even—courteous. It did not threaten. No, only his ugly words threatened. She wondered if the serpent in the garden of Eden had been as beautiful as Jean-Pierre de Fountaine—and as deadly.

"You are blackmailing me," she said.

"But what an odious word, *madame!* Shall we say, instead, that I am here only to spare you pain? That sounds so much more civilized, does it not?

"And I am not an unreasonable man, nor am I overly greedy. I think ten thousand pounds would not be excessive, to keep that painting a secret from the world. In fact, I consider you would be getting a bargain."

"Ten thousand?" Sally asked, stunned. "I do not have such a sum!"

"Perhaps not to hand, you don't, but you can get it," he assured her, in the same gentle voice. She shivered.

"Remember, I have seen your jewels. They are magnificent. You can have the diamond-and-sapphire set copied. What they can do with paste these days is astounding. Perhaps *mon cher* Harry won't even be able to tell the difference. And if he can you can make up some tale of gambling debts, or perhaps of money desperately needed by your family in . . . in Ireland, was it not? Just so. You can be as contrite as you like when you confess. And may I suggest a few bewildered, helpless tears? I am sure you will contrive admirably, for Harry is remarkably foolish about you."

"I have no intention of having my jewels copied, sir," Sally told him, holding her head high. "The very idea!"

The count shrugged and spread his hands wide. "But what is to be done, then? Are you really ready to face the humiliation that will ensue if you do not? Face facts, *mon cher madame*. All London is already linking our names. I even saw a caricature of us and Harry today, in one of the print shops. It appeared to be selling briskly, and causing a great deal of merriment.

"And with the painting providing such proof of a liaison, I doubt you could ever live it down. Besides, I beg you to remember that Harry is a jealous man. I suspect you have already suffered because of that failing of his—forced into exile for three long years. Is it not so?"

Jean-Pierre was watching her carefully now, for his last statement had been only a wild guess. When he saw how she paled and started, he knew that for once luck had been with him. And perhaps now his luck would change at the table as well? he wondered. He certainly hoped so.

He saw she was deep in thought, and he rose gracefully and bowed. "I shall, of course, give you time to consider it, *madame*. You have so few options, I doubt it will take you long. And the artist can wait for a few days. But if I do not hear from you by Friday you may be sure the painting will be exhibited, or perhaps even sold to another. There is a lady—ah, I name no names!—who will pay highly to acquire it."

He means Lady Rolls, Sally thought. He had to mean Lady Rolls. Oh, no! She must never be given this weapon!

"Now I shall bid you *adieu*. Of course, I know you will not mention this to *cher* Harry. It would be such a shame to distress him, to say nothing of your own subsequent banishment to the country again, when you have only so recently returned to town. If, that is, you were foolish enough to do so. I am sure you are not. *Madame?*"

Sally did not see his graceful bow, nor did she watch him as he strolled leisurely to the door, or hear him close it softly behind him. She was thinking hard.

Of course, Jean-Pierre himself was the artist. She remembered how eager he had been to see to the framing of Chalon's painting, even his slightly fevered air the day he had shown it to them here in town, all framed and hung. And because she and Harry had lingered in the country for so long, he had had plenty of time to complete his own base version of the work. She shuddered.

She rose then, too distracted to remain sitting quietly. What was she to do? she thought, as she began to pace. What *could* she do? Harry's aristocratic face came to mind, wearing that haughty, cold expression she disliked so much, and she despaired.

But if she did not find some way to pay the count that ten thousand pounds, the painting would be exposed. How could she and Harry ever face society again? The ton was so sure she was unworthy. They would not be surprised to see her unworthiness with their own eyes. And Lady Rolls would make sure they did. The sly caricatures being sold now would be but a bagatelle when compared to an obscene painting. And Harry had told her what a superb copyist Jean-Pierre was. There would be no doubt as to who the couple portrayed were. The count would have been very careful to make sure of that.

Oh, Harry would never believe her, even though he had finally accepted her explanation of what had happened between Sir Thomas and herself. This was much more serious—the evidence more damning.

And even if, by some miracle, she could convince Harry that it was all a lie, it would make no difference. Her arrogant husband might say he did not care what anyone thought of him, or of her, but if he were faced with a scandal of this magnitude, she knew he would never be able to live it down. Indeed, she had no doubt that he would divorce her. There would be no banishment this time. It would be too complete a disaster.

She put her hands to her hot face, telling herself sternly that she would not cry. There was no time for that now. No, she must think, think hard. But oh, how bereft she felt already, how sad. She loved Harry so, she could not bear to bring any trouble to him, nor could she bear to think of losing him.

Why does this always happen to me? she wondered, bewildered. Why must I always lose everyone—everything—I love? My family, my home in Ireland—Anne and Beechlands? Am I cursed in some way?

But no, she would fight this somehow. She would not lose Harry! How she was to keep him, since she did not intend to pay Jean-Pierre a single *sou*, she did not know. But she would try. It was all she could do.

Chapter Twenty

As HE SAT at the breakfast table the next morn ̄
the earl was surprised to receive a note from his ̣
He smiled a little as he opened it. What was she up
to now, the minx? he wondered. And why didn't s ̣
just come down and join him; say what she had to ̣
in person?

He remembered she had been asleep when he had
finally come home from Lord Pritchard's last night
and gone to her room. He had wanted to wake her,
love her, but she had looked so peaceful he had only
dropped a light kiss on her cheek, and gently smoothed
her dark hair away from her face before he had sought
his own bed.

As he read the note, his little smile died away.
Rather formally, Margarite wrote to ask if she might
have an interview with him, and she begged him to
cancel any morning appointments he might have, for
she had a matter of grave import she had to discuss
with him.

Still, Harry felt no alarm. Of course he would cancel
his meetings, nothing could be simpler. But what was
this "matter of grave import"? He cut another piece
of ham, thinking hard. And then he smiled again,
more widely now. Was Margarite going to tell him she
was with child? They had made love with such fre-
quency and abandon, he had been surprised she had
not confessed the thing a month ago. But would she
consider her pregnancy "grave"? He had told her he
would not mind another child, if she didn't.

Well, he thought, as he chewed his ham and refilled
his coffee cup, he supposed he would just have to wait

and see. But he did not linger at the table that morning, and as soon as he had reached the library he sent Wayland to fetch her. Really, he was surprised at how intrigued he was by this little mystery.

When Margarite came in, dressed in a simple morning gown of pale yellow muslin, he did not think she looked well. She was pale, and her eyes were tired, as if she had not had enough sleep. And there were worry lines on her lovely forehead. He came to take her in his arms, so that he could kiss them away.

"Sit down, sweetheart," he said softly. "And do not frown so. Nothing you have to tell me is worth bringing such concern to your lovely face. And I assure you I will take care of it, whatever it is. Truly."

Sally sank into a chair by the fireplace. There was a cheerful blaze in it this morning, but she did not feel its warmth. She wondered if she would ever feel warm again.

She had not slept at all. Oh, she had pretended to when Harry had come in to her, but she had done so only because she did not think she could bear to look into his all-seeing hazel eyes; no, not even though she was longing for the comfort of his arms, his kiss—his love.

After he had left her room she had wept quietly for a long time. And then she had set herself to think of her problem, and how she was to resolve it.

Nothing occurred to her, no matter how she turned it over and over in her mind. And finally, as dawn was breaking at last, she came to a decision. She would have to tell Harry all about it. There was no other way. She would not pay Jean-Pierre, she could not. Therefore it was obvious that Harry would have to be told. He was the only one who might be able to see them safely out of this. She was too young, too inexperienced to handle it herself.

So no matter what happened, no matter how Harry reacted, she would confess. How she wished he trusted her. It would have been so much easier if he did. But even if he cast her off, even if he began to hate her again, at least he would be spared the shame and degradation a public showing of that painting would bring. She knew she would never forget him, would always regret his loss, but her pain would not matter if she was able to save him.

Now she took a deep breath, and looked up from where she had been contemplating her tightly clasped hands.

"Margarite, dear one, as intriguing as this is, I must insist you tell me what is on your mind," Harry said. "I have been trying to guess from the emotions that have been crossing your face, but I am all at sea. What is it?"

Sally stared at him, memorizing his dear face, still so serene, so loving. He was smiling at her, that warm, intimate smile she had come to depend on and need. This might be the last time she would ever see him look that way. Forcing such a depressing thought from her mind, she said, "Jean-Pierre came to call on me last evening after you had gone out. I—I would have refused to see him, except he did not allow Wayland to announce him. He just walked into the drawing room and sat down."

"What did he want?" Harry asked, his eyes intent on her face. She did not think he sounded very interested.

"He came to tell me there is another painting of the two of us in existence, and to demand ten thousand pounds for it," she said baldly.

She noticed that the earl was leaning forward now, his hazel eyes darkening with anger, and she had to swallow before she went on. "The painting is not an exact copy. From what he said I gather it is . . . it is an obscenity. We are—we are portrayed nude, in the act of making love."

She was almost whispering now, and as much as she wanted to she could not look away from Harry's rigid, furious face.

But to her surprise he did not exclaim, or hurry into speech. Instead he leaned back in his chair, apparently deep in thought.

"Why do you tell me this, Margarite?" he asked.

Of all the questions she had steeled herself to answer, this one was a complete surprise. "Why . . . why, because I have no intention of paying blackmail," she said. "But even though there is no truth to the tale that the count and I are lovers, and though I never posed for that portrait, I could see no way to convince society that it was not so. And if its existence becomes known, you will be ruined. I could not bear for that to happen to you. I realized late last night that I had to tell you. I cannot handle this, but perhaps there is something you can do. . . ."

"Oh yes, there is something I can do indeed," he said, frowning darkly now and looking as haughty as he ever had.

Feeling despair, Sally hastened to say, "I do assure you, Harry, I have never been unfaithful to you with Jean-Pierre, or any man, no matter how damning this evidence may be. He is making it all up, as a way to get money. Please, you must believe me!"

To her infinite regret, he did not say he did. He only remarked, slowly and thoughtfully, "Yes, he wants money, of course. But perhaps he wants revenge as well?"

When she did not speak he went on, "He was furious when I cast him off, you know, and he has always been so jealous of you. He does not like competition, my handsome young former friend. And your beauty detracts from his own. What an ego he has!"

Sally felt a slight stirring of hope deep inside her. As angry as he was, Harry did not seem to be directing that anger at her. Could it be that he did believe her? Even trusted her now? She said a little prayer that it might prove so.

The earl rose, and came to draw her to her feet. "I shall take care of the matter, Margarite. I am glad you came to me and told me about it."

He hugged her briefly, then put her aside to go to his desk. "May I suggest you go upstairs, and get back into bed?" he said. "It is obvious you did not sleep last night. I will see that you are not disturbed."

Sally nodded, her eyes still troubled. She saw he

had forgotten her, and she went slowly to the door. Just before she opened it he said, "You were awake last night when I came to you, weren't you? Why did you pretend you were not?"

She did not turn. She couldn't. She did not want him to see the tears in her eyes. "I could not face you then," she said over her shoulder. "I was frightened about how you would take the news. And I was still trying to find a way out of this by myself, so you would never have to know. I . . . I am so very sorry, Harry. I have brought you nothing but trouble."

"Do not be so silly," he said harshly, and she cringed. "You have brought me nothing of the sort! Go to bed now, sleep. When I see you this evening, I am sure I will have much to report. And Margarite, you are not to worry."

Sally turned then. She wanted to run to him, kiss him, tell him how very much she loved him, but she saw he had forgotten her already. Quietly, she left the room. As she went up the stairs, she realized Harry was right. She was exhausted, and now, having unburdened her heart, she would be able to sleep.

Left alone in the library, the earl sat quietly for a long time. Then he opened the center drawer of his desk to take out all the bills that had recently come to the house. He found the one for the framing of the Chalon painting, and he studied it more carefully than he had when he had first received it. Even though he had been more than satisfied with the job, the price demanded for it seemed excessive. At the bottom of the bill were the words "For a special commission."

He nodded, and made a note of the shop's location.

There were some bills of Jean-Pierre's in the pile. Indeed, it was a rare day that did not bring some angry tradesman to the door, and a rare post that did not contain a number of his bills, some of them months overdue. He had formed the habit of forwarding them to Jean-Pierre's rooms once a week, and informing the creditors that he was no longer responsible for Monsieur le Comte.

He riffled through the day's post casually. The usual

invitations, a letter for Margarite from Walter Scott, and two for him from distant friends. And of course, there were the usual bills. Madame Clotilde, Rundell & Bridge—ah! Now, who was a Mr. Anthony Sarles, Esq.?

He opened the bill, and as he studied it his brows rose.

Mr. Sarles, no doubt having sent many a bill to Jean-Pierre, was now appealing directly to his patron. In impassioned words he begged for payment—a very large payment, too, Harry noted—for a particular oil he had done on commission.

"I can only assume that you are the gentleman who ordered the painting, sir, although I have no proof, for the heads were merely sketched in lightly. I was responsible only for the background and the nude figures, done in the style of Chalon.

"The count promised to pay me well, because the painting had to be finished in such a short time. Indeed, I worked night and day for almost a week in order to complete it.

"When I delivered it to your house, still wet, it was late at night, and to a side door. I received no payment, however. Instead, I was told by the foreigner who took it in to send my bill. As I have done, sir, time and time again.

"Please remit at once, or I shall be forced to take further steps. The nature of the painting being such as it is I should dislike making a stir, but a stir will be made if I am not reimbursed."

The note was signed with the usual flourishes, although Harry did not think Mr. Sarles cared to be his "most obedient servant" or anything of the kind. He made a note of the name before he summoned his butler.

Wayland looked puzzled for only a moment when the earl questioned him.

"As near as I can recall, m'lord, your young friend arrived here on the eighteenth of September. It was a Wednesday," he said, frowning a little in concentration.

"Yes, that would be correct. He left Darlington

Hall early on the morning of the eighteenth. Do go on," the earl said. "Was everything as usual from the time of his arrival?"

Wayland frowned harder. "Yes, I believe so," he said slowly. "He changed his attire, and then he left the house. He did return for dinner, however."

"Was he carrying anything then? Perhaps something large, bulky?"

Wayland's face brightened. "Indeed he was. How did you know, m'lord?"

Harry waved a careless hand and the butler continued. "A very large, flat package it was, sir. He had it taken to his rooms."

"When was the next time you saw the count with a package of that size?"

"I didn't," Wayland admitted. Harry hid his disappointment.

"No, but the next day, that valet of his, Henry is his name, left the house with one. Saw him myself, I did. I remember because I remarked on it, trying to be pleasant-like, sir, but he didn't say a word. Surly fellow, he was. None of us liked him."

"I gather you have divined my interest in all large, flat packages by this time, Wayland. But tell me, if you please, of the count's behavior from that time on."

"There is nothing to tell, m'lord," Wayland admitted, looking crestfallen that it should be so. "He lived much as he always did—sleeping late, out till all hours—you know his ways."

Harry nodded. "Cast your mind ahead a week or so, Wayland, if you would be so good. Did the count continue the life of a gentleman then?"

Now the butler almost beamed. "No, sir, he did not. It was quite remarked, such singular behavior, which is why I remember it so well. But then these Frenchies, you know, they're not like us, and as I was telling the others—"

"Yes, yes, but forget all that now," Harry said impatiently. "Exactly what did the count do?"

"Nothing, m'lord," Wayland informed him stiffly, very ashamed of his outburst.

"Nothing?" Harry prompted.

"No, sir. He never left his rooms for a week, he didn't. Everything had to be left at his door, for no one was permitted inside, not even the maids. That Henry took care of him, and we couldn't get a hint of what his master was up to from *him*."

"But of course the count came out eventually."

"Yes, m'lord. He resumed his normal habits then. And yes, on the very first day he did so, he took a large package from the house. I was surprised he didn't send his man again—but of course, he left him on guard."

" 'On guard'? You must be more plain."

"Even though the count had quit his rooms, the servants were still not permitted to enter them, not for another week. And when they did, that valet watched them every moment. Queer do, that," Wayland mused.

"Betty—one of the upstairs maids—told me there was such an odor of paint in them she felt sick. And she had to cart away a number of paint-stained rags. Quite a blaze they made. Bert, the groom, burned them in the mews."

Harry said a little prayer of thanks for the inquisitiveness of English servants. He had known for years that nothing escaped them, and that everything that went on in a household was gossiped about, but today he was grateful for this failing of theirs.

"Thank you, Wayland," he said as he rose. "I will be going out now. Inform Griffen that I shall need my hat, cane, and gloves. And Wayland—see that the countess is not disturbed by anyone today. She is resting."

Wayland bowed himself away.

The earl went first to the shop that had framed the painting Chalon had done. He discovered the reason the bill was so high was that the craftsman had had to complete the framing in only a day.

"Had to put off several other jobs, I did, milord,"

the little man told him. "But that-there count, 'e was insistent, 'e was."

Unfortunately the man could not remember the exact date he had done the work, but Harry felt he had enough proof without it. He went next to Chalon's studio. The artist was conducting a class, but he called a recess when the earl came in. In the main, the students ignored the visitor. All but one. Harry noticed the thin young man staring at him, saw the resentment on his face, and he beckoned to him.

"Mr. Sarles?" he asked. At the man's surprised nod he said, "I would have a word with you in private later, sir. For now, Monsieur Chalon, I find I have a further commission for you. The painting you did of my countess and the Comte de Fountaine is most faithful to them, and beautifully executed, but it does not please me."

"Indeed?" the master said, ruffling up indignantly.

Harry put an arm around his shoulders and walked him a little apart, where he could be seen talking to him at length. Eventually Chalon nodded—even smiled a bit.

Harry beckoned to Mr. Sarles then and took him outside, shutting the door of the studio to give them some privacy. Their conversation was a lengthy one, but at its conclusion both men were smiling. The earl, because he had received the information he wanted, and Mr. Sarles, because finally he had been paid.

As he went down the stairs, leaving the grateful artist beaming after him, Harry told himself it was just as he had suspected. Jean-Pierre was a superb copyist, true, but he did not have the skill to do nude figures, even if he had been able to procure models.

Quite satisfied with his sleuthing, Harry hailed a hackney and was driven to White's.

He was not surprised to find the club crowded at this hour, nor did he appear at all upset when several gentlemen ignored him. Leisurely looking around, he saw a friend of his about to dine alone, and he went to join him. He had missed luncheon, and he was hungry.

Jeremy Fitton did not appear overjoyed to see him, and after they had ordered their meal Harry inquired as to the reason for his frown.

"To be plain with you, man, don't like to see you made a fool of," Fitton told him, still looking gloomy. "Seen the latest from the print shops?"

As the waiter set down their plates, Harry admitted he had not.

"Ought to pay more attention to things," his friend said gruffly. "Makes you look like a cuckold, damn me if it doesn't!"

"Do you have one of those prints, Jerry?" the earl asked, as he cut his mutton.

"No, but Keating does. He was showing it to me earlier. Waiter! Waiter!"

As the servant hurried up, Fitton ordered him to find Mr. Keating and bring him here. As they waited for that gentleman to appear, both diners tucked into their meals.

Mr. Keating seemed most reluctant to produce the print, but Fitton would not take no for an answer.

"Show it to him, man, go on!" he said, pointing his laden fork at him as he stood hesitating by the table. Reluctantly, Mr. Keating took the print from his pocket and spread it out on the table.

"Yes, that certainly is me, isn't it?" the earl asked, seemingly more interested in the gravy he was pouring on his potatoes and sprouts. "Quite unmistakably me. And it is the countess and Jean-Pierre as well. A very poor likeness of Margarite, however. Not a bit flattering, and she is so beautiful, too. Do you think I should sue?"

"Aren't you upset, man?" Fitton demanded, his face turning red. "Gad, if it were *my* wife being portrayed in such a way, I'd be livid!"

"Calm yourself, Jerry," the earl said, as he speared the last brussel sprout and popped it into his mouth. Then he beckoned both men to lean closer, and interested observers, of whom there were a great many, watched him talking to them for some minutes, even chuckling as he did so.

"No!" Mr. Keating could be heard to exclaim. "Why, you don't mean . . . But, good heavens!"

"Whoever would have thought it?" Mr. Fitton mused, grinning a little. "Are you sure?"

"Very sure. It is quite, quite true," Harry said, wiping his mouth on his napkin before he rose. "Give you good day, sirs."

The two men stared after him as he left, waving to a few other acquaintances as he did so. Jeremy Fitton's table became a very popular place for the next half hour or so, and as for Mr. Keating, his eyes were shining with an unholy light as he hurried away to tell his own particular set of friends the most juicy item of gossip he had heard in years.

It was after three in the afternoon when the earl knocked on the door of the house where the count now resided. The landlord would have denied him, according to orders, if Harry had not mentioned his title and assured him he was a very old and dear friend of the gentleman he sought, reinforcing these statements with a handsome tip.

"Top o' the stairs, second door to the right, milord," he was told, and he made his leisurely way upstairs.

The door was opened very cautiously by Henri, who found himself staggering backwards as the earl shoved the door wide. "Come, come, Henri, your know me!" Harry said. "Why such caution? Tell your master at once that I am here."

"There is no need for him to tell me. I recognized your voice," Jean-Pierre said, coming into the room and sneering. "That will be all, Henri. Leave us."

Neither man spoke until they were alone.

"So, she told you, did she?" the count asked, folding his arms across his chest.

"Naturally," Harry said. "I want the painting."

"But of course, *mon cher*. I don't care who buys it, as long as I get paid for it."

"I am desolated to have to tell you that I have already paid for it," the earl said. "I gave Mr. Sarles his money earlier today."

"Sarles?" the count asked, sneering again. "But there was no need for that."

"I know I should expect that kind of comment from you, with your nonexistent sense of honor," Harry told him, watching the young man carefully. It really was too bad, he mused. Jean-Pierre had been given almost everything else a man could want, but unfortunately that most important part of a man's character was, in his case, completely missing. Well, he thought philosophically, no one is perfect.

"I won't part with it, you know," Jean-Pierre said. "Not without being paid. And the price is still ten thousand pounds, *mon ami*."

"May I see it?" Harry asked, removing his gloves and lounging against the center table.

The count hesitated only for a moment. Harry could tell he was torn between the danger of revealing where the painting was hidden and his longing to show off his expertise. His conceit, as always, carried the day.

"I see no harm in that. And perhaps when you do see it you will realize how . . . mmm . . . valuable it is to you."

As he spoke, he went to a large armoir set against the wall and drew the painting from its depths. He propped it up on a chair, smiling a little as he did so. The earl could see he was very proud of his work. As well he should be. The heads were perfect. It was Margarite and the count to the life.

"Now you have seen it, I am sure you will agree that it would not do to have it fall into another's hands," the count pointed out.

The earl ignored him as he moved forward, still studying the painting, his face expressionless. "As usual, you have copied another man's work perfectly. The heads are outstanding. My compliments.

"But that is not Margarite's body, as you would have known if you had ever seen it. Or perhaps I should say, if Sarles had? This woman is too coarsely made, the skin too ruddy. And those fleshy breasts and thighs—no, no, that is not Margarite."

"Perhaps not, but who will know that?" Jean-Pierre

countered. "And I should warn you I have several er, interested customers for the painting. Come, come, Harry! You must see that you have to pay me, or you will be ruined."

"Ruined? I?" the earl asked, his voice astounded. "You can't be serious! You know I don't give a ha'-penny what people say of me.

"But it won't come to that. Let me explain why. I have all the proof I need that you masterminded this entire, vicious lie, enough so I can take you to court for it any time I choose. But that will not be necessary.

"No, for in your greed and thirst for revenge you forgot how well I know you. And, as well, you forgot a confession you made to me late one night in Naples, after too many bottles of wine. I made mention of that confession in White's only an hour ago. The club was crowded today. By now I am sure you are being discussed everywhere, and by tomorrow you'll be a laughingstock."

He chuckled a little, ignoring the count's white, furi-ous face, his hissed curse. "I wonder what the print shops will make of this most astonishing piece of news? No doubt it will be difficult to, er, portray it. But somehow I am sure they'll find a way, don't you?"

He sighed a little then. "Dear, dear, can it be that I still have some lingering fondness for you, do you suppose, that I come to warn you? How distressing if that were so.

"I suggest you set Henri to packing at once. Perhaps you should even help him. It will hasten your depar-ture. For somehow, I cannot help but feel life would be much more pleasant for you in France from now on. Forget England. You'd never live it down, you know."

The count burst into a torrent of violent French curses. Harry waited patiently until he was through.

"No doubt," he said easily. Then his voice grew colder, and his expression hardened as he said, "You should never have tried to match wits with me, Jean-Pierre. You were out of your class."

*   *   *

When the earl left the count's rooms fifteen minutes later he was carrying a large, bulky package, well wrapped up in heavy paper and twine. He hailed a hackney, a sweet smile of satisfaction on his face for a job well done, and gave the driver orders to take him to St. James's Square.

He found his countess waiting for him in the drawing room. Tea had been served, although she did not appear to have eaten anything. But he thought she looked much better, rested now, even though she was not smiling, and she was eyeing the large package he carried with misgiving.

He winked at her before he turned to his hovering butler and said, "Please bring me a knife, Wayland. A very sharp knife."

"Should you like one of the footmen to open the package for you, m'lord? Or perhaps, if it is a matter of some delicacy, you would like me to do it?" the butler asked.

Harry saw he was trying very hard to conceal his curiosity, and he could hardly blame him for it, not after the questions he had been asked this morning. He hesitated, as if he were contemplating the possibility. When Margarite's face paled, he relented.

"No, I think not. I shall do it myself," he said.

While he waited for the knife to be brought, he went to take his wife in his arms and kiss her.

"Mmmm . . . you always smell so good," he said softly. "I've missed you today."

"Is it . . . is it all right?" she whispered. "Is that the painting? How did you get it away from him?"

"I'll tell you later, when we won't be interrupted. Do pour me a cup of tea, my dear."

As she began to do so, he held up his hand. "No, on second thought, I think we shall both have some sherry. This is a celebration, is it not?"

Sally smiled as he went to pour them a glass, and she smiled again as he toasted her with his eyes before he sipped it.

After Wayland had brought the knife to the earl he

bowed himself away, closing the double doors of the drawing room tightly behind him. Harry reminded himself that such a discreet man deserved a raise in salary.

He rose then and cut the twine around the painting, and ripped the paper aside. Sally watched him, putting down her glass and leaning forward. But when the painting was exposed, and Harry had stepped back, she put both hands to her face in horror.

"Oh, Harry, how perfectly dreadful," she whispered. "Oh, my dear, I had no idea. . . . Good heavens! Oh, take it away from my sight!"

"My dear Margarite, you are too nice," he told her, a twinkle in his eyes. "Aren't you even going to admire Jean-Pierre's technique? Er, as an artist, I mean?"

She had covered her eyes, and now she lowered her hands to peer at him. "You really want me to look at that . . . that abomination?" she asked.

"Since it is an abomination, certainly," he said coolly. "You will observe how carefully the heads have been done, how precisely copied. As for the bodies, well, you can see that the female's is not anything like yours. You are exquisite, beautifully formed, my goddess. But that poor woman, bah! Just look at those breasts. . . ."

"Stop it!" Sally said, covering her eyes again.

"The artist—a very nice young man, my dear, who does this sort of thing to feed his family until he gains fame—is quite adequate, even though no painter is better than his subjects unless he idealizes them. But I was hard put not to laugh when I saw how he had portrayed the count. He is, er, very well endowed, wouldn't you say?"

"I wouldn't say anything about it, and I wish you wouldn't either," Sally said firmly. "Please, Harry, get rid of it!"

"But I thought you might like to do that," he told her, picking up his sherry to sip it again. "Or if you like, we could do it together."

Sally came toward him then and picked up the

knife. "I will be glad to start," she said, her face still flushed. "Please hold it steady."

She waited until he had a firm grip on the frame before she began to slash the canvas. Harry noted that her first cut destroyed a very tender part of Jean-Pierre's anatomy, and he winced.

Seeing how hard it was for her, how she struggled, he motioned her aside so that he could finish the job. In no time, the count's attempt at blackmail lay in shreds on the carpet.

"We can't leave it like that," Sally said, her voice still worried. "You can tell what it was, even now!"

Harry bundled up the pieces and went to feed them to the fire. It took quite a while for all of the painting to burn, but Sally did not take her eyes from the fire until there was nothing left of those shreds of canvas but ashes. Only then did she take her seat again. Ignoring the peculiar odor in the room, she downed her sherry in one very unladylike gulp.

"Tell me about it," she said. "How did you get it? Did you give him ten thousand pounds?"

"Of course not," her husband said, taking her glass to replenish it. "How insulting of you. Do you take me for a flat? I got it for the price of two tickets on the next channel packet. Jean-Pierre, you see, is retiring permanently to France."

Sally gave him such a glowing smile that he bent and kissed her before he handed her her glass again.

"I shall drink to his journey with glee," she said. Then she thought for a moment, her brow furrowed. "But why would he give it up to you, just like that?" she asked. "It was such a potent weapon for him."

"He had very little choice, my dear," Harry said. "You see, I told him how I had gone to White's and how, while I was there, I had revealed a secret about him that only I knew. I thought he would faint when I mentioned it, he turned so pale. He immediately agreed to my scheme, and ordered his valet to start packing."

"But why?" Sally asked, still perplexed. "What secret?"

Harry went over to where the wrapping paper was still strewn on the carpet, and bent to pick it up.

"It all came out when we were first in Italy two years ago," he said absently. "He'd had too much to drink one evening, and he grew careless. He confessed he was only pretending to be a great lover; that it was all a sham. You see, the poor boy is impotent, and always has been. He must have forgotten he told me about it, for we never discussed it again. But I remembered today, and—*ooooph!*"

Intent on the wrapping paper, Harry had not noticed his countess rising from the sofa, nor her flushed face as she ran toward him. When she launched herself straight at him, he was in no way prepared for the attack. He went down with a crash, bringing a small table with him, a furious Sally landing on top of him to pound his chest with her fists.

In her anger, she had forgotten her little fear of him, had never even considered the impropriety of what she was doing. It was as if she were finally attacking the bully of her childhood, Thady O'Brien . . . her drunken, abusive husband, Leo Mannion . . . her weak da . . . the pious, greedy Colonel Jenkins . . . even the arrogant viscount Harry had been, who had thought to buy her for ten thousand pounds. All the men in her life who had brought her such pain and sorrow.

"You knew that! You knew that all the time, but you never told me!" she accused him breathlessly, struggling to sit on him so she could beat him harder. "Oh, how could you? How could you have let me spend all this time worrying? I could kill you!"

"Mar-Margarite, no! No, stop it!" he said, now that he had his breath back. He tried to catch her hands in his, but in her fury she was too quick for him.

"No, I won't!" she said, pounding him even harder. "And to think I have been so happy today, because I thought that at last you *trusted* me! But you didn't, did you? It was just that you *knew* I couldn't have been unfaithful to you with the count. Ooh, I *hate* you!"

Cautiously, Wayland opened the drawing room door to step inside. He had knocked twice and waited, but neither the earl nor the countess had heard him. Both he and the footmen in the hall had heard those loud crashes and, remembering the knife he had brought, Wayland was concerned. Motioning to the footmen to keep to their posts, he had decided to investigate. It was something he was to regret for the rest of his life.

For lying flat on his back on the carpet, surrounded by wrapping paper, an empty frame, and various broken ornaments, and now laughing helplessly, was his generally haughty, austere master. And sitting astraddle him, grasping his hair in her hands, was his countess. She looked as if she were trying to bang his head on the carpet, and with her gown above her knees, and her unpinned curls, she appeared the complete wanton.

Just then, she raised her eyes and encountered Wayland's stunned gaze. He about-faced immediately.

"I . . . I beg your pardon, m'lord, m'lady," he said in his plummy voice, staring straight ahead at the closed door and wishing desperately that he were on the other side of it. "I heard a crash, and I . . ."

Sally took a deep breath. Harry was still laughing so hard, she knew he wouldn't be any help. "That is quite all right, Wayland," she said in her grandest and coolest voice. "It was good of you to be concerned, but the earl and I do not care to be disturbed right now."

"Certainly, madam," the butler said, easing to the door. As a fresh burst of the earl's demented laughter echoed through the room he almost ran out, and he did not take a deep breath until he had the door closed tightly behind him.

He felt a little better as he glared at the avid, interested faces of the footmen. At least, he told himself, wild 'orses couldn't get a word from *him* about what he had just witnessed. He still had his pride.

Inside the drawing room, Sally was struggling to get up so she could pull her skirts down, but Harry would not let her go. His hands held her waist firmly, and, only chuckling now, he smiled up into her eyes.

"Forgive me for laughing, Margarite," he said. "But it was so comical! The look on Wayland's face! And your voice when you told him we did not care to be disturbed! I was overcome.

"No, stay right where you are, madam. This is a very provocative position. I like it. But what a shame we have so many clothes on. Perhaps that can be remedied?"

"Let me up, Harry," she whispered, darting little glances to the door. She was horrified suddenly at what she had done. Why, she had behaved no better than a common bawd! "I am so embarrassed," she said. "To think Wayland saw us this way! And he might still come back!"

Taking pity on her, Harry released her, and she scrambled away. As she brushed her skirts down, still breathing hard, he said, "He won't do that, not after your frigid, regal order. You were superb! And let me assure you, by tomorrow he will have forgotten the incident completely. He is a most superior butler."

To his surprise Margarite turned away from him then, to stand with her back to him, her head bent. He could see the tender nape of her neck under her loose curls, and he went and put his arms around her so he could kiss it. Still she remained rigid in his arms, and he sensed she was trying to contain her sobs.

"I am sorry, Margarite," he whispered in her ear. "Of course I trust you. Why do you think I told you this morning that you were not to worry about it further? And I did not need proof of Jean-Pierre's impotence to convince me you were blameless. Truly."

Sally turned then, to search his eyes. She seemed to be reassured by what she saw there, for she smiled a little and blinked away her tears.

"Oh, Harry," she said, shaking her head. "You are the most impossible man! Whatever am I to do with you?"

He bent to whisper in her ear again, and the suggestion he made caused her to blush a vivid rose.

Chapter Twenty-One

THE NEXT MORNING, Sally discovered that Harry's prediction proved correct. Wayland was his usual superior self, and not by a single quiver of his features, nor the veriest inflection in his voice, did he betray he had ever witnessed her astride his master on the drawing room floor last evening. She was relieved.

That day she noticed that the painting of her and the count had disappeared from the entrance hall. When she questioned Harry about it, he told her he had sent it back to Chalon so that the unworthy de Fountaine might be painted out of the scene. Sally smiled. As admired as the painting had been, and as lovely as she herself knew it was, it would only have been a reminder to her of the agony and doubt she had just endured. It would have been a reminder as well of the obscene painting Jean-Pierre had had done. She doubted she would ever forget it, even though it was now nothing but ashes that one of the housemaids had carried out to the dust bin early this morning.

Two days later, the Earl and Countess of Darlington were to attend a ball given by the Duke and Duchess of Barrington of Berkeley Square. All society seemed to have been invited, and Sally had ordered a new gown for the occasion. It was of the creamy white that Harry had mentioned he would like to see her in sometime—an almost plain, graceful float of silk. She intended to wear her diamond-and-sapphire set with it.

But as she was dressing for the ball, Harry came from his own rooms bearing a velvet box. She dismissed her maid at once. The woman was awkward in the earl's presence still, and apt to color up when he invaded her mistress's rooms. Sally hoped she would grow accustomed in time, for Harry did so with such great regularity.

"Open it, Margarite," Harry said, handing her the box and bending to kiss her cheek. "I think they will look splendid with the new gown."

Sally gasped as a set of rubies came to light. The oval-shaped pendant was huge, and in its depths it glowed a deep, vivid red. There were ear bobs and a bracelet as well.

"Harry, how beautiful!" she whispered. "But why do you give them to me? There is no special occasion that I know of for such a gift."

"But I don't need one. I just wanted to," he told her, as he took the pendant on its fine gold chain from the case, to fasten it around her neck.

As he stood back and admired it where it nestled just above her cleavage, he added, "Although I will admit I did have a reason for this particular gift."

"What was it?" she asked, staring down at it in wonder.

But Harry was already returning to his own rooms. "I will tell you later, my dear," he said over his shoulder. "Make haste now, or we'll be late. And I especially want all London to marvel at you this evening, beauty."

To Sally, it seemed that no one spoke of anything else at the ball but the Comte de Fountaine, and his hurried departure from England.

"My dear, what a surprise it was!" Lady Pritchard exclaimed, as she stood chatting with the Countess of Darlington and some others.

Sally schooled her expression to one of polite interest, for the lady was by no means the first to speak to her of the count this evening.

"And when you consider that Fanny Reynolds boasted for weeks that she was the count's mistress, and Lady Gower implied such things . . . Well! I am not a bit surprised to see that neither of them has come tonight.

"But *impotent*! My word! Did you know?"

"No, for Harry did not tell me," Sally said. "I think that originally he had intended to spare Jean-Pierre any pain, at least until those caricatures of us started appearing. Obviously, it was the count himself who began the rumor that we were lovers, as a way to get revenge. He was so angry when Harry discarded him, because of his impossible debts."

Another lady nearby had been listening avidly, and now she came closer to say, "And there have been some whispers of a painting, too, m'lady. I am sure I heard that correctly. I must admit I quite long to see it. I have heard it is very naughty!"

"A painting?" Sally asked, her eyes very wide, very innocent. "Oh no, madam, you have been misinformed. There is no painting. How could there be? I never posed for any but that one of the two of us that Harry commissioned."

"Monsieur Chalon told me he is to redo that painting of you and the count," Mr. Jannings told her. "I was at his studio today to arrange for him to take my wife and my children's likeness. But why would he do such a thing? The painting was exquisite."

Sally stared at his fat, eager face, and she sincerely pitied Mrs. Jannings her husband. "You had better ask the earl about that, sir," she said. "Oh, there is Lady Elizabeth! You must all excuse me. There is something I have been longing to ask her. . . ."

It was a very long evening, but somehow tonight, Sally did not mind. She felt light and happy and carefree, and she had only to catch Harry's eye to know that all was right with her world at last. Well, almost all, she reminded herself, as she danced with a worshipful Mr. Danvers. For as yet Harry had not said he loved her, and she still had a little suspicion that, in spite of his words, he did not really trust her either. Someday, she told herself, smiling up at the eager beau who partnered her and who wasn't aware that she was not seeing him at all, someday he will tell me. I can wait.

It was after supper that her rubies were remarked. She and Harry were seated at a large table for eight, and now, replete, and with all the ices and comfits devoured, the party had remained to sip champagne and chat.

"I say, what an outstanding set of jewelry you are wearing, my dear countess," Lord Pritchard remarked, his eyes twinkling. "But I am surprised. My wife and I have often remarked how handsome you appear in your sapphires. They are such a match for your eyes."

"Haven't you learned yet that a lady can never have too many jewels, Matthew?" Harry drawled, his eyes alight with some hidden amusement. "But to tell truth, I bought those for Margarite because they were so perfect—the only jewel that could do her justice."

"Why is that?" Jeremy Fitton asked, as his wife sighed in envy.

"You are not familiar with the Bible, sir?" Harry asked.

"What? Well, of course I've read parts of it," his friend blustered. "But what has the Bible to say about your wife's jewels?"

"Many things," Harry instructed him. "There is a verse in the Old Testament that describes Margarite completely."

The assembled guests clamored to know what that might be, but Harry only shook his head. "I send you to Proverbs, Chapter Thirty-one, the tenth verse. And now I beg you will excuse us. I hear a waltz, and I would dance it with my countess."

To cries of "Unfair!" the earl rose and bowed to his friends. "Remember, Proverbs thirty-one, verse ten," he said, drawing Sally's arm through his own and strolling away.

In the ballroom again, Sally looked up at him as he took her left hand and put his arm around her waist.

"I see you don't intend to tell me either, Harry," she said. He nodded, looking not even a bit penitent.

"But you know we may not reach home again until

the early hours of the morning. Would you condemn me to Bible study then?"

He turned her expertly in time to the music. "I may relent in your case, my dear. And then again, I may not. Come, this is a festive evening, is it not? Let us enjoy ourselves. Do you know, I think the waltz is my favorite dance? I get to hold you so close."

Sally could see he had no intention of telling her anything more about the rubies, not then, and she promised herself she would not wheedle. Harry was having such a good time, she hated to spoil it.

Still, as he drew her up from her curtsy after the dance had ended, she could not resist saying, "I shall have a much more festive evening if you let me in on your secret, Harry, and I vow I won't tell a single soul."

He bent to kiss her hand. Then, still holding it, and her eyes with his own as well, he said, his voice serious now, " 'Who can find a virtuous woman? For her price is far above rubies.' "

As Sally's eyes glowed with delight, he continued, "It goes on to say something like 'the heart of her husband doth safely trust in her,' etc. And, 'she will do him good and not evil all the days of her life.' "

"Oh, Harry," Sally breathed, her eyes brimming with tears. "What a lovely thought."

"Yes, I quite agree with you, madam. I was very proud of myself for remembering that verse, although it took me a devil of a time to find it yesterday."

"No doubt it was good for you," Sally told him, trying for a light tone, when all she wanted to do was take him in her arms and kiss him.

As they left the floor arm-in-arm, suddenly she smiled. "Oh, my dear, when this becomes known—as of course it will, now you have made sure of that—how my reputation will improve!"

"That was my intention, Margarite," he said. "I may not care what the ton says of either of us, but since you do, I thought it might help.

"And here is the ever-adoring Mr. Danvers again.

I assume you must be promised to him for the next dance? What I am forced to endure!"

Sally laughed at him and kissed him with her eyes, before she turned to accept Mr. Danvers's escort.

She read the entire chapter of Proverbs the next morning after breakfast, and her eyes filled with tears as she did so. Harry did trust her after all—he did! She had never been so happy!

She spent most of that day in her own suite. The earl had gone to Tattersall's and then on to his club, and she told the servants she was not to be disturbed, no matter who called to discuss the ball or Harry's gift.

She had something else to do. Something much more important.

Sally did not mention how she had spent her day when she and the earl met at dinner. They were enjoying a quiet evening at home, and she had decided to wait until later to give him her surprise.

After he joined her in the drawing room, she came and kissed him before she handed him a few sheets of paper.

"What is this, Margarite?" he asked as he took them.

"Why, the ending to my fairy tale," she said. "You do remember the one I wrote for you, don't you, my Prince of the West Wind?"

"I hope it has a happy ending now," he remarked, one brow quirked.

"Yes, it does, because now it can," she said, her eyes shining. "The prince and princess make up their differences after he gives her a ruby ring, which becomes her last and finest talisman. And of course, they live happily ever after." She paused before she said, a little shyly, "As I think we can live, happily ever after. Oh, Harry, I do love you so!"

"Sweetheart," he murmured, putting the sheets down so he could take her in his arms. After she had been thoroughly kissed, he asked, "Do you know what finally proved to me that I could believe in you?

It was that you dared to come and tell me about Jean-Pierre and that painting. That showed me you did indeed trust me. I don't think anyone has ever trusted me, never mind loved me, before."

He fell silent then, wondering why Margarite didn't look happier. Indeed she seemed quite pensive, almost lost in thought.

"What is it?" he whispered, turning her chin and tipping it up with his hand. "Are you troubled, my dear? About what?"

Sally sighed. Forced to look into his eyes, she said, "I think it is because you have never told me you love me. No, not even once."

He looked startled. "But that's impossible! Of course I have, I must have! All those things I whisper to you while we make love, the sweet names I call you. Surely you are mistaken!"

"No, I'm not," she said sadly. "I . . . I would remember. I have waited so long to hear you say it."

To her regret, he did not speak at once. Instead he drew her close again, and his mouth covered hers in a quick but passionate kiss. Sally swallowed hard, as his lips traced her jawline up to her ear. I must not cry, she told herself fiercely. I must not be bitter because he cannot love me!

"Margarite," he breathed in her ear, his deep voice sending shivers racing over her skin, "Margarite, I not only admire and adore you, I do most truly love you. I have since first meeting. You see, it wasn't only to thwart my mother that I married you."

She drew back a little, to stare up into his eyes. They burned with a light so intense she knew he was speaking the truth.

"No," she murmured, her own eyes glowing with happiness, even as she shook her head and moved away from him. "No, I am not Margarite! I am Sally!"

There was a long pause, and she held her breath.

"Very well," he said with a sigh. "I see that nothing but my complete capitulation will do for you, madam. And since I changed your name once, I suppose I can do it again. No doubt I will grow accustomed in time, for . . . er, *Sally*, I would love you no matter what you were called."

She came back into his arms in a rush, her own arms flung around his neck so that she could bury her hands in his hair and whisper to him. She felt tears of happiness springing to her eyes now, and she blinked them away as his mouth captured hers again and she lost herself in his embrace.

Later, still held tightly in his arms, she began to think of other things she might change now that she had been so successful with this first, most important one. Why, no doubt in time she could change his attitude toward his children—*all* his children. And perhaps she could do something about his arrogance, his pride.

She smiled a little to herself then. No, not that. She could never change that, for it was part of him. She wasn't even sure she wanted to, anyhow. For without it, Harry wouldn't be her Prince of the West Wind. Volatile, restless, unpredictable—and oh, so dearly loved.

Afterword

The story you have just read was based in part on the life of a real woman in England, in the early 1800s. She was a Sally Powers, who became Marguarite, the Countess Blessington.

Accounts of her life vary considerably, although most sources agree she was born in Ireland and sold into marriage at the age of fifteen by her needy parents. Her husband was a drunkard who abused her. Sally left him and returned to her childhood home, and later, when her father had been hung for murder, she was rescued by a British captain who took her to England with him. A few years later she was discovered there by the future Earl of Blessington, who did indeed buy her from that captain for ten thousand pounds. He married her after learning of her husband's death, he having fallen from a prison window in a drunken stupor. Who was it who said "truth is stranger than fiction"?

I have used all of these facts in my story, and in some cases, embellished them. The rest is all invention.

The Countess Blessington did not have a happy life, even after her second marriage. The earl wasted most of his fortune before he died suddenly, leaving her heavily in debt and responsible for the French dandy he had befriended, a Count D'Orsay. Eventually the countess was forced to flee her creditors, and she died less than a month later, alone in Paris. Some say she died of a broken heart.

When I first read of her I was fascinated, and yes, I pitied her. By all accounts she was an outstanding beauty, and so witty, talented, and kind that what happened to her did not seem fair, and I was inspired to write this story.

I hope the lady would approve the happy ending I have given my Countess Darlington, instead of her own sad one. And I hope my readers will approve it as well.

ABOUT THE AUTHOR

Barbara Hazard is the award-winning author of twenty-five regency romances. *A Handful of Dreams* is her fourth historical romance. It was preceded by its sequel, *Call Back the Dream,* and *The Heart Remembers* and *Midnight Magic.* All are available in NAL/Onyx editions. There are over three million of her books in print, both here and abroad.